Sabine Baring-Gould

Urith

A Tale of Dartmoor

Sabine Baring-Gould

Urith
A Tale of Dartmoor

ISBN/EAN: 9783337081089

Printed in Europe, USA, Canada, Australia, Japan

Cover: Foto ©Andreas Hilbeck / pixelio.de

More available books at **www.hansebooks.com**

URITH

A TALE OF DARTMOOR

BY

S. BARING GOULD

AUTHOR OF "MEHALAH," "ARMINELL," "OLD COUNTRY LIFE," ETC.

———

London
METHUEN AND CO.
18, BURY STREET, W.C.
1891

URITH:

A TALE OF DARTMOOR.

CHAPTER I.

DEVIL TOR.

In the very heart of Dartmoor, far from human habitation, near two thousand feet above the level of the sea, but with no prospect in the clearest weather on any side upon cultivated land, stands at present, as stood two hundred years ago, and doubtless two thousand before that, a rude granite monolith, or upright stone, about fourteen feet high, having on it not a trace of sculpture, not the mark of any tool, even to the rectification of its rugged angles and rude shapelessness.

In every direction, far as the eye can range, extends brown, desolate moorland, broken here and there with lumps of protruding rock, weathered by storm into the semblance of stratification.

A bow-shot from this upright stone rises such a hump that goes by the name of Devil Tor; and the stone in question apparently formed originally the topmost slab of this granite pile. But when removed, by whom, and with what object, remains a mystery. The beauty of a vast upland region lies not in its core, but in its circumference, where the rivers have sawn for themselves valleys and gorges through which they travel to the lowlands in a series of falls, more or less broken. About the fringe, the mountain heights, if not so lofty as in the interior, show their elevation to advantage, towering out of the cultivated plains or undulating woodland at their bases.

In the centre there is less of beauty, because there is no contrast, and it is by comparison that we form our estimates.

In the heart of the upland all is equally barren, and the variations of elevation are small. This is especially the case with the interior of that vast elevated region of Dartmoor, which constitutes bog from which flow the rivers that pour into the Bristol Channel on one side, and into the English Channel on the other.

The monolith, blackened by lichen, standing in such utter solitude, was no doubt thought to bear some resemblance to the Great Enemy of Man, and the adjoining Tor was regarded as his throne, on which he seated himself but once in twelve months, on Midsummer Eve, when the Bale-fires flamed on every hill in his honour. On all other occasions he was erect in this eyrie region, peering east and west, north and south, to see what evil was brewing in the lower world of men.

Devil Tor is reached by very few, only now and then does a shepherd pass that way, as the bogs provide no pasturage. The peat there has grown from hoar antiquity undisturbed by the turf-cutter on account of the remoteness of the spot and the difficulty of transport. The fisherman never reaches it, for it lies above the sources of all streams.

The surface of the moor is chapped and transformed by the chaps into a labyrinth, of peaty hummocks and black and oozy clefts, the latter from six to twelve feet deep, running in every direction, and radiating out of each other at all angles. Why the peat is so cleft is hard to say, there is no running water in the gashes, which in many cases go down to the white granite like the fissures in the body of a leper that in places disclose the bone. It would almost seem as though the bitter cold of this region had chapped its surface, and that no soft warm weather ever came to mollify, and to heal its gaping wounds.

Evening had closed in, but not attended by darkness, for the whole sky was glowing. The moor was on fire.

The season was that early spring in which what is locally termed "swaling" takes place, that is to say, the heather is set fire to after the dry winds of March, so as to expose and to sweeten the herbage.

The recent season had been exceptionally dry, even for so rainless a season, and the fires that had been kindled near the circumference of the moor had run inwards, gained the mastery, and rioted over the whole expanse beyond control. They leaped from bush to brake, they crossed streams, throwing over tufts of flaming bracken, pelting the further shore, till that also was ignited.

They circumvented bogs, they scrambled up moraines of granite, locally termed *clatters*, they ran up the hills on one side, enveloped their rocky crests in lambent flame, and descended the further side in a succession of bounds, and now they raged unchecked in the vast untrodden interior, where the wiry heather grew to shrubs, and the coarse grass and rushes were dust dry. There it ate its way along, a red advancing tide, working to windward, with a low roar and crackle, snapping at every bush, mumbling the tufts of rush, tossing up sparks, flame, and smoke, so that in the general glow and haze every landmark was disguised or effaced.

To no distance could the eye reach, because the whole atmosphere was impregnated with smoke, the smoke red and throbbing with the reflection of the fires over which it rolled. Indeed, the entire firmament was aglow, at one time flashing, at another darkening, then blazing out again as a solar photosphere, responsive to the progress and force of the conflagration.

Crouched at the foot of the great upright stone, that rose over her as the Devil triumphing over his pray, was a girl, with sullen, bewildered eyes, watching the fires as they folded about her, like flame fingers interlacing to close in and squeeze, and press the life out of her.

Her hands were bandaged. She rested her chin on them. She was a handsome girl, but with the features irregular. She had large dark eyes—possibly at this moment appearing unduly large, as they stared with a vacant unconcern at the mingled darkness and flame. Her complexion was by nature a transparent sallow, but now it glowed—almost vermilion in the light of the burning moor. Her brow was broad, but low and heavy. The face was strange. When the long dark eyelashes fell, then there was in the countenance, in repose, a certain pathos, a look of sadness, of desolation; but the moment the eyes opened, this was gone, and the eyes proclaimed a sullen spirit within, underground, a smoulder of fierce passion that when stirred would burst forth into uncontrolled fury—akin to madness. When the lids fell, then the face might be pronounced beautiful, but when they rose, only the sullen, threatening eyes could be seen, the face was forgotten in the mystery of the eyes.

As the girl sat beneath the great black monolith her brooding eyes were turned as a brake exploded into brilliant flame. She watched it burn out, till it left behind only a glow of scarlet ash; then she slowly turned her head towards Devil Tor, and watched the fantastic shapes the rocks assumed in the flicker, and the shadows that ran and leaped about them, as imps doing homage to their monarch's chair.

Then she unwound the bandages about her hands, and looked at her knuckles. They were torn, and had bled, torn as by some wild beast. The blood was dry, and when she wrenched the linen from a wound to which it adhered, the blood began again to ooze. Her wounds were inflamed through the heat of the fires and the fever in her blood. She blew on them, but her breath was hot. There was no water within the engirdling ring of fire in which she could dip her hands. Then she waved them before her face, to fan them in the wind, but the wind was scorching, and charged with hot ash.

Sitting thus, crouched, waving her bloodstained hands, with the bandage held between her teeth, under the black upright stone of uncouth shape, she might have been taken for a witch provoking the fires to mischief by her incantations.

Suddenly she heard a voice, dropped the kerchief from her mouth, and sprang to her feet, as a shock of fear—not of hope of escape—went through her pulses to her heart. Whom was she likely to encounter in such a spot, save him after whom the Tor was named, and which was traditionally held to be his throne?

On the further side of the encompassing fires stood a young man, between her and Devil Tor; but through the intervening smoke and fire she could not discern who he was, or distinguish whether the figure was familiar or strange.

She drew back against the stone. A moment ago she was like a witch conjuring the conflagration, now she might have been taken for one at the stake, suffering the penalty of her evil deeds.

"Who are you? Do you desire to be burnt?" shouted the young man.

Then, as he received no reply, he called again, "You must not remain where you are."

With a long staff he smote to right and left among the burning bushes, sending up volumes of flying fiery sparks, and then he came to her, leaping over the fire, and avoiding the tongues of flame that shot after him maliciously as he passed.

"What!" he exclaimed, as he stood before the girl and observed her. Against the ink-black, lichened rock, her face, strongly illumined, could be clearly seen. "What! Urith Malvine?"

She looked steadily at him out of her dark, gloomy eyes, and said, "Yes, I am Urith. What brings you here, Anthony Cleverdon?"

"On my faith, I might return the question," said he, laughing shortly. "But this is not the place, nor is this the time, for tossing questions like shuttlecocks on Shrove Tuesday. However, to satisfy you, I will tell you that I came out in search of some ponies of my father's—scared by the fires and lost. But come, Urith, you cannot escape unaided through this hoop of flame, and now that you are contented with knowing why I am here, you will let me help you away."

"I did not ask you to help me."

"No, but I am come, unasked."

He stooped and caught her up.

"Put your arms around my neck," said he. "The fire will not injure me, as I am in my riding boots, but your skirts invite the flame." Then he wrapped together her gown about her feet, and holding her on his left arm, with the right brandishing his staff, he fought his way back. The scorching breath rushed about them, ten thousands of starry sparks, and whirled round and over them. He took a leap, and bounded over and through a sheet of flame and landed in safety. He at once strode with his burden to the pile of rocks where were no bushes to lead on the fire—only short swath, and a few green rushes full of sap.

"Look, Urith," said he, after he had recovered breath, "between us and the next Tor—whose name, by the Lord,

I don't know, but which I take to be the arm-chair of Lilith, the Devil's grandam—do you see?—the very earth is a-fire."

"How, the earth?"

"The peat is so dry that it has ignited, and will smoulder down into its depths for weeks, for months, mayhap, till a Swithurn month of rains has extinguished it. I have known a moor burn like this all through the summer, and he that put an unwary foot thereon was swallowed like the company of Korah in underground fire."

The girl made no reply. She had not thanked the young man for having delivered her from the precarious position in which she had been.

"Where am I?" she asked, turning her head about.

"On Devil Tor."

"How far from home?"

"What—from Willsworthy?"

"Yes, from Willsworthy, of course. That is my home."

"You want to find your way back? How did you come here?"

"You ask me two questions. Naturally, I want to get to my home. As for how I came here—on my feet. I went forth alone on the moor."

"And lost your way?"

"Certainly, or I would not be here. I lost my way."

"You cannot by any possibility return direct over the bog and through the fire to Willsworthy. I could not guide you there myself. No man, not the best moor-shepherd could do this at such a time. But what ails your hands? You have hurt yourself."

"Yes, I have hurt myself."

"And, again, what induced you to come forth on the moor at such a season as this?"

The girl made no answer, but suddenly looked down, as in confusion.

She was seated on the rock of the Tor. Anthony Cleverdon stood somewhat below, on the turf, with one hand on the stone, looking up into her face, that was in full illumination, and he thought how handsome she was, and what a fortunate chance had befallen him to bring him that way to rescue her—not from death, but from a position of distress and considerable danger. Even had she

escaped the fire, she would have wandered further into the
recesses of the waste, becoming more and more entangled
in its intricacies, without food, and might have sunk exhausted on the charred ground far from human help.

As Anthony looked into her face and saw the sparks
travel in her eyes as the reflections changed, he thought of
what he had said concerning the hidden fire in a moor, and
it seemed to him that some such fire might burn in the
girl's heart, of which the scintillations in her eyes were the
only indication.

But the young man was not given to much thought and
consideration, and the notion that started to his mind disappeared from it as suddenly as it flashed out.

"You cannot remain here, Urith," he said. "I must
take you with me to Two Bridges, where I have stabled my
horse."

"I should prefer to find my way home alone."

"You are a fool—that is not possible."

She said nothing to his blunt and rude remark, but re-
volved in mind what was to be done.

The situation was not a pleasant one. She was well
aware that it would be in vain for her to attempt to discover the way for herself. On the other hand, she was reluctant to commit herself to the guidance of this youth,
who was no relation, not even a friend, only a distant acquaintance. The way, moreover, by which he would take
her home must treble the distance to Willsworthy. That
way would be, except for a short portion of it, over high
road, and to be seen travelling at night with a young man
far from her home would be certain to provoke comment,
as she could not expect to traverse the roads unobserved
by passengers. Although the journey would be made by
night, the packmen often travelled at night, and they were
purveyors, not only of goods, but of news and scandal.
She could not calculate on reaching home till past midnight; it would be sufficient to render her liable to invid-
ious remark were she to make this journey with such a
companion alone by day, but to do this at such a time of
night was certain to involve her in a flood of ill-natured
and ugly gossip. This thought decided her.

"No," she said, "I will stay here till daylight."

"That you shall not."

"But if I will?"

"You will find another will stronger than your own."

She laughed. "That can hardly be."

"Why do you refuse my guidance?"

"I do not want to go with you; I prefer to remain here."

"Why so?"

She looked down. She could not answer this question. He ought not to have asked it. He should have had the tact to understand the difficulty. But he was blunt of feeling, and he did not. Without more ado, he caught her in his arms and lifted her off the rock.

"If I carry you every step of the way," he said, roughly, "I will make you come with me."

She twisted herself in his grip; she set her hands against his shoulders and endeavoured to thrust him from her.

He threw aside his staff, with an oath, and set his teeth. Her hands were unbandaged. She had not been able to tie them up again, but she held the kerchiefs that had been wrapped round them in her fingers, and now they fell, and in her struggles her hands began to bleed, and the kerchiefs became entangled about his feet, and nigh on tripped him up.

"You will try your strength against me—wild cat?" he said.

She writhed, and caught at his hands, and endeavoured to unclinch them. She was angry and alarmed. In her alarm and anger she was strong. Moreover, she was a well-knit girl, of splendid constitution, and she battled lustily for her liberty. Anthony Cleverdon found that he had to use his whole strength to hold her.

"You are a coward?" she cried, in her passion. "To wrestle with a girl! You are a mean coward! Do you mark me?" she repeated.

"On my soul, you are strong!" said he, gasping.

"I hate you!" she said, exhausted, and desisting from further effort, which was vain.

"Well!" said he, as he set her down, "which is the strongest—your will or mine?"

"Our wills have not been tested," she answered, "only our strength; your male muscles and nerves are more powerful than those of a woman. God made them so, alack! That which I knew before, I know now, that a man is stouter than a woman. Boast of that, if you will—but as for our wills!" she shrugged her shoulders, then stooped and recovered her kerchiefs, and began impatiently, to cover her confusion, to re-adjust them about her hands, and to twist them with her teeth.

"And you will remain unbent, unbroken—to continue here in the wilderness?"

"My will is not to go with you."

"Then I use the advantage of my superior strength of nerve and muscle, and make you come along with me."

She took a step forward, still biting at the knots, but suddenly desisted, turned her head over her shoulder, and said, sullenly, "Drive—I am your captive." The step she had taken was acknowledgment of defeat.

"Come, Urith," said he, picking up his fallen staff, "it was in vain for you to resist me. No one opposes me without having in the end to yield. Tell me the truth—captive—captive if you will, tell me what brought you out on the moor? Was it to see the fires?"

"No, I ran away."

"Why did you run away?"

She was silent and strode forward, still pulling and biting at the knots.

"Come, answer me, why did you run away?"

"I was in a passion, slave-driver! Why do you say to me, 'Come, Urith?' I do not come, I go—driven forward by you."

"In a passion! What about?"

"My mother and Uncle Solomon worried me."

"What about?"

"That I will not tell you, though you beat me with your long stick."

"You know well enough, little owl, that I will not strike you."

"I know nothing, save that you are a bully."

"What! because I will not leave you on the moor to perish? Be reasonable, Urith. I am doing for you the best I can. I could not suffer you to remain uncared for on this waste. That would indeed be inhuman. Why, at sea it is infamy for a sailor to leave a wrecked vessel uncared for if he sights it."

There was reason in what he said. That she admitted

in her heart. In her heart, also, she was constrained to allow that the difficult situation into which she had fallen was due to her own conduct. Anthony Cleverdon was behaving towards her in the only way in which a generous lad could behave towards one found astray in the wilderness. But she was angry with him because he was too dull to see that there were difficulties in the way in which he proposed to restore her to her home, difficulties which she could not, in delicacy, express.

Anthony did not press her to speak further. He led the way now, and she followed; whereas, at first, she had preceded, in her angry humour, and to maintain the notion that she was being driven against her will. Occasionally he turned to see that she had not run away. She was chary of speech, out of humour, partly with him—chiefly with herself.

The way led from one granite tor to another, through all the intricacies of fissured bog, till at length the two travellers reached a sensible depression or slope of the land, and now the water, instead of lying stagnant in the clefts, began to run, and presently in a thousand rills filtered down a basin of turf towards a bottom, where they united in a river-head.

The aspect of the country at once changed. It was as when a fever-patient passes from incoherent and inarticulate mutterings into connected syllables, and then to clearly distinct sentences. The wandering veins and seams in the bog had found direction and drift for their contents, acquired a cant down which the water ran, and valley, stream, and river were the definite result.

"Now," said Anthony, "our course is clear; we have but to follow the water."

"How far?"

"About four miles."

"And then?"

"Then I will get my horse, and we shall have a direct course before us."

"What, the high road to Tavistock?"

"No. You shall not go that way."

"By what way then will you take me?"

"By the Lyke-Way."

CHAPTER II.

THE LYKE-WAY.

The whole of Dartmoor Proper is included within the bounds of a single parish, the parish of Lydford. The moor belongs to the Duchy of Cornwall, and at Lydford stood the Ducal Castle. For two hundred years this castle has been in ruins, but stands a monument of possession, and just as the estate has been eaten into and pillaged through a long course of years, so has the castle of the Duke been broken into and robbed, to furnish cottages with stone, and cowstalls with timber.

Parishes when first constituted followed the boundaries of manors, consequently, as the Duke of Cornwall claimed the entire Forest of Dartmoor, that whole forest was included within the parish limits. It is the largest parish as to acreage in England, and that with the scantiest population in proportion to its area.

In former times the moor attracted miners, it does so still, but to a very limited extent ; extensive operations were anciently carried on in every stream bed in quest of tin.

The vast masses of upturned refuse testify to the vastness of the mining works that once made the moors teem with people. The workers in the mines lived in huts merely constructed of uncemented granite blocks, thatched with turf ; the ruins of which may still be inspected. But even these ruins are comparatively recent, though dating from the Middle Ages, for there were earlier toilers on the same ground, and for the same ends, who also lived on the moor, and have also left there their traces ; they dwelt in circular beehive huts, like those of the Esquimaux, warmed by a central fire, and covered in by a conical roof that had a smoke-vent in the midst. Tens of thousands of these remain, some scattered, most congregated within circular enclosures, and hundreds of thousands have been, and are being, annually destroyed. In connection with these are the megalithic circles and lines of upright stones, cairns that contain tombs made of rude stone blocks set on end, and covered with slabs equally rude.

Who were the people that made of Dartmoor at a remote period a scene of so much activity? Probably a race that occupied Britain before the British, and which was subjugated by the inflowing, conquering Celts.

Throughout the Middle Ages, down to the Civil Wars, the tin was much worked, and men living on the moor also died there; and dying there had to be buried somewhere, and that somewhere was properly in the parish churchyard.

Now, as there is but a single road across the moor from Tavistock to Two Bridges, where it forks, one road going to Moreton, the other to Ashburton, and as the main road was of no great assistance to such as desired to reach Lydford for the sake of their burying their dead, a way was made, rudely paved, and indicated where not paved by standing stones, for the sole purpose of conveying corpses to their final resting place.

This way, of which at present but faint traces exist, was called the Lyke-Way. Since the establishment of the prison at Prince's Town, first for French captives in the European War, then for Irish and English convicts, a church has been erected, and a graveyard enclosed and consecrated, for the convenience and accommodation of those who live and those who die on Dartmoor. The Lyke-Way has accordingly been abandoned for three-quarters of a century; nevertheless it is still pointed out by the moor-men, and is still occasionally taken advantage of by them.

In former days, when for weeks the moor was covered with snow, and its road and tracks deep in drifts, corpses were deliberately exposed to the frost, or were salted into chests, to preserve them till the Lyke-Way was once more passable.

Where the Lyke-Way touches a stream, there double stepping-stones were planted in the bed, for the use of the bearers, occasionally a rude bridge was constructed, by piling up a pier in midwater, and throwing slabs of granite across, to meet in the midst on this pier; but these were always wide enough to permit of the bearers to cross the bridge with the bier between them.

It is not to be marvelled at that superstition attaches to this road, and that at night, especially when the moon is shining, and the clouds are flying before the wind, the moor-men aver that there pass trains of phantom mourners along this way, bearing a bier, gliding rather than running, shadows only, not substantial men of flesh. And as, in the old days, the funeral train sang hymns as they went along with their load, up hill and down dale, so do the moor-men protest at the present time that when the phantom train sweeps along the Lyke-Way, a solemn dirge is wafted on the wind of such overwhelming sadness, that he who hears it is forced to cover his face, and burst into tears.

It is said that if one be daring enough to hide behind a rock on the side of the corpse-track when the phantom procession is on the move, so as to suffer it to pass near him, he will see his own face upturned to the moon on the bier that goes by. Then must he make the best of his time, for within a year he will be dead.

Along the Lyke-Way, as the nearest way to her home, and also to his own, in defiance of the superstition that clung to it, did Anthony Cleverdon purpose to conduct Urith.

When she heard him suggest this way she shivered, for she was, though a strong-minded girl, imbued with the belief of the age. But the power to resist was taken from her. Moreover, along that way there was less chance than on any other of encountering travellers, and Urith shrank from being seen.

On reaching the point where she and her companion touched the Lyke-Way, a point recognisable only by Anthony, who was familiar with it—for here it was but a track over smooth turf, then Cleverdon bade his companion seat herself on a stone and await him. He would, he said, go to the tavern and fetch his horse.

Her opposition to his determination had ceased, not because her will was conquered, but because she was without an alternative course to cling to, without a purpose to oppose to his. She was weary and hungry. She had rambled for many hours before Cleverdon had discovered her, and had eaten nothing. Fatigued and faint, she was glad to rest on the stone, and to be left alone, that she might unobserved give way to the tears of annoyance and anger that welled up in her heart.

In an access of inconsiderate wrath—wrath is ever inconsiderate—she had run away from home—run from a sick mother—and she was now reaping the vexations that followed on what she had done. Her annoyance was aggravated, not tempered, by the thought that no one was to blame for the unpleasant predicament in which she was placed but her own self.

As Urith sat, awaiting the return of Anthony, gazing around her, it appeared to her that the scene could hardly be more awful at the consummation of all things. The whole of the world, as far as she could see, was on fire ; it looked as if a black crust were formed over an inner glowing core, like the coal-dust clotted in a blacksmith's forge above the burning interior. There were wandering sparks ranging over it, and here and there a quiver of lurid flame. All that was needed to excite to universal conflagration was a thrust with an iron rod, a blast of concentrated wind, and then the crust would break up, and through its rents would flare out rays of fire too dazzling to look upon, that would swallow up all darkness and dissolve mountain and granite into liquid incandescent lava, and dry up every river with a breath. There was water near the rock where Urith sat, and she again unwound her hands and dipped the bandages in the cool stream.

She was thus engaged, when softly over the velvet turf came Anthony, leading his horse.

"Let me look," said he, bluntly ; "let me tie up your rags. How did you injure your knuckles ?"

She obediently held out her hands.

"I did it myself."

"How? Against the rocks ?"

"No—with my teeth."

"What! You bit your hands ?"

"Yes. I bit my hands. I was in a rage."

"We men," said Anthony, "when we are angry, hurt each other, but you women, I suppose, hurt your own selves ?"

"Yes. We have not the strength or the means to hurt others. Not that we lack the will—so we hurt ourselves. I would rather have bitten some one else, but I could not, so I tore my own hands—with my teeth."

"You are strange beings, you women," said Anthony.

Then he threw the bridle on the ground, and set his foot on it, so as to disengage his own hands.

He took hold of Urith's wrist, and the kerchiefs, one after the other, and arranged the bandages, and fastened them firmly. Whilst thus engaged, he suddenly looked up, and caught her sombre eyes fixed intently on him.

"Would you hurt me—bite and mangle me?" he asked, with a laugh.

"Yes—if you gave me occasion."

"And if I gave you opportunity?"

"Assuredly, if I had the occasion and the opportunity."

"Which latter I would not be such a fool as to allow you."

"Opportunities come—are not made and given."

"You are a strange girl," he said; holding her hands by the bandaged knots at the wrists, and looking into her gloomy eyes; "I should be sorry to rouse the wild best in you—there is one curled up in your heart—that I can see. Your eyes are the entrance to its lair."

"Yes," answered Urith, without shrinking, "it is true there is a wild beast in me."

"And you obey the wild beast. It stretched itself and sniffed the moor air—than away you ran out into the wilderness."

He continued to study her face; that exercised a strange fascination upon him.

"Yes; I was in one of my fits. I was angry, and when I am angry I have no reason—no thought—no feelings, nothing save anger. Just as the moor now is—all fire; and the fire consumes everything. I could not hurt my mother—I did not want to hurt my Uncle Solomon. That other—— He was beyond my reach, and so I bit myself."

Anthony made an attempt to shake himself free from the sensation that stole over his senses, a sensation of giddiness. The effort was ineffectual, it lacked resoluteness, and again the spell settled over him; he was falling into a dream, with his hands on her wrists, and her pulses throbbing against his fingers, a dream woven about him, enlacing, entangling mind and heart and consciousness; a dream in which he was losing all power of seeing anything save her eyes, of hearing anything save her breathing, of feeling anything save the dull throb of her pulse—a dream

2

in which he was being caught and bound, and thrown powerless at her feet—a dream of mingled rapture and pain and undefined terror. She had called herself his captive a little while ago, and now she, without a word or a movement, was subjecting him absolutely.

How long he stood thus fascinated he could not conjecture, he was startled out of it by his horse jerking his bridle from under his foot, and then at once, as one starting out of a trance, he passed into a world of other sensations, he heard the rush of water and the wail of wind, he saw the fires about him, and Urith's eyes no longer filled the entire horizon.

"Come," said he, roughly, as he caught the bridle, "get on the horse ; we must waste no more time talking folly." He put his hands under her foot, and with a leap she was in the saddle.

"You can ride of course," said he, churlishly ; he detested the spell that had been thrown over him ; the conviction that he had been very nearly falling wholly into her power.

"Of course I can ride—I am a moor-maid."

With his hand at the bit he urged the horse on, and strode forward, looking down at the turf, without speaking. The sudden drunkenness of brain that had come over him left its vapours that were not withdrawn wholly and at once. But Anthony was not a man to brood over any sensation or experience, and when Urith asked, "Did you find your father's colts?" he recovered his good humour and gaiety, and answered in his wonted tone, "No, the fire must have driven them further north, maybe they are lost in Cranmeer." Then, with a laugh, he added, "I have been like Saul seeking my father's beasts, and like Saul, have found something better." He looked up at her with a flashing eye.

She turned her head away.

"You came to the moors alone?" she asked.

He did not reply, but pointed to the west. "The wind is shifting, I hold. The direction of the smoke and flames is changed."

She did not observe that he evaded giving her a reply to her question.

The way now dipped into a broad valley, where the fire had already burnt, and had exhausted itself.

It lay before them a dark trough, and yet scintillating in points where ashes glowed after the flames had exhausted themselves. An auroral light pervaded the sky overhead, especially bright above the hills to the east, and against it the granite piles of rock on the mountain tops, stood forth as ruined castles crumbling away in the conflagration, and above one huge block, like an altar, smoke rose in columns intermingled with flame, as though on it a gigantic sacrificial oblation were being made.

"I suppose you were angry with me when I snatched you off Devil Tor, and you strove to free yourself?" said Anthony.

"Not angry, but reluctant," she replied; "for I knew that you wished me well, and that your violence was kindly meant."

He drew the reins sharply and arrested the horse, then turned, put his arm over the neck, and looked up at Urith.

"Verily," said he, "I have the fancy that I should like to put you into one of your fits—as you term them."

"Indeed," she answered; "it is a cruel fancy, for my fits end in some hurt. When the devil entered into the child it cast him into the fire or into the water, and tore him before it came out. You see what one fit has cost me"—she extended her bandaged hands. "But you do not feel how they sting and burn. It may have been rare sport for such as looked on to see this child half scorched by the fire, half smothered by the water, and prostrate, mangled by the devil—but I question if any one would have had the heart to invoke the devil to possess the child; yet that is what you would do."

"Nay," said Anthony, a little confounded by her vehemence and the charge against him; "nay, I would not have you again hurt."

"Then would you stand to be torn yourself?"

"What—would you tear and bite me?"

"I cannot say. When I have one of my fits on me I do not know what I am about."

"Are you repentant for your action afterwards?"

"Assuredly I am repentant when I have gnawed my hands, for they are full of pain."

He turned away. The girl disturbed him. The young man was not accustomed to meet with damsels who were

not honey and cream, smiles and allurements—the frank
avowal of savagery in Urith, mingled with the consciousness that she exerted over him a certain fascination against
which he had no counter-spell, caused him uneasiness.
He turned abruptly round and went forward with lowered
head, and the vapours recently lifted from his brain began
to settle over them again.

Presently he came to the side of a foaming tumbling
river. He halted, and, without looking into Urith's face,
said——

"Now we have come to the Walla, and my cob has been
restive at crossing water to-day, shall I help you to dismount? You can go over by the stepping-stones. I must
ride him across."

He put forth his hand, but she slipped to her feet unas-
sisted, and handed to him the crop or long-lashed whip
that had hung at the saddle-bow, but which she had taken
in hand.

"Yes," he said, "I shall require the crop." Then he
leaped into the saddle and spurred the horse down into the
water.

Urith tripped along the stones till she reached a broad
block in the midst of the river. She found no difficulty in
crossing, as the light overhead mirrored itself in the water,
making of the Walla a very Phlegethon. But for the same
reason Anthony's cob objected to enter. He reared and
plunged, and when whipped and spurred, wheeled about.

Urith watched the futile efforts of her companion.

Presently she called to Anthony, "The cob will go into
the water if you pat him. You further frighten him by
your violence when he is already frightened. The river
seems to roll down fire and blood."

"What!" laughed Anthony; "will you teach me how to
manage a horse?"

"I have had to do with horses every whit as much as
yourself," she replied. "Remember, I am the Wild Maid
of the Moors."

He made no reply, but again essayed to force the cob to
enter the water. Suddenly Urith, still stationed in mid-
stream, uttered an exclamation of surprise, not unmingled
with alarm.

She saw black figures emerge on the hill shoulder, visible against the lurid sky, and then descend along the Lyke-Way, coming along the same track, in the same direction.

At once there rushed upon her the stories she had heard of ghostly trains of mourners, sweeping at night along this road, and of the ill-luck that attended such as cast eyes on them.

"Look!—look!" she exclaimed, now in real terror. "Who are they?—what are they? They are following us, Anthony Cleverdon! Do not let us see them more. Do not let them overtake us."

CHAPTER III.

CAUGHT UP ON THE WAY.

Anthony looked back. Strange was the appearance of the moor side, half-lighted by the skies reddened with the reflection of fires beyond the hills, but with its surface travelled over by sparks. An imaginative mind might have thought that mountain gnomes were alert, and were rambling torch in hand over the moor. Now one red spark wandered along in solitude, then out flashed a second, and ran to meet it ; as if they were the lights of comrades hailing each other. Suddenly a score sparkled and danced in a ring, and were as suddenly extinguished. Or it might be supposed that the spirits of the primeval tin-workers had returned to earth once more, and were revisiting their ancient circles and avenues of stone, to perform in them the rites of a forgotten religion.

To the south-east rose Mistor, one of the loftiest summits on the moor, on whose rocky crest, scooped out by wind and water, is a huge circular bowl, called by the natives the Devil's Fryingpan, in which he prepares the storms that lash and explode on the moor. And now it really seemed as though the Spirit of the Tempest were at work, brewing in his bowl.

In the strange after-glow that partially lighted the hill-side could be seen dark figures descending the Lyke-Way, and approaching the ford where Anthony was vainly endeavouring to force his cob to cross. Anthony uttered an oath, and then redoubled his attempts to drive the brute into the water. But it came to the edge, snuffed, and recoiled.

"What is it?" asked Urith, still watching the pursuing shadows.

Urith ran back over the stones.

"Only some folks coming after us. By heaven! I wish I could get this cursed beast over."

"If you take the bridle on one side, I on the other, and coax the horse, we can cross by the double stones, and he can go in the middle."

"As the bearers with the dead," said Anthony.

Urith patted the frightened beast, talked to him, praised him, and taking the bridle, quietly led him down to the stream. Ever and anon, she turned to look back, and saw the shadowy figures rapidly nearing. Who could they be? Would they recognise her? Were they such as would be likely to recognise her? What, if they knew her, would they think of her being at such a time, and in such a place, alone with Anthony Cleverdon?

Would it be advisable to step aside, and let these travellers pass without seeing her? But she was too ashamed to make such a proposal to her companion. So, as she was caressing the horse, and urging him into the water, these pursuers, whoever they were, drew nearer. She could distinguish that they were mounted.

Anthony stood on the stepping-stones on one side, Urith on those upon the other. The frightened horse cautiously put his hoofs in, snuffed at the water, began to drink, recovered confidence, and allowed himself to be led along through the stream.

They were past the middle of the river when the pursuers came to the side of the stream, and a loud male voice exclaimed——

"There is the runaway, and by God—not alone!"

Urith shuddered, her hand twitched at the bridle, and made the horse start. She knew the voice well. It was not a pleasant one, harsh, and with mockery and insult in its tones. As her hand contracted, so did her heart, and sent a rush of blood tingling to her temples.

"That is Fox Crymes!" she said to her companion, "the last, the very last man I would have had see me here."

" Why the last ? " asked Anthony, stepping on the bank, and leading the horse up on the land. " Why the last that you would have see you, Urith ? "

"Because it was on his account I ran away."

" What," laughed Anthony, "Then it is Fox whom you would have bitten, had he allowed you to fasten your teeth on him ? "

Urith's colour deepened ; if Anthony had had pity, he would not have said this. If he had looked in her face, he would have seen how dark it was with shame and vexation.

"You wring all out. You are cruel—yes, Fox Crymes," she muttered.

" And I am not surprised. I would like to thrash him," said Anthony. "For one thing, for coming up with us now."

The pursuing party consisted of but three, Fox—his real Christian name was Anthony—and two others, Bessie, the sister of Anthony Cleverdon, and Julian, Fox Crimes' half-sister. Both Crymes and Cleverdon had the same Christian name. Old Cleverdon, the father, had been sponsor to Crymes, and in compliment to him had received at the font his godfather's name.

Fox was the only son of Fernando Crymes. Since childhood he had borne the nickname, partly because of his red hair, partly because of his pointed features, also, in a measure, because it was thought that somewhat of the craft and subtlety of Reynard was intwined in his nature. He did not object to the designation ; it had attached itself to him at an early age, when it conveyed no meaning to his mind, and in mature years he accepted it without demur, and was perhaps a little proud that he should be credited with superior shrewdness.

After the death of Fox's mother, old Fernando Crymes had married an heiress—a Glanville—and by her had a single daughter, Julian, at whose birth this second wife had died. Fernando Crymes, though belonging to a very ancient and estated family, had frittered away such remains of the property as had come to him, and would have been reduced to threadbare circumstances had not his second marriage rehabilitated him. He was trustee for his daughter, and lived on her estate. His son, Anthony, was but too well aware that the portion of goods that would fall to himself must be small, whereas his half-sister would be wealthy. The consciousness of this disparity in their prospects affected their relations to each other. Julian was disposed to imperiousness, and Fox let no opportunity pass of saying or doing something to annoy her.

"You have played us a scurvy trick, Anthony," said Fox, as he splashed through the river, and came up with the two on the further bank; then pushing close to Urith, whom Anthony had remounted on his saddle, he peered rudely into her face. He uttered an exclamation of rage as he recognised her, and turned away towards Cleverdon, and said, in a rasping tone, "We awaited you at the tavern an endless age, ever expecting you to come and let us know whether you had found the colts or not. I assured your sister and mine that you were after game of some sort, and the colt-seeking was a mask, but they would not believe me. Finally, I went to the stable, and found that you had slipped away without a word."

"Was I bound to let you know I was going home?" asked Anthony Cleverdon, without an effort to disguise his ill-humour.

"Bound, certainly, by all the ties of breeding and good-fellowship," answered Fox. "But, in good faith, when a woman is concerned, all other considerations are thrown to the winds."

Then he fell back, and addressing his sister Julian and Bessie Cleverdon loud enough to be overheard by those in front, he said, "I never doubted but that Anthony came after something other than colts, and to make a mock of us. I told you as much when we were at the Saracen's Head, and you scouted my words. You said the Fox was ever suspicious, but the Fox has his eye and his nose, and ear keen, and I saw, and smelt, and heard what was hidden to duller senses."

Cleverdon turned round. He was angry, but he said nothing.

Fox Crymes went on, tauntingly. "There is game of all sorts on the Moor; but, good Lord! it is sometimes hard to say which is the game and which the sportsman, and which has been in pursuit of the other."

"Silence that malicious tongue of yours, or I will silence it for you," said Anthony, angrily.

"O! I am always to be threatened whenever I draw my bow, but you—are to be scatheless, whatever your conduct be."

"You fight unfairly, with poisoned weapons."

"And you retaliate, like a wild man, with a bludgeon," answered Crymes. "Are we to hold our hands when treated by you as it has pleased you? You invited us to attend you to the Moor and spend with you a merry day, and then you desert us. Are we not free to question why we are thus treated?"

Then Bessie rode forwards beside Urith, and asked, "Tell me, how came you here?"

"She lost her way in the smoke, and no marvel," said Anthony Cleverdon. "I discovered her strayed among the bogs, and engirded with flames; and had I not done so, she would have stayed all night."

"But what brought her on to the moors?"

"The same occasion that brought you, Bess—she came to see the fires. She became distraught with the smoke, wandered, and lost all knowledge of her direction."

"It is well, brother, that you found her," said Elizabeth; and then, in a lower tone, "Brother, brother, speak to Julian. You have been short of courtesy to-day, and she resents it."

Anthony shrugged his shoulders.

"I will ride alongside of Urith," said Elizabeth Cleverdon. "You must not allow it to be observed that you lack manners, brother Anthony. You persuaded Julian and me to come with you and see the moor on fire, and you have left us to ourselves, and now disregard her markedly."

Whilst the brother and sister were in conversation near the horse on which Urith was mounted, Julian Crymes passed them with averted head, and took the lead along the Lyke-Way. Anthony, admonished by Bessie, strode forward after her, but with a frown and curl of the lips.

Julian Crymes was a handsome dark-haired girl, with a rich, warm complexion, and full lips and rounded chin. Her eyes were large, with that droop in the lids that gives an impression of sensuous languor.

She heard Anthony tread at her side, but did not deign to cast on him a look, neither did she throw a word at him.

Indeed, she was angry and offended, her bosom was heaving, her blood was simmering, and her lips she bit to prevent their quiver. Anthony was out of humour at having been caught up by the party, and was conscious that he had not behaved with civility, but was too proud in himself, too indifferent to the feelings of others, to acknowledge himself to be in the wrong, and to make amends for his lack of courtesy to others.

Accordingly they pursued their way, side by side, she riding with averted head, he pacing with knitted brows and downcast eyes, in silence, and for some considerable distance.

The situation was irksome. Each, instead of speaking, was endeavouring to catch what was said in the rear, each with suspicion that Fox was saying something behind their backs which would cause the left ear to tingle.

Julian was the first to find the situation intolerable, and to break from it. She turned her head over her shoulders and said,

"Bessie could hardly be persuaded to leave the Saracen's Head, even when she heard that you had taken your horse and had ridden away. She has a marvellous faith in you, not shaken by a thousand evidences that you are wanting in those qualities on which faith can be reared. After this day's experience, even if I at any time shared in her estimation of your qualities of cavalier, I shall cease to do so for the future. The first obligation of a cavalier is to be mannerly towards ladies."

"You had Fox with you. I found Urith lost in the morasses, and was forced to help a damsel who was in jeopardy—that, I take it, is the first duty of a cavalier. You were in no straits and she was. You had help, she none."

"You might have called us to aid you in extracting her from the morass, or in assisting her to reach her home afterwards."

Anthony made no reply to this. No reply was possible.

"Come!" said Julian, the pent-up anger in her heart flashing forth. "Have you no apology to offer for your misconduct?"

"What would you have me say?"

"Nay! It is not for me to put the words into your mouth."

"I have told you my reason."

"A poor and pitiful reason, ungarnished with excuse to hide its sorry nature. If the reason be bad, so much the more should it be trimmed with excuses."

"If I have offended you, I am sorry. I cannot help it."

Julian tossed her head. She was highly incensed. He made no attempt to mollify her.

Fox came alongside.

"I hope, Julian," he said, "that you have soundly rated Anthony for his ill-conduct."

She did not answer.

"We might have had a merry canter home over the turf," continued Fox, "had not Anthony spoiled our fun by setting all our tempers on the edge. But it may be that it better comports with the character of the Lyke-Way that we should travel over it rather as mourners than as merry-makers, and that, forsooth, we are, bearing dead fellow-ship between us."

"There is no occasion for that," said Anthony.

"In truth there is, though you who have slain it may not be aware."

"I have no desire to spoil your mirth," said Cleverdon. "Ride on yourself, Fox, with your sister, and leave me behind."

"Julian and I are the worst of company together. We snarl and snap at each other when a third, not of the family, is not by to control us. We will certainly not leave you. I can see that Julian is already in no agreeable mood, and I dare not venture myself in her company un-protected."

"I—!" said Julian Crymes, tossing her head, "I—you mistake, Tony, I am merry."

Fox Crymes laughed mockingly, and spurred on his horse, leaving his sister with Anthony. Bessie brought up the rear with Urith. The train was, as he said, more in character with the way than if it had been composed of merrymakers. Urith and Bessie spoke together in a low tone; now that Fox had ridden forward, silence again fell on Anthony and Julian. He could not have seen the face of Julian had he essayed to do so, for he walked on the off-side, and she kept her head averted, and he his eyes depressed. She was glad that her face was hidden from observation, so agitated was it with disappointment, wounded pride, and jealousy.

Then Fox, ahead, began to sing to himself in strident tones a snatch of an old ballad, and every word in it fell on Julian's heart as a drop of burning phosphorous that no water will extinguish, but that burns down where it has fallen, burying itself, till it has exhausted its fire.

> If I of marriage spake one word,
>   I wot it was not true.
> Man loveth none so easy won,
>   So over fond as you.
> All in your garden grows a herb,
>   I think they call it rue ;
> There willows weep o'er waters deep—
>   That is the place for you.

The tears of mortification rushed into Julian's eyes. Her bosom heaved, and sharply she wheeled her horse about, rode back to those that followed, and said to Bessie, in a voice quivering with emotion, "Go on to the two Anthonys. I want a word with Urith."

Without demur Elizabeth left her place and passed Julian, who drew up across the road to force Urith to rein in. Urith looked at her with some surprise. She did not know Julian except by sight ; she had never spoken to her in her life. And now this latter stayed her course as though she were a highwayman demanding her purse.

Julian at first was unable to speak, choked by her passion. She panted for breath and laboured for words, and both failed her. With nervous hands she plucked at her gloves, and dragged rather than drew them off.

"Will you allow me to go forward ?" asked Urith coldly.

Then all at once Julian broke forth into a stream of words, disconnected, fiery with the fury that raged within.

"You would snatch him away ! You ! And you do not know, or you do not care, that he and I are destined for each other—have been ever since our cradles. Who are you to come between us ? What are you, Urith Malvine, but a half-savage moor-girl ? I have heard of you. Folks have tongues, and tell tales. Why did you come forth on the moor, but because you were aware that he was here ? You came to play the forlorn damsel—to attract the pity and ensure the attention of this knight-errant. Are you crafty? I am not. I am straightforward, and do not deign to wear a false face, and put the domino on my heart. I have heard of you; but I never supposed you were crafty." She half-started up her stirrups: "Would we might fight out our quarrel here, on this spot."

She had reared her arm with her whip, the horse started, and she sank back on her seat; she had exhausted her words for the moment. Her blood tumbled, roared, flowed in her arteries like the river on the moor behind them.

"You are mistaken," said Urith with composure. "You flare forth unprovoked; or is it that you are angry with me because I have refused to have anything to say to your brother?"

"To Fox!" Julian laughed contemptuously. "I respect you for that. I never supposed that you or any sane girl would care for him. But the wherefore of his rejection I did not know till this day. I little suspected that Fox was cast aside because you were questing him who is mine—is mine, do you hear? Do you understand that he is not, and never shall be, yours? He is mine, and neither you nor any other shall pluck him from me. I would we might fight this out together with these weapons!" She reverted to the thought that had occupied her when the horse started and interrupted the thread of her ideas. "You, I see, have Anthony's crop that I gave him on his birthday; and I have but this lady's switch. I do not consider the difference. Just as we are—as we sit on our horses, here, on the turf and heather, with our whips— would to God we might fight it out!"

Again she paused for breath, and panted, and put both her hands to her bounding heart—the hand that held the whip and that in which was the bridle and her gloves.

Then she began to cut with her whip, and the horse she rode to curvet.

"Even with this little lash I would fight you, and slash you up and down across your treacherous face; and if you struck me I should not feel the blows—but there, it would not be seemly. Alack the day in which we are fallen— when we are covered with a net of such delicacy that we may not lift hand or foot to right ourselves!"

She drew a long breath and laid both her hands on the whip and bridle over the mane of the horse, and, leaning forward, said—

"But who—what could interfere if we went a race down the hillside among the bogs and rocks, so that one or other would be flung at a stumble of our steeds, and dash out the brains from our heads on the boulders? Would that please you? Would that approve itself to you? I should draw rein and laugh were that to chance to you." Then in an explosion of jealousy and rage, she dashed her gloves in the face of Urith. "I dare you! Yes, I dare you to wrest him from me!"

Urith sat on the horse unmoved. She was surprised, she was not angry. This was the foaming over of boiling passion, but not a frenzied paroxysm such as came upon herself. The charges brought against her were monstrous, untrue—so monstrous and so untrue that they bore no sting that could pain her.

She replied in her rich deep tones, and with composure. "You mistake. I will not take up your challenge. What is Anthony to me? What am I to him? You are beautiful, clever, and rich—and I," she laughed, "I am but an ungroomed, undisciplined moor colt, who never gave a thought to her looks, whether fair or foul. I am without wit, without scholarship, living with my mother on our poor manor, so poor in means as to be hardly accounted gentle, yet, by birth, too gentle to be esteemed boors. No, I will not contest with you. We are furnished unequally for a contest, you have the long whip and I but the switch."

At that moment the wind, blowing strongly, carried a tuft of ignited gorse overhead, and as it bore the tuft, fanned into fragrance, and the glare momentarily kindled the faces of the two girls planted in opposition.

Each saw the other clearer than in daylight, for the light fell on their faces and the background was sable, unillumined. As Urith looked, she saw how handsome was her opponent, with fluttering locks, her colour heightened by wrath, her full lips trembling, her eyes flashing. She thought that if she were to match herself against such an one she would come away with ignominious defeat; and Julian, by the same light, and at the same moment, formed her opinion of the rival facing her, recognised her strength, her charm, and felt that she was a girl who would jeopardise her hold over Anthony, and imperil her happiness.

Both were strong women, one threatening, the other reluctant to fight. Would they come into real conflict? Would the reluctance of the one be overborne? Would the threat of the first lead to action? And, if they fought, which would win?

"No," said Urith, "I do not covet the prize. So much for one thing. For the other, as I said, the odds are unequal."

"Then," said Julian, "return me my gloves."

"I suppose they have fallen. Would you have me dismount to search the grass for them? Get off your horse yourself, or call Fox to your aid. I will not stoop to look for them for you."

"You have my gloves. They are not on the ground. Return them to me, or I——"

Then Urith impatiently whipped her horse and thrust Julian aside. "This is arrant folly," she said; "I want to be at home. I will be stayed by you no longer."

CHAPTER IV.

THE SUSPENSE.

The ill-assorted, discordant party pushed on as fast as possible along a road that, as it neared inhabited country, became rough and uncertain, and under a sky of diminished light, for the heather on this portion of the moor had been burnt early in the day, and hardly any of the embers remained aglow.

No combination was possible that would content all, for every one except the good-humoured Bessie had some private grudge against another, and Bessie herself was depressed by the general dissatisfaction.

Anthony Cleverdon was vexed that he had not been left to convey Urith to her home undisturbed, though he admitted to himself that for her sake the present accidental arrangement was the best. Julian Crymes, still incandescent in her anger and jealousy, was unwilling to speak to Anthony, and unwilling to allow him to leave her side to address a word to, and show attention to, Urith. When she did speak to him, it was in a taunting tone, and his answers were curt, almost to rudeness.

The temper of Fox Crymes, never smooth, was now fretted to considerable asperity ; for he was smarting under the sense of rejection. He had asked for the hand of Urith, and had been refused, and he saw, or suspected that he saw, a reason for his rejection—an attachment for Anthony Cleverdon. Fox was vain and conceited, and envious of his namesake, who had superior physical powers, a finer person, and a better fortune than himself. He was not sorry that his half-sister was disappointed, for whatever might distress her, gave pleasure to him. However, the occasion of her distress on this occasion was something that wounded him as well as her.

Fox loved Urith, as far as he was capable of loving, but the jealousy he now felt was no measure of his love ; like the famous Serpent's Egg, it was bred of a score of parents. It was the produce of mortified vanity, of envy of Anthony Cleverdon's superior gifts of nature and fortune, of disappointed avarice, quite as much as of rejected love.

Fox Crymes' suit for Urith was not instigated wholly by his admiration for her charms ; it sprang quite as much out of his desire to obtain the small patrimony which would fall to her on her mother's decease.

Willsworthy was an ancient manor, never of great importance, and without fertility, yet not despicable in the eyes of a poor gentleman. It lay on the extreme limits of cultivated land, or rather it may be said to have occupied the debateable ground between the waste and culture. It occupied a hill that ran as a spur out of the moorland, between torrents, and seemed to be what, no doubt, it was, a portion of wilderness snatched from savagery, and hedged in. It possessed no good soil, it lay too high for wheat to ripen on it, it was destitute of these pasture meadows by the waterside, where the grass grows knee-deep, and is gold-sprinkled in spring with buttercups ; it was dominated by rugged tors, and stood near the entrance of the gorge of the Tavy, where it roared and leaped, and shot as it came down into the lowlands, and with it came down the cold blasts that also roared and whirled, and beat about the lone Manor of Willsworthy.

Mrs. Malvine talked disparagingly of her farm, her brother Solomon Gibbs averred it was an estate on which to starve, and not to live. Urith accepted their verdict as final, she knew the need for money that ever prevailed in her house; and yet Fox Crymes cast greedy eyes upon the estate. He saw that it possessed capabilities that were disregarded by the widow and her brother. The manor owned considerable rights. It had the freedom of the moor, to send out upon it an unlimited number of sheep and cattle and colts; at a time when English wool was fetching a high price, and was exported to the Mediterranean, to Cadiz, to Leghorn, to Palermo, to Marseilles; this was important— it afforded exceptional opportunities of making money. There needed but the initial outlay on the stock, their keep was free. Not only so, but sheep in lowlands were, in wet seasons, afflicted with disease which slew them in great numbers, which sometimes exterminated entire flocks. But sheep on the moor were never known thus to suffer; they enjoyed perfect immunity from the many maladies which attend keeping them on cultivated land.

The climate in the West of England is so mild that it was possible to let the sheep run on the moor through the major portion of the year, only for a few months in the depth of the winter, possibly only when snow lay on the moor, was it needful to provide them with food; and the meadows of Willsworthy, though they did not produce rank grass, yet produced hay that was extraordinary sweet and nutritious, and in sufficient abundance to support a large number of sheep and cattle for the short time during which they were debarred from foraging for themselves. Anthony Crymes saw plainly enough, that if he had the management of the estate of Willsworthy he would make it a mine of gold; and that the reason why it did not now flourish was the lack of capital in the acres, and mismanagement. Anthony Crymes knew that some money would come to him from his father, not indeed much, but just sufficient for his purpose, should he acquire this property —and he was very ambitious of obtaining it.

At present, Mrs. Malvine entrusted the conduct of the farm to her brother Solomon who belied his name; he was a man without any knowledge of farming, and with no interest save in his violin, and who took delight only in good company. The farm was allowed to take its course, which was naturally a retrograde one—a relapse from former culture into pristine wilderness.

At the period of this tale, some two hundred years ago, every squire farmed, if not his entire estate, at all events a portion of it. Men of ancient pedigree, proud of their ancestral properties and mansions, of their arms and their alliances, did not disdain to ride to market and cheapen cattle.

The Civil War ruined most of the squires who had taken up arms for the King, litigation ruined others; then came in the great merchants and bought the old owners out, and established themselves in their room. They understood nothing of farming, and esteemed it despicable and unworthy of their new-fangled gentility to pursue it.

With the gall of envy bitter in his heart did Fox see the other Anthony walk alongside of Urith, and assume towards her an intimacy to which he himself had never attained. The girl had ever avoided him, had treated him with coldness tinged with ill-disguised disdain. She had not made that effort to veil her dislike which will gloss over a repulse. Fox saw another man better favoured than himself, reach at a bound a position he had laboriously tried to mount, and had failed.

Hall, or as the country-folk called it "Yall," was the house of the Cleverdons. It had belonged to the Glanville estates—had been bought by old Judge Glanville, in the reign of Elizabeth, who had founded the family. The Glanvilles had flourished for awhile, and had spread over the country-side, taking up estate after estate, and had collapsed as suddenly as they had risen. The Cleverdons had been farmers, renting Hall, and when that estate was sold old Cleverdon by some means got together sufficient money to purchase it, and since the purchase had laid out considerable sums to transform what had been a modest farmhouse into a pretentious squire's mansion.

Old Anthony was in that transitional state in which, passing from one rank of life to another, he was comfortable in neither. He was sensitive and ambitious—sensitive to slights, and ambitious to push himself and his son into a better social position than that which had been occupied by his ancestors ; and, indeed, by himself in early life. The Crymes family had been connected with the Glanvilles by marriage, and now old Anthony schemed on the acquisition of another portion of the Glanville property, through the marriage of his son and heir with Julian Crymes. The old man's success had fostered his ambition. He indulged in a dream of the Cleverdons, by skilful management, assuming eventually the position once maintained by the Glanvilles.

The Civil Wars had produced vast displacement in the social strata. The old gentry were failing, and those who had taken part with neither side, but had waited on their own interests in selfish or indifferent neutrality, were rewarded by emerging, where others were falling into ruin, into ripe prosperity. After that Anthony Cleverdon, the elder, had acquired the freehold of Hall, he had become a widower, and showed no disposition to take to himself another wife. His marriage had not been a happy experience, and none had felt the disagreement in it more than Elizabeth, his eldest daughter, who, after her mother's death, had been called to manage the household. If the opinion of Magdalen Cleverdon were to be taken—the unmarried sister of Anthony, senior—who lived in a small house in Tavistock, the blame of the unhappiness of her brother's married life lay with his wife ; but then the judgment of Magdalen was warped and partial. When Anthony brought home his young wife, she—Magdalen— had endeavoured to remain at the head of the house, to interfere where she could not direct, Mrs. Cleverdon had taken a very decided line, and refused all intermeddlement, and Magdalen, after a sharp struggle for supremacy, had left the house routed. Disappointment had embittered her estimate of her sister-in-law.

But there were other and more substantial grounds for her charging her sister-in-law with having rendered the marriage an unhappy one. Mrs. Anthony had been a portionless girl, the daughter of a poor parson ; Margaret Penwarne might have been regarded as a suitable match socially, but pecuniarily, she was most unsuitable, especially to an ambitious and money-grasping man.

What her brother could see to admire in Margaret Penwarne, Miss Cleverdon protested she never could see—she entirely forgot that Margaret had been endowed with surpassing beauty.

Others beside Magdalen Cleverdon had marvelled at the choice of Anthony, knowing the character of the man. What could induce a man, whose main features were ambition and greed, to select as his partner one who had not a penny, nor was connected with any of the gentle families of the neighbourhood? Magdalen had not reckoned on the girl's beauty; the others who wondered had not counted on Anthony's ambition, which would exert itself in other directions than they considered. His ambition was deeply tinctured with, if it did not originate in, personal vanity. Vanity is but ambition in a fool's cap, and that of Cleverdon was well hung with bells. Because he considered himself the richest man in the neighbourhood of his class, he esteemed himself also irresistible as a wooer. He had been treated with considerable severity by his father in his early years, for the old man had been a strait Puritan, though not such an one as to risk any money for his cause, or compromise his safety for it in any way. He allowed his son no freedom, consulted his wishes in no particular, and allowed him no pocket-money. When the old man died, Anthony was left with a good deal of hoarded money, and freedom to act as he listed. His fancy was taken by Margaret Penwarne, and his vanity and ambition stimulated by the knowledge that she was already the object of the attentions of Richard Malvine, the son of a neighbouring parson, without profession and without inheritance. Richard Malvine was a handsome man, and Margaret Penwarne certainly was attached to him, but the marriage could not be thought of till Richard had a competence on which to support himself and a wife. Anthony Cleverdon entered the list against the handsomest young man in the district, but he had money and a good farm to set against good looks. He and Richard had been together at the Grammar School, and had been rivals there, Richard ever taking the lead, and on one occasion had thrashed Anthony severely. It was with eagerness that Cleverdon seized the opportunity of gratifying his malice by snatching from Malvine the girl of his heart, and it flattered his vanity to have it said of him that he had won the most beautiful girl of the district

over the head of the handsomest man. Margaret struggled
for some time between her affection and her ambition ; the
urgency of her father and mother prevailed, she cast off
Malvine and accepted Cleverdon.

Anthony Cleverdon's pride was satisfied. He had gained
a triumph, and was wrapped up in the sense of victory for
a while, then the gloss of novelty wore off, and he began to
regret his precipitancy in taking to him a wife who brought
nothing into the family save good looks. The thriftiness
of the father now came out in the son. He did not grudge
and withhold money where he could make display, but he
cut down expenses where no show was made, to the lowest
stage of meanness. Margaret's father died. She thought
to take her mother to live with her at Hall, but to this her
husband would not consent, nor could she wring a silver coin
from him wherewith to assist her mother, reduced to great
poverty. This occasioned the first outbreak of domestic
hostilities. Margaret was a woman of temper, and would
not submit tamely to the domination of her husband. His
sister Magdalen took sides against her, and fanned the embers of strife when they gave token of expiring. If Margaret had been of a meek and yielding temperament, the
marriage might not have been so full of broils ; her husband
would have crushed her, and then ignored her. But her
spirit rose against him, and stirred the discord that was
only temporarily allayed. She could not shut her eyes to
his infirmities, she would not condescend to flatter him. In
her heart she contrasted him with the man she had loved
and had betrayed ; her heart never warmed to her husband;
on the contrary, indifference changed into hatred. She
made no scruple about showing him the state of her mind,
she pitilessly unmasked his meannesses, and held them up
to mockery ; she scoffed at his efforts to thrust himself into
a position for which he was not born ; he found no more
penetrating, remorseless critic of all he did, than his own
wife.

Anthony Cleverdon believed, and was justified in believing, that his old rival, Richard Malvine, stood between him
and domestic peace, as a shadow that blighted and engalled
his relations to his wife ; that, though he had triumphed
formally over his rival, that rival had gained the lasting and
substantial success. Anthony Cleverdon might prize him-

self as high as he pleased, but he could no longer blind himself to the fact, that his money bags which had won his wife for him, were unavailing to buy her affections, and secure to him the fruits of his triumph.

This consciousness stimulated his hatred of Malvine to fresh acridity, and in his meanness, he found a base satisfaction in humiliating his wife by every means in his power, and on every available opportunity.

The birth of Bessie did not serve to unite the pair, for Anthony Cleverdon had set his heart on having a son, and when, after the lapse of a considerable interval of time, the desired son arrived, it was too late to serve as a link of reconciliation. Mrs. Cleverdon died shortly after his birth, her only regret being that she had to leave her daughter, whom she loved with double passion, partly because her desolate heart naturally clung to some object, and had none other to which to attach itself, partly also because little Bessie was totally disregarded by her father.

Richard Malvine consoled himself for his disappointment by marrying Marianne Gibbs, of Willsworthy; he took her for the sake of Willsworthy, as Margaret Penwarne had taken Anthony Cleverdon for the sake of Hall. He was a feckless man, who had lived at home in the parsonage with his father, had hunted, had shot, and had never earned a penny for himself. He died, thrown from his horse, in hunting, a few years after his marriage, leaving an only child, Urith.

The death of the mother produced no alteration in the conduct of Anthony Cleverdon towards her daughter. What love he had in his heart was bestowed on his son— the heir to his name and estate.

In nature all forces are correlated. Indeed it is said that force is a pure and unique factor, and that light, heat, sound, etc., are but various manifestations or aspects of the one primal force. It would be hard to say whether old Anthony's love for his boy might not be considered as another phase of his ambition. He had never himself been a firm-built, handsome man; undersized and of mean appearance, he had felt the slight that this physical defect had entailed on him. But the young Tony was robust of constitution, burly of frame, and had inherited his mother's beauty. At Hall, from the hour of his birth, young Anthony had become a sovereign, and every one was placed beneath his footstool. Every inmate of the house laboured to spoil him, either because he was himself provocative of love, or out of a desire to curry favour with the father. He tyrannised over his sister, he was despotic with his father, he was wayward and exacting with the servants. Nothing that he did was wrong in his father's eyes ; he grew up into manhood demanding of the outer world, as a right, that which was accorded to him in his home as a favour.

CHAPTER V.

THE GLOVE TAKEN UP.

Every member of the little party felt sensible of relief when they came out on the high road and left the moor behind. For some time all had been silent ; the efforts to start and maintain conversation had signally failed, and a funeral party would have been livelier.

As soon as the hoofs of the horses rang on the roadway, the fetters that had bound the tongues were thrown aside, and words a few were interchanged.

After ten minutes or a quarter of an hour a little tavern by the wayside was reached, named the Hare and Hounds ; and then Anthony Cleverdon laid his hand on the bit of the horse Urith rode.

"My cob must bait here," he said—"at least, have a mouthful ; so must you. I will go in and see what can be provided, and bid the landlady lay the table."

"I thank you," said Urith ; "but I desire to go home at once. The distance is in no way considerable. I know where I am. But surely I hear my uncle's voice."

That individual appeared at the open door. He was a stout man, with a very red face and a watery eye. His wig was awry. He stood with a pipe in one hand and a tankard in the other.

"Aha !" shouted Solomon Gibbs. "I said the truth ! I knew that it was in vain for me to go in quest of you on the moors, niece. Told your mother so ; but she wouldn't believe me. Come on—come, and let's be jolly—drive away dull melancholy! I knew that you must come on to the road somewhere; and, if on to the road, then to the inn. For what is the inn, my boys, but the very focus and acme to which all gather, and from which all radiate? Come in—come in."

"I wish to push on," said Urith.

"How can you without my cob?" asked Anthony roughly. "I have said—she baits here. You, also—you must be perishing for food. We all are; have been mum all the way home—no fun, no talking. So, come in."

"That is right—urge her, young man, to follow the advice of age and experience," shouted Mr. Gibbs.

Then he began to sing:

> Come my lads, let us be jolly,
> Drive away dull melancholy,
> For to grieve it is a folly
>   When we're met together.

> So, my friends, let us agree,
> Always keep good company,
> Why should we not merry, merry be
>   When we're met together?

He brandished his tobacco-pipe over his head, in so doing striking his wig with the stem, and at once breaking the latter, and thrusting the wig over his ear, and then dived into the alehouse again. He was half tipsy.

"You are right," said Elizabeth to Urith. "You must go on. Your mother is anxious, probably in a state of serious alarm."

"My uncle's horse is in the stable, I doubt not," answered Urith, "and as he will not be disposed to leave till he be unfit to accompany me, I will borrow the horse, and send it back by a servant."

"I will accompany you," said Elizabeth, "and the serving man that brings back the horse can accompany me. The distance is inconsiderable, yet you must not at night travel it alone. Fox and Julian have, I see, turned their horses' heads homewards without bidding us a farewell. I cannot stay outside whilst Anthony is within, and I do not care to enter when men are drinking."

"Your brother will hardly leave you alone outside,"

"My brother will probably forget all about me when he gets with Mr. Gibbs and others who can sing a good song and tell a merry tale."

She said this without any reproach in her tone. She was so accustomed to be neglected, forgotten, to find herself thrust aside by her brother, that she no longer felt unhappy about it ; she accepted it as her due.

Urith sent a stable-boy for Mr. Gibbs' horse, and having mounted it, gratefully accepted Bessie Cleverdon's company for the ride of three miles to Willsworthy.

Urith knew Bessie very little. Old Mr. Cleverdon did not care that his children should associate with the Malvines. His bitterness against the father, Richard, overflowed all his belongings—wife and child and estate ; but he published no reasons for his dislike to association with the owners of Willsworthy, who, moreover, on account of their poverty, kept to themselves. The Cleverdons mixed with those who were in prosperous circumstances, and kept themselves, or were kept, aloof from those on whom Fortune turned her back. Mrs. Malvine had for some time been a woman in failing health, and, having no neighbours, Urith had grown up accustomed to be solitary, and not to know the value of the friendship, or at least the companionship, of girls of her own age and rank. She was too proud to associate, like her Uncle Solomon, with those of a lower grade, and she had not the opportunity of forming acquaintanceship of those fitted to be her comrades.

As Urith rode beside Bessie, her heart stirred with a sensation of pleasure strange to her. There was a kindness, a sympathy in the manner of Elizabeth Cleverdon that found a way at once to Urith's heart, and she warmed to her and shook off reserve. And Elizabeth on her side was touched by the simplicity, the loneliness of the girl's mind, and when they reached the entrance gates to Willsworthy she held out her hand to Urith, and said :

"This must be the beginning of our friendship. I do not know how it is that we have not met before, or rather, have not met to make acquaintance. Promise me that you will not let this be the beginning and the ending of a friendship."

"That lies with you," said Urith, with timidity. It was

to her too surprising a glimpse into happiness for her to trust its reality.

"If it lies with me," said Elizabeth, "then you may be assured it will be warm and fast; expect to see me again soon. I will come over and visit you. But here—let us not part thus. Give me a kiss and take mine."

The girls drew their horses alongside each other and kissed. The tears came into Urith's eyes at this offered and given pledge of kindness. It was to her a wholly new experience, and was to her of inexpressible value.

Then Urith called a serving man, alighted, and delivered her horse up to him that he might attend Bessie Cleverdon on her way back to the Hare and Hounds, and leave it there for her uncle when it pleased Mr. Solomon Gibbs to return home.

Bessie found that her brother was angry and offended when he came out of the alehouse and discovered that Urith had departed without a word; he had felt himself obliged to wait for his sister, because it would not be seemly to allow her to ride home in the dark alone; but he vented his ill-humour on her when she appeared. Bessie bore his reproaches with patience. She was accustomed to be found fault with by her father, and less frequently, nevertheless sometimes, and always unreasonably, by her brother.

"I've promised the ostler a shilling to attend you to Hall," said Anthony. "There is Fox returned, and there is Solomon Gibbs here, and—I don't feel inclined to go home."

"Father will be ill-pleased at your remaining away so long," remonstrated Bessie.

"Father has seen so little of me to-day that another hour's absence won't signify. The weather is going to change—we shall have a thunderstorm. Get home as fast as you can. Here, Samuel, attend my sister."

Then Anthony returned to the alehouse.

At Willsworthy, Urith had stood for a moment in the porch in hesitation. She knew that she deserved to be reproached for her conduct, and she expected it. Her mother was not a person to spare words. She was repentant, and yet was certain that directly her mother addressed her with rebuke her spirit would rise up in revolt.

To her surprise, when she did enter her mother's room, Mrs. Malvine said no more than this, "Oh, Urith! what a many hours you have been absent. But, my child, what is that? You have gloves hanging to your dress."

Urith stooped and looked. It was as her mother had said—the gloves of Julian Crymes had not fallen to the ground, they had been caught by the tags in the gown of Urith, and hung there. She disengaged them, and held them in her hand. She had unwittingly taken up the gage.

CHAPTER VI.

MAGDALEN'S PLANS.

Magdalen Cleverdon had come out for that day from Tavistock to visit her brother at Hall. She did not appear there very often, but made a point of duty to visit Hall once a quarter. Old Anthony had not interfered when his wife resisted the interference of her sister-in-law, and discouraged her visits to the house, and after his wife's death he had not invited her to be more frequent in her expeditions thither; nor had he shown her the slightest inclination to defer to her opinions, and attend to her advice.

Magdalen's visits can hardly have conduced to her own pleasure, so ungracious was her reception when she appeared, except only from Bessie, who was too tender-hearted to be unkind, unconciliatory to any one. Anthony, senior, regarded and spoke of his sister as an old and stupid harridan, and the younger Anthony took his tone from his father, and did not accord to his aunt the respect that was due to relationship and age.

Although one of her periodical visits to Hall usually brought on Magdalen a rebuff, yet she did not desist from them, partly because it satisfied her curiosity to see how matters fared in the old house, and partly, if not chiefly, because she gave herself in Tavistock considerable airs as the sister of the Squire of Hall, and she liked to appear to her neighbours as if on the best of terms with her kindred there.

Magdalen had never been pretty. Her's was one of

those nondescript faces which Nature turns out when inventive faculty is exhausted, and she produces a being, much as a worn-out novelist writes a tale, because she is expected to be productive, though she has nothing but hackneyed features to produce. Or her face may be said to have resembled a modern hymn-tune that is made up of strains out of a score of older melodies muddled together, and void of individual character. Magdalen had, however, not a suspicion that her personal appearance was unattractive. If she had not been sought in marriage, that was due wholly to the inadequate manner in which she had been provided for by her father's will; he had, she held, sacrificed her to his ambition to make a rich man of Anthony.

She was a short, shapeless woman, with a muddy complexion and sandy hair, now turning grey, and therefore looking as if it were full of dust. Her eyes were faded, so were the lashes. She had bad teeth, and when she spoke she showed them a great deal more than was necessary. Any one conversing with her for the first time found nothing in her to notice except these teeth, and carried away from the interview no other recollection of her than one of—teeth.

She made a point of being well-dressed when she made her periodical visits to Hall, to show her consequence, and to let her brother see that she held herself in condition equal to his pretensions.

When she learned that her nephew and niece were not at Hall, but had gone to the moor for the day to watch the fires, and to endeavour to recover some colts that had been turned out on it by old Cleverdon, she expressed her satisfaction to her brother.

"It is as well, Tony," she said, "for I want to have a talk with you; I am thinking——"

"What? Talk first and think after? That is the usual way," said Cleverdon, rudely.

Magdalen tossed her chin. She did not think it prudent to notice and resent her brother's discourtesy. She was not likely to gain much by flattering or humouring him; but to quarrel with him was against her wishes.

"Really, Tony, I have your interests so much at heart——"

"I never asked you to cupboard them there ; but, if they be there, turn the key on them, and let them abide where they are."

"You are clever and witty—that every one knows—and you like to snap your lock under my eyes and make me wince as the sparks fly out ; but I know very well there is no powder in the barrel, and I do not mind. You really must attend to me, brother. There has been so much small-pox about, and it has been so fatal, that upon my word, as a woman, you should lend me your ear."

"What has the small-pox to do with my interests ?"

"Much. Have you made your will, or a settlement of the property ?"

"What now !" exclaimed Anthony Cleverdon roughly." "You came to scare me with thoughts of small-pox, and want me to draw my will, and provide for you ?"

"About that latter point I say nothing, though I do feel that I was ill-treated by my father. You had the kernal and I had the rind of the nut."

"I dispute that altogether. You are an incumbrance on the estate that I feel heavily."

"I am likely to encumber it somewhat longer," said Magdalen, not showing resentment at his brutality. " I do not fear the small-pox. I have had it, and it has marked me ; though not so as to disfigure. The Lord forbid ! "

Observing that her brother was about to make a remark, and being confident that it would be something offensive, she hastily went on : " But what, Tony—what if it were to attack your Anthony ? " What if it were to take him off ? You have but a single son. To whom would Hall go then ? "

Old Squire Cleverdon started to his feet, and strode, muttering, about the room.

"Ah ! It is a thought to consider. The Knightons have lost their heir, and he was a fine and lusty youth. Our Anthony is so thoughtless ; he runs where he lists, and does not consider that he may be near infection. Please the Lord nothing may happen ; but suppose that he were carried off, who would have Hall ? Bessie ? "

"Bessie ! Are you mad ? " Old Cleverdon put his hands in his breeches-pocket and turned and scowled at his sister.

"No. I reckon Bessie would be put off with scant treatment, like myself. Then, Luke?"

"Luke!" Cleverdon burst out laughing. "Never a parson here in Hall, if I can help it. A shaveling like he——"

"Then, who would have it?"

"Not you, if you are aiming thereat," said Cleverdon.

"I was not aiming at that. Such a prospect never rose before me. I do not want Hall. I could not manage the estate."

"I shall take care you have not the chance."

"I have no doubt you will. But consider what are the accidents of life. If you were to lose Anthony——"

"But I shall not. Anthony is flourishing, and not a thought of small-pox, or the falling sickness, or the plague about him. He is sound as a bell; so have done with your croak, you raven. I will call up the servants and have in dinner. You can eat, I suppose?"

"Yes, I can eat, and digest your unkindness; but I cannot forget my anxiety. I am considering the welfare of the family. I am looking beyond myself and yourself. You have raised the Cleverdons from being tenant-farmers into being gentlefolks. You have been to the Heralds to grant you a coat of arms and a crest, and, now every one calls you the Squire, who used to call your father a farmer. You have altered Hall into a very handsome mansion, that no gentleman of good degree need be ashamed to live in. I consider all that, brother, and then I think that you are no fool, that you have wonderful wits to have achieved so much, and I am only anxious lest after having achieved so much for the family and the name of Cleverdon, all should go down again, as it did with the Glanvilles—just because there was no heir male."

"Have done with your croak—here comes dinner."

During the meal old Anthony was very silent. He pulled long and often at the tankard, and neglected the courtesies due to his sister as a guest. She observed that he was uneasy, and was wrapped in thought. What she had said had stuck, and made him uncomfortable. She was too shrewd to revert to the topic during dinner, and when it was over he went out, and left her alone. She knew her brother's ways, his moods, and the turns of his mind, and

was convinced that he would come back to her presently
and broach anew the subject.

She leaned back in the arm-chair, and indulged herself
in a nap. The doze lasted about three-quarters of an hour.
Whilst she slept her brother was walking about the farm,
in great restlessness of mind and body. He was quick-
witted enough to see that Magdalen was right. He could
not count on matters not falling out as she had said, and
then all his labour to build up the Cleverdons would come
down like a pack of cards. His son was the main prop of
the great superstructure raised by his pride and ambition.
If his son, by the dispensation of Providence, were to fail
him, he had none to sustain the succession save his daughter
Bessie and his cousin Luke, a delicate, narrow-chested lad,
who had been an encumbrance thrown on him, had been
reared by him, and sent to school by him, and then thrust
into sacred Orders as the simplest way of providing for
him, and getting him out of the way. Hall to pass to Bessie
or to Luke! The idea was most distasteful to him.

He returned to the oak parlour, where he had left his
sister, and shook her until she roused from her nap.

"Sit up—gather your senses! You do not come here
to sleep like a frog," said old Anthony with his wonted
rudeness.

"I beg pardon, brother. I was left alone and had nought
to occupy my mind, and dozed for a minute."

"I say to you, Mawdline!"—Squire Cleverdon paced
the room with his hands knotted behind his back, writhing
with the inward agitation of his nerves—"I tell you Mawdline, that you did not come here to scare me about small-
pox without some design lurking behind. Let me hear it.
You have emptied the pepper-box, now for the salt-
box."

"I do not know anything of a design behind," answered
Magdalen, rallying her scattered senses, and then plunging
into the main communication with less caution than if she
had been fully awake; "but I think, brother, you should
get them both married as quickly as you may."

"Both!—what Anthony and Bess?"

"To be sure. Anthony might take Julian at any time;
and for Bessie——"

Cleverdon laughed. "I never heard that Bessie had a

gallant as yet, and she never had good looks to lure one. If Tony takes a wife that is sufficient."

"No, brother, it is hardly sufficient. He might, if he married, chance to have no children. Besides, it is well to have alliances on all sides. If only I had married——"

"Fernando Crymes," muttered her brother. "You tried hard for him before he took his first wife."

Magdalen tossed and shook her head. "You indeed misunderstand me. You try to provoke me, brother; but I will not be provoked. I am too desirous to advance the family to be browbeat by you and forced to hold silence. Elizabeth is getting forward in years, and she might be the means of alliance to a good family that would help to give ours firmer hold in the position it has won. There is Anthony Crymes, for instance."

"What!—Fox for Bessie? This is sheer folly."

"Yes, Fox. What against him?"

"Nay, naught other against him, save that he does not lay his fancy to Bessie."

"I am not certain of that. Why else has he rid this day to the moor? He has not gone for love of his sister, that all the world knows. Now see this, brother Tony. If you was to marry Anthony to Julian, and Bessie to Fox, then you would be close allied to one of the best families of the country-side, and he who would lift a word against you would rouse all the Crymes that remain. They were not unwilling to draw to us, or else why did Squire Crymes bid you to be his son's godfather? Fox will not be rich, but he will have something from his father, and that will be enough with what you let Bessie have to make them do well. Then, if there come a family of children on either side, it is well, for there will be a large kindred in the district, and if there be none on one side, but only on the other then what property there is, this way or that, does not fall out of the family."

"If Bessie is to be married, we might look elsewhere for one richer."

"Where will you look? Who among the neighbours is old enough or young enough? Some are over her age. You would not give her to Master Solomon Gibbs. Some be too young and hot-blooded to care for her, not very well favoured, and without much wealth."

Old Anthony stood still before the window and looked out.

"Then," said Magdalen, "there's another side of the matter to be considered. What if Bessie should set her heart on some one of whom you would not approve?"

Old Anthony laughed mockingly. "Not much chance of that I reckon."

"Do you reckon?" asked his sister, with some heat. "Yes, you men make up your minds that we spinsters have no hearts, go through no trials, because you do not see them. As our love is not proclaimed on the house-tops you assume that it does not exist in the secret chambers of the heart. If you are forced to admit that there is such a thing in us, you suppose it may be killed with ridicule, as you put salt on weeds. As for your own headlong, turbulent passions, they brook no control, they are irresistible, but we poor women must smother our fires as if always illicit, like a chimney in a blaze that must be choked out with damp straw stuffed in. You men never consider us. You permit a pretty girl to love, and you consider her feelings somewhat—just somewhat; but it never occurs to your wise heads, but shallow thoughts, that the plain faces and the ordinary-favoured girls may have hearts as tender and susceptible as those who are regarded as beauties. Now, as to Bessie——"

"Well, what as to Bessie?" asked Anthony roughly. He knew that his sister was lightly lifting the corner of a veil that covered her past, and he knew how that by a little generosity on his part, he might have made it possible for her to marry.

"As to Bessie?" resumed Magdalen, "I can only speak what I suspect. I have thought for some time she was fond of her cousin."

"What—of Luke?"

"Of Luke, certainly."

Old Anthony turned angrily on her, and said, "A pack of folly! He is her cousin."

"I said so. Does that prevent her liking him? Have you aught against that?"

"Everything. I will not hear of her marrying a pigeon-breasted, starveling curate. I will speak to her."

"If you meddle you will mar. Take a woman's advice, and say not a word."

4

"Then be silent on this matter."

"If you marry Tony," said his sister, "what are you going to do with Elizabeth? Fernando Crymes has Kilworthy for his life, so that the young people will, I doubt not, live here; and Julian will no more let Bessie remain than would your Margaret suffer me."

"She shall abide here as I choose it."

"No, indeed. You may will it; but women's wishes, when they go contrary, can make a bad storm in the house, and spoil it as a port of peace. You take my counsel and mate the twain together—the one to Julian and the other to Fox."

"Pshaw!" said the old man turning away from the window. "Because I was godfather to Fox, it does not follow that he wants to be my son."

Then the old man came over to the table that stood near his sister, seated himself, and began to trifle with a snuff-box upon it.

"I shall not part with Bess," he said, "till Tony is matched."

"Then let him be matched with speed," said Magdalen sharply. "How know you but that, if you delay, Julian Crymes may turn her fancy elsewhere. She is a wayward hussy."

"Pshaw! Where is there such a lad as my Tony? He is the chiefest of all the youths about. Not one can compare with him. Are you mad to think of such a thing?"

"There is no reckoning on a maid's eyes; they do not see like ours. Moreover, there is no saying what freak might take your Tony, and he might set his mind on some one else."

"No fear of that," answered the squire roughly. "He knows my will, and that is law to him."

"Indeed! Since when? I thought that the cockerel's whimsies and vagaries set the law to the house; and that you, and Bess, and every one of the family danced to such tune as he whistled."

"I reckon he knows his own interests," said the old man grimly. He was angered by his sister's opposition.

"None can trust to that in young men," answered his sister, "as you ought best to know, brother."

Old Anthony winced, and became purple at this allusion

to his own marriage. He started up, struck the snuff-box across the table, then seated himself again, and said grimly: "I asked you, sister, if you could eat and digest a good, wholesome dinner, and I gave it you ; but, by Heaven, you have come here and fed me with unwholesome and unsavoury diet that I cannot digest, and that gives me a worry and heartburn. I wish you had never come."

CHAPTER VII.

IN THE HARE AND HOUNDS.

In the tavern with the sign of the Hare and Hounds, a fire of peat was burning on the hearth. A huge oak settle occupied the side of the fireplace opposite to the window; and beneath and before the window was a long table, the end of which admitted of being drawn out so as to make it serve as a shuffle-board for the use of such as liked to play at that game so popular in the reign of Elizabeth, illicit in the time of the Commonwealth, and at the epoch of my story almost obsolete, except in stray corners remote from fashion.

The settle was of a construction then usual, now rarely met with, and therefore deserving a description as a domestic curiosity. The seat was on hinges, and could be raised, disclosing beneath it a cavity like a clothes chest ; the settle back opened in compartments and revealed sides of bacon and hams that had been smoked, and there awaited cutting up. Above the heads of those who sat in the settle was a sort of projecting roof to cut off all down draught ; but this also served as a cupboard for vinegar, salt, spices, and other groceries. The chest, that was also seat, to a mother with an infant, was of extraordinary service ; when she was engaged at the fire, baking or cooking, she raised the lid or seat and buttoned it back, then she planted the babe in the box, where it lay warm and secure, close to her, without the chance of coming to harm. If the child were in the age of toddledum, then it ran up and down in the box with the little hands on the edge, saw its mother, crowed to her, watched her proceedings, and ran no risk of falling into the fire, or of pulling over and breaking the crockery. Altogether the settle was a great institution, and the march of culture, instead of improving it, has abolished it. More is the pity.

The fireplace was of granite uncarved, but rudely chamfered, very wide and very deep, so deep as to allow of a seat recessed in the wall at the side, in which a chilly old man might sit and toast his knees, protected from the down draught and falling soot by the arched roof of the recess. It used to be said of one of these great fireplaces, in which wood and peat were burned, that a necessary accompaniment was an old man and a pair of tongs, for the logs when burnt through in the midst fell apart, and required some one at hand to pick the ends up, and reverse them on the hearth, and to collect and repile the turfs when they fell down. At the fire-breast burnt, what was called a "spane," that is, a slip of deal steeped in resin, which lighted the housewife at her operations at the fire. But the " spane " emitted more smoke than light. Opposite to the ingle-nook was the "cloam" oven, that is, the earthenware oven let into the wall for baking.

In more ancient times ovens were constructed with enormous labour out of granite blocks, which were scooped out in the middle, but the disadvantage attendant on granite was that it became in time resolved into sand by heat, and crumbled away like sugar.* These were rapidly got rid of when the earthenware oven was introduced, and hardly a specimen remains. Not so, however, with the stone frying-pan, which is only just, and not altogether, superseded. Housewives contend that the iron pan is not so good at frying as the scooped-out pan of stone, and that rashers of bacon done in the latter are incomparably superior to those burnt in iron. Thus, it will be seen that in the West we are only recently, in some particulars emerging from the Stone-Age, but it is with a leap over that of Bronze into the era of Iron.†

---

* Such a granite-oven was discovered in the author's own house in an old and long-abandoned chimney-back, in 1866. It was impossible to preserve it.

† Two such stone frying-pans are to be seen in the Museum at Launceston. The one was given by a gentleman from his kitchen, where it had been long in use, the other was found among the ruins

The walls of the "mug-house" of the Hare and Hounds were well white-washed and ornamented with a quantity of broadside ballads, the illustrations very generally bearing no intelligible relation to the letterpress.

A single rush-candle burning on the table, served to light the room. The servant-wench was expected to act as snuffer, and she regularly at intervals of ten minutes left the work on which she was engaged, cooking, washing, drawing ale, and like the comet that sweeps up to and about the sun, and then dashes back into obscurity, so did she rush up to the candle, snuff the wick between the fore-finger and thumb, and plunge back to the work on which she was engaged, at the fire, in the back-kitchen, or in the cellar.

At the fire and about the table were seated Anthony Cleverdon, Fox Crymes, the host of the Hare and Hounds. Mr. Solomon Gibbs, also a quaint old grey-haired man in sorry garb, and a couple of miners from the moor.

At the time of the tale, and, indeed for a century after, it was customary for men of all classes to meet at the ale-house, parson and Squire, surgeon, farmer, and peasant, comrades all in merry-making—and at that period there was no social-democracy, no class-hatreds—how could there be, when all classes met, and gossiped, and smoked, and boozed together? No good thing comes without bringing a shadow after it. Perhaps it is well that parson and Squire do not now go to the tavern to take pipe and glass with yeoman and ploughboy, but—the misfortune is that there has come class-alienation, along with this social amelioration of the better sort.

Mr. Solomon Gibbs was at the table. He had occupied the corner of the settle all the afternoon, searching for his niece in the bottom of his tankard, but after a while, as evening settled in, he declared he felt the heat too greatly by the fire, and then withdrew to the table. In fact, when occupying the settle, his can of ale had stood on a three-legged stool between his feet, and whenever he lusted after a drink he was obliged to stoop to take it up. As the ale got into his head, he found that this stooping produced a

of Trecarrel—probably coeval with the buildings, the middle of the sixteenth century.

fulness of the veins that made him giddy, and he had fallen
forward once on his hands, and upset the stool and his ale.
Then he deemed it advisable to retire to the table, but
as men never give direct and true reasons for their proceedings, he explained to those who were present that——

"There was thunder in the air, and when there was, he
was liable to fits of giddiness; moreover, the heat of the
fire was insufferable."

His wig was very much awry; underneath it was a strong
stubbly growth, for Mr. Gibbs had not had his head shaved
for a fortnight. His mulberry coat was much stained with
ale, and the elbows were glossy.

The old man in the threadbare coat occupied a chair
near the table, and he stood up, turned his eyes to the
ceiling, extended his arms rigidly before him, planted his
legs apart, and began to sing a song at that time exceedingly popular, "The Catholic Cause;" his voice ranging
through an extensive scale, from bass to falsetto.

> O the Catholic Cause! now assist me, sweet Muse,
>   How earnestly I do desire thee!
> Faith I will not go pray to St. Bridget to-day,
>   But only to thee to inspire me.

The singer was interrupted by a groan from all in the
room, and a shout from Mr. Solomon Gibbs, "Calvinist
Géneva and Hollands for me! Catholic French Claret is
thin—deuced thin liquor!"

> Then the Church shall bear sway, the State shall obey,
>   Which in England will be a new wonder!
> Commons, Nobles, and Kings, and Temporal things
>   Shall submit, and shall truckle under!

The miners jumped to their feet, and began to swear that
they'd rather be crushed in their adits, than live to see that
day.

"Things are coming fair on towards it, sure as the
clouds have been rolling up, and portending a thunder-
storm," said the host.

"Ah!" growled Solomon; "give the Devil his due.
Old Noll, who didn't sit by right Divine, knew how to
make Britain free and honoured."

"No Dutch in the Medway, then! No burning of Spithead and His Majesty's fleet under His Majesty's nose," said the old singer.

"'Tis a pity," said one of the men present, "that there were not a few more drowned on the Lemon and Ore than those who did. Nay, rather, that certain who escaped should not have sunk, and such as drowned should not have escaped."

This had reference to a sandbank near Yarmouth, on which the frigate bearing the Duke of York had struck, when about a hundred and thirty persons were drowned.

"Here!" called Sol Gibbs. "Here's bad luck to Lemon and Ore for doing the work so foully!" and he put his jug of ale to his lips.

"Lemon and Ore," said each who drank, "better luck next time."

"Folks do say," put in the landlord, "that the King, God bless him, was really married to Lucy Walters. If that be so, why then the Duke of Monmouth should be King after him." Then he shook his head, and added, "But, Lord! I know nought about such matters."

"Here's a health to the Protestant Duke!" said the miners, and looked about them. "Now, my masters! Won'ty all drink to the Protestant Duke?"

"To be sure I will—drink to any one," said Solomon Gibbs.

"Why should he not have married her?" asked the singer. "Didn't the Duke of York marry Mistress Ann Hyde? And Lucy Walters was a gentlewoman every whit as much. When the Duke of Monmouth was born, then His Majesty was Prince Charles, in France, with small chance of coming to his own again; for Old Noll was then in full flower, and making the earth quake at the name of England."

"When the Duke of Savoy was persecuting the Protestants, did not Old Noll hold up his finger, and at the sight of his nail the Duke stayed his hands?" said Anthony Cleverdon. "By the Lord! If it had been in my time, I would have drawn the sword for them."

"When all the giants are dead, every Tom Thumb boasts he would have been a Jack of Cornwall," sneered Fox Crymes.

"What is that you say?" asked Anthony, hotly.

"I was merely saying that it ill becomes a man of spirit to boast of what he would have done had things been other than they are."

"Do you mean to hint that I am a coward?"

"I hinted nothing of the sort. I made a general observation. If the time should come when your sword would be wanted to sustain the Protestant cause, I make no doubt that you will be ready to prop it up—on the point."

"No quarrels here," shouted Solomon Gibbs; then he sang:—

Let nothing but harmony reign in your breast,
Let comrade with comrade be ever at rest.
We'll toss off our bumper, together we'll troll,
Give me the punch-ladle—I'll fathom the bowl.

Then he called to the united assembly, "What say you all —shall we have a punch-bowl? *Nem. con.* Carried. That is it which lacked to establish sweetest concord. Landlord! Bring us the needful, and we'll brew.

From France cometh brandy. Jamaica gives rum,
Sweet oranges, lemons from Portugal come.
Of ale and good cyder we'll also take toll,
Give me the punch-ladle—I'll fathom the bowl.

The host called to his wife to produce the requisite ingredients, and went in quest of the ladle, which he kept upstairs, as it had a silver piece of Charles I. let into it.

"I ax," said one of the miners, throwing out his arm as if proclaiming defiance, "how it came about that London was burnt? Warn't them Poperies seen a doing of it—a firing it in several places?"

"And Sir Edmondbury Godfrey—weren't he cruelly and bloodily murdered by 'em?" asked the second.

"Ay! and whose doing is it that that worthy gentleman, my Lord Russell, has been done to death? That every one knows. 'Tis said the Earl of Bedford offered a hundred thousand pounds to save his life; but the Catholic Duke would not hear of his being spared. And the Duke of York will be King after his present Gracious Majesty. By heavens! I would draw sword for the Protestant Duke and swear to his legitimacy."

"I'll tell you what it is," said Fox Crymes, "if this sort of talk is going on here, I'm off and away. If you are not speaking treason, you go pretty nigh to it, too nigh it for safety, and I'll be off."

"There are no informers and spies here," said the yeoman.

"I reckon us be all true Protestants and loyal to the Crown and Constitution. The Constitution! God bless it!"

"You can't go, Fox," said Anthony, "for here comes the storm we have been expecting." He spoke as a flash illuminated the room, and was followed by a boom of near thunder, then down came the rain like the fall of a waterspout on the roof.

> Our brothers lie drowned in the depths of the sea,
> Cold stones for their pillows, what matters to me ?

Mr. Solomon Gibbs was erect, supporting himself on the table by his left hand, whilst he mixed the bowl of punch and stirred it, and sang in snatches :

> We'll drink to their healths and repose to each soul,
> Give me the punch ladle—I'll fathom the bowl.

"Now, then, landlord! Where's the lemons? Bless my soul, you're not going to make us drink unlemoned punch? As well give us a King without a Crown, or a parson without a gown."

> Your wives they may fluster as much as they please—
> Haven't got one, I'm thankful—a sister don't count—
> Let 'em scold, let 'em grumble, we'll sit at our ease,
> In the ends of our pipes we'll apply a hot coal.
> Give me the punch ladle—I'll fathom the bowl.

—So ! the lemons at last? Where's a silver knife to cut them with? Bless my soul! How it rains! I thank Providence the water is without, and the spirit is within."

"This rain will dowse the fires on the moor," said the yeoman.

"And would have washed your Tory zeal out of you,"

laughed Anthony, "had you gone out in it just now, shocked at our Whiggery."

"Oh! you," sneered Fox, "you took good care to say nothing. You were wise not to come within seeing distance with a pair of perspective glasses of Tyburn gallows, where men have been hung, disembowelled, and drawn for less offence than some of the words let drop to-night."

"Now—no more of this," shouted Mr. Solomon Gibbs, "I am president here. Where the punch-bowl is, there is a president, and I waive my sceptre, this ladle, and enforce abstention from politics, and all such scurvy subjects. You began it, Taverner, with your damnable ballad of the Catholic cause, and you shall be served last. Comrades! 'To the King, God bless him!'"

"And the Protestant cause!" shouted Taverner.

"Ay, ay, which His Majesty swore to maintain," said the miners.

"Bar politics!" cried Mr. Gibbs, "or, curse it, I'll throw the punch out of the door. I will, I swear I will. Taverner, give us something cheerful—something with no politics in it to set us all by the ears."

"Shall I give you something suitable to the evening, Mr. Gibbs?"

"Certainly—tune up. I wish I had my viol with me to give a few chords; but I set out to look for my niece who had strayed, and I forgot to take my viol with me."

The grey-haired ballad-singer stood up, cleared his throat, and with the utmost gravity sang, throwing marvellous twirls and accidentals into the tune, the following song:

> My Lady hath a sable coach
>   And horses, two and four,
> My Lady hath a gaunt bloodhound
>   That runneth on before.
> My Lady's coach has nodding plumes,
>   The coachman has no head.
> My Lady's face is ashen white,
>   As one that long is dead.
>
> "Now, pray step in," my Lady saith,
>   "Now, pray step in and ride!"
> "I thank thee, I had rather walk,
>   Than gather to thy side."

The wheels go round without a sound
 Of tramp or turn of wheels,
As a cloud at night, in the pale moonlight,
 Onward the carriage steals.

" Now, pray step in," my Lady saith,
 " Now, prithee, come to me."
She takes the baby from the crib,
 She sets it on her knee.
The wheels go round, etc.

" Now, pray step in," my Lady saith,
 " Now, pray step in, and ride,"
Then deadly pale, in wedding veil,
 She takes to her the bride.
The wheels go round, etc.

" Now, pray step in," my Lady saith,
 " There's room I wot for you."
She waved her hand, the coach did stand,
 The Squire within she drew.
The wheels go round, etc.

" Now, pray step in," my Lady saith,
 " Why shouldst thou trudge afoot ? "
She took the gaffer in by her,
 His crutches in the boot.
The wheels go round, etc.

I'd rather walk a hundred miles,
 And run by night and day,
Than have that carriage halt for me,
 And hear my Lady say :
" Now, pray step in, and make no din,
 I prithee come and ride.
There's room, I trow, by me for you,
 And all the world beside." *

---

* Published with the traditional melody in " Songs of the West,
Traditional Songs and Ballads of the West of England," by S. Baring-Gould and H. Fleetwood Sheppard (Methuen, Bury Street, London, 1889). ·

CHAPTER VIII.

ST. MARK'S EVE.

The ballad of the "Lady's Coach," sung to a weird air
in an ancient mode, such as was becoming no more usual
for composers to write in, and already beginning to sound
strange and incomplete to the ear, at once changed the tenor
of the thoughts of those in the tavern, and diverted their
conversation away from politics into a new channel. The
wind had risen, and was raging round the house, driving
the rain in slashes against the casement; and puffing the
smoke down the chimney into the room.

"You came back from the moor along the Lyke-Way,
did you?" asked the farmer of Anthony.

"Yes; it is many miles the shortest, and there was plenty
of light."

"I wouldn't travel it at night for many crowns," said the
yeoman.

"Why not!" asked one of the miners. "What is there
to fear on the moor? If there be spirits, they hurt no
one."

"I should like others to risk it before me," said the yeoman.

"Anthony took good care not to ride it alone," muttered
Fox, with a side glance at young Cleverdon.

"You forced yourself on me," answered Anthony, sharply.

"Of course you wanted to be quite alone—I understand,"
sneered Fox.

"You can comprehend, I hope, that your company is no
advantage to be greatly desired on the Lyke-Way or elsewhere," retorted Anthony, angrily. "It is possible enough
that it was distasteful to others beside myself."

"And your society was infinitely preferable. I make no
question as to that," scoffed Fox.

"Now, no quarrels here. We have banished politics.
Must we banish every other topic that arises?" asked Solomon Gibbs. "What is this that makes you bicker now?"

"Oh, nothing!" said Crymes. "Anthony Cleverdon and
I were discussing the Lyke-Way, and whether either of us

cared to go along it at night. I shrink from it, just as does
Farmer Cudlip. Nor does Cleverdon seem more disposed
to walk it."

"I am not disposed to travel over it in rain and wind, in
the midst of a thunder-storm. I would go along it any
other night when moon and stars show, to allow of a man
finding his road."

"I'll tell you what," said the yeoman; "there's worst
places than the Lyke-Way on such a night as this."

"Where is that?"

"Do you know what night it be?"

"A very foul one."

"Ay, no doubt about that! after a fair day. But this is
St. Mark's Eve, and I'll tell you what befel my grandfather
on this night some years agone. 'Twas in Peter Tavy, too
—it came about he'd been to the buryin' of his uncle's
mother's sister's aunt, and, as he said hisself, never enjoyed
hisself more at a buryin'. There was plenty o' saffron cake
and cyder, and some bottles of real old Jamaica rum, mellow—Lor' bless you—soft and mellow as a cat's paw. He
lived, did my grandfather, at Horndon, and it were a night
much such as this. My grandfer had rather a deal stayed
wi' the corpse, but he was a mighty strict and scrupulous
old man, and he knowed that his wife—my grandmother as
was—would expect him home about—well, I can't say for
sartain, but, anyhow, some hours afore daybreak. Us poor
fellers in this world o' misery and trial, can't a'ways have
what we desires, so my grandfer had to sacrifice hisself on
the alter of dooty, and not to bide with the corpse and the
Jamaica rum, not to mention the saffron cake. 'Tes surprising, gentlemen," said Farmer Cudlip, looking round at
Cleverdon, Crymes, and Solomon Gibbs, "'tes surprising
now, when you come to reckon up, how soon one comes to
the end o' eating cake, and yet, in Jamaica rum, and punch
—I thanky' kindly, Mr. Gibbs, to fill me the glass. Thanky',
sir!—As I was saying, in drink one's capacity is, I should
say, boundless as the rolling ocean. Ain't it, now, Mr.
Gibbs?"

"Ah! Solomon the Wise never said a truer word," answered Solomon the Foolish.

"'Tes curious, when you come to consider, now," said the
farmer; "for meat and drink both goes the same way and

into the same receptacle; yet how soon one is grounded on cake, but can float, and float—I thank you Mr. Gibbs, my glass is empty—float forever in liquor."

"We should like to hear what your grandfather did," said Cleverdon, laughing.

"What he did? Why, he sot down," said Cudlip. "After leaving the house of tears and bereavement, he was going home, and was very tired, his legs began to give way under him. And as he came along by the wall o' Peter Tavy Church, sez he to hisself, 'Why, dash me if it bain't St. Mark's Eve, and many a time have I heard tell that they as wait on that eve in the church porch is sure to see go by in at the door all they that is sure to die in the rest o' the year.' Well, gentlemen, my grandfer, he knowed he was a bit late, and thought his wife—my grandmother—wouldn't take it over kindly, so he thinks if he could bring her a bit of rare news, she'd mebbe forgive him. And, gentlemen, what more rare news could he bring than a tale of who was doomed to die within the year? So he went in at the churchyard-gate, and straight—that is to say, as straight as his legs, which weren't quite equal, could take him—to the porch, and there, on the side away from the wind, he sot hisself down."

"I wouldn't have done it," said one of the miners, nudging his fellow; "would thou, Tummas?"

"Not I," responded his comrade. "If it had been the Lyke-Way, that's different. I'd walk that any night. But to go under a roof, in the churchyard—it were tempting o' Providence."

"Go on with your story," said Solomon Gibbs. "Those that interrupt lose a turn of filling from the bowl."

"Well, then," continued Cudlip, "my grandfather was seated for some time in the porch, and uncommon dark it was, for there are a plenty of trees in the churchyard, and the night was dirty, and the sky covered with clouds. How long he sat there I cannot tell, but long enough to get uneasy; not that he was afraid, bless your souls, of what he might see, but uneasy at being there so long and seeing nothing, so that he must go home to my grandmother without a word o' explanation or information that might pacify her, should she be inclined to be troublesome. Just as he was about to get up, in a mighty bad temper, and to go home, cursing the fools who had got up the tale of St. Mark's Eve, why, looking along the avenue in the yard, what should he see but some curious long, white things, like monstrous worms, crawling and tumbling, and making for the church porch. You will understand, gentlemen, that my grandfather thought he would do better to wait where he was, partly, because he did not wish to pass these worm-like creatures, but, chiefly, that he might have something to report to his missus, to make her placable and agreeable."

"But what where they?" asked Anthony Cleverdon.

"I'll tell you, Master Anthony. They was human arms, from the shoulder, walking of themselves; first they laid along from shoulder to elbow, then the hand from elbow forward lifted itself and looked about, and then came down flat on the palm, and lifted all the hinder part from the elbow-joint till it stood upright, and then turned a somersault, and so on again, two steps, as it were, and then a somersault; a coorious sort of proceeding, I take it."

"Very," said Crymes, with a sneer.

"There was about nine of 'em coming along, some fast as if racing each other, some slow, but creeping on, and overtaking the others that was going too fast, and fell over on the elbow-joint, when up went hand and shoulder kicking in the air like a beetle on his back. My grandfather felt that now sartainly he'd have news to tell his old woman. Presently a lot of the arms was about the step to the church porch, shy-like, not knowing whether to come in or no—some standing up on the shoulder and poking the hands in, some curlin' of themselves up on the step, as a-going to sleep, and some staggering about anyways. At last one of the boldest of them made a jump, and came down on my grandfather's knee, and sat there, with the shoulder part on his knee, like as a limpet fastens on a rock, or the end of a barnacle on a log of wood, and there it sat and curled itself about, and turned the hand just as it saw out of the nails—which was very white, and served as eyes. It was curious, my grandfather said, to see the fingers curling one over the other, just as a fly preens its wings. My granfer' couldn't make it out at first, till at last he saw it was pulling and picking at a gold ring on the last finger but one. It was a very broad ring—and direct-

ly my granfer' knowed it, and said, 'Why, blazes!' said
he, 'that's Mistress Cake's wedding ring!' And no sooner
had he said that, than the arm jumped off his knee and
went on to the church door, and he saw it no more. Now,
it is a fact, gentlemen, that Mistress Cake, of Wringworthy,
died a month later of the falling sickness. But he had not
a moment for consideration, as in came another arm, that
stood at his foot bowing to him with the hand, and then
patting him on the shin. This arm didn't like to seem to
make so bold as to come up and sit on his knee, so my
granfer stooped and looked at it. It stood up on the
shoulder, and it had very strong muscles; but rather stiff,
they seemed, wi' age, for they cracked like when the arm
bent itself about, which it did in a slow and clumsy
fashion. 'Twas a brown arm, too, and not white, like
Madam Cake's; and the hand was big, and broad, and
hairy, and it turned itself over and showed the palm, and
then it held up one finger after another, which was all
covered with warts. Then my granfer said, 'Lor' bless and
deliver! but this be the hand of Ploughman Gale!' And,
sure enough, I reckon it was. It seemed quite satisfied,
and folded itself up, and made a spring like a cricket—
went out of sight to the church door."

"I should like to know how your grandfather saw all
this," said Anthony Cleverdon, "if it was, as you say, a
dark night, and it was in the church porch?"

"No interfering!" exclaimed Mr. Gibbs. "You've forfeited. Here's your glass, Master Cudlip. Go on."

"There's not much more to be said," continued the
yeoman. "One or two more arms came on, and granfer
said there was a sight o' difference in their ways: some
was pushing like, and forward; and others rayther hung
back, and seemed to consider small bones of themselves.
Now it was a fact that all those he saw and named belonged to folks as died within the year, and in the very order
in which they came on and presented themselves before
him. What puzzled him most to name was two baby-arms
—purty little things they was—and he had to count over
all the young children in the parish before he could tell
which they was. At last, up came a long, lean, old, dry
arm, tossing its hand in a short, quick, touchy fashion, and
went up on grandfer's knee without so much as a 'By your

leave.' And there it sat, and poked its hand about, wi' all the fingers joined together like a pointed serpent's head. It moved in a queer, irritable, jerky manner, that was familiar, somehow, to my grandfather. After a bit he put his head down to look at the elbow, where he fancied he saw a mole, when—crack! the hand hit him on his cheek such a blow that he tumbled over, and lay sprawling on the pavement; and he knew, by the feel of the hand as it caught him, that it was—my grandmother's. When he had picked himself up, he saw nothing more, so he went home. You may be very sure of those two things, gentlemen— [Thank you, Mr. Gibbs. I'll trouble you to fill my glass. Talking has made me terrible dry]—he never told his missus that Madam Cake's arm had sat on his knee, nor that he had seen and recognized her *own* arm and hand."

"I wouldn't go on this night to the church porch, not for a king's crown," said one of the miners. "Did not your grandfather suffer for his visit?"

"Well," answered the yeoman, "I reckon he did ever after feel a sort o' cramp in his knees—particularly in wet weather, where the arms had sat—but what was that to the relief? My grandmother died that same year."

"I wouldn't go there for any relief you might name," said the miner again, who was greatly impressed by the story. "I've heard the pixies hammering down in the mines, but I think naught of them. As for the Lyke-Way, what goes over that is but shadows."

"Some folks are afraid of shadows," said Fox, "and don't think themselves safe unless they have at least a woman with them for protection."

"You are again levelling at me!" exclaimed Anthony Cleverdon. "I have no fear either of shadows or substances. If you choose to come out and try with me, you will see that I am not afraid of your arm, and that I can chastise your tongue."

"Oh! my arm!" laughed Crymes. "I never supposed for a moment you dreaded that. But it is the arms without bodies, moving like worms in the churchyard at Peter Tavy, on this St. Mark's Eve, you are more likely to dread."

"I am not afraid of them," retorted Cleverdon.

"So you say; but I do not think you seem inclined to show you are not."

"Do you dare me to it?"

" I don't care whether you go or not. If you do, who is
to stand surety for you that you go where I say—to the
churchyard of Peter Tavy?"

" One of you can come and see."

" There !" laughed Fox, " crying off already ! Afraid to
go alone, and appealing for company."

" By heaven, this is too bad !" cried Anthony, and started
to his feet.

"Don't go," shouted Mr. Solomon Gibbs. "It's folly,
and break up of good company."

" There's good company with Fox Crymes girding at me
at every minute. But, by heaven, I will not be jeered at
as a coward. Fox has dared me to go to Peter Tavy
churchyard, and go I will—alone, moreover."

" No such thing," said the host; "it is too bad a night.
Stay here and help finish this brew; we'll have another
bowl, if Mr. Solomon approves—and Mr. Cudlip."

" I will go," said Anthony, thoroughly roused, and rendered doubly excitable by the punch he had been drinking.

" You have done wrong to spur him," said Gibbs, addressing Crymes.

" Faith ! I am a sceptic," said Fox. " I disbelieve altogether in the walking arms, and I shall be glad to learn
from a credible witness whether the same be a mere fiction
and fancy, or have any truth in it. Master Cudlip's grandfather lived a long time ago."

" I do not believe in it either," said Cleverdon; " but
although I did I would not now be deterred. Fox casts
his gibes at me, and I will show him that I have metal
enough to make such a trifling venture as this."

He threw on his coat, grasped his long walking-stick,
and went out into the storm. A furious gale was sweeping
about the little hamlet of Cudlip town, where stood the
tavern. It was not possible to determine from which
quarter the wind came, it so eddied about the inn and the
open space before it. Anthony stood against the wall outside for a moment or two till his eyes accustomed themselves somewhat to the dark. Every few moments the
glare of lightning in the sky illumined the rocky ridges of
White Tor and Smeardun, under which Cudlip town lay,
and the twisted thorns and oaks among blocks of granite

that strewed the slopes before the three or four old farm-houses that were clustered about the inn.

Then Anthony, having satisfied himself as to his direction, set down his head against the wind, and strode forward, with his staff feeling the way. On his right, below in this valley, roared the Tavy, but the song of the water was mixed up with that of the wind so inextricably that Anthony, had he tried it, could not have distinguished the roar of one from that of the other. The lane was between stone walls and hedges of half stone and half earth, in summer adorned with magnificent foxgloves. For a while the rain slackened, and where the walls were high Anthony had some shelter against the wind. Peter Tavy Church lay outside the village, and he would reach it without passing another house.

The principal fury of the storm seemed to be concentrated over White Tor, a lofty peak of trap rock fortified in prehistoric times, and with beacons and cairns of angular fragments piled up within the enclosure. In one place a huge fang of black rock stood upright, and was split by lightning, with a block of basalt fallen into the cleft, where it swung among the rocks. Over the cairns and embankments the thunder-cloud flamed white, and threw out dazzling fire-bolts. Anthony stood one moment, looking up at the Tor; it was as though the spirits of the air were playing at tossball there with thunderbolts. Then he again pushed forward. The wind, the cold—after the warmth of the tavern and the spirits he had drank—confused his brain, and though he was not intoxicated, yet he was not judge of his actions. At the next explosion of the electric fluid he saw before him the granite tower of the church, and the trees in the churchyard bare of leaves.

Those in the tavern became grave and silent for a moment after Anthony left.

"It is a folly," said one of the miners; "it is tempting heaven."

"I don't care whether he sees aught or not," said Cudlip; "my grandfather's story is true. It don't follow because Anthony Cleverdon comes back having seen nothing that my grandfather told an untruth. Who can tell? perhaps nobody in the parish will die this year. If there is to be no burials, then no arms will be walking."

"I hope he's not gone the wrong road and tumbled into the river," said Solomon Gibbs.

"I'll tell you what he will do," said Fox. "He will let us sit expecting his return all night, and he will quietly take himself off to Hall, and laugh at us for our folly to-morrow."

"Not he," said the innkeeper; "that's not the way with Master Cleverdon. *You* might have done that, and we should not ha' been surprised."

"I would have done it, most assuredly. If Tony does not, then he is more of a fool than I took him. He loves a bit of brag as much as another, and with brag he went forth."

"There is no brag in him," said Taverner, the ballad-singer. "Every one knows what Anthony Cleverdon is; if he says he will do a thing, he will do it. If we wait long enough, he will return from the churchyard."

"Or say he has been there."

"If he says it, we will believe him—all but you, Mr. Crymes, who believe in nobody and nothing."

"Now, we have had threats of quarrel already more than once; I must stop this," said Solomon Gibbs. "Storm outside is sufficient. Let us have calm within over the sea of punch."

"Oh!" said Fox, contemptuously, "I don't quarrel with old Taverner; no man draws save against his equal."

"Punch! more punch!" shouted Gibbs. "Landlord, we are come to the gravel. And, Taverner! give us a song, but not one so dismal as 'My Lady's Coach.' That set us about speaking of St. Mark's Eve, and sent Cleverdon on this crazy adventure."

"What shall I sing?" asked the songman, but he did not wait for an answer. He stood up and began:—

> Oh! the trees they are so high,
> And the trees they are so green!
> The day is past and gone, sweet love,
> That you and I have seen.
>   It is cold winter's night,
>   You and I must bide alone,
>   Whilst my pretty lad is young,
>   And is growing.

The door was burst open, and Anthony entered, with the water pouring off him. He was blinded with the rain that had beat in his face, as he came toward Cudlip's town. In his arms he bore something like a log.

"There!" said he, and cast this object on the table, where it struck and shattered the porcelain punchbowl, sending its last contents over the table and the floor.

"There!" shouted Anthony, "will you now believe I have been in the churchyard?"

"By the Lord!" shouted Solomon Gibbs, "this is past a joke. This is a mortal insult."

That which Anthony had cast on the table was one of the oak posts which marked the head of a grave, square, with a sort of nick and knob on the top. Such a post as was put up by those who could not afford granite tombstones.

"It is an insult! It is an outrage!" roared Gibbs, "look there!" He pointed to the inscription on the post—it ran thus :—

RICHARD MALVINE,
OF WILLSWORTHY, GENT.

CHAPTER IX.

WILLSWORTHY.

The night of storm was succeeded by a fresh and sparkling morning. The rain hung on every bush, twinkling in prismatic colours. There still rose smoke from the moor, but the wind had shifted, and it now carried the combined steam and smoke away to the east. The surface of Dartmoor was black, as though bruised all over its skin of fine turf. Hardly any gorse bushes were left, and the fire had for more than one year robbed the moor of the glory of golden blossom that crowned it in May, and of the mantle of crimson heath wherewith it was enfolded in July.

Luke Cleverdon, Curate of Mary Tavy, walked slowly up the hill from the bridge over the brawling River Tavy towards Willsworthy. He was a tall, spare young man, with

large soft brown eyes, and a pale face. His life had not
been particularly happy. His parents had died when he
was young, and old Cleverdon, of Hall, had taken charge of
the boy in a grumblingly, ungracious fashion, resenting
the conduct of his brother in dying, and encumbering him
with the care of a delicate child. Luke was older than
young Anthony, and possibly for a while old Anthony may
have thought that, in the event of his wife giving him no
son, Hall and his accumulations would devolve on this frail,
white-faced, and timid lad. The boy proved to be fond of
books, and wholly unsuited for farm life. Consequently
he was sent to school, and then to College, and had been
ordained by the Bishop of Exeter to the Curacy of Tavy
St. Peter, or Petery-Tavy, as it was usually called. His
uncle had never shown him affection, his young cousin,
Anthony, had been in everything and every way preferred
before him, and had been suffered to put him aside and
tyrannise over him at his will. Only in Bessie had he
found a friend, though hardly an associate, for Bessie's interests were other than those of the studious, thoughtful
boy. She was a true Martha, caring for all that pertained
to the good conduct of the house, and Luke had the dreamy
idealism of Mary. The boy had suffered from contraction
of the chest, but had grown out of his extreme delicacy in
the fresh air of the country, and living on the abundant
and wholesome food provided in a farm. His great passion
was for the past. He had so little to charm him in the
present, and no pursuit unfolding before him in the future,
that he had been thrown as a lad to live in the past, to
make the episodes of history his hunting fields. Fortunately for him, Dartmoor was strewn with prehistoric antiquities; upright stones ranged in avenues, in some in-
stances extending for miles, with mysterious circles of
unhewn blocks, and with cairns and kistvaens, or stone
coffins, constructed of rude slabs of granite. Among these
he wandered, imagining strange things, peopling the solitude, and dreaming of the Druids who, he supposed, had
solemnised their ritual in these rude temples.

Old Cleverdon was angered with the pursuits of his
nephew. He utterly despised any pursuit which did not
lead to money, and archæology was one which might, and
often did, prove expensive, but was not remunerative from

a pecuniary point of view. As soon as ever Luke was
ordained and established in a curacy, the old man considered that his obligation towards him had ceased, and he
left the poor young man to sustain himself on the miserable salary that was paid him by his non-resident Rector.
But Luke's requirements were small, and his only grief at
the smallness of his stipend was that it obliged him to
forego the purchase of books.

He was on his way to Willsworthy, four miles from the
parish church, at the extreme end of the parish, to pay a
pastoral visit to Mistress Malvine, who was an invalid.
Before reaching the house he came to a ruined chapel, that
had not been used since the Reformation, and there he
suddenly lighted upon Urith.

His pale face flushed slightly. She was seated on a mass
of fallen wall, with her hands in her lap, occupied with her
thoughts. To her surprise, on her return late on the
preceding night, before the breaking of the storm, her
mother had not followed her accustomed practice of covering her with reproaches ; and this had somewhat disconcerted Urith. Mrs. Malvine was a woman of not much
intelligence, very self-centred, and occupied with her ail-
ments. She had a knack of finding fault with every one,
of seeing the demerits of all with whom she had to do ; and
she was not slow in expressing what she thought. Nor
had she the tact to say what she thought and felt, and have
done with it, she went on nagging, aggravating, exaggerat-
ing, and raking up petty wrongs or errors of judgment
into mountains of misdemeanour, so that when at one
moment she reproved such as had acted wrongly, she invariably in the next reversed positions, for she rebuked
with such extravagance, and enlarged on the fault with
such exaggeration as to move the innate sense of proportion
and equity in the soul of the condemned, and to rouse the
consciousness of injustice in the accused.

Such a scene had taken place the previous day, when
her mother, aided by the blundering Uncle Solomon, had
driven Urith into one of her fits of passion, in which she
had run away. When Mistress Malvine discovered what
she had done—that she had actually pressed her child
beyond endurance, and that the girl had run to the wilderness, where she could no more be traced, when the day

and evening passed without her return, the sick woman became seriously alarmed, and faintly conscious that she had transgressed due bounds in the reprimand administered to Urith for rejecting the suit of Anthony Crymes. Consequently, when finally the girl did reappear, her mother controlled herself, and contented herself with inquiring where she had been.

Luke Cleverdon knew Urith better than did his cousins; in his rambles on the moor, as a boy, he had often come this way, and had frequently had Urith as his companion. The friendship begun in childhood continued between them now that he was curate in charge of souls, and she was growing into full bloom of girlhood.

He now halted, leaning both his hands on his stick, and spoke to her, and asked after her mother.

Urith rose to accompany him to the house. "She is worse; I fear I have caused her trouble and distress of mind. I ran away from home yesterday, and might have been lost on the moor, had not"—she hesitated, her cheek assumed a darker tinge, and she said—"had not I fortunately been guided aright to reach home."

"That is well," said Luke. "We are all liable thus to stray, and well for us when we find a sure guide, and follow him."

For a young man he was gaunt. He was dressed in scrupulously correct clerical costume, a cassock and knee-breeches, white bands, and a three-cornered hat.

Urith spoke about the fire on the moor, the bewilderment caused by the smoke, and then of the storm during the night. He stood listening to her and looking at her; it seemed to him that he had not before properly appreciated her beauty. He had wondered at her strange temper —now frank, then sullen and reserved; he did not know the reason why this was now for the first time revealed to him—it was because in the night a change had taken place in the girl, for the first time she had felt the breath of that spirit of love which like magic wakes up the sleeping charms of soul and face, gives them expression and significance. Not, however, now for the first time did the thought cross his mind that, of all women in the world, she was the only one he could and did love. He had long loved her, loved her deeply, but hopelessly, and had fought many a hard battle with himself to conquer a passion which his judgment told him must be subdued. He knew the girl — wild, sullen, undisciplined — the last to mould into the proper mate for a village pastor. Moreover, what was he but a poor curate, without interest with patrons, without means of his own, likely, as far as he could judge, to live and die, a curate. He knew not only that Urith was not calculated to make a pastor's wife, but he knew also that hers was not a character that could consort with his. He was studious, meek, yet firm in his principles; she was hardly tame, of ungovernable temper, and a creature of impulse. No, they could not be happy together even were circumstances to allow of his marrying. He had said all this to himself a thousand times, yet he could not conquer his passion. He held it in control, and Urith, least of all, had a notion of its existence. She exercised on him that magic that is exercised on one character by another the reverse at every point. The calm, self-ruled, in-wrapped nature of Luke looked out at the turbulence or the moroseness of the wild girl with admiration mingled with fear. It exercised over him an inexplicable but overpowering spell. He knew she was not for him, and yet that she should ever belong to another was a thought that he could not bear to entertain. He walked at her side to the house listening to her, but hardly knowing what she said. The glamour of her presence was on him, and he walked as in a cloud of light, that dazzled his eyes and confused his mind.

Willsworthy was a very small and quaint old manor house —so small that a modern farmer would despise it. It consisted of a hall and a couple of sitting-rooms and kitchen on the ground floor, with a projecting porch, with pavise over it. The windows looked into the little court that was entered through old granite gates, capped with balls, and was backed by a cluster of bold sycamores and beech, in which was a large rookery.

Mrs. Malvine was in the hall. She had been brought down. She was unable to walk, and she sat in her armchair by the hearth. The narrow mullioned lights did not afford much prospect, and what they did reveal was only the courtyard and stables that fronted the entrance to the house. To the back of the house was, indeed, a walled gar-

den ; but it was void of flowers and suffered from the neglect which allowed everything about Willsworthy to sink
into disrepair and barrenness.   It grew a few pot-herbs,
half-choked by weeds.   There was no gardener kept ; but
a labourer, when he could be spared off the farm, did something in a desultory fashion to the garden—always too late
to be of use to it.

"Peace be to this house !" said Luke, and passed in at
the door.

He found that, for all his good wish, nothing at the moment was farther removed from Willsworthy, than peace,
Solomon Gibbs had slept long and heavily after his carouse,
and had but just come down the stairs, and had just acted
the inconsiderate part of telling his sister of the outrage
committed by Anthony Cleverdon on her husband's grave.
The poor widow was in an hysterical condition of efferves-
cent wrath and lamentation.

The story was repeated, when Luke and Urith appeared,
in a broken, incoherent fashion—the widow telling what
she knew, with additions of her own, Solomon throwing in
corrections.

Urith turned chill in all her veins.   Her heart stood still,
and she stood looking at her uncle with stony eyes.
Anthony Cleverdon, who had behaved to her with such
kindness—Anthony, who had held her in his arms, had
carried her through the fire, who had looked into her
face with such warmth in his eyes—he thus insult her
father's name and her family !   It was impossible, incredible.

Luke paced the little hall with his arms folded behind
his back.   He had heard nothing of this at Peter Tavy
when he left it.   He hoped there was some mistake—some
exaggeration.   What could have been Anthony's object?
Mr. Solomon Gibbs's account was certainly sufficiently involved and obscure to allow of the suspicion that there was
exaggeration, for Mr. Solomon's recollection of the events
was clouded by the punch imbibed overnight.   But the fact
that the headpiece of the grave had been brought to the
tavern by his cousin could not be got over.   Luke's heart
was filled with commiseration for the distress of the widow,
and pain for Urith, and with bitterness against Anthony.
He had nothing but platitudes to say—nothing that could

pacify the excited woman, who went from one convulsion into another.

Suddenly the door was thrust open and in, without a knock, without permission, came Anthony himself—the first time he had crossed that threshold.

Urith's arms fell to her side, and her fists became clenched. How dare he appear before them, after having committed such an offence? Mistress Malvine held up her hands before her face to hide the sight of him from her eyes.

"I have come," said Anthony, "I have come because of that bit of tomfoolery last night."

Luke saw that his cousin was approaching the widow, and he stepped between them. "For shame of you, 'Tony!" he said, in quivering voice. "You ought never to show your face after what has been done—at all events here."

"Get aside," answered Anthony roughly, and thrust him out of the way.

"Madame Malvine," said he, planting himself before the hysterical widow, "listen to me. I am very sorry and ashamed for what I did. It was in utter ignorance. I was dared to go to the churchyard last night when the ghosts walk, and Fox said no one would believe me that I had been there unless I brought back some token. We had all been drinking. The night was pitch-dark. I got up the avenue under the trees, and pulled up the stake nearest to the church porch I could feel. Whose it was, as Heaven is my witness, I did not know. I was wrong in doing it; but I was dared to do something of the kind."

"You must have known that my brother-in-law lay on the right-hand side of the porch," said Solomon Gibbs.

"How should I know?" retorted Anthony. "I am not sexton, to tell where every one lies. And on such a pitch-black night too, I could find my way only by feeling."

"Your offence," said Luke, sternly, "is not against this family only, but against God. You have been guilty of sacrilege."

"I will ask you not to interfere," answered Anthony. "With God I will settle the matter in my own conscience. I am come here to beg forgiveness of Mistress Malvine and of Urith."

He turned sharply round to the latter, and spoke with a

deep flush in his cheek, and with outstretched arm. "Urith! you will believe me! You will forgive me! With my best heart's blood I would wipe out the offence. I never, never dreamed of injuring and paining you. It was a misadventure, and my cursed folly in sitting drinking at the Hare and Hounds, and of allowing myself to be taunted to a mad act by Fox Crymes, who is my evil genius."

"It was Fox Crymes who urged you to do it?" asked Urith, her rigidity ceasing, and the colour returning to her cheeks and lips.

"He goaded me to the act, but he had nothing to do with my bringing your father's headpiece to the tavern—that was the devil's own witchcraft."

"Mother," said Urith, "do you hear; it was Fox Crymes's doing. On him the blame falls."

"You believe me, Urith—I know you must! You know I would not injure you, offend you, grieve you in any way. You must know that, Urith—you do in your heart know it; assure your mother of that. Here, give me your hand in pledge that you believe—that you forgive me."

She gave it him at once.

"Now see, Mistress Malvine, Urith is my testimony— Good God! what is the matter?"

Mrs. Malvine had fallen back in her chair, and was speechless.

CHAPTER X.

LUKE CLEVERDON.

Luke Cleverdon left the house. He could no longer endure to remain in it. He saw the flash in Urith's eye as she put her hand in that of Anthony in answer to his appeal. He had seen sufficient to shake and wring his heart with inexpressible pain. He walked hastily down the hill, but stopped at the ruined chapel, and entered there. The old broken altar lay there, one of its supports fallen. Luke seated himself on a block of granite, and rested his arm against the altar-slab, and laid his head on his arm. That he had long loved Urith he knew but too well for his peace of mind, but never before had his passion for her so flamed

up as at that moment when she took his cousin's hand.
What had occurred on the previous day on the moor was repeated again; a smouldering fire had suddenly caught a
great tuft or bush, almost a tree, of gorse, and had mounted
in a pillar of flame.

Was Anthony in all things to be preferred to him? In
the house at Hall, Luke had submitted without demur to
be set aside on all occasions, for Anthony was the son, and
Luke but the nephew, of the old man; Hall would one day
be the inheritance of Anthony, and in Hall the son of old
Anthony's brother had no portion. But now that he had
left his uncle's house, now that he was independent, was
Anthony still to stand in his way, to lay his hand on and
claim the one flower that Luke loved, but which he dared
not put forth his hand to pluck?

Timid and humble-minded as Luke was, he had never
considered that he could win the affections of any girl, least-
ways of one such as Urith. But it was a delight to him to
see her, to watch the unfolding of her mind, and character,
and beauty, to know that she was a wild moor-flower, regarded by no one else but himself, sought by none, or, if
sought, rejecting such seekers with disdain. He was so
simple and single in his aims, that it would have well contented him to merely admire and humbly love Urith, never
revealing the state of his heart, asking of her nothing but
friendship and regard. But—when, all at once, he saw
another stand beside her, take her hand, and seize on her
heart with bold temerity, and by his boldness win it—that
was too much for Luke to endure without infinite pain,
and a battle with himself. If he had formed any ideal picture of the future, it was the harmless one of himself as the
friend, the gentle, unassuming, unasserting friend of Urith,
suffered by her, after some little resistance, to divert her
headlong character, brighten the gloomy depths of her
strange mind. He knew how greatly she needed an ad-
viser and guide, and his highest ambition was so to help
her that she might become a noble and generous woman.
That he had not formed this hope out of pure pastoral zeal
he knew, for he who taught others to search their own
consciences, not lightly, and after the manner of dissem-
blers with God, had explored his own heart, and measured all
its forces; but till this moment he had never realized that

there was a selfishness and jealousy in his love, a selfishness which would have kept back Urith from knowing and loving anyone, and a jealousy intense and bitter against the man who obtained that place in Urith's heart to which he himself laid no claim, but which he hoped would be forever empty.

He tried to pray, but was unable to do more than move his lips and form words. Prayers did not appease the ardor, lessen the anguish within. As he looked up at the moor he saw now that it was still smoking. The storm of rain in the night had not quenched the fires, nor could the dews of Divine consolation put out that which blazed within his breast.

He had never envied Anthony till now. When he had been at school, he had been but scantily furnished with pocket-money. There had been many little things he would have liked to buy, but could not, having so small a sum at his disposal; on the other hand, Anthony could at all times command his father's purse, had spent money as he liked, had wasted it wantonly, but Luke had accepted the difference with which they had been treated without resentment; yet, now that Anthony had stepped in between him and Urith, something very much like hatred formed like gall in his heart.

He tried to think that he was angry with his cousin for having given Mistress Malvine pain, with having been guilty of sacrilege, but he was too truthful in his dealings with himself to admit that these were the springs of the bitterness within.

Suddenly he looked up with a start, and saw Bessie before him, observing him with sympathetic distress. His pale forehead was covered with sweat-drops, and his long, thin hands were trembling. They had been clasped, the one on the other, on the altar-stone, and Luke's brow had rested on them, his face downward; thus he had not seen Bessie when she approached.

"What is it, Luke?" she said, in kindly tones, full of commiseration. "Are you ill, dear cousin?"

He looked at her somewhat vacantly for a moment, gathering his senses together. As in bodily pain, after a paroxysm, the mind remains distraught for a moment, and is unable to throw itself outward, so it is with mental pain to an even greater degree. As Bessie spoke, Luke seemed to be brought, or to bring himself, by an effort, out of a far-off world into that in which Bessie stood surrounded by the old chapel walls, hung with hartstongue leaves, still green, untouched by winter frost.

"What are you suffering from?" she asked, and seated herself at his side.

"It is nothing, cousin," he answered, and shook his head to shake away the thoughts that had held him.

"It is indeed something," she said, gently; "I know it is; I see it in your white and streaming face." She took his hand in hers. "I know it from your cold hand. Luke, you have had no one but me to talk to of your troubles in boyhood, and I had none but you to tell of my little girlish vexations. Shall we be the same now, and confide in each other?"

O, false Bessie! knowing she was false, as she said this. The keen eye of her Aunt Magdalen had seen what Bessie supposed was hidden from every one, that she loved her cousin Luke. But to Luke would that secret assuredly never be entrusted. It was to be a one-sided confidence.

"Are you ill? Are you in bodily pain?" she asked.

He shook his head—not now to shake away thought, but in negative. He passed his disengaged hand and sleeve over his brow, and was at once composed. "I am sorry you saw me like this, Bessie. I thought no one would come in here."

"I have come to see Urith, after last night. I promised her I would come some time, and I thought that I would ask if she were quite well, for the day was to her long and trying."

"Do not go on there now," said Luke gently, releasing his hand. "There has something happened. You have not heard, but it will be noised everywhere shortly, and the shock has been too much for Mistress Malvine; she has fallen into a fit."

"Then I had better go on, cousin; I may be of help to Urith."

"You have not heard ——" Then he told her of what Anthony had done the preceding night. Bessie was greatly disturbed; the act was so profane, and so inconsiderate. The inconsiderateness might, indeed, partially excuse the act, but hardly redeem it from sacrilege, and was certain to arouse general and deep indignation; the inconsiderateness showed an unbalanced mind, wanting in ordinary regard for the feelings of others.

"And yet," said Elizabeth, "this is not what has made you so unhappy. You have not told me all."

Luke remained silent, looking before him. "Bessie," said he, "has it never been observed by you that Anthony had an affection for Urith?"

"Never," answered Elizabeth; "I do not see how there could have sprung up such a liking. They hardly ever can have spoken to each other before yesterday, though they may have met; as, for instance, seen each other in church. I never heard Anthony name her."

"He does not tell you what he has in his heart."

"I did not believe that he had any particular regard for any one. He has not been a person to seek the company of young maidens; he has affected to utterly scorn them, and has held himself aloof from their company."

"I think—I am sure that he likes her," said Luke slowly.

Then Bessie turned her face and looked at him steadily.

"Oh, Luke! Luke!" she exclaimed, and there was pain in her tone. "I have read your heart. Now I know all." And now that she had discovered his secret, Luke was glad to be able to pour out his heart into her sympathetic ear, to tell her how that he did love Urith, but also how that he had never dreamed of making her his wife.

"My wife!" said he, with a sad smile; "that is not a name I shall ever be able to give to any woman. It is not one that any woman would care for me to call her by."

Bessie listened as he talked, without a sign in her face of other emotion than pity for him. Not in the slightest did she raise a fold of the veil that concealed her heart, the rather did she wrap it round her the more closely.

After a while Luke rose relieved. He took Bessie's hand in his, and said, "Now, dear cousin, you must make me a promise. When you have any trouble at heart, you will come and tell me." She pressed his hand and raised her eyes timidly to his, but made no other answer.

They walked together down the hill, and then, at the bridge, parted. When they parted, Bessie's eyes filled with tears.

But the heart of Luke was relieved, and he walked homewards encouraged to fight out the battle with himself, and overcome the jealousy with which he began to regard his cousin Anthony.

CHAPTER XI.

THE GLOVES AGAIN.

Anthony remained at Willsworthy. He had behaved exceedingly badly, had wounded the good lady of the house where most susceptible to pain, and so acutely that she had fallen into unconsciousness ; yet he remained on. He was accustomed to consult his own wishes, not those of others, and to put on one side all considerations of expediency and good feeling, where his own caprice was concerned.

Urith and the servant wench had carried Madame Malvine to her room, and Solomon Gibbs had dashed off to the stables to get his horse, so as to summon the surgeon from Tavistock.

Anthony was alone in the little hall, and he leaned his elbows on the window-sill and looked out. There was nothing for him to see ; nothing to interest him in the barn wall opposite, which was all that was commanded by the window ; so he turned his eyes on a peacock butterfly that had hybernated in the hall, and now, with return of spring, shook off sleep and fluttered against the leaded panes, bruising its wings in its efforts to escape into the outer air. There were no flowers in the window ; nothing at all save some dead flies and a pair of lady's riding-gloves folded together.

Anthony looked round the hall. It was low, not above seven feet high, unceiled, with black oak unmoulded rafters. There was a large granite fireplace, no sculptured oak mantelpiece over it ; nothing save a plain shelf ; and above it some arms, a couple of pistols, a sword, a pike or two, and a crossbow. The walls were not panelled save only by the window, where was the table, and where the family dined. The walls elsewhere were plainly white-

washed, and had not even that decoration that was affected
at the tavern—ballads with quaint woodcuts pasted against
them.   There was no deer park attached to the house;
there never had been even a paddock for deer, consequently
there were no antlers in the hall.

Near the window was a recess in the wall over a granite
pan or bowl partly built into the wall.   At first sight it
might be taken as a basin in which to wash the hands;
but it had no pipe from it to convey the fouled water
away.   Such pans are found in many old western farm-
houses and manor halls, and their purport is almost forgotten.   They were formerly employed for the scalding of
the milk and the making of clouted cream.   Red-hot char-
coal was placed in these basins, and the pans of milk
planted on the cinders.   The pans remained there, the
coals being fanned by the kitchen maid, till the cream was
formed on the surface, and in this cream-coat the ring of
the bottom of the pan indicated itself on the surface.   This
was the token that the milk had yielded up all its quo-
tient of fatty matter.   Thereupon the pan was removed to
the cool dairy.   The presence of the granite cream-pro-
ducer showed that the hall served a double purpose: it
was not only a sitting- and dining-room, but one in which
some of the dairy processes were carried on.   Moreover,
near the entrance-door was what was called the "well-
room," entered from the hall.   This was a small lean-to
apartment on one side of the porch, paved with cobble-
stones, in which was a stone trough always brimming with
crystal moorland water, conducted into it from outside,
and, running off, was carried away outside again.   As this
was the sole source whence all the water-supply required
for the house was obtained—for dairy, for kitchen, and for
table—it may be imagined that the hall was a passage-
room, traversed all day long by the servant-wenches with
pails, and pans, and jugs.

Such an arrangement was suitable enough in the time
before the Wars of the Roses, when Willsworthy was built;
but its inconvenience became apparent with the improved
social conditions of the Tudor reigns, and in the time of
Elizabeth an addition had been made to the house, so that
it now possessed two small parlours looking into the garden
at the back; but these Anthony had not seen.   In these

some attempt was made at ornament. A manor house
before the Tudor epoch rarely consisted of more than a
hall, a lady's bower, kitchen, and cellars, on the ground-
floor ; Willsworthy had been enlarged by the addition of a
second parlour, with the object of abandoning the Hall, to
become a sort of second kitchen.

But the family had been poor, and continued in its ancestral mode of life. The second parlour had its shutters
shut, and was never used, and Madame Malvine sat, as had
her husband, and the owners of Willsworthy before them,
in the Hall, and endured the traffic through it, and the
slops on the stone floor from the overflowing pails.

The paving of the Hall was of granite blocks, rudely
fitted together, and was strewn with dry brown bracken.
We marvel at the discomfort of ancient chairs, because the
seats are so high from the ground. We forget that the
footstool was an attendant inseparable from the chair, when
ladies sat in these stone-floored halls. They were necessary
adjuncts, holding their feet out of the draught, and off the
stone.

Small and mean as the manor house would appear in
one's eyes now, yet it was of sufficient consequence in early
days to have its chapel, a privilege only accorded to the
greater houses, and wealthiest gentry. The chapel was
now in ruins. It had not been used since the Reformation.

Anthony became impatient of waiting. He would not
leave, and he was vexed, because he was kept loitering at
the window without some one to speak to.

He was tired of looking at the butterfly battering its
wings to pieces, so he took up the gloves and unrolled
them—a pretty pair of fine leather ladies' gloves, reaching
to the elbow, and laced with silk ribbon and silver tags.
Elegant gloves ; more handsome, Anthony thought, than
suited the usual style of Urith's dress. He had nothing
else to do but turn them inside out, unfold, and refold
them.

As he was thus engaged, he thought over an interview he
had had that morning with his father. With all his faults,
and they were many, the young man was open and direct,
and he had told his father what he had done the night
before.

To his surprise, directly old Cleverdon heard that he had

pulled up Richard Malvine's head-post, and thrown it on
the tavern table before the topers, he burst into an exultant
laugh, and rubbed his hands together gleefully.

When, moreover, Anthony expressed his intention of going to Willsworthy to offer an apology, the old man had vehemently and boisterously dissuaded him from so doing.

"What are the Malvines?" he had said; "a raggle-taggle,
beggarly crew. I won't have it said that a son of mine
veiled his bonnet to them. That was a fair estate once, but
first one portion and then another portion has been sold
away, and now there is but enough to starve on left.
Pshaw! let them endure and pocket the affront. If they
try to resent it, and prosecute you in court of law, I will
throw in my money-bag against their moleskin purse, and
see which cause then has most weight in the scales of
justice."

The intemperance of his father's conduct and words had
on young Anthony precisely the opposite effect to that intended. It opened the young man's eyes to the gravity of
his conduct. Without answering his father he went to
Willsworthy, leaving the old man satisfied that he had
overborne his son's resolution to make amend for his offence. Whether this would have happened had not Urith
produced so strong an impression on his heart the previous
day, and enlisted him on her side, may well be questioned;
for the visit of apology involved an acknowledgment of
wrong-doing which was not readily made by Anthony. He
was thinking over, and wondering at, his father's conduct,
when Urith entered the hall, and expressed surprise at seeing him.

"I tarried," said he, "to know how it fared with your
mother."

Urith replied, somewhat stiffly, "The shock of hearing
what you have done has given her a fit."

"She has had them before."

"Oh, yes. She cannot endure violent emotion, and your
behaviour——"

"I have said I am sorry; what can I do more? Tell me,
and I will do it. The stake was rotten, and broke off. If
you will, I will have a stone slab placed on the grave at my
own cost."

Urith flushed dark.

"That I refuse in my mother's name and in mine. We will not be beholden to you—to any stranger—in such a matter; and after what has been done, certainly not to you."

Anthony stamped with impatience.

"I have told you I am sorry. I never made an apology to any one in my life before. I supposed that an apology offered was at once frankly accepted. I have told you it was all a mistake. I intended no ill. It was a pitch-black night—I could not see what I laid hold of. My act was, if you will, an act of folly—but have you never committed acts of folly? You ran away from home yesterday. Did not that trouble your mother, and occasion greater perturbation of feeling?"

Urith looked down. "Yes," she said, "one foolery followed another. First came mine, then yours. The two combined were too much for my mother to endure."

"We are a couple of fools; be it so," said Anthony. "Now that is settled. Young folks' brains are not ripened, but are like the pith in early hazel nuts. It is not their fault if they act foolishly. That is settled. You believed my account. I never lie, though I be a fool."

"Yes, I have accepted your account, and I, in part, forgive you."

"In part! By Heaven, that is a motley forgiveness—a fool's forgiveness. I must have a complete one. Come here. Come to this window. Why should I shout across the hall to you, and you stand with your back turned to me, as though we were on opposite sides of the Cleave?" He spoke with as much imperiousness as if he were in his own house, commanded her as though he expected of her as ready submission as was accorded him by his sister.

"What do you want with me? I do not care to go near a man subject to such outbreaks of folly."

"You are one to declaim!" said Anthony, scornfully. "You who run away, and bite your knuckles till they are raw."

Urith's brow darkened. "You might have spared me that taunt," she said; "you would have done so had you been generous."

"Come over here," commanded Anthony. "How can I measure my words when I have to throw them at you from a furlong off? It is like a game of quoits when one has not strid the distance, and knows not what force to employ."

Urith without further demur came to him. This was a new experience to her to be addressed in tones of command; her mother scolded and found fault, and gave, indeed, orders which she countermanded next moment, so that Urith had grown up with the habit of following her own desires, and disregarding the contradictory or impossible injunctions laid on her.

"Come here, Urith," said Anthony; "I do not see why we have been such strangers heretofore. Why do you never come to Hall?"

"Because Hall has never come to Willsworthy."

"But my sister; you would like Bessie—I am sure of that."

"I like her now."

"Then you will come and see her at Hall?"

"When she has first been to see me, and has asked me to return the visit."

"She shall do that at once."

"She has promised to come here. She was very kind to me last night."

"She is a good creature," said Anthony, condescendingly.

"And no fool," threw in Urith.

"I don't say she is clever, but what brains she has are full ripe. She is considerably older than I am."

To this Urith made no response.

Then Anthony took up the gloves, drew them out, and passed them under the ribbon of his hat.

"I was your true knight yesterday, achieving your deliverance, and every true knight must wear either his lady's colours or some pledge to show that she has accepted him as her knight. That, I have heard say, is how some crests were given or taken. Now I have assumed mine—your gloves. I take them as my right, and shall wear them in your name."

"They are not mine," said Urith; "you will do me a favour if you will take them for me to her to whom they of right belong, and say that I return them to her. She lost them last night, and I found them. I never go near Kilworthy—never have an opportunity of seeing her—and

her brother I am not likely to see. Therefore I beseech
you to convey them to her from me."

"To whom? Not Julian?"

"Yes, to Julian."

Anthony muttered an oath.

"I will take them from my hat and throw them under
foot," he said, angrily. "I did not ask for a favour of
Julian Crymes, but for something of yours, Urith."

"You did not ask any one for a favour," she replied,
gravely. "You took the gloves unasked."

He pulled them from his hat, and was about to cast them
back on the window-sill, when Urith arrested his hand.

"No," she said; "I asked you a favour, and you will
not be so discourteous a knight as to refuse it me."

"You take me as your knight!" exclaimed Anthony, with
a flash of pleasure from his eyes that met hers, and before
which hers fell.

"My errand boy," she said, with a smile, "my foot-page
to carry messages from me. You will take the gloves to
Julian Crymes."

"Not in my hat, but in my belt—thus," said Anthony,
passing them under his girdle. Then, after a pause, he
said, "You have given me nothing."

"Yes, I have."

"What? Only another maid's gloves?"

"Something else. My forgiveness."

"Full?"

"Yes—full. Go now, and take the gloves."

"I shall return another day for something of your own."

Still he loitered; then suddenly looked up, with a laugh.
"Mistress! What is your livery? What is your colour?"

"My colour! Yellow—yellow as the marigold, for I am
jealous."

"Then, here is my hat. You shall put your badge in it."

"Not till I admit your service."

"You have—you have given me a commission."

Urith laughed. "Very well. There are marsh marigolds in the brook. You shall have them."

CHAPTER XII.

AND AGAIN.

Anthony went home to Hall. He was on foot—if he must go to Kilworthy and return the gloves to Julian Crymes, he would ride. They hung in his girdle. His hat was gay with marsh marigolds. A sudden, overwhelming intoxication of happiness had come over Urith. She was loved, and loved in return. Her heart had hitherto known no love, or only that which was rendered as a duty to an exacting and trying mother. The world to her had become wider, brighter, the sky higher. The condition in which her mother was was forgotten for a moment, for a moment only, as with fluttering heart and trembling fingers, and pulses that leaped and then were still, she picked the marigolds and put them in his cap. Then he was gone, and she returned at once to her mother's room.

Anthony wore his hat ajaunt as he strode into the yard of Hall, and when he saw his sister Bessie in the door, he called to her to come to him, to save himself the trouble of taking a dozen steps to her out of his way to the stable.

She obeyed the summons at once.

"Bess!" said he, "I have made a promise for thee. I have been to Willsworthy, and have said that thou wilt go there to-day."

"Oh, Anthony!" said Elizabeth, in return. "How could you do as you have done concerning the headpiece?"

"There, there! that is finished and done for. I sent it back the same night. I called up the sexton to help me. But the matter is at an end, and I will not have it stirred again. Do you hear, you must go to Willsworthy to-day. I have passed my word."

"I cannot, Tony. I was on my way there when I met Luke, and he told me what you had done. Then for shame I could not go on, but returned home."

"I went there and made my peace," said Anthony. "Do not blow a drop of soap into a vast globe. It is all over and mended. I said I was sorry, and that was the end of the matter."

"But Luke told me that Mistress Malvine has had a fit because of it."

"She has had the like before, and has recovered; she will be herself again to-morrow—and, it matters not! sickly and aged folk must expect these accidents. You shall go to Willsworthy to-day."

"I cannot indeed, brother, for my father has forbidden it."

"Forbidden you going there?"

"Yes, brother, when I came back, he asked where I had been, and when I told him he was wrath, and bade me never go there again. He would not, he said, have it appear that he was begging off from the consequences of what you had done."

"I have begged off. That is to say—I explained it was all a mistake. I meant no wrong, and so it is covered up and passed over."

"That may be, Tony, but against my father's command I cannot go."

"It is such folly," said Anthony, "I will go see him myself. You shall go there. I told Urith that I would send you. My father shall not make my word empty."

He went by her.

She caught his arm, and said, in a low tone, "Brother, why do you make so much now of Urith Malvine? And you treating her as your true love?"

"True love!" repeated he, scornfully. "That is the way with all you woman-kind. If one but sees a handsome girl, and speaks two words to her, at once you arrive at the notion that we have chosen each other as true lovers, passed rings and promises, and wished for a marriage licence. Let me go by."

He walked into the house, and to his father's room, which he entered without announcing himself.

The old man sat by the fire. His account-books were on the table, at his side. The fire was of turf and wood.

"What is this, father?" began Anthony, in his imperious fashion, "That you have forbidden Bess to go to see the Malvine family, and the Madame is ill, had a falling fit this morning."

"It is not for us to make a scrape and a cringe to the like of them," answered the old man, raising himself in his chair by a hand on each arm, as he had sunk together in the seat. "I take it the Cleverdons need not stoop to that beggar brood."

"I did wrong," said Anthony, shortly. "And I have been to Willsworthy, and said I was sorry. I offered to put up a monument of stone to Master Richard Malvine at our own cost."

"You did!"

"Yes, father, I did, I would do it at my own expense."

"You have not a penny but what I allow you, and not one penny would I hand out for such a purpose."

"Then it is as well that my offer was refused."

"I bade you forbear going to that house when you spake of it this morning."

"You advised me not to go; but my conscience spoke louder than your voice, father, and I went."

"How were you received?" asked old Cleverdon, with a malignant leer.

Anthony shrugged his shoulders: "The old Madam fell into a fit at the sight of me. There was also Luke there."

"Oh, Luke!" said Anthony senior, with a sneer. "He may go there; but no son or daughter of mine. We do not consort with beggars. That is enough. You have been. Do not go again. If they bring the matter into a court of law I am well content—more than content, for it will bring them to utter beggary, and they will have, maybe, to sell, and I will buy them out." He turned to the fire and laughed at the thought. Then, turning his face round again over his pointed shoulder, he said, in an altered tone, "I am glad you are in here; you do not often give me a chance of a talk, and now I wish to speak with you of serious matters. You are getting to be a man, Tony —quite a man—and must think of settling in life. It is high time for us to have the arrangement with Julian Crymes——"

"What arrangement?"

"Oh, you know. It has been an understood thing. You have not been ignorant, though you may affect to know nothing about it. Fine property hers! All the Kilworthy estate after her father's death. He has it for his life. But there is money. A good deal, I doubt not, will go with her hand at once. If we had that we could clear the mortgage off Hall."

Anthony frowned, and folded his arms.

"I am against delaying marriage till late," continued old Cleverdon ; " so I propose that you have a talk with Julian at once, and get her to say when it is to be. Some time this year ; but not in May—May marriages are unlucky." The old man chuckled, and said, "I reckon your honeymoon you will find a harvest moon."

"I have no fancy for Julian Crymes," said Anthony ; " I never had."

"Pshaw ! Of course you have a fancy for Kilworthy. It will fit on with Hall bravely ; and so the old Glanville property will come together all in time to the Cleverdons."

"I am not going to take Julian for the sake of Kilworthy. That you may be assured of," said Anthony.

" Oh, yes, you will ; but I dare say you want to keep out of chains a little longer. If so, I do not press you. Nevertheless, in the end it comes to this—you must take Julian and her estate."

"I will have neither one nor the other," said Anthony. "I do not want to marry—when I do I will please myself."

"You will consult my wishes and my plans," said the father. "But there, I have said enough. Turn the thing over in your head ; the girl likes you, small blame to her— you are the bravest cockrell in the district, and can crow loud enough to make all others keep silence."

"I will never take Julian," again said Anthony. "It is of no use, father, urging this ; she has been thrown at me, and has thrown herself at me. I may have prattled and laughed with her, but I never cared much for her. I shall never take but the maid that pleases me ; I give you assurance of this, father."

"Well, well, that will suffice. I was too early in speaking. Take your time ; in the end you will see through my spectacles. Now I am busy ; you may go."

Anthony left. He was irritated at his father for endeavoring to force him to marry Julian Crymes, irritated with him for his depreciatory tone when speaking of the Malvines, irritated with him for not allowing his sister to go to Willsworthy.

At the present moment he felt very reluctant to go to

Kilworthy and see Julian, to return to her the pair of gloves. After she had been thrust on him and he had declined to think of her, he felt out of humour for a visit to her ; he had lost command of himself, in his annoyance, and might speak with scant courtesy.

"If I could light on Fox I would give him the gloves," said Anthony, as he mounted the horse.

He rode out on a down near Hall, and there drew rein, uncertain whether he would go direct to Kilworthy or not.

"No," said he, "I will ride first to Peter Tavy and see that the head-post of Master Malvine be secure. I will give the sexton something to have the foot scarfed, that it may not fall over or give way. After that I can go to Kilworthy." So he turned his horse's head in the direction of the inn, the Hare and Hounds at Cudliptown, where he would fall into the road to Peter Tavy.

In his irritation at what his father had proposed, he forgot about the bunch of flowers in his hat. He left them there disregarded, fretting in his mind at his father's attempt to force him to a union that was distasteful to him. He liked Julian well enough ; she was a handsome girl. He had admired her, he had played the lover—played without serious intent, for his heart had not been touched — but now he entertained an aversion from her, an aversion that was not old ; it dated but from the previous day, but it had ripened whilst his father spoke to him of her.

Anthony was this day like a charged electric battery, and any one that came near him received a shock. His father had seen that the mood of the young man was not one in which he would bear to be contradicted ; the old man was aware that his son would discharge his feelings against him quite as readily as against another, and he, therefore, had the discretion not to press a point that irritated Anthony, and was like to provoke an outburst.

And now, as Anthony rode over the down, past many old tumuli covering the dead of prehistoric times, he had no eyes for the beauty of the scene that opened before him, eyes for no antiquities that he passed, ears for none of the fresh and pleasant voices of early spring that filled the air ; he was occupied with his own thoughts, grumbling and muttering over the matters of dissatisfaction that had risen up and crossed him. He had apologised for the outrage committed on Richard Malvine's grave, but he could not excuse himself of having occasioned a shock to Mistress Malvine. He was angry with his father for the slighting manner in which he spoke of the Malvines, for having forbidden Bessie going to them, for having endeavoured to force him into an engagement with Julian. He would please himself, murmured Anthony to himself; in such a matter as this he would brook no dictation. His liking for Urith was too young to have assumed any shape and force, and he had no thoughts of its leading any further. Such as it was, it had been fed and stimulated by opposition—the interference on the moor, the opposition of his father, the difficulties put in his way by his own act—but then Anthony was just the man to be settled in a course by encountering opposition therein.

He crossed the river, reached Cudliptown, and saw the surgeon's horse hitched up outside the tavern. The doctor had been to Willsworthy, and had halted at the Hare and Hounds for refreshment on his way home.

Anthony at once dismounted. He would go in there and ask tidings of the health of the widow.

He fastened up his horse and entered the tavern, in his usual swaggering, defiant manner, with his hat on, and a frown on his brow. He found in the inn, not the surgeon only, but James Cudlip, and to his surprise Anthony Crymes.

The relationship in which Anthony Cleverdon stood to Fox was intimate but not cordial. They had known each other and had associated together since they were children; they had been at school together; they hunted, and rabbited, and hawked together. Anthony was not one who could endure to be alone, and as he had no other companion of his age and quality with whom to associate, he took up with Fox rather than be solitary. But when together they were ever bickering. Fox's bitter tongue made Anthony start, and with his slow wit he was incapable of other retort than threat. Moreover, from every one else young Anthony received flattery; only from Fox did he get gibes. He bore in his heart a simmering grudge against him that never boiled up into open quarrel. Fox took a malicious delight in tormenting his comrade, whom he both envied and disliked.

That Anthony Crymes had paid his addresses to Urith, and had been refused, was unknown to Anthony Cleverdon, to whom Crymes confided no secrets of his heart or ambition.

When Anthony caught sight of Fox at the table, he checked the question relative to the condition of Madame Malvine that rose to his lips, and came over to the settle.

"Why! what a May Duke have we here!" exclaimed Fox Crymes, pointing with a laugh at Anthony's cap. "What is the meaning of this decoration?"

Instead of replying, Anthony called for ale.

"And wearing his mistress' gloves as well!" shouted Crymes.

"They are not my mistress' gloves," answered Anthony, hastily, and in a tone of great irritation. "If you would know, Fox, whose they are, then I tell you, they belong to your sister."

"How came you by them? And wherefore wear them?"

"I was on the lookout for you, Fox, to return them to you for her. I do not want them. She lost them over-night."

"And where did you find them? On the moor?"

"They were given to me by the finder. Will that satisfy you? I will answer no more questions."

Crymes saw that Anthony Cleverdon was in an irascible mood—such a mood as gave him special opportunities of vexing Anthony and amusing himself.

"And now about your posie of golden cups?" he asked tauntingly.

"I said I would answer no more questions."

"It is not necessary. I know very well where you have been."

"I have been home—at Hall," said Anthony, going over to the table from the settle, where he felt himself uneasy with all eyes fixed on him. He pulled the gloves out of his belt and laid them before him, and drew them their full length on the table, then smoothed them with his finger. He wished he had not entered the inn; his face was clouded, and his muscles twitched, Crymes enjoying his evident annoyance. He sat on the further side of the table, with his mug of beer by him.

"I know very well where you have been," said he again, with his twinkling, malicious eyes fixed on Anthony. "So was I the day before yesterday; and also came off with a posie—but a better one than yours."

"It is a lie!" burst from the irritated young man, starting. "Urith never——" Then he checked himself, as Fox broke into ironical laughter at the success of his essay to extract from Anthony the secret of his bunch of marigolds. Anthony saw that he had been trapped, and became more chafed and hot than before.

"Do you know what she meant by giving you those flowers?" asked Crymes, and paused with his eyes on the man he was baiting.

Anthony answered with a growl.

"You know what they are called by the people?" said Crymes. "Drunkards. And, when you were presented with that posie, it was as much as to say that none save one to whom such a term applied would have acted as you had done last night by your offence against a dead man's grave, and by adding insult to injury by your visiting the widow and child to-day."

The blood poured into Anthony's face and dazzled his eyes. A malevolent twitch of the muscles of the mouth showed how Fox enjoyed tormenting him.

"Go again a little later in the season, and Urith will find another, and even more appropriate, adornment for your hat—a coxcomb!"

Yeoman Cudlip and Surgeon Doble laughed aloud, so did the serving wench who had just brought in Anthony's ale.

The young fellow, stung beyond endurance, sprang to his feet with a snort—he could not speak—and struck Fox across the face with the gloves.

Crymes uttered a cry of pain and rage, and with his hand to his eye drew the hunting-knife from his belt, and struggled out of his place to get at Anthony. The surgeon and yeoman threw themselves in his way and disarmed him, the girl screamed and fled to the kitchen.

"He has blinded me!" gasped Fox, as he sank back into a seat. "I cannot see."

Anthony was alarmed. Water was brought, and the face of Crymes washed. One of the silver tags of the glove had struck and injured the right eyeball.

CHAPTER XIII.

WIDOW PENWARNE.

There are epochs in the lives of most men when a sad fatality seems to dog their steps and turn athwart all that they do. Anthony had come to such an epoch suddenly since that ride and walk along the Lyke-Way. He had allowed himself to be taunted into a foolish visit to the churchyard on St. Mark's Eve, when there he had desecrated a grave, then he had thrown Madame Malvine into a fit, had disagreed with his father, and now had injured the eye of his comrade.

Anthony's anger cooled down the moment he was aware of what he had done, but this was not a piece of mischief that could be put to rights at once, like the replacing of the headpiece of the grave. His presence in the room was a distraction and cause of irritation to the man he had hurt, now in the hands of the surgeon, and he deemed it advisable to leave the inn, mount his horse, and ride away to Peter Tavy Church, where he desired to have a word with the sexton and carpenter relative to the old head-post of Malvine's grave.

Peter Tavy Church, or the Church of St. Peter on the Tavy, is a grey granite edifice, mottled with lichen, with moorstone pinnacles, and a cluster of fine old trees in the yard. Externally the church is eminently picturesque, it was beautiful within at the time of our tale, in spite of the havoc wrought in the period of the Directory; of more recent times it has undergone a so-called restoration which has destroyed what remained of charm.

For a long time it has been matter of felicitation that the old opprobrium attaching to the men of the West Country of being wreckers has ceased to apply; the inhumanity of destroying vessels and their crews for the sake of the spoil that could be got from them has certainly ceased. But we are mistaken if we suppose that wrecking as a profession or pastime has come to an end altogether. The complaint has been driven inwards, or rather, wrecking is no longer practised on ships, which the law has taken under its protection, but on the defenceless parish churches.

The havoc that has been wrought in our churches within the last thirty years is indescribable. In Cornwall, with ruthless and relentless activity, the parish churches have, with rare exceptions, been attacked one after another, and robbed of all that could charm and interest, and have been left cold and hideous skeletons. I know nothing that more reminds one (speaking ecclesiologically) of the desert strewn with the bones of what were once living and beautiful creatures, scraped of every particle of flesh, the marrow picked out of their bones, the soul, the divine spark of beauty and life, expelled for ever.

No sooner does a zealous incumbent find himself in the way of collecting money to do up his church, than he rubs his hands over it and says, "Embowelled will I see thee by and by." Falstaff was fortunately able to get away from the knife. Alas! not so our beautiful old churches. The architect and the contractor are called in, and the embowelling goes on apace. All the old fittings are cast forth, the monumental slabs broken up, the walls are scraped and painted, plaster everywhere peeled off, just as the skin was taken off St. Bartholomew, and the shells are exulted over by architect, contractor, parson, and parishioners, as shells from which the bright soul has been expelled—*sans* beauty, *sans* interest, *sans* poetry, *sans* everything. The man of taste and feeling crosses the threshold, and falls back with the same sense as comes on the reader of a young lady's novel, as at a mouthful of bread from which the salt has been omitted, of something inexpressibly flat and insipid. Before its restoration, Peter Tavy Church had the remains of a beautiful roodscreen nicely painted and gilt, and an unique pew of magnificent carved oak for the manorial lord to sit in, with twisted columns at the angles supporting heraldic lions.

Anthony Cleverdon dismounted from his horse at the church-yard, hitched up his beast, and entered the graveyard. He saw the sexton there, and talking to him was an old woman in threadbare dress, grey hair, very dark piercing eyes, bent, and leaning on a staff. She was a stranger, at all events, he did not know her, and yet there was a something in her features that seemed peculiar to him.

7

The sexton said something to her, and she at once came down the church path to meet Anthony, extending to him her hand.

"Ah!" she said. "I can see, I can see my Margaret in your face—you have her eyes, her features, and the same toss of head. I know you. You have never, maybe, heard of me, and yet I am your grandmother. Have you come here to see your mother's grave? I am glad, I am glad it is cared for, not, I ween, by your father. Which of you thinks of the mother, and has set flowers on the grave—see, it is alight with primroses?"

"I believe that was Bessie's doing," answered Anthony; then involuntarily he looked at her shabby gown, patched and worn.

"I would like to see Bessie. Is she like you? If so—she is like your mother. Ah! my Margaret was the handsomest girl in all the West of England. You have not forgotten your mother, I hope, young man."

"I do not remember her—you forget she died shortly after I was born."

"How should I know?" The old woman took his hand, and held it fast as she peered into his face with eager eyes. "How should I know, when your father never took the trouble to let me know that my own, my dear and only child, was dead? If I had known she was ill, I would have come to her, though he took, as he threatened to take, the pitchfork to me, if I crossed his threshold. I would have come and nursed her; then, maybe, she would not have died. But he did not tell me. He did not ask me to her burial, and not till long after did I hear she was no more. He was a hard and a cruel man."

The clear tears formed in the old woman's eyes, and trickled down her cheeks.

"I have been ill all the winter, and very poor; but that was not known, and if known would not have concerned your father. When I got better, I came here to ask if I might be buried, when I die, near my Margaret. Or are you Cleverdons too great and fine now for that? Well—you will let me lie at her feet, though I was her mother, just as I have seen a dog put under the soles of the figures in old churches. You are her son, you are my own grandchild, though you have never known me and cared for me, and given me a thought. Please the Lord, you are not hard as your father, and you will grant me this."

"I did not know I had a grandmother," said Anthony. "If there is anything you want, it shall be done."

"No, I do not suppose that your father ever spoke of me. Your mother's father was the parson here, and died leaving no money. I had to leave, and become a housekeeper to maintain myself, and what little money I then earned has been expended in my illness. Now, will you let me see Bessie? She is good, she remembers her mother, and thinks of her."

Anthony endeavoured to withdraw his hand from the grasp of the old woman, but she would not suffer it; she laid the other caressingly on his, and said,

"No, my boy, you will not be unkind, you will not go from me without a promise to bring me Bessie. I must see her."

"You shall come to Hall, and see her there."

She shook her grey head. "Never! never! I could not bear to be in that house where your mother, my poor Margaret, suffered. Moreover, your father would not endure it! He threatened to take the pitchfork to me—when your mother was alive."

"He would not do that now," said Anthony. "But as you will. I will bring Bessie to you. Where shall I find you?"

"I am staying at Master Youldon's. He knew my dear husband in the old times, and knew me, and does not forget old kindnesses."

"Very well. You shall see Bessie. I have some business with the sexton."

Then he withdrew his hand from the old woman, and went to the grave of Richard Malvine, where he gave directions what was to be done to that and the headpiece.

Widow Penwarne came to him.

"What is this?" she asked. "What have you to do with this grave?"

"I have some orders to give concerning it," answered Anthony, vexed at her interference. "I will speak with you later, madam."

"But what does the grave of Richard Malvine matter to you?" again she asked. "Ah!" she exclaimed, and went and picked some of the primroses from the mound over her daughter, and then strewed them over the grave of Richard, "Ah!" she said.   "Here lie two whose hearts were broken by your father—two for whom he will have to answer at the Judgment Day, and then I will stand up along with them, and point the finger at him, and accuse him. If there be a righteous God, then as He is righteous so will He judge and punish!"

"Why, well, now, is not this strange?" exclaimed Anthony.   "Here comes my sister Elizabeth.   I wonder much what has brought her."

Bessie appeared, with a wreath of spring flowers in her hand.   She had ridden, attended by a serving-man.   She was surprised and pleased to see Anthony at Richard Malvine's grave.

"Oh, brother!" she said, "I have been so troubled over what has been done that I set to work to make a garland to hang on the grave, as some token of respect, and regret for what had been done."

"What, you also!" exclaimed the old woman, and went to her and clasped her hands.   "You are Bessie Cleverdon, the dear child of my Margaret.   Let me kiss you, ay, and bless you."   She drew the head of Elizabeth to her and kissed her.

"This is our grandmother, Bessie," exclaimed Anthony.

"Ay!" said the old woman, studying the girl earnestly with her dark, eager eyes.   "Yes, I am the grandmother of you both ; but you are not like my Margaret, not in face, and yet not like your father—please God in heaven—not like him in soul!" she said, with vehemence.

"Let us go aside," said Anthony, "out of earshot of the sexton, if you cannot speak of my father without such an overflow of spleen."

"Then we will go to your mother's grave," said Madame Penwarne. "I see you stand by your father ; but I can see this in you—that you will stand by him so long as he does not cross your will.   Let him but oppose you, young man, where your headstrong will drives, and there will be trouble between you.   Then, maybe, your father will begin to receive the chastisement from the hand of the Lord that has been hanging over him ever since he took Margaret to Hall.   That is a strange turn of the wheel, that his two children should meet at the grave of Richard Malvine to care for its adornment. And I warrant you do not know, either of you, what is owing to him who lies there—ay! and to her who rests at our feet."

"I can't understand riddles," said Anthony, "and it is no pleasure to me to hear hard words cast at my father. If you are in poverty, grandmother, you shall be helped. I will speak to my father about you, and when I speak he will listen and do as is fitting. Of that be assured. If you have anything further to say of my father, say it to him, not to me."

"I will take nothing, not a farthing of his," answered the old woman, sharply.

"Why not, grandmother?" asked Bessie, gently, and kissed the old woman's quivering cheek. "It will be the greatest unhappiness to Anthony and me to think that you are not provided for in your age, and in comfort. We shall not be able to rest if we suppose that you are in want. It would fill us with concern and self-reproach. My father is just, and he also——"

"No," said the old woman, interrupting her, "just he is not. Moreover, he owes me too much—or rather he owes my dead daughter, your mother, too much—he cannot repay it: not one thousandth part with coin. You, Elizabeth, are older than your brother. You must know that your mother's life was made miserable, that she had no happiness at Hall."

"And I trust and believe," said Bessie, "that my dear mother, in the rest of Paradise, has long ago forgotten her troubles, and forgiven my father if he had in any way annoyed her."

"Do not be so sure of that, child," exclaimed the old woman, with vehemence. "If I were to go out of this life to-morrow, I should go before the throne of God to denounce your father, and I would call Richard Malvine and your mother as witnesses against him. Shall I tell you what he did? These who lie here—he yonder, where you have placed the garlands, and my poor Margaret—loved each other, and would have been happy with each other. But her father died, I was poor, and then for the sake of his money, Margaret was persuaded to take Anthony Cleverdon, and give up Richard Malvine."

"If that be so——" began young Anthony.

"It is so," said the old woman, vehemently.

"Then the blame lies with you," said he. "You pressed her to take the rich man and refuse the poor. My father was guiltless."

The widow drew back and trembled; but presently recovered herself and said, "That may be—I bear in part the blame. But if he had been kind to her it would have been other. I would not reproach him; but it was not so, and Bessie was old enough to remember that little love passed between them, that he was hard, and cruel, and unkind. He broke her heart—and there she lies."

"I am not here," said Anthony, "to hear my father reproached. I respect you as my grandmother; but you have doubtless a jaundiced eye, that sees all things yellow. I will see what can be done for you. It does not befit us that the mother of our mother should be in want."

As they spoke, from out of the church came Luke Cleverdon. His face was pale, and his eyes were sunken. The sexton had not known that he was in the sacred building. Luke came towards the little group, treading his way among the graves with care. The tomb of the Cleverdons was near the chancel south window. He extended his hand to Mistress Penwarne, saying, "I was within. It was not my fault if I heard much that was said; and now I have but come into your midst, Anthony, Bessie, and you, Madame, to make a humble petition. I am curate in charge here; the rector is not resident. I live in the old parsonage, that must be so familiar to Mistress Penwarne —every room hallowed with some sweet recollection—and I am alone, and need a kinswoman to be my housekeeper, and "—he smiled at the old woman—"be to me as a mother. Madame, will you honour my poor roof by taking up your abode therein? It is, forsooth, more yours than mine, for there you lived your best days, and to it you are attached by strongest ties; but I am but a casual tenant. It is not mine—I am but the curate. Here we have no continuous city, and every house is to us but a tavern on our pilgrimage where we stay a night."

CHAPTER XIV.

THE CLEAVE.

Throughout the day Willsworthy was full of visitors. Never before had it been so frequented. The act of Anthony Cleverdon had been bruited through the neighbourhood, and aroused general indignation against the young man and sympathy for the widow.

Mistress Malvine was sufficiently recovered in the afternoon to receive some of those who arrived in her bedroom, and Mr. Solomon Gibbs entertained the rest in the hall. Those who had known the Malvines well—these were not many—and those who knew them distantly, persons of the gentle class, of the yeoman and farmer ranks, all thought it incumbent on them to come, express their opinions, and inquire after the widow. Not only did these arrive, but also many cottagers appeared at the kitchen door, full of sympathy—or at all events, of talk. It really seemed as if Willsworthy, which had dropped out of every one's mind, had suddenly claimed supreme regard.

It was a source of real gratification to the sick woman to assume a position of so much consequence. It is always a satisfaction to hear other persons pour out the vials of wrath and hold up hands in condemnation of those who have given one offence, and Madame Malvine was not merely flattered by becoming the centre of interest to the neighbourhood, but was influenced by the opinions expressed in her ear, and her indignation against Anthony was deepened.

Wherever in the house Urith went, she heard judgment pronounced on him in no measured terms, the general voice condemned him as heartless and profane. Question was made what proceeding would be taken against him, and abundance of advice was offered as to the course to be pursued to obtain redress. Urith was unable to endure the talk of the women in her mother's room, and she descended to the hall, there to hear her Uncle Solomon, amongst farmers and yeomen, tell the story of Anthony's deed with much exaggeration, and to hear the frank expressions of disapproval it elicited.

Then she went into the kitchen, where the poorer neighbours were congregated. Everywhere it was the same. Condemnation fell on Anthony. No one believed that he had not acted in wilful knowledge of what he was about.

Urith could not fail to observe that there was a widespread latent jealousy and dislike of the Cleverdons in the neighbourhood, occasioned partly, no doubt, by the success of the old man in altering his position and entering a superior class, but chiefly due to his arrogance, hardness, and meanness. All the faults in Anthony's character were commented on, and his good qualities denied or disparaged.

Urith could with difficulty restrain herself from contradicting these harsh judges, and in taking on her the defence of the culprit, but she saw clearly that her advocacy would be unavailing, and provoke comment.

She therefore left the house. Her mother was so much recovered as not to need her. Whether the old lady acted wisely in receiving so much company after her fit, Urith doubted, but her mother had insisted on the visitors being admitted to her room, and under the excitement she rallied greatly.

To be away from the clatter of tongues, she left the farm and went forth upon the moor.

To the north of Willsworthy rises a ridge of bold and serrated rocks that rise precipitously above the River Tavy, which foams below at a depth of three hundred feet; they present the appearance of a series of ruined towers, and are actually in places united by the remains of ancient walls of rude moorstone, for what purpose piled up, it is not possible to say.

A bar of red porphyritic granite crosses the ravine, and over this leaps the river into a deep pool, immediately beneath the boldest towers and pinnacles of rock that overhang. Among these crags, perched like an eagle above the dizzy abyss, sat Urith on a rock, listening to the roar of the river wafted up to her from beneath. Away to the north and east of the moor extended shoulder on shoulder, to the lonely peak of Fur Tor that rises in uttermost solitude near the sources of the Tavy, amidst all but untraversable morasses. She was glad to be there, alone, away from the lips that spit their venom on the name of Anthony.

The human heart is full of strange caprices, and is wayward as a spoiled child. The very fact that the whole country side was combined to condemn Anthony made Urith in heart exculpate him — that every mouth blamed him made her excuse him. It was true that he had acted with audacious folly, but there was merit in that audacity. What other youth would have ventured into the churchyard on such a night? The audacity so qualified the folly as almost to obliterate it. He had been challenged to the venture. Would it have been manly had he declined the challenge? Did not the blame attach to such as had dared him to the reckless deed? She repeated to herself the words that had been spoken in her mother's house about him, so extravagant in expression, exaggerated in judgment as to transcend justice, and her heart revolted against the extravagance and forgave him. If all the world stood up in condemnation, yet would not she. Her cheeks flushed and her eyes sparkled. She recalled his chivalry towards her on the moor; she heard again his voice; recollected how he had held her in his arms; she felt again the throb of his heart, heard his breathing as he strode with her through the flames, as he wrestled with her for the mastery; and she laughed aloud, she rejoiced that he had conquered. Had she overmastered him, and her will had been submitted to by him, she would have despised him. Because he was so strong in his resolution, so determined in carrying it out, she liked and respected him.

There flashed before her something like lightning—it was his eyes, lifted to hers, with that strange look that sent a thrill through all her veins and tingled in her extremities. That look of his had revealed to her something to which she dare not give a name, a something which gave him a right to demand of her that morning testimony to his integrity of purpose, a something that constrained her, without a thought of resistance, to give him what he asked, first her hand in witness that she believed him, then the bunch of flowers in token that she accepted him as her knight. As her knight?

Her heart bounded with pride and exultation at the thought! He her knight! He, the noblest youth in all the region round, a very Saul, taller by the head **and** shoulders than any other, incomparably handsome, **more** manly, open, generous, brave—brave! who feared neither man nor midnight spectre.

Yet—when Julian Crymes had charged her with attempting to rob her of her lover, she, Urith, had repelled the charge, and had declared that she did not value, did not want him. Nor had she then; but the very violence, the defiance of Julian, had forced her to think of him—to think of him in the light of a lover. The opposition of Julian had been the steel stroke on her flinty heart that had brought out the spark of fire. If anything had been required to fan this spark into flame, that had been supplied by the chattering, censorious swarm of visitors that afternoon.

And Anthony? How stood he?

At that moment he was weighed down with a sense of depression and loneliness such as he had never felt previously. He had been accustomed to be flattered and made a great deal of. His father, his sister, his cousin, the servants, Fox Crymes, every one had shown him deference, had let him see that he was esteemed a man born to fortune and success; he had been good at athletic exercises, good in sport, a good horseman, taller, stronger than his compeers, and heir to a wealthy gentleman. But all at once luck had turned against him; he had committed blunders and had injured those with whom he had come in contact; possibly blinded Fox, had offended the Malvine family, thrown the old dame into a fit, had quarrelled with his father, brought down on his head the reproach and ridicule of all who knew him. Then came the encounter with his grandmother, and the discovery of the wrong done to his mother and to the father of Urith by his own father. Bold, self-opinionated as Anthony was, yet this sudden shock had humbled him and staggered him: he had fallen from a pinnacle and was giddy. A sort of irrational, blind instinct within him drove him back in the direction of Willsworthy. He felt that he could not rest unless he saw Urith again, and—so he explained his feeling—told her more fully the circumstances of the previous night's adventure, and heard from her own lips that her mother was not seriously injured in health by the distress he had caused her, and that she, Urith, forgave him.

His imagination worked. He had not been explicit enough when he came to Willsworthy. The fainting fit of the mother had interrupted his explanation. Afterwards he had forgotten to say what he had intended to say, and what ought to have been said. When he was gone, Urith would consider it strange that he had been so curt and reserved, she would hear her Uncle Solomon's stories, tinged with rum punch past recognition of where truth shaded into fiction.

Moreover, he felt a craving for Urith's sympathy; he wanted to acquaint her with what he had done to Fox Crymes before the story reached her embellished and enlarged. To his discredit it would be told, and might prejudice her against him. He must forestall gossip and tell her the truth himself.

So he rode in the direction of Willsworthy, but when he came near the place, an unusual diffidence stole over him—he did not dare to venture up to the house, and he hung about the vicinity in the road, then he went out on the moor, and it was when on the down that he thought he caught sight of her at some distance in the direction of the Cleave.

A labourer came by. "Who is that yonder?" he asked.

"I reckon any fool knows," answered the clown. "That be our young lady, Mistress Urith."

"Take my horse, fellow," said Anthony, and dismounted.

He went over the moor in pursuit of the girl, and found her seated on the rock with a foot swinging over the precipice. She was so startled when he spoke to her as almost to lose her balance. He caught her hand, and she rose to her feet.

They stood on a ledge. Two towers of rock rose with a cleft between them like a window. The shelves of the granite were matted with whortleberry leaves, now all ranges of colour from green, through yellow to carmine, and with grey moss. A vein of porphyry penetrating the granite striped it with red, and Nature had tried her delicate pencil on the stone, staining or stippling it with her wondrously soft-toned lichenous paints. Below, at the depth of five hundred feet, the river roared over its red porphyry barrier, throwing into the air foam bubbles that were caught by the wind and carried up, and danced about, and sported with as are feathers by a wanton child. The great side of Stannon Down opposite, rising to sixteen hundred feet, was covered by flying shadows of forget-me-not blue and pale sulphurous gleams of sun. As the light glided over it, it picked out the strange clusters of old circular huts and enclosures, some with their doors and lintels unthrown down, that were inhabited by an unknown race before history began.

Anthony put his arm round Urith. "We stand," said he, "on the edge of a chasm; a step, a start, and one or other—perhaps both—fall into the abyss to sheer destruction. Let me hold you; I would not let you go—if you went, it would not be alone."

Urith did not answer; a trembling fit came on her. She stood, she felt, at the brink of another precipice than that before her eyes.

"I could not keep away," said Anthony. "I have got into trouble with every one, and I was afraid that you also would be set against me; so, after I had been to see about your father's grave, that all was right there—and Bessie had laid a garland of flowers on it—then I came back here. I thought I must see you and explain what I forgot to say this morning."

"You need say no more about that matter," answered Urith. "I told you at the time that I believed your word. You said you intended no ill. I am sure of that, quite sure. I know it is not in you to hurt."

"And yet I have hurt you and your mother, and also Fox Crymes." Then he told her how he had struck him, and that he was afraid he had seriously injured his eye.

"And you have brought back the gloves!" exclaimed Urith.

"Yes; here they are."

"You have not fulfilled my commission?"

"I will do it if you wish it; I have not done it yet. I was going to give Fox the gloves; I did not desire to see Julian. You must understand that my father has been speaking to me to-day about Julian—it seems he has set his mind on making a pair of us. I do not know what Julian thinks, but I know my own mind, that this is not my taste. After he had spoken to me about her, I could not go on direct to her house and see her. My father would think that I gave in to him, and—I should have been uneasy myself."

Urith said nothing, she was looking down at the tossing, thundering torrent far below.

"I never cared much for Julian," continued Anthony, "and after yesterday I like her less."

"Why so?" Urith looked up and met his eyes.

"Why so? Because I have seen you. If I have to go through life with any one, I will take you in the saddle behind me—no one else."

Urith trembled more than before; a convulsive, irrepressible emotion had come over her. Sometimes it happens when the heavens are opened with a sudden flare of near and dazzling lightning, that those who have looked up have been struck with blindness. So was it now; Urith had seen a heaven of happiness, a glory of love—a new and wondrous world open before her, such as she had never dreamed of, of which no foretaste had ever been accorded her, and it left her speechless, with a cloud before her eyes, and giddy, so that she held out her hands gropingly to catch the rock; it was unnecessary, the strong arm of Anthony held her from falling.

The young man paused for an answer.

"Well!" said he. "Have you no word?"

None; she moved her lips, she could not speak.

"Come," said he, after another pause, "they who ride pillion ride thus—the man has his leather belt, and to that the woman holds. Urith, if we are to ride together on life's road, lay hold of my belt."

She held out her hands, still gropingly.

"Stay!" she said, suddenly recovering herself with a start. "You forgot; you do not know me. Look at my hands, they are still torn; I did that in one of my fits of rage. Do you not fear to take me when I go, when crossed, into such mad passion as these hands show?"

Anthony laughed. "I fear! I!"

Then she put her right hand to lay hold of his girdle, but caught and drew out the gloves.

"I have these again!" she exclaimed. "Even these gloves cast at me in defiance. Well, it matters not now. I refused to take them up, yet I could not shake them off; now I take them and keep them. I accept the challenge."

She grasped him firmly by the girdle, and with the other hand thrust the gloves into her bosom.

"I do not understand you," said Anthony.

"There is no need that you should."

Then he caught her up in his arms, with a shout of exultation, and held her for a moment hanging over the awful gulf beneath.

She looked him steadily in the eyes. She doubted neither his strength to hold her, nor his love.

Then he drew her to him and kissed her.

It is said that the sun dances on Easter day in the morning. It was noon now, but the sun danced over Urith and Anthony.

"And now," said the latter, "about your mother. Will she give her consent?"

"And your father?" asked Urith.

"Oh, my father!" repeated Anthony, scornfully, "whatsoever I will, that he is content with. As to your mother ——"

"I know what I will do," said Urith; "Luke has great influence with her. I will tell him all, and get him to ask her to agree and bless us. Luke will do anything I ask of him."

CHAPTER XV.

FATHER AND SON.

When Anthony came home, he found that his father had been waiting supper a while for him, and then as he did not arrive, had ordered it in, and partaken of the meal.

The old man's humour was not pleasant. He had been over that afternoon to Kilworthy, and had heard of his son's act of recklessness. Fears were entertained for Fox's sight in one eye. He was ordered to have the eye bandaged, and to be kept in the dark.

When Anthony entered the room where was his father, the old man looked up at him from the table strewn with the remains of his meal, and said, roughly, "I expect regular hours kept in my house. Why were you not here at the proper time? About any new folly or violence?"

Anthony did not answer, but seated himself at the table.

"I have been to Kilworthy," said the old man, "I have heard there of your conduct."

"Fox insulted me. You would not have me endure an insult tamely?" His father's tone nettled the young man.

"Certainly not; but men pink each other with rapiers, instead of striking with lace tags."

"That is the first time any one has let fall that I am not a man," said Anthony.

There was always a certain roughness, a lack of amiability in the behaviour of father to son and son to father, not arising out of lack of affection, but that the old man was by nature coarse-grained, and he delighted in seeing his son blunt and brusque. He—young Tony—was no milksop, he was proud to say. He was a lad who could hold his own against any one, and fight his way through the world. The old man was gratified at the swagger and independence of the youth, and at every proof he gave of rude and over-bearing self-esteem. But he was not pleased at the brawl with Fox Crymes; it was undignified for one thing, and it caused a breach where he wished to see union. It threw an impediment in the way of the execution of a darling scheme, a scheme on which his heart had been set for twenty years.

"I do not know what it was about," said the father, "more than that I had heard you had been squabbling in an alehouse about some girl."

"The insult or impertinence was levelled at me," said Anthony, controlling himself; "I did not mean to injure Fox, on that you may rely. I struck him over the face because he had whipped me into anger which I could not contain. I am sorry if I have hurt his eye. I am not sorry for having struck him, he brought it on himself."

"It is not creditable," pursued old Cleverdon, "that your name should be brought into men's mouths about a vulgar brawl over some village drab or house wench."

The blood surged into Anthony's face, he laid down his knife and looked steadily across the table at his father.

"On that score," said he, "you may set your mind at rest. There has been no brawl over any village wench."

"I can quite understand," said the father, "that Fox Crymes was jealous and did not measure words. He can pepper and spice his speeches till they burn as cantharides. What is he beside you? If you cast a fancy here or there, and there be naught serious in it, and it interferes with his sport, he must bear it. But, Tony, it is high time you was married. We must have no more of these wrangles. Whose name came up between you? Was it his sister's? I can well understand he does not relish her marriage. There has ever been rough water between them. She has the property—and when old Justice Crymes dies—where will he be? Was that the occasion of the dispute?"

"No, father, it was not."

"Then it was not about Julian?"

"About Julian? Certainly not."

"Nor about some village girl?"

"Nor about any village girl, as I have said."

"Then what was it about? or rather, about whom was it?"

"There is no reason why you should not know," answered Anthony, with coolness, "though that is a side matter. Fox told me that a suitable ornament for my cap was a coxcomb. That is why I struck him."

The old man laughed out. "You did well to chastise him for that."

"As you asked what girl's name was brought up, I will tell you," said Anthony. "It was that of Urith Malvine."

"Urith Malvine!" scoffed old Cleverdon, his eyes twinkling malevolently. "Not surprised at that light hussy bringing herself into men's mouths in a tavern."

"Father!" exclaimed the young man, "not a word against her. I will not bear that from you or from any man."

"You will not bear it!" almost screamed old Anthony. "You—you! make yourself champion of a beggar brat like that?"

"Did you hear my words?" said the young man, standing up. "No one—not even you—shall speak against her. It was because Fox sneered at her that I struck him; he might have scoffed at me, and I would have passed that over."

"And you threaten me? You will knock out my eye with your tags?"

"I merely warn you, father, that I will not suffer her

name to be improperly used. I cannot raise my hand against you, but I will leave the room."

"It is high time you were married. By the Lord! you shall be married. I will not be rasped like this."

"I will marry when I see fit," said Anthony.

"The fitness is now," retorted his father. "When a young gallant begins to squabble at village mug-houses about——"

"Father!"

"The near time is ripe. I will see Squire Crymes about it to-morrow."

"I am not going to take Julian Crymes."

"You shall take whom I choose."

"I am to marry—not you, father; accordingly, the choice lies with me."

"You cannot choose against my will."

"Can I not? I can choose where I list."

"Anyhow, you cannot take where I do not allow. I will never allow of a wife to you who is not of good birth and rich."

"Of good birth she is—she whom I have chosen; rich she is not, but what matters that when I have enough."

"Are you mad?" screamed the old man, springing from his chair and running up and down the room, in wild excitement. "Are you mad? Do you dare tell me you have chosen without consulting me—without regard for my wishes?"

"I shall take Urith, or none at all."

"Then none at all," snapped old Cleverdon. "Never, never will I consent to your bringing that hussy through my doors, under my roof."

"What harm has she done you? You have not heard a word against her. She is not rich, but not absolutely poor —she has, or will have, Willsworthy."

"Willsworthy! What is that compared with Julian's inheritance?"

"It is nothing. But I don't want Julian, and I will not take her for the sake of her property. Come, father, sit down, and let us talk this matter coolly and sensible."

He threw himself into a chair, and laid his hands on the arms, and stretched his legs before him.

The Squire stopped, looked at his son, then staggered

8

back to his chair as if he had been struck in the breast. He thought his son must have lost his wits. Why—he had not known this girl, this daughter of his most deadly enemy, not more than a day, and already he was talking of making her his wife! And this, too, to the throwing over of his grand opportunity of uniting the Kilworthy property to Hall!

"Come, father, sit down, and keep cool. I am sorry if you prefer Julian to Urith, but unfortunately the selection has to be made, not by you, but by me, and I greatly prefer Urith to Julian. Indeed, I will not have the latter at any price—not if she inherited all the Abbey lands of Tavistock. You are disappointed, but you will get over it. When you come to know Urith you will like her; she has lost her father—and she will find one in you."

"Never!" gasped the old man; then with an oath, as he beat his fist on the table, "Never!"

Bessie heard that high words were being cast about in the supper-room, and she opened the door and came in with a candle, on the pretence that she desired to have the table cleared if her brother had done his meal.

"You may have all taken away," said Anthony. "My father has destroyed what appetite I had."

"Your appetite," stormed the old man, "is after most unwholesome diet; you turn from the rich acres to the starving peat-bog. By heaven! I will have you shut up in a mad-house along with your wench. I will have a summons out against her at once. I will go to Fernando Crymes for it—it is sheer witchcraft. You have not seen her to speak to half-a-dozen times. You never came to know her at all till you had played the fool with her father's grave, and now——. By Heaven, it is witchcraft! Folks have been burnt for lighter cases than this."

Bessie went over to her father, and put her arms round him, but he thrust her away. She looked appealingly to her brother, but Anthony did not catch her eye.

"I do not see what you have against Urith," said Anthony, after a long pause, during which the old man sat quivering with excitement, working his hands up and down on the arms of his chair, as though polishing them. "That she is not rich is no fault of hers. I have seen her often, and have now and then exchanged a word with her, though only yesterday came to see much of her, and have a long talk with her. I did her a great wrong by my desecration of her father's grave."

"Oh! you would make that good by marrying the daughter. Well, you have put out Fox's eye. Patch that up by marrying his sister." The old man's voice shook with anger.

Anthony exercised unusual self-control. He knew that he had reached a point in his life when he must not act with rashness; he saw that his father's opposition was more serious than he had anticipated. Hitherto he had but to express a wish, and it was yielded to. Occasionally he had had differences with the old man, but had invariably, in the end, carried out his own point. He did not doubt, even now, that finally his father would give way, but clearly not till after a battle of unusual violence; but it was one in which he was resolved not to yield. His passion for Urith was of sudden and also rapid growth, but was strong and sincere. Moreover, he had pledged himself to her, and could not draw back.

Bessie was resolved, at all costs, to divert the wrath of her father from Anthony, if possible to turn his thoughts into another channel; so she said, stooping to his ear,

"Father; dear father! We met to-day our grandmother in the churchyard."

The old man looked inquiringly at her.

"Madame Penwarne," exclaimed Bessie.

He had forgotten for the moment that she could have a grandmother on any other side than his own, and he knew that his mother was long dead.

"Yes, father," said Bessie. "And she says Anthony is the living image of our dear, dear mother."

The old man turned his eyes slowly on his son. The light of the candle was on his face, bold, haughty, defiant, and wonderfully handsome. Yes! he was the very image of his mother, and that same defiant smile he had inherited from her. The old man in a moment recalled many a wild scene of mutual reproach and stormy struggle. It was as though the dead woman's spirit had risen up against him to defy him once more, and to strike him to the heart.

Then Anthony said, "It is true, father. We both of us met her; and it is unfit that she should find a shelter elsewhere than in this house. Something must be done for her."

"Oh! you will teach me my duty! She is naught to me."

"But to us she is. She is the mother of our mother," answered Anthony, looking straight into his father's eyes, and the old man lowered his; he felt the reproach in his son's words and glance.

Then he clenched his hands and teeth, and stood up, and wrung his hands together.

Presently, with a gasp, he said, "Because I married a beggar, is this mating with beggars to be a curse in the family from generation to generation, entailed from father to son. It shall not be; by heaven! it shall not be. You have had your own way too long, Anthony! I have borne with your whimsies, because they were harmless. Now you will wreck your own happiness, your honour, make yourself the laughing-stock of the whole country! I will save you from yourself. Do you hear me? I tried the sport, and it did not answer. I had wealth and she beauty, and beauty alone. It did not answer. We were cat and dog—your mother and I. Bessie knows it. She can bear me witness. I will not suffer this house to be made a hell of again."

"Father," said Anthony, "it was not that which caused you unhappiness—it was that you had interfered with the love of two who had given their hearts to each other."

Bessie threw herself between her father and brother. "Oh, Anthony! Anthony!" she cried.

"You say that!" exclaimed the old man.

"I do—and now I warn you not to do the same thing. Urith and I love each other, and will have each other."

"I tell you I hate the girl—she shall never come here."

"Father," said Anthony—his pulses were beating like a thundering furious sea against cliffs, as a raging gale flinging itself against the moorland tors—"father, I see why it is that you are against Urith. You nourish against her the bitterness you felt against her father. You laughed and were pleased when I had dishonoured his grave. That surprised me. Now I understand all, and now I am forced to speak out the truth. You did a wrong in taking our mother away from him whom she loved, and then you ill-

treated her when you had her in your power. You have
nothing else against Urith—nothing. That she is poor is
no crime."

Bessie clasped her arms about the old man. "Do not
listen to him," she said. "He forgets his duty to you,
only because he has been excited and wronged to-day."
Then to her brother: "Anthony! do not forget that he is
your father, to whom reverence is due."

Anthony remained silent for a couple of minutes, then
he stood up from his chair, and went over to the old man.
"I was wrong," he said. "I should not have spoken thus.
Come, father, we have had little puffs between us, never
such a bang as this. Let it be over; no more about the
matter between us for a day or two, till we are both cool."

"I will make an end of this affair at once," said Squire
Cleverdon. "What is the good of putting off what must
be said?—of expecting a change which will never take
place. You shall never—never obtain my consent. So
give up the hussy, or you shall rue it."

"Nothing is gained, father, by threatening me. You
must know that. I have made up my mind." He folded
his arms on his breast.

"And so have I mine," answered old Cleverdon, folding
his arms.

Father and son stood opposite each other, hard and fixed
in their resolves—both men of indomitable, inflexible determination.

"Hear mine," said the Squire; "you give the creature
up. Do you hear?"

"I hear and refuse. I will not, I cannot give up Urith.
I have pledged my word."

"And here I pledge mine!" shouted the old man.

"No—no, in pity, father! Oh, Anthony, leave the room!"
pleaded Bessie, again interposing, but again ineffectually;
her brother swept her aside, and refolded his arms, confronting his father.

"Say on!" he said, with his eyes fixed on the old man.

"I swear by all I hold sacred," exclaimed the father,
"that I will never suffer that beggar-brat to cross my
threshold. Now you know my resolution. As long as I
am alive, she shall be kept from it by my arms, and I shall
take care that she shall never rule here when I am gone.

Now you know my mind, marry her or not as you please.
That is my last word to you."

"Your last word to me!" repeated Anthony. He set
his hat on his head, the hat in which hung the utterly
withered marsh marigolds. "Very well; so be it." He
walked to the door, passed through, and slammed it behind
him.

<hr>

CHAPTER XVI

MOTHER AND DAUGHTER.

Luke Cleverdon walked slowly, with head bowed; towards Willsworthy. The day was not warm, a cold east
wind was blowing down from the moor over the lowlands
to the west, but his brow was beaded with large drops.

Anthony had come to him the night before, and had
asked to be lodged. He had fallen out with his father,
and refused to remain at Hall. Luke knew the reason.
Anthony had told him. Anthony had told him more—that
Urith was going to request his, Luke's, intercession with
her mother.

Neither Anthony nor Urith had the least suspicion of the
burden they were laying on the young man. It was his
place, thought Anthony, to do what could be done to further his—Anthony's—wishes. Luke was under an obligation to the family, and must make himself useful to it when
required. That he should employ his mediation to obtain
an end entirely opposed to the wishes of the old man who
had housed and fed, and had educated him, did not strike
Anthony as preposterous. For the moment, the interests,
credit of the family were centred in the success of his own
suit for Urith, his own will was the paramount law, which
must be obeyed.

Urith thought of Luke as a friend and companion, very
dear to her, but in quite another way from that in which
she regarded Anthony. Luke had been to her a comrade
in childhood, and she looked on him with the same child-
like regard that she had given him when they were children; with her this regard never ripened into a warmer
feeling.

Anthony had slept soundly during the night. Care for the future, self-reproach, or self-questioning over the past had not troubled him. His father would come round. He had always given way hitherto. He had attempted bluster and threats, but the bluster was nothing, the threats would never be carried out. In a day or two at the furthest, the old man would come to the parsonage, ask to see him, and yield to his son's determination.

"I don't ask him to marry Urith," argued Anthony. "So there is no reason why he should lie on his back and kick and scratch. There is no sense in him. He will come round in time, and Bessie will do what she can for me."

But Luke had not slept. He was tortured with doubts, in addition to the inward conflicts with his heart. He asked himself, had he any right to interfere to promote this union, which was so strongly opposed by the father—so utterly distasteful to him? And, again, was it to the welfare of his cousin, and, above all, of Urith, that it should take place?

He knew the character of both Urith and Anthony. He was well aware how passionate at times, how sullen at others, she was wont to be. He attributed her sullenness to the nagging, teasing tongue, and stupid mismanagement of her mother, and the blunderheadedness of her uncle—interfering with her liberty where they should have allowed her freedom, crossing her in matters where she should have been suffered to follow her own way, and letting her go wild in those directions in which she ought to have been curbed. He knew that this mismanagement had made her dogged and defiant.

He knew, also, how that his cousin, Anthony, had been pampered and flattered, till he thought himself much more than he was ; did not know the value of money ; was wilful, impetuous, and intolerant of opposition. Would not two such headstrong natures, when brought together, be as flint and steel? Moreover, Luke knew that Anthony had been regarded on all sides as the proper person to take Julian Crymes. It had been an open secret that such an arrangement was contemplated by the parents on both sides, and the young people had, in a measure, acquiesced in it. Anthony had shown Julian attentions which were only allowable on such an understanding. He may have meant nothing by them; nevertheless, they had been sufficiently marked to attract observation, and perhaps to lead the girl herself to conclude that his heart was touched, and that he only tarried a few years to enjoy his freedom before engaging himself.

But Luke was so sensitively conscientious that he feared his own jealousy of his cousin was prompting these suspicions and doubts; and he felt that his own heart was too perturbed for him at present to form a cool and independent survey of the situation.

As he expected and feared, so was it. Urith arrested him on the way up the hill to Willsworthy. She knew he would come to see her mother, and was on the lookout for him. She asked him to plead her cause for her, and in his irresolution he accepted the office, against his better judgment, moved thereto by the thought that he was thus doing violence to his own heart, and most effectually trampling down and crushing under heel his own wishes, unformed though these wishes were.

Luke found Mistress Malvine in her bedroom. She had been greatly weakened by the fit on the previous morning, still more so by the exhaustion consequent on the visits of the afternoon. However ill and feeble she might be, her tongue alone retained its activity, and so long as she could talk she was unconscious of her waning powers. In the tranquillity that followed, when her acquaintances and sympathisers had withdrawn, great prostration ensued. But she had somewhat rallied on the following morning, and was quite ready to receive Luke Cleverdon when announced.

She was in her bed, and he was shocked to observe the change that had come over her. She held out her hand to him. "Ah, Master Luke!" she sighed, "I have need of comfort after what I have gone through; and I am grateful that you have come to see me. Whatever will become of my poor daughter when I am gone! I have been thinking and thinking, and wishing that it had pleased God you were her brother, that I might have entrusted her into your hands. You were here and saw how she went on and took sides with that Son of Belial, that Anthony, when he came concerning the grave of my dear husband. She has

no heart, that child. I know she will be glad when I am
gone, and will dance on my tomb. I have not spared her
advice and counsel, nor have I ever let her go, when I have
my rebuke to administer, under half an hour by the
clock."

"Madam," said the young curate, "do not now make
boast of the amount of counsel and admonition you have
administered; it is even possible that this may have been
overdone, and may have had somewhat to do with the temper
of your daughter. It is now a time for you to consider
whether you are prepared, should it please God to call
you——"

"Oh!" exclaimed Mrs. Malvine, "I am thankful to say
I am always prepared. I have done my duty to my husband, to my brother, and my child. As for Urith, I have
perfectly fed her with my opinions on her conduct in every
position and chance of life. My brother has, I am sure,
also not to charge me with ever passing it over when he
comes home drunk, or gets drunk off our cider, which is
no easy matter, but it can be done with application. I
have always, and at length, and with vehemence, told him
what I think of his conduct."

"You must consider," said the curate, without allowing
himself to be drawn into admiration for the good qualities
of the sick woman, "you must consider, madam, not how
much you have harangued and scolded others, but how
much you deserve rebuke yourself."

"I have never spared myself, heaven knows! I have
worked hard—I have worked harder than any slave. There
are five large jars of last year's whortleberry jam still un-
opened in the store-room. I can die happy, whenever I
have to die, and not a sheet unhemmed, and we have
twenty-four."

"There are other matters to think of," said Luke, gravely, "than whortleberry jam—five pots, sheets—twenty-four,
rebuke of others—unmeasured, incalculable. You have to
think of what you have left undone."

"There is nothing," interrupted the sick woman, "but
a few ironmoulds in Solomon's shirts, which came of a
nail in the washing-tray. I gave the woman who washed
a good piece of my mind about that, because she ought to
have seen the nail. But I'll get salt of lemon and take that

out, if it please the Lord to raise me up again; at the same time, I'll turn the laundress away."

"It is by no means unlikely that heaven will not raise you up," said the curate, "and in your present condition, instead of thinking of dismissing servants for an oversight, you should consider whether you have never left undone those things which you ought to have done."

"I never have," answered the widow, with disdain, "except once. I ought to have had Solomon's dog Toby hung, but I was too good, too tender-hearted, and I did not. The dog scratched, and was swarming with fleas. Solomon never cared to have him kept clean, and I told him if he did not I would have Toby hung, but I did not. I have, I admit, this on my conscience. But, Lord! you are not comforting me at all, and a minister of the Word should pour the balm of Gilead into the wounds of the sick. Now, if you would have Urith up and give her a good reprimand, and Solomon also, and if you would hang that dog—that would be a comfort to my soul, and I could die in peace."

"With your complaint, Mistress Malvine, you must be ready to die at any moment—whether in a true or false peace depends on your preparation. I am not here to lecture your brother and daughter, and hang a dog because it has fleas, but to bid you search and examine your own conscience, and see whether there be not therein inordinate self-esteem, and whether you have not encouraged the censorious spirit within you till you have become blind to all your own defects, in your eagerness to pull motes out of the eyes of others."

"There! bless me!" exclaimed the widow. "Did you hear that? The soot has fallen down the chimney. I told Solomon to have the chimney swept, and, as usual, he has neglected to see to it. I'll send for him and give him what I think; perhaps," she added, in a querulous tone, "when he considers that the words come from a dying sister he may be more considerate in future, and have chimneys swept regularly."

"I have," said the young curate, "one question on which I require an answer. Are you in charity with all the world? Do you forgive all those who have trespassed against you?"

"I am the most amiable person in the world, that is why I am so imposed on, and Solomon, and Urith, and the maids, and the men take such advantage of me. There is that dog, under the bed, scratching. I hear it, I feel it. Do, prithee, Master Luke, take the tongs and go under the bed after it. How can I have peace and rest whilst Toby is under the bed, and I know the state his hair is in?"

"You say you are on terms of charity with all the world. I conclude that you from your heart forgive my cousin Anthony his unconsiderate act on St. Mark's Eve."

"What!" exclaimed the sick woman, striving to rise in her bed, "I forgive him that—never—no, so help me Heaven, never."

"So help you Heaven!" said Luke, starting up, and answering in an authoritative tone, whilst zeal-inspired wrath flushed his pale face. "So help you Heaven, do you dare to say, you foolish woman! Heaven will help to forgive, never help to harbour an unforgiving spirit. If you do not pardon such a trespass, committed unintentionally, you will not be forgiven yours."

"I have none—none to signify, that I have not settled with Heaven long ago," said the widow, peevishly. "I wish, Master Luke, you would not worry me. I need comfort, not to be vexed on my deathbed."

"I ask you to forgive Anthony, will you do so?"

She turned her face away.

"Now listen to me, madam. He has fallen into disgrace with his father. He has had to leave his home, and his father will have no word with him."

"I rejoice to hear it."

"And the reason is this—the young man loves your daughter Urith." He paused, and wiped his brow.

The widow turned her face round, full of quickened attention.

"That he did not purpose a dishonour to the grave you may be assured, when you know that he seeks the hand of Urith. How could one who loves think to advance his suit by an outrage on the father's memory? It was an accident, an accident he deplores most heartily. He will make what amends he can. Give him your daughter, and then he will have the right of a son-in-law to erect a handsome and suitable tomb to your husband, and his father."

As he spoke, he heard the steps creak, Urith was ascending the stairs, coming to her mother, to throw herself on her knees at her side, clasp her hand, and add her entreaties to those of Luke Cleverdon.

"Help me up!" said Mrs. Malvine.

Then the curate put his arm to her, and raised her into a sitting position. Her face had altered its expression from peevishness to anger. It was grey, with a green tinge about the nose and lips, the lines from the nostrils to the chin were deep and dark. Her eyes had a hard, threatening, metallic glimmer in them.

At that moment Urith appeared in the doorway. Luke stood, with his hand to his chin, and head bowed, looking at the woman.

"You are here, Urith!" said she, holding out her hand towards her spread out. "You have dared—dared to love the man who has dishonoured your father's grave. You have come here to ask me to sanction and bless this love." She gasped for breath. Her face was livid, haggard; but her dark eyes were literally blazing—shooting out deadly-cold glares of hate. The sweat-drops ran off her brow and dropped upon the sheet. The lips were drawn from the teeth. There was in her appearance something of unearthly horror. "You shall never—never obtain from me what you want. If you have any respect for your father's name—any love lingering in your heart for the mother that bore you—you will shake him off, and never speak to him again." She remained panting, and gulping, and shivering. So violent was her emotion that it suffocated her.

"I know," she continued, in a lower tone, and with her hands flat on the coverlet before her, "what you do not—how my life has been turned to wormwood. His mother stood between me and my happiness—between me and your father's heart; and, after what I have endured, shall I forgive that? Aye, and a double injury—the wrong done by Margaret Penwarne's son to my husband's grave?—Never!"

She began to move herself in bed, as though trying to scramble up into a standing posture, and again her hand was threateningly extended. "Never—never shall this come about. Urith! I charge you——"

The girl, alarmed, ran towards her mother. The old woman warned her back. "What! will you do violence to me to stay my words? Will you throttle me to prevent them from coming out of my lips?"

Again she made an effort to rise, and scrambled to her knees: "I pray heaven, if he dares to enter my doors, that he may be struck down on my hearth—lifeless!"

She gave a gasp, shivered, and fell back on the bed. She was dead.

CHAPTER XVII.

THE COUSINS.

Some days passed. Mistress Malvine had been buried. No direct communication had taken place between Anthony and his father. The gentle Bessie, full of distress at the breach, had done what she could to heal it; but ineffectually. Each was too proud and obstinate to make the first advance. Bessie's influence with her father was of the slightest—he had never showed love towards his plain daughter; and Anthony was too much of a man, in his own idea, to allow himself to be guided by a woman. Luke was perplexed more than ever. Urith was now left wholly without proper protection. Her uncle was worse than useless—an element of disorder in the household, and of disintegration in the pecuniary affairs of the family. The estate of Willsworthy did not come to him. It had belonged to his mother, and from his mother had gone to his sister, and now passed to his niece. It was a manor that seemed doomed to follow the spindle. But, though it had not become his property, he was trustee and guardian for his niece till she married; and a more unsatisfactory trustee or improper guardian could hardly have been chosen. He was, indeed, an amiable, well-intentioned man; but was weak, and over-fond of conviviality and the society of his social inferiors, from whom alone he met with deference. He had been brought up to the profession of the law; but, on his father's death, had thrown up what little work had come to him that he might be with his mother and sister, as manager of the estate. When his sister married Richard Malvine he was again thrown on his own resources, and lived mainly on subventions from his sister and friends, and a little law business that he picked up and misman- aged, till his brother-in-law died, when he returned to Willsworthy, to the mismanagement of that property which Richard Malvine had barely recovered from the disorder and deterioration into which it had been brought by Solo- mon Gibbs's previous rule. The old fellow was unable to stick to any sort of work, to concentrate his thoughts for ten minutes on any object, was irresolute, and swayed by those with whom he associated. His sister lectured and scolded him, and he bore her rebuke with placid amiability, and promises of amendment; promises that were never fulfilled. One great source of annoyance to his sister was his readiness to talk over all family matters at the tavern with his drinking comrades, to explain his views as to what was to be done in every contingency, and dilate on the pecuniary difficulties of his sister, and his schemes for the remedy of the daily deepening impecuniosity. This public discussion of the affairs of the family had done much to bring it into disrepute. Those who heard Mr. Gibbs over his cups retailed what they heard to their friends and wives with developments of their own, and the whole neighbourhood had come to believe that the Malvines were a family irretrievably lost, and that Willsworthy was a poor and intractable estate. Those who used their eyes—as Crymes—did not share in this latter opinion, they saw that the property was deteriorated by mismanagement, but they all readily accepted the opinion that bankruptcy was inevi- table to the possessors at that time of Willsworthy.

Luke Cleverdon, knowing all the circumstances, and hav- ing gauged the character and abilities of Solomon Gibbs, was anxious concerning the future of Urith. She had ten- dered a dubious, sullen, and irregular submission to her mother, but was not likely to endure the capricious, unin- telligent domination of her uncle. His sister had, moreover, exercised a very considerable restraint on Solomon. He always lived in wholesome dread of her tongue; when re- lieved of every restraint, there was no reckoning on what he might do with the money scraped together. Urith her- self was unaccustomed to managing a house. Her mother had been an admirable disciplinarian in the house, and kept everything there in order, and Urith had run wild.

Her mother had not attempted to join her with herself in domestic management, and had driven the girl into a chronic condition of repressed revolt by her unceasing fault-finding. The girl had kept herself outside the house, had spent her time on the moors to escape the irritation and rebellion provoked by her mother's tongue.

The only tolerable solution would have been for Luke to have made Urith his wife, and taken on himself the management of the property, but such a solution was now impossible, for Urith's heart was engaged. It had never been a possibility to Luke's imagination, for he had sufficient cool judgment to be quite sure that he and Urith would never agree. He was quiet, reserved, devoted to his books or to antiquarian researches on the moor, and she had an intractable spirit—at one time sullen, at another frantic—with which he could not cope.

Besides this uncongeniality of temperament, he had no knowledge of or taste for agricultural pursuits, and to recover Willsworthy a man was needed who was a practical farmer and acquainted with business. If he were, moreover, to live at Willsworthy and devote himself to the estate, he must abandon his sacred calling, and this Luke could not justify to his conscience. The choice of Urith, fallen on Anthony, was unobjectionable as far as suitability for the place went. Anthony had been reared on a farm, and was familiar with all that pertained to agriculture. He had energy, spirit, and judgment. But the strong unreasoning opposition of old Squire Cleverdon, and the refusal of Urith's mother to consent to it, made Luke resolve to do nothing to further the union.

Luke spoke to Anthony on the matter, but was met with airy assurance. The old man must come round, it was but a matter of time, and as Mistress Malvine was but recently dead, it could not be that the daughter should marry at once. There must ensue delay, and during this delay old Cleverdon would gradually accustom himself to the prospect, and his anger cool.

Time passed, and no tokens of yielding on the part of the father appeared. Luke spoke again to his cousin. Now Anthony's tone was somewhat altered. His father was holding out because he believed that by so doing he would prevent the marriage, but he was certain to relent

as soon as the irrevocable step had been taken. **Just as**
David mourned and wept as long as the child was sick, but
washed his face, and ate and accommodated himself to the
situation when the child was dead, so would it be with the
Squire. He would sulk and threaten so long as Anthony
was meditating matrimony, but no sooner was he married
than the old man would ask them all to dinner, kiss, and
be jolly.

Luke by no means shared his cousin's sanguine views.
Mistress Penwarne was in the house, and from her he
learnt the circumstances of the marriage and subsequent
disagreement of old Anthony and Margaret ; and he could
to some extent understand the dislike the old Squire had
to his son's marrying the daughter of his rival. He knew
the hard, relentless, envious nature of the man, he had
suffered from it himself, and he doubted whether it would
yield as young Anthony anticipated. It was true that
Anthony was the Squire's son and heir, that he was the
keystone to the great triumphal Cleverdon arch the old
man had been rearing in imagination ; it was certain that
there would be a struggle in his heart between his pride
and his love. Luke was by no means confident that old
Cleverdon's affection for his son would prove so mastering
a passion as to overcome the many combined emotions
which were in insurrection within him against this union,
and impelling him to maintain his attitude towards his son
of alienation and hostility.

When Luke spoke to Anthony of the difficulties that stood
in his way, Anthony burst forth impatiently with the words,
"It is of no use you talking to me like this, cousin. I
have made up my mind, I will have Urith as my wife. I
love her, and she loves me. What does it matter that
there are obstacles ? Obstacles have to be surmounted.
My father will come round. As to Urith's mother, the
old woman was prejudiced, she was angry. She knows
better now, and is sorry for what she said."

"How do you know that ? "

"Oh ! of course it is so."

"But do you suppose that Urith will go in opposition to
her mother's dying wish ?"

"She will make no trouble over that, I reckon. Words
are wind—they break no bones. I appeal from Alexander

drunk to Alexander sober, from the ill-informed and peppery old woman, half-crazed on her death-bed, to the same in her present condition. Will that content you?"

"You have not spoken to Urith on this matter?"

"No—I have not seen her since the funeral. I have had that much grace in me. But I will see her to-day, I swear to you. I will tell you what I think," said Anthony, with vehemence. "You are as cold-blooded as an eel. You have never loved—all your interest is in old stones, and pots and pans dug up out of cairns. You love them in a frozen fashion, and have no notion what is the ardour of human hearts loving each other. So you make one difficulty on another. Why, Cousin Luke, if there were mountains of ice I would climb over them, seas of fire, I would wade through them, to Urith. Neither heaven nor hell shall separate us."

"Do not speak like this," said the curate, sternly. "It is a tempting of Providence."

"Providence brought us together and set us ablaze. Providence is bound to finish the good work and unite us."

"There has been neither consideration nor delay in this matter, and Providence, maybe, raises these barriers against which you kick."

"I will kick them over," said Anthony.

"Yes," said Luke, with a touch of bitterness; "always acting with passion and inconsideration. Nothing but head-long folly would have led you to do violence to Master Malvine's grave. The same rash impetuosity made you injure Fox Crymes' eye; and now you will throw yourself head-long into a state of life which involves the welfare of another, just because you have a fancy in your head that may pass as quickly as it has arisen."

"I am not going to listen to a sermon. This is not Sunday."

"I do not believe you will make Urith happy."

"No, not in the fashion you esteem happiness. Certainly not in that. In grubbing into barrows after old pots and counting grey stones on the moor. No. Urith would gape and go to sleep over such dull happiness as this. But I and she understand happiness in other sort from you. We shall manage somehow to make each other happy, and I defy my

9

father and the ghost of old Madam Malvine to stand between us and spoil our bliss."

Luke bowed his head over the table, and put his hand before his eyes, that his cousin might not observe the emotion that stirred him at these cutting but thoughtlessly uttered words of his cousin. He did not answer at once. After some pause he said, without looking up, "Yes, you may be happy together after your fashion, but something more than passion is wanted to found a household, and that is, as Scripture tells us, the blessing of the parents."

"My father is all right," said Anthony. "He has set his head on my uniting Kilworthy to Hall, and trebling the family estate. He can't have that, so he is growling. But Urith does not come empty; she has Willsworthy. If we do not extend the kingdom of Cleverdon in one direction, we shall in another. My father will see that in time, and come round. The weathercock does not always point to the east; we shall have a twist about, a few rains, and a soft west, warm breeze of reconciliation. I will make you a bet —what will you take?"

"I take no bets; I ask you to consider. In marriage each side brings something to the common fund. What do you bring? Urith has Willsworthy."

"And I Hall."

"No; recollect your father's threat."

"It was but a threat—he never meant it."

"Suppose he did mean it, and perseveres; you will then have to be the receiver, not the giver."

"The place is gone to the dogs. I can give my arms and head to it, and bring it round from the kennel."

"That is something, certainly. Then, again, you are wilful, and have had your way in all things. How will you agree with a girl equally wilful and unbending?"

"In the best way; we shall both will the same things. You don't understand what love is. Where two young creatures love, they do not strive, they pull together. It is of no profit talking to you, Luke, about love; it is to you what Hebrew or Greek would be to me—an unintelligible language in unreadable characters. I will be off to see Urith at once."

"No," said Luke, "you must not go to Willsworthy; you will cause folks to talk."

"I care nothing for their talk."

"If you care nothing for what people say, how is it you fell out with and struck Fox? You must consider others besides yourself. You have no right to bring the name of Urith into discredit. Do you not suppose that already tongues are busy concerning the cause of your quarrel with your father?"

"But I must see her, and come to some understanding."

"I will go to Willsworthy at once, and speak to her of your matter. I have not done so hitherto—I have only sought to comfort her on the death of her mother."

"I do not desire a go-between," said Anthony, peevishly. "In these concerns none can act like the principals."

"But I cannot suffer you to go. You must think of Urith's good name, and not have that any more put into the mouths of those who go to the pot-house. It has been done more than enough already. Stay here till I return."

Luke took up his three-corner hat and his stick and went forth. On reaching Willsworthy he did not find Urith in the house, but ascertained from a maid-servant that she was in the walled garden. Thither he betook himself across the back courtyard. The rooks were making a great noise in the sycamores outside.

He found the girl seated on the herb-bank in the neglected garden, with her head on her hand, deep in thought. She was pale, and her face drawn; but the moment she saw Luke she started up and flushed.

"I am so glad you are come. You will tell me something about Anthony?"

She was only glad to see him because he would speak of Anthony, thought Luke; and it gave a pang to his heart.

"Yes," said he, taking a seat beside her, "I will speak to you about Anthony."

She looked him full in the face out of her large, earnest, dark eyes. "Is it true," she asked, "what I have been told, that he has fallen out with his father, and is driven from Hall?"

"He has taken himself off from Hall," answered Luke, "on your account. His father refuses to countenance his attachment to you."

"Then where is he? With you?"

"Yes, with me. I have come to know your mind. He

cannot always remain with me and at variance with his father."

"On my account this has happened?" she said.

"Yes, on your account. How is this to end?"

She put her hands to her brow, and pressed her temples. "I am pulled this way and that," she answered, "and I feel as if I should go mad. But I have made my resolve, I will give him up. I have been an undutiful daughter always, and now I will obey my mother's last wishes. In that one thing that will cost me most, I will submit, and so atone for the wrong I did all the years before."

"Then you determine to give up Anthony, wholly?"

The colour came and went in her cheek, then deserted it entirely. She clasped her hands over her knee—she had reseated herself—and she said in a low voice, "Wholly."

"You give me authority to tell him this?"

"Yes. It can never be that we can belong to each other after what my mother said. You heard. She hoped if he ever passed through this door, that he might be struck dead on the hearth."

"They were awful words," said Luke, "but——"

"They were her last words."

Luke returned to his home and found Anthony there, pacing his little parlour, to work off his impatience. When he heard what Luke had to say, he burst into angry reproach. "You have spoken like a parson! It was wrong for you to meddle, I knew no good would come of it! I will not hear of this! I will go to Urith myself!"

"You must not."

"I will! Nothing shall stay me." He caught up his hat and swung out of the room.

CHAPTER XVIII.

A LOVER AND HIS LASS.

Anthony strode along the way to Willsworthy. That way took him past Cudliptown. The landlord was at the door of his inn.

"What! pass my house without a step inside?" asked

he. "There's Master Sol Gibbs there and Moorman Ever."

"I cannot stay," answered Anthony.

"Oh !" laughed the taverner, "I see ;" and he began to whistle a country song—"An evening so clear."

Instantly the strains of a viol-de-gamba were heard from within taking up the strain, and Uncle Solomon's voice singing lustily :

> An evening so clear
> I would that I were,
> To kiss thy soft cheek
> With the faintest of air.
> The star that is twinkling
> So brightly above,
> I would that I were
> To enlighten my love !

Anthony walked on. His brow knitted, and he set his teeth. The innkeeper had guessed that he was going to Willsworthy, and suspected the reason. That idiot Solomon Gibbs had been talking.

As he strode along, the plaintive and sweet melody followed him ; all that was harsh in the voice mellowed by the distance ; and Anthony sang to himself low, as he continued his course :

> I would I were heaven,
> O'erarching and blue,
> I'd bathe thee, my dearest,
> In freshest of dew.
> I would I the sun were,
> All radiance and glow,
> I'd pour all my splendour
> On thee, love, below !

He remembered how—only a few weeks agone—when he had been at the tavern with some comrades, and songs had been called for, he had expressed his impatience at this very piece, which he said was rank folly. Then he had not understood the yearning of the heart for the loved one, had not conceived of the desire to be all and everything to its mistress. Now he was expelled from his father's house, threatened with being disinherited, and was actually with-

out money in his pocket wherewith to pay for ale or wine
at the tavern, had he entered it. He who had been so free
with his coin, so ready to treat others, was now unable to
give himself a mug of ale. That was what had driven
him past the tavern door without crossing the threshold,
or rather that was one reason why he had resisted the invitation of the host. Yes—he had suffered for Urith, and
he rather plumed himself on having done so. She could
not resist his appeal when he told her all he had risked for
her sake.

Besides, Anthony was stubborn. The fact of his father's
resistance to his wish had hammered his resolution into
inflexibility. Nothing in the world, no person alive or
dead—neither his father nor her mother—should interfere
to frustrate his will. Anthony's heart beat fast between
anger and impatience to break down every obstacle ; he
sang on, as he walked :—

> If I were the waters
>   That round the world run,
> I'd lavish my pearls on thee,
>   Not keeping of one.
> If I were the summer,
>   My flowers and green
> I'd heap on thy temples,
>   And crown thee my Queen.

He had reached the ascent to Willsworthy, he looked up
the lane—and saw Urith in it ; outside the entrance gates
to the Manor House. She was there looking for her uncle,
who had been required about some farm-business. She
saw Anthony coming to her, with the sun glistening on him
over the rude stone hedge hung with fern. She heard his
song, and she knew the words—she knew that he was ap-
plying them to her. For a moment she hesitated, whether
to meet him or to retire into the house. She speedily
formed her resolution. If there must be an interview, a
final interview, it had better be at once, and got over.

The evening sun was low, the moor peaks over the manor house were flushed a delicate pink, as though the
heather were in bloom. Alas ! this year no heather would
wrap the hills in rose flush, for it had been burnt in the
great fire. High aloft the larks were shrilling. She could

hear their song in broken snatches between the strophes of Anthony's lay as he ascended the hill.   He had seen her, and his voice became loud and jubilant:—

> If I were a kiln,
>   All fire and flame,
> I'd mantle and girdle thee
>   Round with the same.
> But as I am nothing
>   Save love-mazed Bill,
> Pray take of me, make of me,
>   Just what you will.

He had reached her.   He held out his arms to engirdle her as he had threatened, and the flame leaped and danced in his eyes and glowed in his lips and cheek.

She drew back proudly.

"You have had my message?"

"I take no messages—certainly none sent through parsons.   The dove is the carrier between lovers, and not the croaking raven."

"Perhaps it is as well," said Urith, coldly.   She had nerved herself to play her part, but her heart was bounding and beating against her sides like the Tavy in one of its granite pools beneath a cataract.   "I sent by Master Luke Cloverdon to let you know that we must see each other no more."

"I will take no such message.   I will—I must see you. I cannot live without."

"My mother's wishes must be followed.   I have promised to see and speak to you no more."

"You promised!   To whom?   To her?"

Urith was silent.

"I will know who twisted this promise out of you.   Was it Luke?   If so his cassock and our cousinship shall not save him."

"It was not Luke."

"It was your mother?"

"I did not actually promise anything to my mother. But—I must not shrink from telling you—I have made the promise to myself, we can be nothing to each other."

"Unsay the promise at once—do you hear?   At once."

"I cannot do that.   I made it because I considered it

right. Your father is against our—acquaintance——" She hesitated.

"Go on—he is against our being lovers, and more against our marrying. But what of that? He always gives way in the end, and now the only means of bringing him to his senses is for us to go before the altar."

"My mother, with her last breath, warned me from you."

"I know perfectly well for what reason. My mother and your father were to each other what are now you and I; then, by some chance, all went wrong, and each got wed to the wrong person. Neither was happy after that, and my father on one side and your mother on the other, could not forget this, so they have carried on the grudge to the next generation, and would make us do the wrong that they did, and give you to—the Lord knows who?—perhaps Fox Crymes; and me, certainly, to Julian. I have seen what comes of wedding where the heart is elsewhere. I will not commit the folly my father was guilty of. Julian Crymes shall take another, she shall never have me. And you, I reckon, have no fancy for another save me; and if your mother had made any scheme for you, she has taken it with her to the grave, and you are not tied to make yourself unhappy thereon."

As he spoke, Urith retreated through the gateway into the court, and Anthony, vehement in his purpose, followed her.

They were as much alone and unobserved in the little court as in the lane, for only the hall windows and those of an unused parlour looked into it. But Anthony raised his voice in his warmth of feeling. "Urith," said he, "I am not accustomed to take a No, and what I am not accustomed to I will not take."

"No!" she answered, and looked up, with a kindling of her eye. "And what I say, to that I am accustomed to hold; and what I am accustomed to hold, that hold I will. I say No." She set her foot down.

"And I will not take it. I throw it back. Why, look you, you have said Yes. We are pledged to each other. You and I on The Cleave. There I have you, Urith. You passed your word to me, and I will not release you."

She looked on the paved ground of the court, with grass

sprouting between the cobble-stones, and played with her foot on the pebbles. Her brows were contracted, and her lips tight closed. Presently she looked up at him steadily, and said—

"It is for the good of both that I withdraw that word, stolen from me before I had weighed and appraised its worth. I will not be the cause of strife between you and your father, and I dare not go against the last words of my mother. Do you know what she said? She prayed that you might be struck dead on the hearth should you dare enter our doors again."

"Very well," said Anthony, "let us see what her prayer avails. Stand aside, Urith."

He thrust her away and walked forward to the entrance of the house, then he turned and looked at her and laughed. The sun shone on the porch, but it was dark within. He put out his hands and held to the stone-jambs, and looking at Urith with the dazzling evening sun in his eyes, he said—

"See now! I defy her. I go through!" and walking backwards, with arms outspread, he passed in through the porch, then in at the second doorway.

Urith had remained rooted to one spot, in astonishment and terror. Now she flew after him, and found him standing in the hall on the hearthstone, his head above the dark oak mantel, laughing, and with his legs wide apart, and his hands in his belt.

"See, Urith!" he jeered, "the prayers are of no avail. Prayers bring blessings, not curses. Here am I on the hearthstone, alive and well. Now—will you fear an idle threat?"

He laughed aloud, and broke out into a snatch of song.

> "If I were a kiln,
> All fire and flame,
> I'd mantle and girdle thee
> Round with the same."

Then he caught her round the waist and drew her towards him; but by a sharp turn she freed herself from his grasp.

"No," she said; "one must give way, and that shall not be I."

"Nor I," he said, resolutely, and the blood rose in his cheeks; "I am wholly unwont to give way."

"So am I."

"Then it is—which is strongest."

"Strongest in will—even so; there I doubt if you will surpass me."

"I tell you this is folly, mad folly," said Anthony, with violence; "my happiness—my everything depends on you. I have broken with my father. I am too proud to go back to Hall and say to him, 'Urith has cast me off, now she finds that I am penniless.' What am I to do? I cannot dig, to beg I am ashamed, and I have no stewardship in which to be dishonest. If I cannot have you, I have nothing to live for, nothing to work for, nothing, and no one to love." He stamped on the hearthstone. "By heavens, may I be struck dead here if only I get you, for without you I will not live. Let it be as your mother wished, so that I have you."

She remained silent, with hands clasped, looking down—her face set, colourless, and resolved with a certain dogged, sullen fixity.

"Am I to be the laughing-stock of the parish?" asked Anthony, angrily. "Turned out of Hall, turned out of Willsworthy! My father will have naught to do with me because of Urith Malvine, and Urith Malvine will have naught to say to me because of Squire Cleverdon. This is too laughable—it would be laughable if it concerned another than me—but I am the sufferer, I am the ball tossed about and let drop by every hand. I will not be thus treated. I will not be the generally rejected. You must and you shall take me."

"Listen to me, Anthony," said Urith, in tones that hardly vibrated, so complete was her self-control. "If you will not ask your father's pardon——"

"What for? I have done him no harm."

"Well, then, if you will not, go to your father and say I will not take you, and therefore all is to be as before."

"No, that I will not do; I will have you even against your will. You may give me up, but I will not so lightly let you fall."

"Hear me out. If you will not do this, go away from this place."

"Whither?"

"Nay, that is for you to decide. I should say, were I a man, that I could always find a where—in the King's army."

Anthony laughed scornfully. "In the King's forces, that on the accession of the Duke of York will be employed to put down the Protestants, and treat them as they have been treated in Savoy and in France? No, Urith, not at your wish will I do that; but if the Duke of Monmouth or the Prince of Orange were——

Urith held up her hand. In at the door came her uncle, red and wine-flushed, carrying his viol.

"Halloo!" shouted Mr. Solomon Gibbs, "*in vino veritas.* Hussey, you don't understand Latin. I have learnt something—slipped out unawares from Moorman Ever. To-morrow—What think you? A Drift."

"A Drift!" For the moment Urith forgot all about the presence of Anthony, in the excitement of the announcement.

"A Drift!" Anthony tossed up his head and clasped his hands, and forgot Urith and all else, for a moment, in the excitement of the announcement.

"Ay," said Uncle Solomon; "and Tom Ever would have bitten out his tongue when he said it, he was so vexed."

CHAPTER XIX.

A DRIFT.

A Drift? What is a Drift?

The vast expanse of Dartmoor, occupying nearly a hundred and fifty thousand acres, for the most part, but not altogether, belongs to the Duchy of Cornwall. Considerable, and, in many cases, fraudulent encroachments have been made on Duchy property—slices taken out of it in past times—and the Duchy agents bribed to turn their eyes away; or simply taken and secured to the squatters by prerogative of long squatting unmolested. The main mass of moor constitutes the ancient and Royal forest of Dartmoor; but much waste land exists outside the forest bounds in the possession of private owners, or as common land, over which the lord of the manor has but manorial rights.

Around the circumference of the moor are, and always have been, stationed certain men having a position under the Duchy, corresponding to that of foresters elsewhere. But, as there are no trees on Dartmoor, these men have no care of timber ; nor have they, as foresters elsewhere, the custody of the deer, as there are no red deer in this Royal forest. Red deer there were in times past ; but they were all destroyed at the close of the last century, when large plantations were made on the moor and in its confines, because the deer killed the young trees.

On account of the rugged and boggy nature of Dartmoor, no Royal hunters had come there since the Saxon kings ; consequently, no pains were taken to preserve the deer, and every moorman and squire neighbouring on the wilderness considered that he had a right to supply himself with as much venison from off it as he could eat, and every farmer regarded himself as justified in killing the deer that invaded his fields and swarmed over his crops. The men answering to foresters elsewhere, living under the Duchy, and posted around the borders of the moor, inherited their offices, which passed in families for generations, and it is probable that the Evers, the Coakers, and the Widdecombes of to-day are the direct descendants of the moormen who were foresters under the Conqueror—nay, possibly, in Saxon times.

They are a fine-built race, fair-haired, blue-eyed, erect, better able to ride than to walk, are bold in speech, and perhaps overbearing in action, having none above them save God and the Prince of Wales—*the* Duke, the only Duke above their horizon.

Around the forest proper is a wide tract of common land, indistinguishable from moor proper, and this does not belong to the Duchy, but the Duchy exerts, for all that, certain rights over this belt of waste. The parishes contiguous on the moor have what are termed Venville rights, that is to say, rights to cut turf and to free pasturage on the moor ; the tenants in Venville may be said to have the right to take anything off the moor that may do them good except green oak and venison, or more properly, vert and venison. This has led to the most ruthless destruction of prehistoric antiquities, as every farmer in Venville carries away as his right any granite-stone that commends itself to him as a gate-post, or a pillar to prop a cowshed ; sheep, bullocks, and horses are turned out on Dartmoor, and the horses and ponies live in all weathers on the wilderness, defy all boundaries, and ask for no care, no shelter, no winter quarters. Bullocks and sheep have their lairs, and want to be levant and couchant, and to be cared for in winter, and therefore are not driven on to the moors till spring, and are driven off in autumn.

The moor is divided into regions, and over each region is a moorman. In each quarter of the moor a special earmark is required for the ponies turned out in that district, a round hole punched in the ear, through which is passed a piece of distinguishing tape, scarlet, blue, white, and black. Ponies wander widely : a herd will disappear from one place and appear at another like magic, in search after pasture ; but the moormen of each region claim the fines on the ponies belonging to their region, and, to a certain extent, exercise some sort of supervision over them.

Although every tenant in Venville has an undisputed right to free pasturage, yet it is usual for him to fee the moorman for each horse or beast he sends out, and, if this be refused, he may find his cattle stray to a very remarkable extent, and be liable to get " stogged " in the bogs and be lost.

As horses, etc., that are driven on parish commons, or on moors belonging to private individuals, very often leave these quarters for the broader expanse of the Royal Forest, it is necessary, or deemed advisable, on certain days arbitrarily determined on, without notice to anyone, to have a "Drift." A messenger is sent round in the night or very early in the morning to the Venville tenants, from the moorman of the quarter, to summon them to the Drift ; on certain tors are upright holed stones, through which horns were passed and loudly blown, to announce the Drift. All the neighbourhood is on the alert—dogs, men, boys are about, squires and farmers armed with long whips, and formerly with pistols and short swords and bludgeons.

All the ponies and colts on the quarter, not only on Dartmoor Forest, but on all the surrounding zone of waste

land, are driven from every nook and corner by mounted
horsemen and dogs, towards the place of gathering, which
is, for the western quarter, Merrivale Bridge. The driving
completed, a vast number of ponies and horses of all ages,
sizes, colours, and breeds, and men and dogs, are collected
together in a state of wild confusion. Then an officer of
the Duchy mounts a stone and reads to the assembly a
formal document with seals attached to it. That ceremony
performed, the owners claim their ponies. Venville tenants carry off theirs without objection ; others pay fines.
Animals unclaimed are driven off to Dinnabridge Pound,
a large walled-in field in the midst of the moor, where they
remain till demanded, and if unclaimed are sold by the
Duchy.*

To this day a Drift causes violent altercations ; formerly
free fights between Venville tenants and those who were outside the Venville parishes were not uncommon, and blood
was not infrequently shed. That a Drift should excite a
whole neighbourhood to the utmost may be imagined. The
dispersion of the horses by the fire on the moor occasioned
the Drift at this unusual time of early spring.

The morning was windy, clouds large and heavy were
lumbering over the sky, turning the moor indigo with their
shade, and where the sun shone the grey grass, as yet un-
tinged with spring growth, was white as ashes.

On the top of Smerdon stood a gigantic moorsman, with
lungs like blacksmith's bellows, blowing a blast through a
cow's horn that was heard for miles around. But the yelp-
ing of dogs, the shouts of men proclaimed that the whole
world was awake and abroad, and needed no horn to call to
attention. Men in rough lindsey and frieze coats and
leather breeches, high boots, with broad hats, wild-looking
as the horses they bestrode, and the hounds that bayed
about them, galloped in all directions over the turf, shouting and brandishing their long whips. Colts, ponies of
every colour, with long manes and flowing tails, wild as any
bred on the prairies, leaped, plunged, raced about, snorting, frightened, and were pursued by dogs and men.

Although there was apparent confusion, yet a rude order

---

* See an article on Venville rights on Dartmoor, by W. F. Collier,
Esq , in the Devon Association Transactions for 1887.

might be observed. All the men were moved by one common impulse—to drive the horses and ponies inwards, and though these frightened creatures often broke the ring that was forming and careered back to the outer downs whence they had been chased, to be pursued again by a host of dogs and men, yet there was observable a rough chain of drivers concentrating towards a point on the Walla, spanned by a bridge under Mistor.

The whole neighbourhood was there—Anthony had come, ashamed to be seen afoot, and yet unwilling not to be there. He saw one of his father's servants on his own horse, and he demanded it; the fellow readily yielded his saddle, and Anthony joyously mounted his favorite roan. Fox Crymes was there with his eye bandaged, and glancing angrily at Anthony out of the one uninjured eye. Old Squire Cleverdon did not come out, he could no longer sit at ease on horseback, and had never been much of a rider. Mr. Solomon Gibbs was out in a soiled purple coat, and with hat and wig—as was his wont—awry. And Urith was there. She could not remain at home on such an occasion as a Drift. Her uncle was not to be trusted to recognise and claim the Willsworthy cobs. He was not to be calculated on. There was a tavern at Merivale Bridge, and there he would probably sit and booze, and leave his colts and mares to take care of themselves. There was no proper hind at the manor, only day-labourers, who were poor riders. Therefore Urith was constrained to attend the Drift herself.

She was the only woman present; Julian Crymes had not come out. When Anthony saw Urith he approached her, but she drew away.

"Why, how now !" shouted Fox. "Whose horse are you riding?"

"My own," answered Anthony, shortly.

"Oh! I am glad to hear it. I understood that you had been bundled out of Hall without any of your belongings ; but your father, I suppose, allowed you to ride off on the roan?"

"I will thank you to be silent," said Anthony, angrily.

"Why should I, when even dogs are open-mouthed? And as for Ever and his horn, he is calling everyone to speak in a scream, so as to be heard at all. Were you allowed to take off oats and hay as well?"

Anthony spurred his horse, to be out of ear-shot of his tormentor; but Fox followed him.

"What was it all about?" he asked. "All the countryside is ringing with the news that you and your father are fallen out, and that he has turned you out of doors; but opinions are divided as to the occasion."

"Let them remain divided," answered Anthony, and dug his spurs in so deeply that his horse bounded and dashed away. Fox no longer attempted to keep up with him, but turned to attach himself to Urith. She saw his intention, and drew near to her uncle, who was in conversation with Yeoman Cudlip.

They were now riding through a broad vale or dip between a range of serrated granite heights to the east, and the great trap-rounded pile of Cox Tor crowned with vast masses of cairn piled about the blistered basaltic prongs that shot through the turf at the summit. These cairns were probably used as beacons, for all were depressed in the middle to receive the heaps of fern and wood that were ignited to send a signal far away to the very Atlantic on the north, from a warning given on the coast of the English Channel.

The turf was free from masses of boulder, but was in places swampy. At the water-shed was a morass with a spring, and from this point the stream had been laboriously worked in ancient times for tin; the bed was ploughed up and thrown into heaps in the midst of the course.

"Look yonder," said Cudlip. "Do you see that pile o' stones with one piece o' granite atop standing up? There's P. L. cut on that. Did you ever hear tell how Philip Lang came by his death there? and how he came to lie there? For I tell y' there he is buried, and it is the mark where Peter Tavy parish ends and Tavistock parish begins, and they say he do lie just so that the parish bound goes thro' the middle of him. It all came about in the times of the troubles between the King and the Parliament. Sir Richard Grenville was in Tavistock, and was collecting men for the King; and Lord Essex came up with the Roundheads, and there was some fighting. Then some of the train bandmen were out here, and among them was Philip. He was a musketeer; but, bless your soul! he didn't know how to use the piece, and I've heard my father say that was the way with many. It was an old matchlock, and to fire it he had a fuse alight. Lord Essex was skirmishing round the country and Sir Richard had set a picket at this point. Well, Philip Lang, not knowing but the enemy might surprise him from one side or the other, had his fuse alight, and his musket charged. But by some chance or other, the fuse was uncoiled, and the lighted end hung down behind him and touched the horse on the croup. The beast jumped and kicked, and Lang could not make it out, for the fuse was behind him. Every time the horse bounded, the burning end struck him again in another spot, and he sprang about, and ran this way and that, quite mad; and Philip Lang, who was never a famous rider, let go his matchlock, and had hard to do to keep his seat. But, though he had dropped the musket, the fuse was twisted round him and kept bobbing against the horse, and making it still madder. Then the beast dashed ahead across the valley, and went head over heels down into the old miners' works, and Philip was flung where you see that stone, and he never breathed or opened his eyes after. 'Twas a curious thing that he fell just on the boundary of both parishes, and there was no saying whether he lay in one or the other. There was mighty discussion over it. The Peter Tavy men said the body belonged to Tavistock, and the Tavistock men said it belonged to Peter Tavy; and neither parish would bury him, for, you see, he was a poor man, without friends or money."

"Say, rather," threw in Fox, "without money and friends."

"As you like," answered the yeoman, and continued. "Well, it was thought that the parishes would have to go to law over it, to find out which would have to bury him, but after a deal o' trouble they came to an agreement to bury him where he fell, and three Peter Tavy men threw stones over him on one side, and three Tavistock men threw stones the other; and when the stone was set up the Peter Tavy men went to the expense of cutting one letter, P, and the Tavistock men went to the cost of the other letter, L."

" Come, " said Mr. Solomon Gibbs, " we are fallen into the rear. "

They pricked on, and descended the slope to the River Walla, that foamed and plunged over a floor of broken granite at some depth below. In the valley, where was the bridge, two or three mountain-ash trees grew; there was an inn and by it a couple of cottages. Here was now a scene of indescribable confusion and noise. The wild, frightened horses and ponies driven together, surrounded on all sides by the drivers, were leaping, plunging over each other, tossing their manes and snorting. The ring had closed about them. Every now and then a man dashed among them, on foot or mounted, when he recognized one of his own creatures, and by force or skill separated it from the rest, shouted to the drivers, who instantly opened a lane, and he drove the scared creature through the lane of men back on to the free wild moor. To effect this demanded daring and skill, and the men rivalled each other in their ability to claim their animals, and extricate them from the midst of the crowd of half-frantic creatures plunging and kicking. Neither Urith nor Solomon Gibbs had any intention of attempting such a dangerous feat, but purposed waiting till all other horses had been claimed, when they would indicate their own creatures, and the good-humoured moor-men of their quarter would discharge them. Accordingly they remained passive observers, and the sight was one full of interest and excitement; for the extrication of the horses claimed was a matter of personal danger, and demanded courage, a quick eye, great resolution, and activity.

Fox Crymes had no intention of venturing within the ring; he was standing on foot near Anthony's horse. Anthony was awaiting his time when he would rush in to the capture of his father's colts. All eyes but those of Urith were riveted on the struggle with the horses. There were some tall men, or men on large horses, between her and the herd of wild creatures, and as she could not well see what went on within the ring, she looked towards Anthony.

She was a little surprised at the conduct of Fox. In the first place, he seemed to be paying no attention to what was engrossing the minds and engaging the eyes of the

rest. He held a little back from Anthony, and was striking a light with a flint and a steel which he had taken from
his pocket.

What could be his purpose?

Urith was puzzled. Fox was no smoker.

She noticed that he had a piece of amadou under the
flint, and the sparks fell on it; it kindled, and Fox enclosed it within his hollowed hand and blew it into a glow.

Then he looked hastily about him, but did not observe
Urith. His bandaged eye was towards her, or he must
have seen that she was watching him, and watching him
with perplexity.

Then he took three steps forward.

Urith uttered a cry of dismay.

Fox had thrust the fragment of burning amadou into
the ear of the horse Anthony rode.

CHAPTER XX.

A BLOODY HAND.

The effect on Anthony's horse was instantaneous. With
a snort it bounded into the air, threw back its head, then
kicked out and began to dance and revolve, put its head
down between the fore-legs, then reared into the air, every
violent motion fanning the burning bunch of amadou into
stronger heat.

Anthony was taken by surprise, but maintained his seat.
The horse quickly scattered those around. One man,
struck by the hoofs, was drawn away in a state of unconsciousness. Some men were driven in among the enclosed
ponies, but quickly ran away; and, in less time than it
takes to write, the circle of lookers-on had reformed, en-
closing Anthony on his maddened steed in the same arena
with the wild cobs and colts.

A scene of indescribable confusion ensued. The tortured horse bounded in among the throng of ponies, and
threw them, if possible, into wilder disorder. All that
could be seen for some moments was a tumult of heads,
flying manes, hoofs, beasts leaping on and over each other,

and Anthony with difficulty, and in extreme danger, carried up and down above the sea of horses' heads and heels. If he had fallen, his brains would have been dashed out in one minute.   He knew this, and endeavoured to force his horse by deep spur out of the tangle ; but, agonised by the fire in its ear, it disregarded rein and spur.   Of its own accord, however, it disengaged itself, or by chance found itself free for an instant from the surrounding tossing, plunging mass of its fellows ;   and then, with a scream rather than a snort, it dashed right among the surrounding men.   They divided at once—not a man ventured forward to catch the rein and stay the mad beast.

In front was the river, with the low wall of the bridge over it, and under the arch, among huge masses of granite, leaped, and roared, and tumbled the Walla, as mad as the frightened moorland ponies—of a rich brown, but transparent, colour, where not whipped into foam.

Anthony's horse was dashing at the wall.   The brute's head was now round biting itself, then down between its fore-hoofs, in a frantic paroxysm of kicks.   Then it rushed forward, halted, spun round, then leaped with all four feet into the air, uttering screams.   Everyone was cowed—no one dared approach, and yet the situation of Anthony was critical.   Another bound, maybe, and his horse would be over the wall, and roll with him among the masses of rock big as haystacks, over and among which the river dashed itself to threads and flakes of foam, or went down into one of the wine-dark pools, where the eddies swirled and dissolved their foam before taking another leap.

Instinctively, overawed by one of those waves of feeling which come on men and beasts alike, all sounds ceased, the men no longer spoke, nor did the dogs bark.   Only the churning of the colts' and ponies' feet was heard within the living ring of men, and the tinkle, tinkle, tinkle of a sheep-bell beyond the river.

The horse was rearing to leap.

At that moment—a shot, and the horse fell like lead. Urith had snatched the pistol from the holster of her uncle's saddle, had leaped to the ground, run forward, and fired.

Silence remained as unbroken as before, save for the tinkle of the sheep-bell, till Anthony disengaged himself

from his fallen horse, stood up, shook himself, and then a
cheer burst from all the men present, who pressed forward
to congratulate him.

"Stay!" said Urith, still on the bridge, and with the pistol in her hand. She was white with emotion, and her
eyes flaming with wrath. "Listen to me—you—all of you.
I saw him do it—I saw him light a ball of tinder and thrust
it into the horse's ear, to drive the beast mad."

She looked round—her flashing eyes sought out him of
whom she spoke.

"I saw him do it, when all were looking elsewhere after
their cobs. He hated him, and he sought this mean, this
cruel, this treacherous revenge on him."

She panted, her heart was beating furiously, and the
blood rushed to her temples, and then ebbed away again,
leaving her giddy.

"Take him!" she cried. "He deserves it. Take him
and fling him among the horses, and let them trample him
down into the dirt. The man who did what he has done
deserves no better."

"Who!—who!—name!" shouted the bystanders.

"Who it was who did this? Did I not name him? It
is he." She had caught sight of him with his bandaged eye.
"Bring him forward—Fox Crymes."

In a moment Fox was hustled forth out of the throng
into the foreground.

"I would," gasped Urith, in quivering fury, "that I had
another pistol, and I would shoot you as I have the horse,
base, vile coward."

Fox looked at her contemptuously out of his one eye.
"It is well that none is in your hand—a maniac should
not be trusted with firearms, or should practise them on
herself."

"What has he done?" shouted Farmer Cudlip. "What
is the charge against him?"

"I say," answered Urith, "that whilst all were engaged
looking for their colts, I saw him light a piece of tinder
with flint and steel, and then thrust it into the ear of the
horse."

Silence followed this announcement. The men had
been too surprised to follow her charge when first
made.

"What do you say to that, Master Crymes?" asked Cudlip.

"It is a lie," retorted Fox. "She did it herself, so as to make a spectacle and appear as the preserver of her lover."

Again silence, save only for the trampling of the enringed ponies. The sheep-bell had ceased; maybe the sheep that bore the bell was lying down.

Urith spoke slowly, in her deepest tones.

"On the moor there is no law—or only the plain law of God that all can understand and obey. He is a murderer in heart. He tried to kill Anthony Cleverdon, and now he —coward that he is—insults me. Take him up and throw him among the horses."

At once a score of hands were laid on Fox Crymes. It was true, there was no law on the moor. There every man was a law unto himself. The Stannary Court sat but once in the year on the top of one of the central Tors, but that took cognisance only of offences against the mining laws. There was no criminal jurisdiction over the moor lodged anywhere—or, it was supposed that there was none. But then—crime was unknown on Dartmoor.

When an act of violence is to be done, especially when sanctioned by some rough rule of justice, there is no lack of hands to commit it.

Fox Crymes was generally disliked, his stinging tongue, his lack of geniality had alienated every acquaintance from him; the farmers present were rude men of the moor confines, brought under little or no control, kings on their own estate, and free of the moor to do thereon what they listed, take thence what they desired, fight thereon any with whom they were at feud, avenge themselves with their own arms for any wrong done to them. Never had a lawyer been invoked to unravel a doubtful claim, or to settle a dispute. Every knot was, if not cut through with a sword, at all events beaten out with the quarterstaff; and every dispute brought to an end by silencing one side with a bludgeon or a pistol.

In one moment, Fox Crymes was caught up, with a roar of many voices giving consent to the execution of the sentence pronounced by Urith, at once accuser and judge.

"Hold off!" cried Fox, and drew his knife; freeing himself by a twist of the body from those who held him, and who shrank back at the flash of steel.

His one eye glared. " I will drive it up to the haft in the first man who touches me ! " he said.

" Strike it out o' his hand ! " shouted Cudlip.

Fox, stabbing with his blade to right and left, backed from his assailants towards the wall. Cudgels were raised and aimed at him, but he dexterously withdrew his arm as each descended. The sight of the drawn weapon kindled the blood of the moor men, and those who had held back at first, now pressed forward to take him.

A shout ! the colts and horses had made a rush, a dash, and had broken through the ring. It was quickly re-formed, and away after those who had escaped rushed some of the men with their whips whirled about their heads.

This caused a momentary diversion. Anthony took advantage to leave his place by the fallen horse, come forward, and with his elbows force his way through to Crymes, and then, planting himself between Fox and his assailants, he shouted :

" No harm has been done. It was a joke. He and I had sport together, and I hit him in the eye and hurt him ; he knows I never designed to injure him. Now he tried a merry prank on me. He designed no hurt to me—but it has gone further than he would, as did mine with him. Hands off—here, Fox, show them we bear each other no malice—here before all, give me your right hand, good friend."

Crymes held back.

Cudgels were lowered, and the men drew away.

Fox slipped his hunting-knive up his sleeve, and sullenly extended his arm.

" You see ! " called Anthony, looking round, and not regarding Crymes. " You see ! We are good friends, and hearty comrades."

Then he clasped the right hand of Fox. As he did so, the blade slipped down the sleeve into the hand of Crymes, and as Anthony clenched his fingers about those of Fox, they closed on the blade in his hand, which was keen, and cut. He felt the knife, but he did not relax his grasp, and when he drew his hand away it was covered with blood.

"It was a mischance," said Crymes, with a malicious laugh. "You did not give me time to sheath the knife."

"Many a mischance falls between us," answered Anthony, hastily, drawing his glove over the wounded hand, lest it should attract attention.

Then he strode up to Urith, who stood palpitating near.

"I have saved you from yourself to-day," he said.

"Yes—I thank you."

"You can thank me but in one way."

"How so?"

"Give me your hand. Take me forever."

She put her hand into his: "I cannot help myself," she said, in a low tone. "Oh, mother, forgive."

Then she loosed her hand, looked on it, and said, "There is blood!"

The blood had oozed through his glove.

"It is my blood," answered Anthony, "on your hand."

CHAPTER XXI.

FIXED.

Squire Cleverdon gave no token of relenting towards his son. Bessie had her brother's interests so at heart that she ventured, without sufficient tact, to approach him on the subject, but was roughly repelled. The old man was irritated when she spoke, and irritated when she was silent; for then her eyes appealed to him in behalf of Anthony. The father held out, believing that by so doing he would break down Anthony's resolution. He did not believe in the power of love, for he had never experienced love. His son had taken a fancy, a perverse fancy for this Urith, as a child might take a fancy for a new toy. When the lad had had time to feel how ill it was to be an exile from his father's house, without money, without authority over serving-men, hampered and clipped in every direction and all sides, he would come to a better sense, laugh at his folly, and return to obedience to his father and to the suit for Julian Crymes and Kilworthy.

His heart overflowed with gall against Urith. The

thought of having a poor daughter-in-law could never have been other than distasteful to him, when he had set his mind on the wealthy Julian ; but there were special reasons which made the acceptance of Urith impossible to him. She was the daughter of the man over whom he had gained a triumph in the eyes of the world, but it was a triumph full of shame and vexation inwardly. It was due to that man that his married life had been one of almost intolerable wretchedness. Not for a moment did he consider himself to blame in the matter ; he cast all the responsibility for his unhappiness on Richard Malvine ; on him he heaped all the hate that flamed out of envy at the personal superiority of the latter, jealousy because he had won the heart of his wife, and held it so firm that he—Anthony Cleverdon—had never been able to disengage it and attach it to himself ; revenge for all the slights and insults he had received from her unsparing, barbed tongue, slights and insults she had known well how to administer, so as to leave rankling wounds which no time would heal. Even now, as he brooded over his quarrel with Anthony, the sneers, the mockery she had launched at him for his meanness, his pride, his ambition, rose up fresh in his memory, charged with new poison, and rankled in him again. But he did not feel anger against his dead wife for that, but against him who had used her as his instrument for torturing him ; and as Richard Malvine was dead, he could but retaliate on his daughter.

Old Cleverdon attributed the worst motives to Urith. Margaret Penrose had married him for his money, and, naturally, Urith Malvine compassed the capture of Anthony, his son, for the same reason ; he did not see how he involved himself in contradiction, in that he charged Urith with her attempt to become the wife of his son for the sake of his wealth, as if it were a deadly crime, whilst he himself acted on no other motive than ambition and money-greed. She had entangled the young fellow in her net, and he would tear this net to pieces and release him. He would break down his son's opposition. He was not one to be defeated in what he took in hand, and no better means could be chosen by him for his purpose than making Anthony feel what poverty and banishment signified. Anthony had hitherto had at command what money he needed, and now to be with empty pockets would speedily bring him to reason. To attempt gentle means with his son never occurred to him; he had been accustomed to command, not to persuade. He became harder, more reserved, and colder than before; and Bessie in vain looked for a gentle light to come into his steely eyes, a quiver to come on his firm-set lips, and a token of yielding to flicker over his inflexible features.

And yet the old man felt the absence of his son, and had little sleep at night thinking of him; but never for one moment did he suppose that he would not in the end triumph over his son's whim, and bring the young man back in submission to his usual place.

Luke had been to Hall to see his uncle, in behalf of, but without the knowledge of, young Anthony.

"Oh! tired of keeping him, are you?" asked the old Squire. "Then turn him out of the parsonage. I shall be the better pleased; so will he be the sooner brought to a right mind."

Nothing was effected by this visit. After it, with bent head, full of thought, Luke took his way to Willsworthy. On entering the house, he found Anthony there, in the hall, with Urith and Uncle Solomon, the latter on the settle smoking, with a table before him on which stood cider. The light from the window was full and strong on the toper's face, showing its blotched complexion. Mr. Gibbs appeared to his best when partially shaded, just as a lady nowadays assumes a gauze veil to soften certain harshnesses in her features.

> I saddled my horse and away I did ride
> Till I came to an ale-house hard by the road-side,
> I called for a glass of ale humming and brown,
> And hard by the fireside I sat myself down,
> Singing tol-de-rol-de-rol, tol-de-rol-dee,
> And I in my pocket had one penny!

Uncle Sol sang in subdued tones till he came to the tol-de-rol! when he drew the pipe from the corner of his mouth and sang aloud, rattling his glass on the table. He was not intoxicated, but in that happy, hilarious mood which was his wont, even out of his cups.

"Oh, uncle! do be silent," pleaded Urith. "Here comes

Mr. Luke, and we want to talk of serious matters, and not of——"

"I in my pocket had one penny!" shouted Uncle Sol, diving into the depths of his pouch and producing the coin in question, which he held out in his open palm; "never got more—never from this confounded place. Squeeze, squeeze, and out comes one penny. Never more. If Anthony can do better with it, let him try. I have done my utmost, toiled and moiled, and at the end of all these years I in my pocket have one penny :—

> I tarried all night, and I parted next day ;
> Thinks I to myself, I'll be jogging away—

but you won't send me off with in my pocket but one penny ? "

"We will not send you off at all, uncle," said Urith. "But here is Master Luke. Let us talk the matter over with seriousness, and without snatches of song."

"I can't help myself, I must sing," said Mr. Gibbs. "You say on, and I will warble to myself. It is your affair rather than mine."

Luke looked at Anthony and Urith, who stood near each other. He folded his hands behind his back, that he might conceal the nervous twitching of his fingers.

"What is it, Anthony?" he asked.

"Luke, we want your help. I know very well that this is early times since the death of Urith's mother; but that cannot be helped. I cannot live on upon you longer. You are poor, and——"

"I grudge you nothing that I have."

"I have a vast appetite. Besides, I like to have money of my own to spend; and I am not like Mr. Solomon Gibbs, who has in his pocket one penny, for I have none."

"I will give you what I can."

"I will not take it, Luke ; what I have and spend shall be mine own. So Urith and I will ask you to make us one, and give me a right to a penny or two."

Luke was confounded ; this was acting with precipitation, indeed. He quite understood that Squire Cleverdon would not receive Urith as a daughter-in-law with open arms, and that he would oppose such an alliance by all means in his power. Like Anthony, he supposed that the old man's violence of language and threats of disinheritance meant nothing. He would cut off his right hand rather than give up his ambitions set upon his son. But in the end he would yield to the inevitable, if inevitable this were. But this haste of Anthony in precipitating the marriage, in disregard to all decency, must incense the old father, and, if anything could do so, drive him to act upon his word.

Luke became, if possible, graver; the lines in his face deepened. He withdrew his hands from behind his back.

"Anthony," said he, "this will not do. You are acting with your usual hot-headedness. You have angered your father, and must seek reconciliation and the abatement of his wrath, before you take such a step as this."

"I said so," threw in Urith.

"My father never will yield so long as he thinks that I may be brought to change my mind. When he finds that I have taken the irrevocable step, then he will buckle under."

"And is it for the son to bid the father do this?" asked Luke, with some warmth. "No, I will be no party to this," he added, firmly, and set his thin lips together.

"I love her, and she loves me; we cannot live apart. God has made us for each other," said Anthony; "my father can't alter that; it is God's will."

Luke did not meet Anthony's glowing eyes, his were resting on the ground. He thought of his own love, and his own desolate heart. For a moment the bitterness therein overflowed; he looked up sharply, to speak sharply, and then his eyes fell on the two young things—Anthony big, sturdy, wondrously handsome, and full of joyous life, and at his side Urith, in her almost masculine and sullen beauty. Yes, they were as though made for each other—the bright, light temper to be conjoined to the dark and sombre one, each qualifying, correcting the exuberance in the other, each in some sort supplementing the deficiencies in the other. The harsh words that were on his lips remained unspoken. On the settle Uncle Sol was murmuring his tune to himself, every now and then breaking forth into a louder gush of song, and then at once suppressing it again.

Perhaps it was God's will that these two should belong to each other; perhaps the old hostility, and wrath, and envy that had embittered the lives of their several parents were to be atoned for by the mutual love of the children. Luke was too true a Christian to believe that the words of hate that had shot like fire-coals from a volcano out of the mouth of Madam Malvine, when dying, could avail aught now. In the better light into which she had passed, as he trusted, in the world of clearer vision and extinguished animosity, of all-enwrapping charity, she must, with inner anguish, repent, and desire to have unsaid those terrible words. The dying utterances of the woman did not weigh with Luke, or, if they had any weight, it was to turn the scale against them. No better comfort to the soul of the dead could be given than the certainty that those words had been reversed and cast aside. Luke passed his hands over his brow, and then said, "I will see your father again, Anthony."

"That will avail nothing ; you have spoken with him already. I tell you he will not alter till he sees that his present conduct does not affect me. What can he say or do after I am married? He may, indeed, cut me off with a shilling ; but he will not do that. He loves me too well. He is too proud of having founded a family to slay his firstborn. Whom could he make his heir but me? You do not suppose he would leave all to you?"

"No," answered Luke. "If he did—as an extreme measure—it would all come to you. I would not keep one penny of it."

"And I in my pocket——"

"Do be quiet, uncle!" pleaded Urith.

"Then what *can* he do? He must come round. He is as certain to come round as is the sun that sets every evening in the west."

"I hope so."

"I am sure of it. I know my father better than do you, Luke. See here. Urith has Mr. Solomon Gibbs as her guardian, and he is quite willing."

"Oh, heartily!—heartily!" shouted Mr. Gibbs. "I'm quite incompetent to guardian any one, especially such a defiant little devil as my niece. She snaps her fingers in my face."

Luke stood biting his thumb.

He was as fully confident as was Anthony that the old

man would not leave Hall away from his son. He might
be angry, and incensed against Anthony; but his pride in
the family position which he had won would never suffer
him to disinherit his son, and leave the estate away from
him—away from the name.

"I cannot—I cannot!" exclaimed Luke, with pain in his
tone, for he felt that it was too great a sacrifice to be required of him that he should pronounce the nuptial blessing over Anthony and Urith. He laboured for breath.
His brow was beaded with sweat. His pale face flushed.

"Anthony! this is unconsidered. You must postpone
all thought of marriage to a later season. Consider that
Urith's mother is but recently dead."

"I know it; but whether now or in three months, or
three years, it makes no matter—I shall love her all the
same, and we belong to each other. But, see you, Luke,
I cannot go on three years—nay, nor three months, and
hardly three weeks—without an occupation, and without
money, and without a position. I am as impatient as you
are for my reconciliation with my father. But we can be
reconciled in one way only—through Urith's wedding-ring.
Through that we will clasp hands. The longer the delay,
the longer the estrangement, and the longer does my father
harbour his delusion. If you will not marry me at once
to Urith——"

"That I will not."

"Then I shall remain here, and work for her as her steward, look after the farm and the estate, and put it straight
for her. Why, this is the time of all the year of the greatest importance to a farmer—the time that my direction is
most necessary. I tell you, Luke, I stay here, either as
her husband or as her steward."

"That cannot be, that must not be," said Luke, with
heat, "and that Urith herself must feel."

Urith did feel it. But Urith's mind was disturbed by
what had taken place. She had no knowledge of the world,
and Anthony's arguments had seemed to her conclusive, so
conclusive as to override her own repugnance to an immediate marriage. She had resolved to give him up altogether, and yet she had yielded; that resolve had gone to
pieces. She had resolved that if she did take him it should
be at some time in the future, but when he pointed out to

her that his only chance of reconciliation with his father
was through marriage, as to abandon her was an impossible
alternative, and that he was absolutely without work, without a position, without means—sponging on his cousin, a
poor curate, then she saw that this, her second resolve,
must go to pieces, like the first.

"Anthony," said Luke ; "you will have to go away for
a year—for some months at the least."

"Whither ?—To whom ?"

"Surely Justice Crymes knows of——"

"How can I accept any help from him when I refuse
his daughter, and when I have blinded his son ?"

"That is true—and your mother had no relatives ?"

"None that I know of but my grandmother, who is with
you."

"Then go to sea."

"I have no taste to be a sailor."

"Be a soldier ?"

"No, Luke, here I can serve Urith—save Willsworthy
from going to destruction. It is not a bad estate, but has
been mismanaged. Here I can be of utility, and here I
can be a help to Urith, and find work that suits me, and
which I understand. It seems plain to me that Willsworthy is crying out for me to come and take it in hand ; and,
unless it be taken in hand at once, a whole year is lost."

"That is true," threw in Solomon Gibbs, whose great
eagerness now was to be disembarrassed of a task that was
irksome to him, and obligations that were a burden. "You
see, I was never reared to the farm, but to the office. I can
draw you a lease, but not a furrow ; make a settlement,
but not a turf-tye. I wash my hands of it all."

"Then, in God's name," said Luke, in grey pallor, and
with quivering features, "if it must be, then so be it.
May be His finger points the way. As you will. I am at
your service—but not for one month. Concede me that."

"From to-day," said Anthony. "So be it. That is
fixed."

CHAPTER XXII.

BANNS.

Sunday morning. A more idyllic and peaceful scene than Peter Tavy Church on Sunday could hardly be found. The grand old granite church with its bold grey tower and rich pinnacles standing among trees, now bursting with leaf; overhead, the soaring moors strown with rock; the river or brook bounding, brawling down between the hills, with a pleasant rush that filled the air with a fresh, never-failing music.

The rooks cawing, pee-whits calling, larks thrilling, wood-pigeons cooing, and the blackbirds piping during the pauses of the church-bells. And within the church, after the service had begun, when the psalm was not sung, as an accompaniment to the parson's prayer came in through the open door, with the sweet spring air and the sunlight, and through the ill-set and cracked wavy-green glass of the windows—that wondrous concert of Nature. As an organist sometimes accompanies the Confession and the Creed and Lord's Prayer, with a subdued change of harmonies on the instrument, so did mighty awakening Nature give its changing burden to this voice of prayer within, without a discord, and never unduly loud.

A quaint old church, with fragments of stained glass in the windows, with old oak-carved benches representing on shields various strange sea-monsters, also rabbits running in and out of their holes, moor-birds fluttering over their young, and along with these symbols of trade, a spit with a goose on it, a flax-beating rack, a sheaf of wheat, and a sickle, and again the instruments of the Lord's Passion, and armorial bearings of ancient families, a queer jumble of subjects sacred and profane, a picture of human life. The screen existed almost intact, richly sculptured and gilt, and painted with the saints and apostles. Above this a great Royal Arms.

The church was full. In the great carved pew, mentioned in a former chapter, were the Crymes family; in another, newly erected, were Squire Cleverdon and his daughter. Urith and her uncle sat in the old bench belonging to the Willsworthy Manor; the family had not had the stray cash at command to replace this with a deal pew, according to the new fashion. Anthony was within the screen, in the rectory seat.

Looking through the screen, he could see his father, with his blue coat—the collar dusted over with powder—his dark eyebrows and sharp features. The old man looked straight before him, and purposely kept his eyes away from the chancel and his son when he stood up during Psalm and Creed.

The Second Lesson was read, and then ensued a pause. Even Anthony's heart gave a leap and flutter then, for he knew what was to follow.

Luke, in distinct tones, but with a voice in which was a slight tremor, announced: "I publish the banns of marriage between Anthony Cleverdon, of this parish, bachelor, and Urith Malvine——"

He was interrupted by a strange noise—something between a cry of pain and the laugh of a madman. Squire Cleverdon, who had risen to his feet on the conclusion of the Lesson, had fallen back in his pew, with livid face and clenched hands.

The curate waited a moment till the commotion was abated; then he proceeded—"Urith Malvine, of this parish, spinster. If any of you know any just cause why these persons may not be joined together in holy matrimony——"

Squire Cleverdon staggered to his feet, and, clasping the back of the pew with both hands, in a harsh voice that rang through the church, cried, "I forbid the banns."

"This is the first time of asking." Luke proceeded, with a voice now firm: "If any objection be raised, I will hear it immediately after Divine Service."

Little attention was given through the rest of public worship to anything save the old father, his son, and to Urith. All eyes wandered from the Cleverdon pew, in which the Squire sat screened, and in which he no more rose, to Anthony in the chancel, and then to Urith, who was deadly pale.

Luke's sermon may have been eloquent and instructive; not a person in the congregation gave heed to it.

11

There was another person present who turned white at the announcement, and that was Julian Crymes; but she speedily recovered herself, and, rising, looked across the church at Urith with eyes that flamed with jealousy and hate. Her hand clenched her gloves, wrapped together in it. Yes, that wild moor-girl had won in the struggle, and she—the rich, the handsome Julian—was worsted. Her heart beat so furiously that she was afraid of leaning against the carved oak sides of the pew lest she should shake them. Her eye encountered that of her half-brother, twinkling with malice, and the sight gave back her self-possession; she would not let Fox see, and triumph over her confusion.

The congregation waited with impatience for the conclusion of the service, and then, after defiling into the churchyard, did not disperse; they tarried to hear the result of the objection raised to the publication.

Urith hastened away with her uncle, but she had difficulty in persuading him to go with her. He had so many friends in the churchyard, there was such a topic for discussion ready; but her will prevailed over his, and after a forlorn look back at his friends, and a shrug of the shoulders, he left with her.

But Anthony remained with head erect; he knew that no objection his father could make would avail anything. He nodded his head to acquaintances, and held out his hand to friends with his wonted confidence; but all showed a slight hesitation about receiving his advances, a hesitation that was so obvious that it angered him. He was at variance with his father, and the father held the purse-strings. All knew that, and none liked to be too friendly with the young man fallen out of his fortune, and out of place.

Fox alone was really friendly. He pushed forward, and seized and shook Anthony's hand, and congratulated him. The young man was pleased.

"Bygones are bygones," said Fox, whose eye was covered with a patch, but no longer bandaged. "My sight is not destroyed, I shall receive it again, the doctor says. As for that affair on the moor, at the Drift—you know me better than to suppose I meant you harm."

"Certainly I do," answered Anthony with warmth. "Just as you knew that when I struck you with the glove,

I had not the smallest desire to hurt you. It was—well, what you like to call it—a passage of arms or a frolic. It is over."

"It is over, and all forgotten," said Fox. "You will not be deterred by your father's refusal to give consent to this marriage?"

"Certainly I will not," answered Anthony. "He will come round in time. It is but a question of time."

There was no vestry. Old Cleverdon waited in the church till Luke had taken off his surplice, and then went up to him in the chancel.

"What is the meaning of this?" he asked, rudely. "How dare you—who have eaten of my bread, and whose back I clothed, take the part of Anthony against me?"

Luke replied gravely, "I have done my office; whoever asks me to read his banns, or to marry him, I am bound to execute my office."

"I will send to the rector, and have you turned out of the cure."

"You may do so, if you please."

Luke maintained his calm exterior. The old man was trembling with anger.

"If you have objections to the marriage, state them," said Luke.

"Objections! Of course I have. The marriage shall not take place. I forbid it."

"On what grounds?"

"Grounds!—I do not choose that it shall take place; let that suffice."

"That, however, will not suffice for me. I am bound to repeat the banns, and to marry the pair, if they desire it, unless you can show me reasons—legitimate reasons—to make me refuse. Anthony is of age."

"He *shall* not marry that hussy. I will disinherit him if he does. Is not that enough? I will not be defied and disputed with. I have grounds which I do not choose to proclaim to the parish."

"Grounds I know you have," answered Luke gravely; "but not one that will hold. Why not give your consent? Urith is not penniless. Willsworthy will prove a good addition to Hall. Your son loves her, and she loves him."

"I will not have it. He shall not marry her!" again broke from the angry man. "He does it to defy me."

"There you are in error. It is you who have forced him into a position of estrangement, and apparent rebellion, because you will not suffer him to obey his own heart. He seeks his happiness in a way different from what you had mapped out; but it is *his* happiness, and he is better able to judge what conduces thereto than are you."

"I do know better than he. Does it lead to happiness to live separated from me—for I will never see him if he marries that hussy? Will it be to his happiness to see Hall pass away into other hands? Never, so help me God! shall he bring her over my threshold—certainly never as mistress. Answer me that."

The blood mounted to Luke's cheeks, and burnt there in two angry spots.

"Master Cleverdon," he said, and his voice assumed the authority of a priest, "your own wrongdoing is turning against you and yours. You did Urith's father a wrong, and you hate him and his daughter because you know that you were guilty towards him. You took from him the woman he loved, and who loved him, and sought to build your domestic happiness on broken hearts. You failed: you know by bitter experience how great was your failure; and, instead of being humbled thereby, and reproaching yourself, you become rancorous against his innocent child."

"You—you, say this! You beggar, whom I raised from the dunghill, fed, and clothed?"

"I say it," answered Luke, with calmness, but with the flame still in his cheek, "only because I am grateful to you for what you did me, and I would bring you to the most blessed, peace-giving, and hopeful state that exists—a state to which we must all come, sooner or later—some soon, some late, if ever we are to pass into the world of Light—a knowledge of self. Do not think that I reproach you for any other reason. You know that I speak the truth, but you will not admit it—bow your head and beat your breast, and submit to the will of God."

The Squire folded his arms and glared from under his heavy eyebrows at the audacious young man who presumed to hold up to him a mirror.

"You will not refrain from reading these banns?"

"Not without just cause."

"And you will defy me—and marry them?"

"Yes."

The old man paused. He was trembling with rage and disappointment. He considered for a while. His face became paler—a dusky grey—and the lines between his nostrils and the corners of his mouth hardened and deepened. Forgetting that he was still in the church, he put his hat on his head; then he turned to walk away.

"I have shown all—all here, that I am against this; I have proclaimed it to the parish. I will not be defied with impunity. Take care you, Luke! I will leave no stone unturned to displace you. And as for Anthony, as he has made his bed so shall he lie—in his pigstye. Never—I call God to my witness—never in Hall."

As he passed through the richly-sculptured and gilt and painted screen, an old woman stepped forward and intercepted him on his way to the church door.

He put out his hand impatiently, to wave her away, without regarding her, and would have thrust past. But she would not be thus put aside.

"Ah, ha! Master Cleverdon!" she exclaimed, in harsh tones. "Look at me. Do you not know me—me, your wife's mother. Me, whom you threatened with the stick should I venture through your doors to see my daughter?"

Old Cleverdon looked at her with a scowl. "Of course I know you—you old beldame Penwarne."

"There is a righteous God in heaven!" cried the old woman, with vehemence—extending her arms to bar his passage. "Now will he recompense to you all the heartache and misery you brought on my child—aye, and through your own child too, That is well! That is well!"

"Stand aside!"

"I will not make a way for you to go," continued the old woman. "If you venture to go away until I have spoken, I will run after you and shriek it forth in the churchyard where all may hear. Will you stay now?"

He made no further attempt to force his way past her.

"You thought that with your money you could buy everything—even my child's heart; and when you found you could not, then you took her poor heart, and trampled on it; you spurned it; and you trod it again and again under your cursed foot till all the blood was crushed out of it." Her eyes glowed, there was the madness of long-retained and fostered hate in her heart. "You made a wreck of her life, and now your own child spurns you, and tramples on all your fatherly love, laughs at your ambition, mocks all your schemes, and flings back your love in your face as something too tainted, too base, to be worth a groat. Ah, ha! I have prayed to see this day. I see it, and am glad. Now go."

She stepped on one side, and the Squire walked down the church. In the porch he found Bessie, or rather Bessie found him, for he did not observe her. She put her hand on his arm, and looked earnestly, supplicatingly into his eyes. He shook off her hand, and walked on.

Half the congregation—nearly all the men, and a good many of the women, were in the churchyard in groups, talking. Fox was with Anthony, but as soon as the Squire appeared, he fell from him and drew back near one of the trees of the church avenue, and fixed his keen observant eye on the old man. But every other eye was on him as well. Cleverdon came slowly, and with that mixture of pomposity and dignity which was usual with him, but which was this day exaggerated, down the avenue, he nodded and saluted with his hat the acquaintances whom he observed, but he said no word of greeting to any one. Presently he came opposite his son, then he stayed his foot, looked at him, and their eyes met. Not a muscle was relaxed in his face, his eye was cold and stony. Then he turned his head away, and walked on at the same leisurely pace.

The blood boiled up in Anthony's arteries. A film passed over his sight and obscured it, then he turned and went down another path, and abruptly left the graveyard.

CHAPTER XXIII.

The marriage had taken place; the banns were no further opposed. Old Cleverdon, indeed, sought a lawyer's advice; but found he could do nothing to prevent it. Anthony was of age, and his own master. The only control over him he could exercise was through the strings of the purse. The threads of filial love and obedience must have been slender, they had snapped so lightly. But the Squire had never regarded them much, he had considered the others tough to resist any strain—strong to hold—in the wildest mood.

He was not only incensed because Anthony defied him, but because the defiance had been open and successful. He had proclaimed his disapproval of the match by forbidding the banns before the entire parish; consequently, his defeat was public.

Urith had been carried, as by a whirlwind, out of one position into another, without having had time to consider how great the change must necessarily be. She had, in her girlhood, hardly thought of marriage. Following her own will, independent, she had not pictured to herself that condition as invested with any charm which must bring upon her some sort of vassalage—a state in which her will must be subordinate to that of another.

The surroundings were the same: she had spent all her days since infancy in that quaint old thatched manor-house; looked out on the world through those windows; seen what of the world came there flow in through the same doors; had sat at the same table, on the same chairs; heard the tick-tick of the same clock; listened to the same voices—of Uncle Sol and the old family maid. The externals were the same; but her whole inner life had assumed a new purpose and direction.

She could think, at first, of nothing save her happiness. That rough home was suddenly invested with beauty and fragrance, as though in a night jessamine and rose had sprung up around it, covered its walls, and were breathing their fragrance through the windows.

The course of her life had not been altered, broken by a leap and fall, but had expanded, because fuller, and at the same time deeper.

Now and then there came a qualm over her conscience at the thought of her mother. She had defied her last wishes, and her marriage had followed on the burial with indecent haste, but in the dazzle of sunshine in which she walked the motes that danced before her served but to intensify the brilliance of the light.

Summer was advancing. The raw winds of early spring were over, and the east wind when it came down off the moor was no longer edged as a razor, but sheathed in velvet. The world was blooming along with her heart, not with a lone flower here and there, but with exuberance of life and beauty.

Her mother had kept but a single domestic servant, a woman who had been with her for many years, and this woman remained on. A charwoman came for the day, not regularly, but as frequently as she could.

The circumstances of the Malvines had been so bad that they could not afford a large household. Mistress Malvine had helped as much as she was able, and Urith, now that she was left mistress, and had introduced another inmate into the house, was called on to consider whether she would help in the domestic work, or keep another servant. She wisely resolved to lend a hand herself, and defer the enlargement of the household till the farm paid better than it did at present. That it would be doubled in value under prudent management, neither she nor Anthony doubted.

She believed his assurances, and his assurances were well-grounded. To make it possible to double its value, however, one thing was wanted, which was not available— capital, to buy sheep and cattle.

Anthony attacked the task with great energy. He knew exactly what was wanted, and he had great physical strength, which he did not spare.

Some of the walls of moonstone—uncemented, unbound together by mortar, piled one on another, and maintaining their place by their own weight—had fallen, and presented gaps through which the moor-ponies and cattle invaded the fields, and their own beasts escaped.

Anthony set to work to rebuild these places. The stones were there, but prostrate, and, through long neglect, overgrown with moss, and embedded in the soil. Urith brought out her knitting and sat on a stone by him, as he worked, in the sun and sweet air. Never had Urith been so happy—never Anthony so joyous. Never before had Urith cared about the preparation of a meal, and never before had Anthony so enjoyed his food. They were like children—careless of the morrow, laughing, and in cloudless merriment. The old servant, who had grumbled and shaken her head over the precipitate marriage of Urith, was carried away by the joyousness of the young couple, unbent, smiled, and forgave the indiscretion.

They received visitors—not many, but some. Urith and her mother had had few acquaintances, and these came to wish the young couple happiness. Those of old Cleverdon kept aloof, or came hesitatingly: they were unwilling to break with the rich father for the sake of the son out of favour. Luke made his formal call. He came seldom ; he had not sufficiently conquered his own heart to be able to look on upon the happiness of his cousin and Urith without a pang. When, a month after the wedding, he met Anthony one day, the latter flew out somewhat hotly in complaint of the neglect with which he had been treated.

"I suppose you also, Cousin Luke, are hedging, and trying to make friends with my father by showing me the cold shoulder."

"You say this!" exclaimed Luke, in pained surprise.

"You have rarely been to see me since my marriage. I hardly know what is going on in the world outside our boundary-walls. But it does not matter—I have a world of work, and of content within."

Luke made no reply.

"There is Bessie, too—I thought better of her—she has not been over to us. I suppose she knows on which side her bread is buttered."

"There you wrong her," answered Luke, hotly. "You little have understood and valued Bessie's generous, unselfish, loving heart, if you can say such a word as that of her."

"Then why has she not been near me?"

"Because she has been forbidden by your father. You know, if you have any grace in you, Anthony, that this prohibition troubles her, and costs her more tears and heartaches than you."

"She should disobey in this matter. I see neither reason nor religion in blind obedience to irrational commands."

"She may serve your interests better by submission. You may be well assured that your welfare is at her heart; and that she seeks in every way to bend your father's stubborn will, and bring him to a reconciliation with you."

"By the Lord, Luke!" exclaimed Anthony, "I wish you would take Bessie yourself. She would make an admirable parson's wife."

Luke paused a moment before he replied, then he answered, in a constrained voice, coldly: "Anthony, in such matters I follow my own impulse, and not the directions of others. You speak thinking only of yourself, and your wish to be able once more to see your sister makes you suggest what might be distasteful to her and unsuitable to me."

"There, there, it was a joke," said Anthony. "Excuse me if I be a little fretted by separation from Bessie. She would be of the greatest possible assistance to Urith, and Urith has no one——"

"There is still one course open to you, which may lead to reconciliation," said Luke.

"And that——?"

"Is to go to Hall and see your father. Try what effect that has on him. It cannot make matters worse, and it may make them better."

"Oh, repeat the story of the Prodigal Son! But I am not a prodigal. I feel no repentance. I cannot say, 'Father, I have sinned against heaven and against thee—make me as one of thy hired servants.' I cannot say what I do not feel. It is he who has transgressed against me."

"And you expect him to come to you, beating his breast; and then you will kill the fatted calf and embrace and forgive him?"

Anthony laughed, with a heightened colour. "Not so,

exactly; but—it will all come right in the end. He can't hold out, and in the end must take me back into favour. To whom else could he leave Hall?"

One market day Anthony and Urith were in Tavistock. Every one was there that he knew; market was attended by all the gentry, the farmers, and tradespeople of the country side; by all who had goods to sell or wanted to buy, and by such as wanted to, or were able to do, neither one the other, but who could exchange news and eat and drink at the ordinary, and perhaps thereat get drunk.

Urith rode to market on pillion behind Anthony, holding to the leather belt about his waist. The day was bright, and as they rode, he turned his head over his shoulder and spoke to her, and she answered him. They were as children full of mirth, only one little cloud on the horizon of each—on that of Anthony the lack of warmth with which his old acquaintance greeted him, a matter that vexed him more than did the estrangement from his father; on that of Urith, the consciousness that she had disobeyed her mother's last wishes; but in the great splendor of their present happiness these little clouds were disregarded.

In Urith's bosom was a rose—the first rose of summer—that Anthony had picked, and he had himself fastened in with a pin to her bodice, and she had kissed his head as he was engaged thereon.

The day was not that of ordinary market; it was the Whitsun fair as well; and, as Anthony approached Tavistock, numbers of holiday makers were overtaken, or overtook him, on his way to the town. The church bells were ringing, for there was Divine Service on such festival days, and this was usually attended by all the women who came to fair, whilst their husbands saw to the putting away of their horses, saving only such as had wares for sale, and these occupied themselves during worship with their stalls, if they had them; if not, with spreading their goods on the ground in such advantageous manner as best to attract purchasers.

"You will come to me to the church porch, Tony!" said Urith, as she dismounted. "In the crowd we may miss each other, and I shall like to go on your arm."

So it was agreed, and Urith entered the church. This, a fine four-aisled building, was in ancient times, as it is now, the parish church; it stood in the shadow of the mighty Minster of the Abbey, dwarfed by it, a stately pile, second only in size in the county to the Cathedral Church of Exeter. Ruins of it remained at the time of this tale, tall pillars and arches, and the main road from Plymouth had, out of wilful wickedness, been run, in the days of the commonwealth, up what had been the nave, and the east end torn down, so that market could be held in the desecrated House of God, under the partial shelter of the vaulted aisles. All is now gone, quarried away to supply every man with stone who desired to rebuild his house; most of it removed for the construction of the stately mansion of the Earls of Bedford, who were possessed of the Abbey property.*

"What—you here! So we see you again?" exclaimed Fox, as Anthony dismounted in the inn-yard. Fox Crymes held forth his hand, and it was warmly grasped by Anthony, who at once looked at his eye. Crymes had discontinued the bandage, but all did not seem right with the orb. "I can see with it," said the latter, observing the look of Anthony, "but with a cloud; that, I fear, will ever hang there."

"You know that I would pluck out one of my own eyes and give it you," said Anthony, with sincerity and emotion. "I shall never forget that unhappy blow."

"Nor I," answered Crymes, dryly.

"Is your sister here?" asked Anthony.

"Yes—in the church. By the way, Tony, how is it that we never see you at the Hare and Hounds? Does not the apron-string extend so far? Or are your legs so clogged with the honey in the pot into which you are dipping for you to be able to crawl so far?"

"Oh, you will see me there some day; but now I am too hard-worked. All Sol Gibbs's muddles to mend, you understand, and neglects to be made up for. I work like a slave?"

"How about your father? Any nearer a reconciliation?" There was a leer in Fox's eye as he asked this.

Anthony shrugged his shoulders.

"I must be off," said he.

"Where to?"

---

* Now the Bedford Inn.

"To the porch. I promised Urith to meet her there."

"Oh! she is pulling at the apron-string. Let me not detain you."

Anthony walked away. He was annoyed. It was absurd, preposterous of Fox to speak to him as if he were in subjection to his wife. The words of Fox left an uneasy feeling in his breast, as if it had been touched by a nettle, a tingle, a sting, nothing to signify—but a perceptible discomfort.

He reached the church-porch as Urith and Julian were leaving the church, and he arrived at a critical moment.

That morning before leaving Willsworthy, Urith had taken her gloves to draw them on, when she found them stuck together with some adhesive matter. On pulling them over she found that the palms and fingers were covered with pitch. It then occurred to her that she had laid her hands on some rails that been recently blackened with pitch to preserve them from decay, by her husband and that it was not dry as she had supposed. The gloves were spoiled—she could not wear them. She was not possessed of another pair, and could not ride to Tavistock with hands uncovered.

Her eyes fell on the pair that had belonged to Julian, and which had been cast at her in defiance. After hesitating for a moment, she drew these on, and resolved to purchase herself fresh gloves in the fair.

On reaching church, she drew off her gloves, and laid them across the rail of the pew.

Julian Crymes was near, in the Kilworthy pew—that belonging to the Glanvilles, as did the pew in Peter Tavy Church also, attached to another house owned by the family in that parish.

Urith did not give her gloves a thought till she saw Julian's eyes fixed on them, and caught a dark glance from her.

Then she coloured, conscious of the mistake she had made, but recovered herself immediately. She had won in the match—a fair one, and had carried off the stakes. A sense of elation came upon her, she held up her head, and returned Julian's look with one of haughty triumph. She saw Julian's colour darken, and her lips tremble; a passage of arms took place in the church, the weapons being but glances of sharp eyes.

What was played and sung neither considered, each was engaged on her own thoughts. Elated Urith was—happiness fills the heart with pride. She—she whom no one hitherto had regarded, had wrested away the great prize against tremendous odds—Julian's beauty, family position, wealth, and the weight of his own father's advocacy. For her sake he had thrown away everything that others esteemed. She had cause to be proud—reason to feel her heart swell with the sense of victory: and who that has won a victory does not desire a public triumph?

No sooner was service over, than Urith, with a little ostentation, drew on the gloves, then took the rose Anthony had pinned to her stomacher, and looking fixedly at Julian, loosened it, pressed it to her lips, and replaced it. Her rival read in the act the very thoughts of her heart. That rose which had been given her was the pledge of Anthony's love.

Julian panted with anger. It was well for her that none was in the pew by her to notice her emotion. At the last Amen she flung open the door, and stepped out into the aisle, at the same moment as Urith, and both made their way to the porch, side by side, without a look at each other. They passed through the doorway together, and saw Anthony standing there.

Instantly—the whole thing was done so quickly as to escape Anthony's notice—Julian turned with flashing eye on Urith, plucked the rose from her bosom, pressed it to her own lips, then threw it on the ground and crushed it under her foot.

There was no time—that was no place for retaliation. Urith's blood rushed to her heart; then she caught her husband's arm, and with him walked away.

All that day a sense of alarm and unrest troubled her. Julian had renewed her defiance; had threatened both her and Anthony. Would this threat be as vain as her former defiance? Urith swallowed her fears, scorned to entertain them—but the sting remained.

In the evening, when about to start on her return, when his horse was ready—"You must wait for me a moment, Tony," she said, and hurried back to the porch.

The rose, trampled out of shape, trodden on by many feet, lay there, soiled and petalless.

If Julian were to snatch him away, were to cast him down under foot and crush him—what would she do? Would she wear him again? Would she stoop to him?

She stood in the grey, cool porch, looking at the battered flower. Then she bent, picked up the rose, and hid it in her bosom.

CHAPTER XXIV.

KILWORTHY.

Anthony helped Urith to the saddle, saying,

"I am not coming home just now. You must ride back alone."

"But why not?" Urith asked, in surprise, and a little disappointment.

"Must I account to you for all my acts?" said Anthony, somewhat testily.

"Not at all," answered Urith; "but surely there is no objection to my asking so innocent a question as that. If, however, it gives you displeasure, I will abide without an answer."

"Oh!" said Anthony, the cloud passing from his face, "I have no reason not to answer. I am going with Fox. He has asked me to return with him to Kilworthy; and as I have seen no one for a couple—nay, for three months, and have well-nigh lost the use of my tongue, I have accepted."

"I do not like Fox. I do not like you to be with him."

"Am I to consult you as to whom I make my friends? He is the only one who has come forward with frankness, and has braved my father's displeasure by showing me a countenance of old friendliness."

"I do not like Fox—I mistrust him."

"I do not," said Anthony, bluntly. "I am not going to take my opinions from you, Urith."

"I do not suppose you will," retorted she, with a little heat; "but do not forget what he did to you at the Drift. That was a false and cowardly act."

"Oh!" laughed Anthony, somewhat contemptuously; "you maidens do not understand the sort of jokes we men play on each other. He meant no harm, and things went worse than he intended. None can have been more vexed at the turn they took than himself. He told me so."

"What! That a horse should go mad when burning touchwood is set in his ear?"

"He did not purpose to put it into his ear. The horse tossed his head, and Fox's hand slipped."

"And his hand slipped when your fingers were cut?"

"No, not his hand, but his knife; it was in his sleeve. You would not have had it slip upwards?"

Urith was silent; she was angered, vexed—angered and vexed at Anthony's easy good-nature. Any excuse satisfied him. So with regard to his father's displeasure; it did not concern him greatly—cost him not an hour's wakefulness. All would come right in the end, he said, and satisfied himself with sanguine hope. His was a buoyant nature, the opposite to her own, which was gloomy and mistrustful. She raised no further objection to Anthony leaving her to return home alone. He was in a touchy mood, and, for the first time since their marriage, answered her testily.

But she made allowance for him. He had been cut off from his friends, he had been forced out of his wonted course of life. He had been pinched for money, obliged to work hard. Was it not reasonable that on a fair-day and holiday he should wish to be with his old companions and make merry, and have a glass of ale or a bottle of sack? Uncle Sol could not or would not accompany her home; he also had friends to detain him, and purposed to pass the evening in an alehouse singing and making merry.

Urith's knowledge of men, their ways, and their fancies, was limited to the study of her uncle; and though she could not believe that her Anthony was a sot and witless, yet she supposed that he partook of the same taste for society and for the bottle, which she regarded as much a characteristic of men as a rough chin and a masculine voice.

Anthony, with unconcern, was on his way to Kilworthy. This ancient mansion stood high, with its back to the north wind; before it the hills fell away in noble park-land studded with oak and beech over a century old—trees that had been planted by Judge Glanville in the reign of Elizabeth—and beyond the valley of the Tavy rose the tumbled, desolate ridges of Dartmoor, of a scabious blue, or wan as ashes.

The side of the hill was hewn away near the house into a series of terraces, one planted with yews, the others rich with flowers. The house itself had that stately beauty that belongs to Elizabethan mansions.

When Anthony arrived along with Fox, he was not a little surprised to see a large company assembled. Many of the young people and their parents of the best families around were there, sauntering in the gardens, or playing bowls on the green.

He was surprised, for Fox had not prepared him to meet company, but he was pleased, for he had been cut off from society for some months, had hardly seen old friends, and now he was delighted to be among them, and—his father being absent—on the old familiar terms. The depression of his spirits gave way at once, and he was filled with cheerfulness and fun ; he played bowls, and when the dew fell, and it was deemed advisable for all to retire from the garden, he was most ready of all for a dance.

Julian was also in high spirits ; she was looking remarkably pretty in a light summer dress. She met Anthony with frankness, and he engaged her for the first dance.

The beauty of the place, the pleasant society, the profusion of good food and wines, united to give Anthony satisfaction. He appreciated all this so much the more, as he had been deprived of these things for some time. It was true that he had enjoyed the company of Urith, but then Urith's circle of associates was almost nothing ; she did not know those people that he knew, was not interested about matters that woke in him curiosity. She could talk only of Willsworthy, and Willsworthy as a subject of conversation was easily exhausted. There was a freedom in the society of those he now met, a want of constraint that delighted him. When one topic ran dry another was started. With Urith conversation flagged, because there was no variety in the subjects of conversation.

Then again the beauty and richness of the place gratified his eye after the bleakness of Willsworthy. There, high on the moor side, only sycamores would grow—here were trees of royal appearance, huge-trunked, with broad expanding branches, the aristocracy of trees as only seen in

English parks, where they are given scope to expand from infancy. At home, moreover, the general narrowness of means and lack of management had not made of the table a place of enjoyment. A meal was necessary, something to be scrambled through and got over. No effort was made by Mrs. Malvine in earlier days to make it a gratification for the palate, and it did not occur to Urith when she was married and mistress of the household that things might in this respect be improved. Anthony was no epicure, but young men as well as old like to have palatable dishes set before them, and to have not only their wives well-dressed and tricked out, but also their dishes. Here also Urith failed. She disregarded personal adornment. Handsome though she was, she would have looked far handsomer had she cared to set off her charms with tasteful dress. She despised all solicitude about dress, and it was a little disappointment to Anthony that she took so little pains to do justice to herself in this respect. Now that he was in the midst of pretty girls, charmingly set off by their light gowns and bright ribbons, he felt as if he had stepped out of association with moths into that of butterflies—out of a vegetable, into a flower-garden.

Again, since his marriage—indeed, ever since he had left Hall, he had felt the irksomeness of being without money, he had discovered the value of coin, and had learned that it could not be thrown away. He had nothing of his own, what coins he had in his pocket came to him from his wife.

Now he was in a house where money seemed to be disregarded. He need not drink sour cider, but take his choice of wines. He was not served at table by one old maid-of-all-work, but by liveried footmen, in the blue and yellow Glanville colours. The table was furnished with abundance of plate, engraved with the Glanville stags or the Crymes martlet. At Willsworthy he had used bone-handled knives and forks, and had eaten off pewter.

He danced with Julian once more. She was bright, sparkling with merriment, full of lively sally, and she looked marvellously pretty. Anthony wondered at himself for not having observed it before, or at not having sufficiently appreciated it.

His sister arrived, somewhat late, and Anthony at once went to her, with both hands extended.

"Is Urith here ? " she asked.

" No."

" Why not ? "

" She was not invited."

"Then why are you here ? "

" For this good reason, that I was invited."

" But, Tony," said Bessie, " you ought not to have accepted unless she was asked as well."

"Nonsense ! Bet," exclaimed Anthony, fretfully. "I am not tied to her apron-strings. We have not met for months, and your first address to me is—a rebuke."

He walked away, annoyed, and rejoined Julian.

What! was he to be debarred visiting his friends—spending a pleasant social evening with them—because he was asked without his wife !

"I say, Tony," said Fox, into his ear, " what do you think of Kilworthy now ? You have thrown it away for the sake of a pair of sulky eyes—aye, and Hall, too ? Well I have always heard say that love was madness ; but I never believed it till I heard what you had done."

Anthony's pleasure was spoiled. The contrast between Kilworthy and Willsworthy had been unconsciously drawn in his mind before ; now it was fixed and brought into prominence, and he saw and realised in a moment the tremendous sacrifice he had made. From this minute he looked on all around him with other eyes. He saw what might have been his position, his wealth—how he would have been esteemed and envied had he followed the course mapped out for him by his father—had he taken Julian instead of Urith.

He looked again at Julian—his eyes insensibly followed her—and again he marvelled that hitherto there had been a veil over them, so that he had not appreciated her beauty. He could not withdraw his eyes : they pursued her whereever she went.

All at once she turned, with the consciousness that he was looking at her. Their eyes met, and he coloured to the temples. He blushed at his thoughts, for he was asking himself whether life, with such comfortable surroundings, would not have been more than bearable—even delightful—at her side.

In a moment he had recovered himself ; but not his lightheartedness—that was gone. He asked for his horse, and then remembered that he had none. Urith had ridden home on his horse, therefore he must walk.

CHAPTER XXV.

GATHERING CLOUDS.

Next day Anthony's brow was clouded, and his manner had lost its usual cheerfulness. He was angry with himself for having been to Kilworthy. Bessie was right, he acknowledged it now—a slight had been put on his wife by his being invited without her. He ought to have seen this before. He ought to have refused the invitation. Then he remembered that he had been told nothing about a party at the house, so his anger was turned upon Fox, who had entrapped him into a false position.

But this was not all. He was ashamed at himself for having for a moment reconsidered his conduct in taking Urith instead of Julian. In vain did he reason with himself that he had done something heroic in resigning such enormous advantages for the sake of a girl; whether he liked it or not, the odious thought lurked in a corner of his heart and would not be expelled—Was Urith worth the sacrifice?

There was much to humiliate him in his present state. He who had been wont to spend his money freely, had now to reckon his coppers and calculate whether he could afford the small outlay that slight pleasures entailed. And then —these coppers were not his, but his wife's. He was living on her bounty, indebted to her for every glass of ale he drank. Of his own, he had nothing. His confidence that his father's obstinacy would give way, and that he would be taken into favour again, was shaken. He began to fear that so long as his father lived he would remain in disfavour. That, on his father's decease, he would inherit Hall, he did not doubt for a moment. There was no one else to whom the old man could bequeath the estate. Bessie was a girl, and Luke a parson—disqualifications absolute.

Most heartily did he wish that the misunderstanding with

his father were at an end. It was a degradation for him—
for him, the heir of the Cleverdons—to be sponging on his
wife. The situation was intolerable. But how was it to be
altered? He could not force his father to reconciliation.
His pride forbade his going to him and acting the prodigal
son. His heart grew hot and bitter against the old man
for his unreasonable and persistent hostility, which had
reduced him to a position so pitiable and humiliating.

Then there arose before his mind's eye the beautiful
grounds and noble mansion of Kilworthy, the pleasant
company there—and Julian. He shook his head impatiently, set his teeth, and stamped on the floor, but he
could not rid himself of the thoughts.

"I do not see, 'fore Heaven, why we should not have a
clean table-cover," he said at dinner; "nor why every dish
should be huddled on to the board at once. I am not a
pig, and accustomed to feed as in a stye."

Urith looked at him with surprise, and saw that displeasure was lowering on his brow.

She answered him gently, but he spoke again in the same
peevish, fault-finding tones. He complained that the pewter dishes were hacked with knives, and the mugs bent out
of shape and unpolished. If they must eat as do servants
in a kitchen, let them at least have the utensils in trim
order.

Urith sought in vain to dispel the ill-humour that troubled him; this was her first experience of domestic disagreement. The tears came into her eyes from disappointment, and then his ill-humour proved contagious. She
caught the infection and ceased to speak. This annoyed
him, and he asked her why she said nothing.

"When there are clouds over Lynx Tor there is vapour
over Hare Tor as well," she answered. "If you are in gloom
I am not like to be in sunshine. What ails you?"

"It is too maddening that my father should remain stubborn," he said. "You cannot expect me to be always gay,
with the consciousness that I am an outcast from Hall."

She might have answered sharply, and the lightning
would then have flashed from cloud to cloud, had not, at
that moment, Luke entered the house.

"Come at last!" was Anthony's ungracious salutation.

"I have not been here often, certainly," said Luke, "for

I did not suppose you wanted me ; the parson is desired by those in sorrow and tears, not by those in perfect happiness."

"Oh ! " said Anthony, " it is not as the parson we want you, but as a cousin and comrade."

Urith asked Luke if he would have a share of the meal just concluded. He shook his head ; he had eaten before leaving the rectory. He had taken his meal early, so as to be sure of catching Anthony at home before he went abroad.

As Luke spoke he turned his eyes from his cousin to Urith, and saw by the expression of their faces that some trouble was at their hearts ; but he had the tact not to advert to it, and to wait till they of their own accord revealed the cause.

"Have you been to Hall lately? Have you seen my father ? " asked Anthony, after a pause, with his eyes on the table.

"I have not been there ; your father will not see me. He cannot forgive the hand I had in making you happy."

" Then you have no good news to bring me ? "

" None thence. I have talked to Bessie——"

" So have I. I saw her yesterday at Kilworthy, and she scolded me instead of comforting me."

" Comforting you ! Why, Anthony, I do not suppose for an instant that she thought you needed comfort."

" Should I not, when my father shuts me out of his house—out of what should be mine—the house that will be mine some day ! It is inhuman ! "

" I can quite believe that your father's hardness causes you pain, but no advantage is gained by brooding over it. You cannot alter his mood, and must patiently endure till it changes. Instead of altering his for the better, you may deteriorate your own by fretful repining."

Anthony tossed his head.

" You, too, in the fault-finding mood ! All the world is in league against me."

" Take my advice," said Luke ; " put Hall out of your thoughts and calculations. You may have to wait much longer than you imagined at one time till your father relents ; you know that he is tough in his purpose, and firm in his resolution. He will not yield without a struggle with his pride. So—act as if Hall were no more yours than Kilworthy."

Anthony winced, and looked up hastily, his colour darkened, and he began hastily and vehemently to rap at the table.

"Kilworthy!" Why had Luke mentioned that place by name? was he also mocking him, as Fox had yestereven, for throwing away his chance of so splendid a possession.

Luke did not notice that this reference had touched a vibrating string in his cousin's conscience. He went on, "Do not continue to reckon on what may not be yours. It is possible—though I do not say it is likely—that your father may disinherit you. Face the worst, be prepared for the worst, and then, if things turn out better than you anticipated, well!—you unman yourself by living for, reckoning on, dead men's boots; make yourself shoes out of your own hide, and be content that you have the wherewithal to cover your feet."

"You think it possible that my father may never come round—even on his death-bed?"

"God grant he may," answered Luke, gravely. "But he entertains an old and bitter grudge against your wife's father, and this grudge has passed over to, and invests her. God grant His grace that he may come to a better mind, for if he goes out of this life with this grudge on his heart, he cannot look to find mercy when he stands before the throne of his Judge."

Anthony continued drumming on the table with his fingers.

"My recommendation is," continued Luke, "that you rest your thoughts on what you have, not on what you have not. And you have much to be thankful for. You have a wife whom you love dearly, and who loves you no less devotedly. You are your own master, living on your own estate, and in your own manor house. So—live for that, care for that, cultivate your own soil, and your own family happiness, and let the rest go packing."

"My own house! my own land!" exclaimed Anthony. "These are fine words, but they are false. Willsworthy is not mine, it belongs to Urith."

"Anthony!" cried his wife, "what is mine you know is yours—wholly, freely."

"Well," said Luke, with heat, "and if Hall had been yours when you took Urith, it would have been no longer mine or thine, but ours. So it is with Willsworthy. Love is proud to receive and to give, and it never reckons what it gives as enough, and accepts what it receives as wholly its own."

Anthony shrugged his shoulders, then set his elbows on the table, and put his head in his hands.

"I reckon it is natural that I should grieve over the alienation from my father."

"You are not grieving over it because it is an alienation from your *father*, but from Hall, with the comforts and luxuries to which you were accustomed there."

"Do you not see," exclaimed Anthony, impatiently, "that it is I who should support my wife, and not my wife who should find me in bread and butter? Our proper positions are reversed."

"Not at all. Willsworthy has gone to rack and ruin, and if it be brought back to prosperity, it will be through your energy and hard work."

"Hard work!" echoed Anthony. "I have had more of that since I have been here than ever I had before."

"Well, and why not? You are not afraid of work, are you?"

"Afraid! No. But I was not born to be a day labourer."

"You were born, Anthony, the son of a yeoman family which has worked hard to bring itself up into such a condition that now it passes for a family of gentry. Do not forget that, and do not blush for yourself when you use the muck-fork or the spade, or you are unworthy of your stout-hearted ancestors."

Anthony laughed. The cloud was dispelled. This allusion to the family and its origin touched and pleased him. He had often joked over his father's pretensions. He put forth his hand to his cousin, who clasped it warmly.

"All well, old friend, you are right. If I have to build up a new branch of the Cleverdons, it is well. I am content. Fill the tankard to the prosperity of the Cleverdons of Willsworthy—and to the dogs with Hall!"

Anthony put his arm round Urith's waist. The clouds had cleared, and, as they rolled off his brow that of Urith brightened also. Luke rose to depart. He would not suffer his cousin to attend him from the door. He went forth alone ; and, when he had passed the gate, he halted, raised his hand, and said, "Peace be to this house !" Yet he said it with doubt in his heart. He had seen a ruffle on the placid water, and that ruffle might forebode a storm.

CHAPTER XXVI.

ON THE TERRACE.

Months had passed. On the 6th of February, 1685, died Charles II., and James, Duke of York, succeeded to the throne. At once, through England, the story was spread that he had been poisoned by the Jesuits to secure the succession for James, and forestall the purpose of the King to declare the legitimacy of his son, the Duke of Monmouth. So great was the suspicion entertained against James, that this slander was very widely believed, and alarm and resentment grew in the hearts of the people. On the very first Sunday after his father's death James went in solemn state to Mass, and at his Coronation refused to receive the Sacrament at the hands of the Archbishop of Canterbury.

When the crown was set on his head it slipped, and nigh fell on the floor ; and this little incident was whispered, then bruited, through England, and was regarded as a token from heaven that he was not the rightful Sovereign. but an usurper.

Then came the punishment of that scoundrel, Titus Oates, richly deserved ; but Oates was a popular favourite, and his chastisement raised him to the pedestal of a Protestant martyr.

It was well known that James aimed at the repeal of the Habeas Corpus Act, and at the toleration—even promotion —of Popery, and the country was in fevered agitation and brooding anger at what was menaced.

Such was the condition of affairs in the spring of 1685.

There had been catching weather, a few days of bright sunshine, and then thunder-showers. Then the sky had

cleared, the wind was well up to the north, and, though
the sun was hot, the air was fresh. It was scented, everywhere except on the moor, with the fragrance of hay.

Julian Crymes was out of doors enjoying the balmy air
and the sloping, golden rays of the evening sun. She had
some embroidery in her hands; but she worked little at it.
Her eyes looked away dreamily at the distant moor, and
specially at a little grey patch of sycamores, that seemed
—so remote were they—against the silvery moor, to be a
cloud-shadow. Behind that grey tuft rose Ger Tor, strewn
with granite boulders; and on one side opened the blue
cleft of the Tavy, where it had sawn for itself a way from the
moor-land into the low country. The dark eyes of the girl
were full to spilling—so full that, had she tried to continue her needlework, she would have been unable to see
how to make her stitches.

Her breath came short and quick, for she was suffering
real pain—that gnawing ache which in its initiation is
mental, but which becomes sensibly physical.

Julian had loved Anthony. She loved him still. When
he had come that evening of the fair to Kilworthy, her
heart had bounded: her head had been giddy with pleasure at seeing him again—above all, at seeing him without
his wife. Towards Urith she felt implacable, corroding
hatred. That girl—with no merit that she could see, only
a gloomy beauty—a beauty as savage as the moors on the
brink of which she lived, and on which Anthony had found
her—that girl had shaken to pieces at a touch her cloud-
castle of happiness, and dissolved it into a rain of salt disappointment.

Anthony was taken from her, taken from her for ever,
and her own hopes laid in the dust. Julian had battled
with her turbulent heart; her conscience had warned her
to forget Anthony, and at times she really felt as if she had
conquered her passion. No sooner, however, did she see
Anthony again, than it woke up in full strength; and
whenever she saw Urith, her jealous rage shook itself and
sharpened its claws.

Her father was away in London, and on the seat beside
her lay a letter she had that day received from him. He
had written full of uneasiness at the political and religious
situation. Recently the Earl of Bath had been down in

the West of England with new charters to towns in Devon and Cornwall, constituting new electoral bodies, or altering the former bodies, and a hurried election had ensued, in which great pressure had been used to obtain the return of the Court party, of Catholics and Tories, by intimidation on the one side and by bribery on the other. Mr. Crymes, however, supported by the authority of the Earl of Bedford, had been returned for Tavistock in the Protestant interest, and he was now in London, sitting in the first Parliament summoned by James II.

Titus Oates, whom the Protestants, or at all events the more ignorant and prejudiced among them, believed in as a faithful witness, had been whipped from Aldgate to Newgate one day, and two days after, again from Newgate to Tyburn, for having revealed the Popish Plot, which was declared to be a fabrication of his own imagination. He and Dangerfield, another of these witnesses, had been pilloried. The King meditated the repeal of the Habeas Corpus and the forcible introduction of the Roman Catholic religion. It was rumoured that there was a rising in Scotland, headed by the Duke of Argyle; there was a great uneasiness in London, and a disturbance of spirits throughout the country. Though the Members of Parliament had been elected in a questionable manner, so as to bring together an undue preponderance of creatures of the Court; yet it had not proved itself as submissive as the King expected. The letter concluded with the words :—" How this will all end, God knows. For myself, I doubt whether there will not be great troubles again even as there were in the times of His Sacred Majesty King Charles I. For mine own part, I would resist even unto blood, rather than see our religion set at naught, and our liberties trampled under foot by Jesuits; and my daily prayer is that the Lord will avert such things from us, and yet with such extravagance and determination do things appear to be pressed forward with this end, that I have not hope myself of a peaceable issue."

Had Mr. Crymes been then beside his daughter, he might have supposed that the sad political outlook had disturbed her mind, and had brought the tears to her eyes and the flush to her cheeks; but she had read his letter with indifference. His gloomy forecasts had hardly affected her at all, for her heart was filled with its own peculiar bitterness.

What prospect of happiness opened before her? She cared for no one; she could care for no one after having given up her heart to Anthony. From childhood she had looked up to him as her allotted husband—she had grown up with a daily-increasing devotion to him. His good looks, his frankness had helped to make of him an idol before whom she bowed down and worshipped. He was swept out of the horizon of her ambition, and it had left that prospect utterly blank and colourless. She had valued her fortune, her home, only as means of enriching Anthony, and giving him a worthy position in the county. Her fortune was now wholly without value to her. She would have been contented to be a beggar with him, if she could have possessed him wholly as her own.

Suddenly she started, and lost her colour; she saw Anthony coming up the drive to the house. He also saw her on the terrace, in her white gown under the yew-trees, and he waved his hat to her. She beckoned to him; she could not help herself. She knew that it would have been right for her to fly up the steps and hide in the walled garden which occupied the slope of the hill above the terraces, but she was powerless to move—to withhold her hand from signing to him to draw near.

He obeyed at once, and came up the steps to the first terrace with a shouted salutation.

How handsome he was! What dark, sparkling eyes! What wavy long hair, that fell over his brow and cheeks as he took off his broad-brimmed hat, so that he was forced to put his hands to his face and brush the thick curly locks back.

Julian did not rise; she sat on her bench as though frozen, and her blood stood still in her arteries. She looked at him with eyes large and trembling between the lashes. Then he came striding towards her, with his hearty salutation, and at once all the blood that had been arrested in her veins, as Jordan when the Ark stood in its course, rushed back in pent-up, burning floods, and so blinded and stunned her that for a moment or two she could neither see nor speak.

After a few moments, during which he stood respectfully

by her, hat in hand, she looked up into his eyes, and asked why he had come.

He was warm with walking, and the drops stood on his brow, and he had a heightened glow in his face. He was handsomer than ever, she exclaimed inwardly, and then thought, "Oh! if he had been mine! been mine! as he ought to have been—as he would have been but for——." Then she checked herself, assumed a coolness she did not feel, and asked, "Has anything else brought you here than the desire to give us honest pleasure at seeing again an old friend?"

"Indeed, Julian," answered Anthony, "I have come on more self-seeking purposes. We are behind with our hay at Willsworthy. The place lies so high, and is so bleak, that we are a fortnight behind you here; and then the weather has played us tricks, so that none has as yet been saved. I want additional help; there are none save our two men and myself. Solomon Gibbs counts naught, and I cannot ask help from Hall, as you well know. I do not desire to ask a favour elsewhere, and so I have come here to see Fox, and ask his help."

"Fox is away—I believe he is at Hall. But I can answer your question, and grant your petition, which I do with a ready heart. How many men do you want? I will send all you desire—I will come myself and help toss the hay— No," she checked herself, as the thought of Urith rose within, "no, I will not go near Willsworthy myself, but I will send the workmen."

"I thank you," answered Anthony. "We do not grow rich shears of hay as you do here; but what does grow is said to be sweet. I hope it may be so, for it is not over-much."

There was a tone of disparagement in reference to Willsworthy that struck Julian.

"I have heard Fox comment on the place," she said, "and he thinks well of it."

"A thing may look well at a distance, that won't bear looking into close at hand," said Anthony.

She looked at him, and his eyes fell. He had not meant more than he had said, but when she thus glanced up with a query in her eyes, he thought that perhaps his words might apply to other things than grass fields and tumble-down farm buildings.

Julian took up the letter from the seat by her, and passed her hand lightly over the seat, as a sign to him to take it.

He did so, without more ado. He was heated and tired with his walk.

Then Julian resumed her embroidery, and bowed her head over it. She waited for him to start some topic of conversation. But he was silent. He who had formerly been full of talk and mirth, had become reserved and grave.

After a long and painful silence, Julian asked, in a low voice, " What is Urith about? "

" I beg your pardon ? " asked Anthony, roused out of a reverie. " Urith—what about Urith ? "

" I asked what she was about."

" I cannot tell. Nothing in particular, I suppose."

The same tone as that in which he had spoken about Willsworthy.

" Your marriage does not seem to have improved your spirits. I miss your olden gaiety."

" I have enough to take that out of me. There is my father's continued ill-humour. What think you of that, Julian? Is there any immediate prospect of his coming to a better mind ? "

" My brother could answer this question better than I, for I have no occasion or opportunity for speaking with your father, whereas Fox is over at Hall twice or thrice in the week."

" What makes him go there ? "

" There you ask me what once more I cannot answer. But let us say he goes in your interest. He is your friend."

" About the only friend I have left," said Anthony, with bitterness.

" Fox is not the man I would choose if I had the selection," said Julian. " I should know him better than most, as he is my brother—that is to say, my half-brother. I thank God—only my half-brother. Take heed to yourself, Anthony, that he does not play you a scurvy trick."

" What can he do ? "

" You are generous and forgiving. Fox is neither. He has not forgiven you that blow with the glove that injured his eye."

" You wrong him, Julian."

" All I can say to you is—do not trust him. I never—
never trust him. If he says one thing he means the con·
trary. Did he tell you that he went to Hall with the end
of persuading your father to forgive you ? "

" He did not even mention to me that he saw my father
often."

" Well," said Julian, drawing a long breath, " whilst we
are together, which is not often now, not as it was, let us
talk of matters more pleasant than the habits and ways of
action of Fox."

" What shall we talk about ? "

" There ! " said Julian, putting her father's letter into his
hand. " Read that. If you cannot find a topic, I must help
you to one."

Anthony read the letter with an elbow on each knee and
his legs wide apart, so that his head was bent low. As he
read, Julian's eyes were on him. Involuntarily a sigh escaped her bosom. If he thought of it at all he attributed
it to sympathy with her father's anxiety ; had he looked
up and seen her face, he would have been undeceived. It
was well for him that he did not.

The letter interested him greatly. Like the bulk of the
young men of the West, he was keenly alive to the political
situation, and was a hot partisan. The gathering together
of the men in taverns led to eager discussion of politics ;
the orderly Government of the Protector, and the extravagance and exactions of the restored Royalty, had aroused
comparison. Under Old Noll the name of England had
been respected abroad, and the English people could not
forget and forgive the humiliation of the Dutch fleet in
the Medway and the burning of Chatham. Those who had
no love for Puritanism were, nevertheless, ardent supporters
of Liberty, and firmly resolved that their country should
not be brought under Roman Catholic despotism. The ill-
treatment of the Waldenses had roused great feeling in
England, collections for them had been made in every
parish church, the Revocation of the Edict of Nantes was
not forgotten, the exiled Protestants filled all England
with the tale of the cruelties and oppression to which they
had been subjected, and had helped to deepen to a dogged
determination in men's hearts the resolve never to suffer the
Roman religion to obtain the mastery again in the land.

Anthony's brow darkened and his lips tightened as he read. When he had done the letter he started to his feet, planted his hat on his head, and exclaimed :

"My God! I wish it would come to blows, and that I could carry a pike."

"Pshaw!" said Julian ; "what excitable creatures you men are concerning matters that move us not a whit. I have forgotten what my father wrote about. Against whom would you trail a pike? With whom come to blows?"

Anthony did not answer, for it was not easy to reply to these questions. He would fight for liberty and religion. But against whom? He dare not breathe even to himself the thought that it would be against his King.

"And, pray, why come to blows?"

"If you had read your father's letter with attention, you would know. For my part, I should hail war, if there were a chance of it, that I might have some occupation for my hands."

"You have the hay," said Julian, ironically.

"I want space to move, air to breathe. I am cramped. I—I do not know what I want," he said, and dashed his hat on the ground again, and threw himself into the seat by Julian.

"How would Urith relish you taking the pike for any cause?"

Anthony did not answer. He was looking sullenly, musingly before him. He had found out what troubled him— what took the brightness out of his life. The circle in which he moved, in which his energies were expended, was too cramped. To make hay! Was that a fitting work to occupy his mind and powers of body? His world—was that to be the little two-hundred-acre estate of Willsworthy?

"You have not been married above two months, and you are already sighing with impatience to be away in a battle-field—anywhere but at home, poor Anthony!" Her face was turned from him that he might not see how her cheeks flamed.

He said nothing. He did not even bid her a good-by ; but he rose, resumed his hat, and walked away, with his head down, absorbed in his thoughts.

CHAPTER XXVII.

MATRIMONIAL PLANS.

Squire Cleverdon did not often visit his sister. She was vastly proud when he did. What she would have liked would have been for him to drive up to her door in a coach and four, the driver cracking his whip on the box; but Squire Cleverdon did not keep a coach. Why should he? He had no womankind to consider in his household. Of the fair and inferior sex there was but Bessie, and Bessie never counted in old Anthony Cleverdon's calculations. Had his wife lived, he probably would have had his coach, like other gentlemen, not to please and accommodate her, but out of ostentation. But as his wife had departed to another world, and Bessie was too inconsiderable a person to be reckoned, he was glad to be able to spare his purse the cost of a coach, which he could hardly have purchased under a hundred pounds. As Magdalen Cleverdon could not see her brother drive up in a coach, she was forced to be satisfied to see him come as he would, on horseback, followed by two serving-men in his livery, and to be content that her neighbours should observe that the Cleverdons maintained so much state as to have men in livery to attend on the head of the house.

She was much surprised one day to see him come on foot without attendants. He was not a man to show his thoughts in his face, which was hard and wooden, but his eyes expressed his feelings when the rest of his face was under control—that is, when he did not screw down the lids and conceal them.

Accordingly Magdalen could not gather from her brother's countenance the purport of his visit, though she scrutinised it curiously.

He seated himself in one of her chairs, near the table, and laid his stick across his knees; Magdalen waited with the deference she usually paid him till he began the conversation; but he also, with unwonted hesitation, deferred his communication to allow her to open the ball.

The silence became irksome to her, and she was the first

to interrupt it, and then with the remark that she was surprised to see him arrive alone, and on foot.

"One does not require to have all the town know I am
here, and know how many minutes I remain," said he rudely,
in reply.

Then again silence fell on both.

After another painful pause, Magdalen began : "Really,
brother, I should like to know for what reason you have
come to do me the honour, and afford me the *pleasure* of your
company. The white witch has a crystal into which he
looks, and in which he reads what he desires to know ; but
you veil your eyes, and I cannot discover, or attempt to
discover, thence what your purport might be in coming
hither."

Old Cleverdon fidgeted in his chair, dropped his stick,
picked it up again, and blurted forth : "I suppose you get
that disobedient son of mine tumbling in here every few
days."

"Indeed, I do not, brother. Do you suppose that I
countenance such rebellious conduct?"

"I did not know. I considered, as he might not show
his face in Hall, that he came here for news about the
place and me."

"I do not deny that I have seen him ; but only rarely.
He never did affect my company greatly, and I cannot say
that he visits me more frequently since his marriage than
he did before."

"I am glad to hear it. How is he getting on in his pigstye."

"I have not been there to see. He and she are content
with it for a while, and make no doubt that in the end you
will forgive them, and be the best of fathers."

"Do they?" exclaimed the Squire, with a harsh laugh
and a flame on his cheek. "Do they think that I have a
head of dough, to be moulded into what shape they list?"
He struck the table with his stick, so as to startle his sister and make her jump in her chair.

"Good heavens, brother ! How excitable you are," said
Magdalen ; "and I dare be bound you do not know that
Mistress Penwarne is taken into the Rectory at Peter Tavy,
as housekeeper to your most dutiful and respectful nephew
Luke—an ancient harridan who, having set her daughter

against you, now does her utmost to make wildfire between your son and you."

" What wildfire burns atwixt us is of his own kindling," said Squire Cleverdon. "And does she reckon on setting herself in my armchair, and ruling in my house, indeed! My son I might forgive had he married any other, but not for having taken Urith."

" One beggarly marriage is enough in the family," said Magdalen. The expression had slipped her tongue without consideration. She saw at once, by the twitching of her brother's muscles, that she had stung and enraged him. She hastened to amend her error by saying, " Yes, you were drawn in by their designing ways. You had not then the knowledge of the world that you now have. Having been entangled by unscrupulous and poor wretches yourself, you would not have your son fall a prey to the like—but he would sow his wild oats, and now must reap his crop."

" Yes," said old Anthony, " he must reap his crop, which will not grow one of oats, but of thistles and nettles. 'Tis a cruel shame that Kilworthy should go from the family."

" It has never been in it."

" That is true—never in actual possession, but so long in prospect as to almost constitute a claim."

" But gone it is. Gone past the possibility of your getting it."

" I am not so confident of that as you seem to be," said Old Cleverdon, snappishly. " In faith, sister Magdalen, you appear wondrous blind. Is there no way of it coming, nevertheless, to be joined to Hall ? "

" None that I can see. If Fox took Bessie to wife, he could not bring Kilworthy with him, for that goes with Julian."

" Exactly. It goes with Julian ; but who will take her ? "

" You have no second son."

" No, I have not."

" Surely you do not dream of making Luke your heir, and marrying him to Julian Crymes ? "

" Luke !—who defied me by marrying Anthony to that hussy ? "

"I thought not, brother, but—as the Lord is my helper
—I see no other way of compassing it."

"It has never lightened on your mind that I might take
a second wife."

"You !"—Magdalen fell back in her chair, and raised
her hands in amazement.   "You, brother Anthony !
You !"

"Even so," he answered, grimly.   "I am not young,
but I am lusty ; I am a man of substance, and I reckon
that Mistress Julian is not so besotted as was my son.
She, I presume, has had a desire like to mine, that the two
estates should be united, so as to make a large domain, and
as she cannot effect this by marrying an unripe fool, she
can gain the same end by taking me, a wise and mellow
man of the world.   The end is the same.   The two properties are united, and Julian Crymes has ever struck me
as having a clear and healthy mind.   So—I doubt not—
she will be as content to have me as that Merry Andrew
and Jack o' the Green, who has thrown himself away at
Willsworthy."

Magdalen's astonishment held her speechless for some
time ; at last, seeing that her brother was offended at the
astonishment she exhibited, she said, "But, brother ! has
she given you any—hopes ? "

"She has not.   I have not approached her on the subject, but I thought that you, as a woman, might sound her.
Yet, I am not without my reasons for believing that my
suit would be accepted—though not immediately.   Fox
Crymes has given me reason to hope."

"Fox !—But what——"

"If you will have patience, Magdalen, and will allow me
to conclude what I was saying, your mind will be more enlightened, and you will cease to express so unbecoming,
such indecorous, so gross incredulity.   You forget my
position and my wealth.   I am not, indeed, a Member of
Parliament, as is my friend Crymes, but I might have been
had my views been more favourable to the Catholic party.
I have seen a good deal of Master Anthony Crymes, my
godson, of late ; he has been to Hall several times in the
week, and then I threw out—in an uncertain way, and as
if in sport—the notion that, as Anthony had proved false,
and had disappointed Julian of her ambition to have the

two estates united, that I would consider about it, and
might persuade myself to accommodate her views by stepping into the position thrown up by my son."

"And what did he say?"

"He did not open his mouth and eyes into a stare unbecoming to the face, and impertinent to me. He accepted
the proposition cordially. He saw nothing strange, preposterous, ridiculous in it. I should like to see," said the
squire, working himself up into a white heat, "I should
like to see anyone, you, sister Magdalen, excepted, who
would dare to find anything strange, preposterous, ridiculous in me, or in any proposition that I make."

"I tender ten thousand excuses," said Magdalen, humbly.
"But, brother, you entirely misunderstand me. If I gaped—"

"You did gape."

"I know I gaped and stared. I admit I opened my eyes
wide, it was with astonishment at your genius, at the clever
and unexpected way in which you overcame a great difficulty, and rallied after a great disappointment."

"Oh! It was that, was it?" asked the Squire, relaxing
some of his severity and cooling.

"On my word as a gentlewoman. I never employed
those words you attribute to me. Indeed I did not. The
only expletives becoming are of a very different quality.
So Fox agreed to the proposal?"

"Most heartily and warmly."

"But, brother, I misdoubt me if Fox has much influence
with his sister. They are ever spitting and clawing at
each other, and it hath appeared to me—and yet I may be
wrong—that whatsoever the one suggests the other rejects;
they make a point of conscience of differing from each other."

"All that," said the squire, "all that have I foreseen, and
I have provided against it. The proposal shall not be
covertly favoured by Fox. He shall, indeed, appear to set
his face against it, but we shall make Bessie our means of
breaking the ice, and drawing us together. I have some
notion of letting Fox become Bessie's suitor—now, when
he is accepted, and has——"

"But—brother!"

"What in the name of the seven stars do you mean by
your buts thrown in whenever I speak? It is indecorous,
it is insulting, Magdalen."

"I meant no harm, brother—all I ask is, has Bessie given her consent?"

"Bessie is not Anthony. What her father chooses, that she is ready to submit to. I have always insisted on her obedience in all things, and without questioning, to my will, and I have no reason to suppose that in this matter she will go against my interests."

"But—brother!"

Master Cleverdon impatiently struck the table. "Did I not tell you, sister Magdalen, that your *buts* were an offence to me? Will you join with Anthony in resistance and rebellion against me—*me*, the head of the house? I have not come here, pray understand, to discuss this matter with you, as though it needed to be considered and determined upon conjointly between us, but to tell you what I have decided upon, and to require you, as you value my regard, and look for any advantages to be gotten from your connection with Hall, to support me, and to exercise all your influence for me, and not against me."

"You cannot suppose for one moment, brother, that I would do anything against you."

"I cannot say. Since Anthony revolted I have lost all confidence in everyone. But I have no time to squander. Understand me. Persuade Bessie, should she show tokens of disobedience—which is catching as the plague—a dislike to submit herself in all things to my wishes, then you may hold up Anthony as a warning to her, and let her understand that as I have dealt by him, so I will deal by her if she resists me. Now you will see what is my intention. When Bessie is married to Anthony Crymes, they will live with me, for Anthony and Julian will be much forward and backward between the two houses, as Bessie is her best of friends; and thus she will come to see much of me and of Hall, and will be the more ready insensibly, so to speak, to slide into my arms, and into the union of the two estates. Not that I suppose at present she has any objection to me, but, as Fox says, she will require some justification before the world for taking the father after having been rejected by the son. If she is often over at Hall, why—all wonder will cease, and it will come about with the smoothness of an oiled wheel."

"I suppose so, brother—but——"

The Squire started up with an oath. "I shall regard you as an opponent," he said, "with your eternal objections. Consider what I have said, act on it, and so alone will you maintain your place in my regard."

Then he left the house, grumbling, and slammed the door behind him, to impress on his sister how ill-pleased he was with her conduct.

Time had not filled the cleft between Anthony and his father; and Fox Crymes had done his best to prevent its being filled or being bridged over; for he now saw a good deal of the old Squire Cleverdon, and he took opportunity to drop a corrosive remark occasionally into the open and rankling wound, so as to inflame and anger it. Now it was a reported speech of Anthony, showing how he calculated on his father's forgiveness; or a statement of what he would do to the house, or with the trees, when his father died and he succeeded to Hall; or else Fox told of some slighting remark on the beggary of everything at Willsworthy, made by a villager, or imagined for the occasion by himself.

The old man, without suspecting it, was being turned about the finger of the cunning young Crymes, who had made up his mind to obtain the hand of Elizabeth and with it Hall. So could he satisfy his own ambition, and best revenge himself on Anthony and Urith.

The wit and malice of Fox acted as a grinding-stone on which the anger of the Squire was being constantly whetted, as if it had not at the first been sharp enough.

The old man could not endure the idea of his property ever falling to the daughter of Richard Malvine—of Malvine blood ever reigning within the walls of his mansion.

He had not yet altered his will, and he could not resolve how to do this. He did not desire to constitute Bessie his heiress. He could not reconcile himself to the thought of Hall passing out of the direct line, of another than a Cleverdon owning the estate where his ancestors had sat for centuries, and which he had made into his own freehold. All the disgust he had felt when Elizabeth was born, and he found himself father of a daughter as his first-born, woke up again, and he could not bring himself to constitute her his heiress. Yet, on the other hand, it was equally, if not more, against his will that it should pass to his revolted son

and the daughter of his mortal enemy. As he was thus
tossing between two odious alternatives, the idea of marrying Julian himself lightened on his mind, and he seized it
with desperate avidity ; yet not without a doubt he refused
to give utterance to, or permit in another. In a vague
manner he hoped that the union of Fox and Bessie might
pave the way to his own marriage with Julian.

CHAPTER XXVIII.

A WIDENING OF THE RIFT.

"Urith," said Anthony, "we are to go together to the
dance at the Cakes ; I have said we would."

"The dance, Anthony ! It cannot be."

"Why not ? Because I particularly desire it ? "

"Nay—not so, assuredly ; but the time is so short since
my mother's death."

"But our marriage makes that as nought. It has turned
the house of mourning into one of merriment—or—it
should have done so. It suffices I intend to go, and I will
take you with me."

"Nay—Anthony, I would not cross you——"

"You do—you object." He spoke with irritation. "Do
you not see, Urith, that this life of seclusion is intolerable
to me ? I have been unaccustomed to the existence which
befits a hermit. I have been wont to attend every merry-
making that took place—to laugh and dance and sing there,
and eat and drink and be happy. I protest that it is to me
as displeasing to be without my amusement as it would be
to a kingfisher to be without his brook, or a peewhit to be
condemned to a cage."

"But cannot you go without me ? " asked Urith, disconcerted.

"No ; it will be noted and remarked on. You are my
wife—you are a bride. You ought to, you must, appear
where others are. Why should you spend all your life in
the loneliness of this—this Willsworthy ? Do you not feel
as cramped by it as must have felt Noah in the Ark ? "

"I do not, Anthony."

"You do not, because you have never been out of the Ark; bred in it, you are accustomed to its confined atmosphere. I am not. I love to meet with and be merry with my fellows, and I cannot go alone. Why, Urith, on the fair day I went to Kilworthy, and there was Bessie. What did she say to me, but—'You should not be here, be at any entertainment in a neighbour's house without Urith?'"

"Did Bessie say that?"

"Yes, she did."

"Then I will go with you to the Cakes, Anthony."

It was customary in former times for the gentlefolks of a neighbourhood to meet at each other's houses, at intervals, for dances and carouses—the young folks for dances, their elders for carouses. On such occasions the burden of entertainment did not fall wholly, or to any serious extent, on the host in whose house the assembly took place. Each guest brought with him or her a contribution to the feast—ducks, geese, capons, eggs, cheese, bottles of wines, pasties, honey, fruit, candles, flowers—very much as at a picnic nowadays, each party invited contributes something. The host actually furnished little more than the use of his house. Even the servants of the guests were expected to assist, and generally attended on their own masters and mistresses, behind whose chairs they stationed themselves.

The Cakes occupied a quaint old barton, named Wringworthy, in a central position for the neighbourhood; and they had an excellent hall for a dance, well appreciated by the young gentlefolks of the neighbourhood.

The evening for the dance arrived. Folk went early to a dance in those days, before the darkness had set in. Many were on the road; none in coaches; all on horseback—the young ladies seated on pads behind their grooms.

Clattering along at a good pace came Fox, riding alongside of Elizabeth Cleverdon. He had gone to Hall to fetch her. She was annoyed : she did not understand the attention, in her simple mind. The idea never entered that he had designs on her hand. She did not wish to feel prejudiced against him ; at the same time she did not like him, and was unable to account to herself for this dislike.

Her father made much of him. Fox was now constantly at Hall, and he made himself companionable to the old man. Bessie with pain contrasted his conduct with that

of her brother, who had never put himself out of the way
to be agreeable to his father—had not courted his society
and sought to be a companion to him. She was grateful to
Fox for his efforts to relieve the old Squire of his desolation by giving him so much of his society.

Fox was her brother's friend, and she had no doubt that
he was at Hall with the purpose of doing his utmost to
further a reconciliation between Anthony and his father.
For this she thanked him in her heart, yet she could not
stifle the dislike that would spring up and assert itself notwithstanding. Nor did she like the look that Fox cast at
her occasionally. He meant no harm, doubtless; he was
but showing her that he was acting as her confederate in
the cause which, as she trusted, both had at heart. Nevertheless, she wished he would not look at her with that cunning, wounding twinkle in his eyes.

Presently Fox and Bessie caught up Anthony riding with
Urith on pillion behind him. Fox greeted them boisterously, and Bessie threw him and Urith a kiss. Anthony
acknowledged Fox's greeting with warmth, but that of his
sister with a little coldness. He was annoyed with her for
her tameness in submitting to her father. There was no
opportunity for more than a word, as Fox urged on his
horse and that of Elizabeth Cleverdon, with his whip, to a
pace with which Anthony was unable to keep up. The old
Willsworthy mare was a clumsy piece of horseflesh, not
comparable in any way with the beasts from Hall and Kilworthy stables. Anthony was aware of this, and somewhat
ashamed.

On reaching the house of the Cakes, the sound of music
was audible—a couple of fiddles, a bass, and a clarionette;
but, in the noise of voices, salutations, and laughter, the
melody was drowned; only occasionally the deep grunt of
the bass, and the shrill wail of the clarionette, like that of
a teething babe, were audible.

The hall was full. It was not large, as we nowadays
reckon size; but it was of sufficient size to accommodate a
good many, and not so large as to make them feel chilled
by the vastness of the space. From the hall opened a parlour, in which were set out card-tables for the elders.

Directly Anthony and his wife entered, Bessie signed to
Urith to sit by her. She was uneasy at the pointed way

in which Fox paid her attention, kept near her, and talked
with her. She could see that his conduct had attracted
notice, and that she was the subject of a good deal of
remark. She was sad at heart—little inclined for merriment ; but she had come as her father desired it ; and always conscientious, and desirous to sink her own feelings
so as not to disturb and distress others, she concealed her
inner sadness, assumed a gentle, pleased manner natural
to her when in company. She had been wont from early
childhood to shut up her troubles within her heart from
every eye, and to wear a composed exterior ; consequently
this was less difficult to her now than it might have been to
others less self-disciplined.

Urith, moreover, was not best satisfied to find herself at
a merrymaking so shortly after her mother's death ; and,
besides, was so wholly unaccustomed to one, that she felt
frightened and bewildered. She snatched at once at the
chance of sitting by Bessie, as a relief to the painful sense
of loneliness and confusion in which she was, confused by
the crowd that whirled about her—lonely in the midst of
it, because strange to most of those composing it. Anthony
was among friends. He knew every one, and was greeted
heartily by all the young people, male and female ; but she
was thrust aside by them as they pushed forward to welcome him, and she was jostled outside the throng which
had compacted itself around him.

At the most favourable time she would have felt strange
there, for her mother had never taken her to any rout at a
neighbour's house ; she had been to no dances, no dinners—
had been kept entirely aloof from all the whirl of bright and
butterfly life that had made country life so enjoyable ; and
now she was oppressed with the inner consciousness of the
impropriety of appearing at a dance at such a brief interval after the earth had closed over her mother. At once,
with nervous self-consciousness, Urith rushed into self-ex-
culpation.

"I would not have come—indeed, I did not wish to
come ; but Anthony insisted. He said he would not come
without me ; you had told him that, and—I did not wish to
stand in the way of his pleasures. He has worked very
hard ; he has been cut off from his usual associates ; he has
had no holiday—so I thought it well to come."

"Yes, you did right. You will find Anthony exacting. That he always was, but good at heart," said Bessie.

"I do not dance myself—I cannot dance," said Urith, in further self-excuse; "so that it will not seem so very strange my being here, if I simply look on."

"You will have to dance—to open the ball with Anthony, I suppose, as you are the bride."

"I! Oh, but I do not know how to dance. I never have danced. I do not understand the figures. I do not distinguish between a brawl, a rant, and a jig."

"That is unfortunate—but it will serve to excuse you; yet I think you must essay to foot it once with Anthony. He is certain to insist on it."

"But I do not know——" Urith flushed. "How can I dance when I have never practised the measures and the paces?"

At that moment Anthony came up.

"Come, Urith," said he; "we must open the ball. All are waiting for you."

"But I cannot, Anthony."

He made a movement of impatience. "Nonsense, you must!" That was in his old imperious manner, which Bessie knew so well.

Bessie said aside to Urith, "Make the attempt. You cannot well go wrong."

Urith stood up—nervous, trembling, turning white and red, and with the tears very near the surface.

"Look here," said Anthony. "Father thinks, because I am thrust out of Hall, that everyone may kick at me—that I am of no account any more. Let us show that it is otherwise. Let them see that I am something still, and that my wife is not a nobody. Come!" He whisked her to her place at the head of the room.

Urith saw that all eyes were on her, and this increased her nervousness. As she passed Fox she caught his malicious eye, and saw the twirl of laughter and cruel jest on his lip.

"I cannot—and let me alone, Anthony," escaped her again. She was frightened.

"Have done. I do not want you here to make a fool of yourself and me; and that you will do if you slink back to your place."

" But I cannot dance, Anthony."

" Folly ! I will put you to-rights. With half a pinch of wit you cannot go wrong."

The music struck up, the clarionette squealed, the violins sawed, and the bass grunted. In a moment Urith was caught away—felt herself swung, flying, she knew not where. She knew not what she was doing. She could neither keep step with the music, nor discover the direction in which she had to go. She saw faces—faces on every side—full of laughter, amusement, mockery. She was thrown adrift from Anthony, was groping for his hand ; could not tell where he was, what she had to do ; got in the way of other dancers, was knocked across the floor, knocked back again ; ran between couples—then, all at once, she was aware of Anthony pushing his way to her, with an angry face, and an exclamation of, " You are no good at all ; get back to your chair. I won't dance with you again and be made a laughing-stock of."

He left her, where he had thrust her out of the dance, to find her way back to Bessie, and strode off to Julian, caught her by the hand, and in a moment was fully engaged.

He was maddened with vexation. It was unendurable to him that he had been the occasion of laughter. Every other girl and woman in the room, however plain, could dance—only his wife not. She alone must sit against the wall ! That it was his fault in forcing her to come against her wishes—his fault in making her attempt to do what she had protested her ignorance of—he did not recognise. The wife of Anthony Cleverdon ought to take a prominent place—ought to be able to dance, and dance well—ought to be handsomer, better dressed, more able to make herself agreeable, than any other woman ! And there she was —helpless ! Handsome, indeed ; but with her beauty disguised by an unbecoming dress ; silent, sulky, on the verge of tears. It was enough to make his heart fill with gall !

On the other hand, here was Julian Crymes in charming costume, bright of eye, fresh of colour, full of wit and banter, moving easily in the dance, light, confident, graceful. Julian was glowing with pleasure ; her dark eyes flashed with the fire that burned in her soul, and the hot blood rolled boiling through her veins.

For some moments after she had taken her seat Urith was unable to see anything. The tears of shame and disappointment filled her eyes, and she was afraid of being observed to wipe them away.

But Bessie took her hand, and pressed it, and said, " No wonder you were agitated at this first appearance in company. No one will think anything of it, no doubt they will say you are a young and modest bride. There, do not be discouraged; the same would have happened to me in your circumstances. What—must I?"

The last words were addressed to Fox, who came up to ask her to dance with him. She would gladly have excused herself, but that she thought a dance was owing to him for his courtesy in coming to Hall to accompany her.

"I am not inclined for more than one or two turns this evening," she said to Fox; "for there are many here younger than I, and I would not take from them the dances they enjoy so much more than myself."

As the tears dried without falling in Urith's eyes, and her heart beat less tumultuously, she was able to look about her, and seek and find Anthony.

It was with a stab of pain in her heart that she saw him with Julian. They were talking together with animation, her great eyes were fixed on him, and he bent his head over her. Urith knew the heart of Julian—knew the disappointed love, the rage that consumed it; and she wondered at her husband for singling this girl out as his partner. Then she reproached herself; for, she argued, that this heart, with its boiling sea of passion, had been revealed to her, not to him. He was unconscious of it.

Urith followed him and Julian everywhere; noted the changes in his countenance when she spoke; felt a twinge of anguish when, for a moment, both their eyes met hers, and they said something to each other and laughed. Had they laughed at her awkwardness in the opening dance?

Elizabeth passed before her on Fox's arm, and, as they did so, she heard Fox say, "Yes, your brother is content now that he is with Julian. You can't root old love out with a word."

Bessie winced, turned sharply round, and looked at Urith, in the hope that this ill-considered speech had not been heard by her. But a glance showed that Urith had not been deaf : her colour had faded to an ashen white, and a dead film had formed over her sombre eyes, like cat-ice on a pool.

Bessie drew her partner away, and said, with agitated voice, "You should not have spoken thus—within earshot of Urith."

"Why not? Sooner or later she must know it—the sooner the better."

Bessie loosened herself from him, angry and hurt. "I will dance with you no more," she said. "You have a strange way of speaking words that are like burrs—they stick and annoy, and are hard to tear away."

She went back to take her place by Urith, but found it occupied. She was therefore unable at once to use her best efforts to neutralise the effect produced by what Fox had said.

Urith's face had become grave and colourless, the dark brows were drawn together, and the gloomy eyes had re-covered some life or light ; but it was that of a Jack-o'-Lantern—a wild fire playing over them.

Anthony danced repeatedly with Julian. The delight of being with him again, of having him as her partner—wholly to herself—if only for a few minutes, filled her with intoxi-cation of pleasure, and disregard of who saw her, and what was said concerning her. Her heart was like a flaming tuft of gorse, blazing fiercely, brightly, with intense heat for a brief space, to leave immediately after a blank spot of black ash and a few glowing sparks ; and Anthony stooped over her enveloped in this flame, accepting the flattering homage, forgetful of his responsibilities, regardless of the future, without a thought as to the consequences. Her bosom heaved, her breath came hot and fast, her full lips trembled.

Urith's eyes were never off them, and ever darker grew her brow, more sinister the light in her eyes, and the more colourless her cheek.

Suddenly she sprang up. The room was swimming around her ; she needed air, and she ran forth into the night. The sky was full of twilight, and there was a ris-ing moon. Though it was night, it was not dark.

She stood in the road, gasping for air, holding the gate. Then she saw coming along the road a dark object, and heard the measured tramp of horses' hoofs. It was a carriage. Along that road, at midnight, so it was said, travelled nightly a death-coach, in which sat a wan lady, drawn by headless horses, with on the box a headless driver.

For a moment Urith was alarmed, but only for a moment. The spectral coach travelled noiselessly; of this that approached the sound of the horse-hoofs, of the wheels, and the crack of the whip of the driver were audible.

The carriage drew up before the entrance-gates of the house, and a gentleman thrust forth his head.

"Ho! there! Do you belong to the house? Run in, summon Anthony Crymes. Tell him his father wants him—immediately."

CHAPTER XXIX.

CAUTIONS.

Urith entered the hall again, and told Fox that his father was without, and wanted him.

"My father!" exclaimed young Crymes. "Oh! he is home from the Session of Parliament, where they and the King have been engaged in offering each other humble pie, for which neither party has a taste. What does he want with me?"

"I did not inquire," answered Urith, haughtily.

Mr. Crymes had not known her in the road, when he called out to her to send his son to him.

Fox was annoyed to have to leave the dance, but he could not disobey his father, so he took his hat and coat, and went forth.

Mr. Crymes was waiting for him, in the coach.

"I heard you were here, on my way. Stirring times, my boy, when we must be up and doing."

"So am I, father; you took me off from a saraband."

"Fie on it! I don't mean dancing. Come into the coach, and sit with me. I have much to say."

"Am I to desert my partners?"

"In faith! I reckon the maids will be content to find another better favoured than thee, Tonie."

Fox reluctantly entered the carriage, but not till he had made another effort to be excused.

"Julian is here, is she to be left without an escort?"

"Julian has her attendants, and will be rejoiced to be free from your company, as when together ye mostly spar."

When the coach was in movement, Mr. Crymes said, "I have come back into the country, for, indeed, it is time that they who love the Constitution of their country and their religion should be preparing for that struggle which is imminent."

"I thought, father," said Fox, "you were sent up to Westminster to fight the battle there. It is news to me that warfare is to be carried on by Cut and Run. I suppose you were in risk of being sent to the Tower?"

The old man was offended.

"It will oblige me if you reserve your sarcasms for others than your own father. I come home, and you sneer at me."

"Not at all; you mistake. I wondered how the Constitution was to be preserved here, when the great place of doctoring and drenching the patient, of bleeding and cupping, is at Westminster, and you were sent thither to tender your advice as to how that same Constitution was to be dealt with."

"The battle is not to be fought there," said Mr. Crymes, "nor with tongues. The field of conflict will be elsewhere, and the weapons keener and harder than words."

"The field of conflict is, I trust, not to be here," remarked Fox; "your sagacity, father, has assuredly taken you to the furthest possible distance from it. As soon as these weapons stronger than tongues are brandished, I shall betake me to Lundy or the Scilly Isles."

"You are a coward, I believe," said Mr. Crymes, in a tone of annoyance. "I expect to find in you—or, rather, but for my experience of you, I might have reckoned on finding in my son—a nobler temper than that of a runaway."

"But, my good father, what other are you?"

"If you will know," said Mr. Crymes, petulantly, "I

14

have come into the country—here into the West—to rouse it."

" What for?"

" For the cause of the Constitution and Religion."

" And when the West is roused, what is it to do? Stretch itself, and lie down to sleep again?"

" Nothing of the kind, Tonie. I do not mind confiding to you that we expect a revolution. It is not possible to endure what is threatened. The country will—it must—rise, or will lose its right to be considered a free and Protestant country." Mr. Crymes waited, but, as his son said nothing, he continued. "The Duke of Monmouth is in the Low Countries, and is meditating an invasion. The Dutch will assist; he is coming with a fleet, and several companies levied in Holland, and we must be organised and ready with our bands to rise as soon as he sets foot in England."

" Not I," said Fox. "If you, father, venture your neck and bowels for Monmouth and the Protestant cause, I content myself with tossing up my cap for King James. Monmouth's name is James as well as his Majesty's, so my cap will not compromise me with either; and, father, I only toss up my cap—I will not risk my neck or bowels for either by drawing sword."

" You are a selfish, unprincipled rogue," said Mr. Crymes. " You have neither regard for your country nor ambition for yourself."

" As for my country, I can best care for it by protecting such a worthy member of it as myself, and my ambition lies in other lines than political disturbance. I have not heard that either side got much, but rather lost, by taking parts in the Great Rebellion, whether for the Parliament or for the King. The only folk who gained were such as put their hands in their pockets and looked on."

" By the Lord!" exclaimed the old gentleman, "I am sorry that I have such a son, without enthusiasm, and care for aught save himself. I tell you the Earl of Bedford secretly inclines to the cause of Monmouth, and has urged me to come down here and stir the people up. Now, when his Lordship——"

" Exactly," scoffed Fox. " Exactly as I thought, he keeps safe and throws all the risk on you. Nothing could so induce me to caution as the example of the Earl of Bedford."

In the meantime, Bessie, at the dance, was in some uneasiness. She had missed Urith when she went out of the house, and, after her return, noticed that her face was clouded, and that she was short of speech. Bessie took Urith's hand in her lap and caressed it. She did not fully understand what was distressing her sister-in-law. At first she supposed it was annoyance at her failure in dancing, but soon perceived that the cause was other. Urith no longer responded to her caresses, and Bessie, looking anxiously into her dark face and following the direction of her eyes, discovered that the conduct of Anthony was the occasion of Urith's displeasure. Anthony was not engaged to Julian for every dance, but he singled her out and got her as his partner whenever he could, and it was apparent that she took no pleasure in dancing with anyone else; she either feigned weariness to excuse her acceptance of another partner, or danced with him without zest, and with an abstracted mind that left her speechless.

Bessie Cleverdon, the last person in the room to think hardly of another, the most ready to excuse the conduct of another, was hard put to it to justify her brother's conduct. He did not come to his wife between the dances, treating her with indifference equal to a slight, and he lavished his attentions on Julian Crymes in a manner that provoked comment.

"They are old friends, have known each other since they were children, have been like cousins, almost as brother and sister," said Bessie, when she felt Urith's hand clench and harden within her own as Anthony and Julian passed them by without notice, engrossed in each other.

"You must think nothing of it—indeed you must not. Anthony is pleased to meet an old acquaintance and talk over old times. It is nothing other," again she protested, as Urith started and quivered. The bride had encountered Julian's eye, and Julian had flashed at her a look of scorn and gratified revenge. She was fulfilling her threat, she was plucking the rose out of Urith's bosom.

Presently, Julian came across the room to Bessie with eyes averted from Urith.

"Come with me," said she to Bessie Cleverdon, "I want

a word with you. I am hot with dancing. Come outside the porch." She put her arm within that of Anthony's sister, and drew her forth on the drive, outside.

When there, Julian said, "Bessie, what is this I hear on all sides. Are you engaged?"

"Engaged! What do you mean?"

"Engaged to Fox. I am told of it by first one and then another; moreover, his attentions to you were marked, and all noticed them; that has given strength to the general belief."

"It is not true. It is not true!" exclaimed Bessie, becoming crimson with shame and annoyance; "who can have set such a wicked story afloat?"

"Nay, I cannot tell that. Who can trace a piece of gossip? But the talk is about, in the air, everywhere. There must be some foundation for it."

"None at all, I assure thee—most seriously, and most honestly, none at all. You pain me inexpressibly, Julian. Deny it whenever you hear it. Contradict it, as you love me."

"I do love thee," answered Julian, "and for that reason I have hoped it was false, for I pity the maid that listens to Fox's tongue and believes his words. If it be true——"

"It is not true; it has not a barleycorn of truth in it."

"But he has been much at Hall, every week, almost every other day."

"Because he is Anthony's friend, and he is doing what he can for him with my father."

Julian laughed. "Nay, never, never reckon on that. Fox will do no good turn to anyone, leastwise to Anthony. He go twice or thrice a week to Hall on other concern than his own! As well might the hills dance. Trust me, if he has been to Hall so oft, it has been that he sought ends and advantages of his own. I never knew Fox hold out the end of his riding-whip to help a friend."

"That may be," said Bessie Cleverdon. "But he has not come for me. I pray let my name be set aside. I have nothing to do with him. He has not so much as breathed a word touching such a matter to me. I pray you deny this whenever you hear it, and to whomsoever you speak concerning it."

Julian laughed.

"I am glad I have thy word that there is naught in it, as far as thou art concerned. I spoke of it to Anthony, and he also laughed me out of countenance thereat. But he trusts Fox. I would not trust him save to trip up or stab in the back, an enemy. Do'st know, Bess, what notion came on me? I fancied that Fox was seeking thee, because he reckoned that the strife between Anthony and his father would never skin over, and that the old man would make thee his heir."

"No! no!" exclaimed Elizabeth, in distress. "Do not say such things, do not think such things. I am certain that you mistake Fox. He is not so bad as you paint him."

"What! you take up the single-stick to fight in his defence?"

"I will fight in defence of any man who is maligned. I cannot think of Fox what you say. I pray say no more hereon. You pain me past words to express, and there really is no ground for what you do say."

"Take care! take care! Bess. I know Fox better than do you, better than does anyone else, and he may yet play you such a move as will checkmate you."

Elizabeth did not answer. The two girls took a turn on the lawn together, and Bessie drew Julian's arm tighter to her side; she even laid her disengaged hand on her shoulder, clinging to her as a supplicant.

The attitude, her manner was so full of entreaty, that Julian halted in her walk, turned to her, and asked, "What is it that you want, Bess?"

"My dear—dear Julian," Elizabeth stroked Julian's arm with her gentle hand, "O Julian! Do, I pray thee, not dance any more with Anthony."

"Why not, Bess?"

Elizabeth hesitated. She was unwilling, almost unable to express her reasons. An unrest was in her bosom, a fear in her heart, but nothing had taken distinct shape.

"My dear, dear Julian, I entreat you not. You should feel that it were fit that my brother should dance this evening with his wife—with Urith."

"She can no more dance than a goose," answered Julian, bluntly.

"That is true—I mean she cannot dance very well ; but it is not seemly that she be left out altogether, and that he should be so much with you."

"Why not? We are old friends."

"Do you not feel, Julian, that it is unfitting? She—I mean Urith—must feel hurt."

"She is hurt !" repeated Julian, with a thrill of triumph in her voice ; but this Bessie did not notice. It never for a moment occurred to her that it could give exultation to Julian to know that she had pained another.

"Indeed, you must consider," pursued Bessie. "The poor young thing has not had the chance of learning to dance, and Anthony is without much thought ; he seeks his pleasure. Young men do not think, or do not understand the hearts of girls. I watched Urith, and I believe that every step you took trod on her heart."

"It did !" Her tone shocked Bessie, who for a moment released her arm and looked in her face, but in the darkness could not see the expression.

"Indeed it did," she continued ; "for, as she could not dance, it seemed a slight to and forgetfulness of her that she was left to sit out, and Anthony amused himself with you and with others. He meant no harm, I know that very well ; but, nevertheless, he hurt her much, and she bled with inward pain. She was shamed, and should not have been shamed before a great many people on her first appearance after her marriage, at a rout."

"You should administer your exhortations, Bess, to Anthony. I have not the custody and responsibility of that wild, vixenish colt, Urith."

"I cannot get a word with Anthony, and you, Julian, are dancing with him three times to any other partner's one."

"Would you have him sit down at her side and twiddle his thumbs, like a disgraced child in a corner?"

"I would have him and you think of the feelings of a young girl who is sad at heart," said · Bessie, gravely. Julian's tone distressed her ; a glimmer of the true condition of affairs entered her mind and filled it with horror and indignation.

"Julian," she said, in a firmer tone, with less of appeal in it and more of command, "at one time I used to think that we were like to become sisters——"

" What, by your taking Fox? It is not too late."

" Do not—do not banter on that subject. You know my
meaning. I did suppose that Anthony would have sought
his happiness in you. But it has pleased God to order it
otherwise. Now he must find his happiness—not at Kilworthy, nor at Hall, but at poor little Willsworthy, that
bleak moor farm, and not with you, but with Urith. He
has sacrificed a great deal for her—lost his home, lost his
father, almost lost me, has given up wealth and position,
and he must be compensated for these losses in his own
new home. It is not right that you—that anyone should
do anything to spoil this chance, to rob him of his com-
pensation in full. Anthony can be nothing to you for the
future. Leave him alone. Do not play with him, do not
draw him away from Urith. He has now already mighty
odds against him; do not, for God's sake, do anything that
may make the odds overwhelming, and blight and ruin his
happiness here and for ever. For, Julian, it is now, in the
first months of marriage, that his state will be determined
one way or the other. Mar the concord between him and
his wife now, and it may never again be found; and that
concord lost, with it to wreck goes the whole life of my
brother. If ever, Julian, you had any love for Anthony,
if now you have any kindly feeling towards him, let him
alone."

She paused and waited for an answer. None came,
Julian walked faster, dragged her up and down the lawn
as she clung to her.

" It was Anthony's doing that Urith came to-night; she
was averse to appear, but he insisted on it. She told him
she could not dance; he forced her to take her place with
him at the head of the room for a measure. Did she ever
seek him out? Never. He thrust himself upon her. When
her mother died, she had no desire to be hurried into marriage, but he overruled all her objections. He, ever
thoughtless, inconsiderate of others, has taken her up out
of her old course of life——"

" Enough, enough about her," said Julian, "when you
speak of her my anger foams. Speak of him, of his happiness jeopardised, and I cool. What! Has it come to this,
that I—I in my gloveless hands hold the fortunes, hold the
hearts of these two, to beat and batter them together, and

crush and break them both? What if I threaten to do it?"

"You are too good at heart to make the threat, or, if made, to make it good."

Julian was silent again. She took several turns in front of the house. The sounds of revelry streamed out to them. Through the open porch door, along with the light, and occasionally in the porch itself, came a flash of colour as a girl stood there in her bright-tinted dress with the blaze of the candles upon her. Bats were wheeling, and their shrill scream pierced the ear.

"Let me alone, Bess," said Julian. "I cannot breathe, I cannot think when you are by me; my head is like a weir, and all my thoughts tumble, boiling, spattering over, beaten to foam."

Elizabeth withdrew to the porch, where she seated herself, and watched the excited girl on the lawn. She had put her hands to her head and was still pacing up and down, now fast, then slowly, according as her passion or her good nature prevailed.

Then out at the door came Anthony, shouting, "Where is Julian? She promised to dance the Mallard with me! Bessie, have you seen her? I claim her for the Mallard."

Julian heard his voice, and stepped back under the shade of a bank of yews. There was before her gravel, and in that gravel a piece of white spar that shone like a flake of snow in the dark. If she stepped out to that piece of spar he would see her, claim her, and—her evil nature would have got the upper hand. Whither would it lead her? She did not ask that. She saw before her now only the alternative of a half-hour's mad pleasure on the arm of Anthony, of cruel triumph over his already humiliated wife, and abandonment of the contest.

The struggle was over with unexpected brevity. The tune of the Mallard struck up, and Anthony went back into the hall without her, to seek for her there, or to find there another partner.

Then Julian heard the burst of voices in song, for the Mallard was a country dance led by two, with chorus by all the performers as they turned their partners, and went in chain with linked, reversed arms, down the room.

SHE: When lambkins skip, and apples are growing,
 Grass is green, and roses ablow,
 When pigeons coo, and cattle are lowing,
 Mist lies white in the vale as snow.

 CHORUS: Why should we be all the day toiling ?
  Lads and lasses along with me !
  Done with drudgery, dust, and moiling,
  Come along to the greenwood tree.

HE: The cows are milked, the teams are a-stable,
 Work is over with set of sun.
 Ye farmer lads, all lusty and able,
 Ere the moon rises begins our fun.

 CHORUS: Why should we, etc.

Julian came to the porch to Elizabeth.

"Go," said she, "tell my servants to make ready. I will return home. I will not go indoors again, till the horses are at the door. My father has returned, and Fox is with him. Be that my excuse."

Bessie put up both her hands to the face of Julian, drew down her head to her, and kissed her. Then she disappeared.

Julian remained without, listening to the ballet.

SHE: O sweet it is to foot on the clover,
 Ended work, and revel begun,
 Aloft the planets never give over,
 Dancing, circling round of the sun.

 CHORUS: Why should we, etc.

HE: So Ralph and Phil, and Robin and Willie,
 Kiss your partners, each of you now ;
 Bet and Prue, and Dolly and Celie,
 Make your curtsey ; lads! make a bow.

 CHORUS: Why should we be all the day toiling ?
  Lads and lasses along with me !
  Done with drudgery, dust, and moiling,
  Come along to the greenwood tree.

CHAPTER XXX.

When Julian Crymes had departed, it appeared to Anthony that the dance had lost its principal charm, and he wearied of it.

"Come, Urith," said he; "I think we will go. It is late." This was almost the only time he had spoken to her since the opening dance.

"I am ready," she answered; "have been for two hours."

He went forth to see after the horse, and had it brought round to the door. He took his place in the saddle, and Urith sat behind him. They rode forth from the grounds into the high road, along which their course lay for a mile and a half, after which it diverged over moor. Anthony did not speak, and Urith remained equally silent. She had her hand on his belt, and he felt the pressure. He was vexed with her; she had not done him credit that evening. She was uncouth, and unfit to associate with people accustomed to social intercourse—unable to take a part in the amusements such as is expected of every young person. She was decently dressed, but without richness and refinement of taste, and in an old-fashioned gown that had been her mother's. The blood rushed into his head as he thought of how folks must have laughed at him and her when she failed in the opening dance. She was the bride of the evening; every one was prepared to concede to her the place of pre-eminence, but she had shown herself wholly incapable of occupying the place offered her. Then how uninteresting she had appeared beside the other girls present! Their faces had been radiant with mirth, hers dull with discontent and ill-humour.

What if he had appeared there with Julian as his bride? How different all would have been! She would have been well, handsomely dressed, and in all the inherited jewelry of the Glanvilles. She would not have sat a whole evening mum against the wall. She would have shown herself queen of the revel. A warm breath, sweet as if laden with gorse essence, fanned his face at the thought, and was followed at once by a sharp and icy blast. Julian had been refused by him with all her wealth, her rank, her accomplishments, her beauty, and what had he acquired instead?

How could he have supposed that Urith was devoid of all those feminine delicacies of manner which enable a woman to place herself at ease in all society? She had thrown a cold, wet blanket over his joy on this first coming forth into the world from his seclusion at Willsworthy. Then Anthony went on spinning at the same dark thread of ideas. He asked himself what there was in Urith that had attracted him, why it was that he had been so infatuated as to throw his luck to the winds so as to possess her. When the head begins to reckon, then the heart is on the way to bankruptcy.

He counted over the advantages he had rejected, measured the sacrifices he had made for Urith's love, and he asked what she could throw into the scale to outweigh all this?

His hand twitched the bridle, and made the horse toss his head and plunge.

Urith also was occupied with her own thoughts. It had been a relief to her to get away from the laughter and music and revelry of Wringworthy; she thought that, could she be away from the heated room and swaling candles, in the cool night air, under the stars, her tranquillity of mind would return. But it was not so. Anthony's silence, her sense of having offended him by her clumsiness, her dread lest his love for her should be cooling; above all, the haunting spectre of a fear lest Julian should be fulfilling her threat, and be weaning from her the heart of her husband, followed her, and filled her blood with fever. But she strove against this fear, fought it with all the weapons at her command. It was impossible that his love, so strong, so unselfish, which had cost him so much, should evaporate, and that his heart should sway about like a weathercock. The resolution wherewith he had pursued his end, that proved him to have a strong character, and not one that is turned about in every direction.

He had some excuse for being out of humour. He was proud of her. He had desired to let all see what a woman he had got as his wife. He was disappointed, and the

depth of his disappointment was the measure of his pride
in her.

But then there rose up before her mind the picture of
Julian on Anthony's arm, with burning cheeks and bright
eyes, looking up in his face, and his eyes resting upon her
with a warmth that should be in them only when fixed on
the face of his wife. Did she not know that glow in his
countenance? That fire in his eye? Had he not looked
at her in the same way before they were married?

"Do you intend to drag me off my horse?" asked Anthony, "that you pull at my belt so roughly?"

"And you, that you draw the rein so short and make
the mare rear?"

Urith knew nothing of the world. It had ever seemed
to her inconceivable that after the bond and seal of marriage the thought of either should stray; that any one
should dare to dream of loving a man who was pledged in
heart and mind and soul to another woman. Yet Julian
as much as told her she still loved Anthony, would use all
her fascinations to draw him to her and away from his
wife. Was Anthony so weak that his conscience would
suffer him to be thus attracted from the place of duty?
No—a thousand times, no. He was not so feeble, so lacking in moral strength as this.

They had turned off the high road upon the moor.
Here was no stoned road, no road that lay white in the
darkness before them, but turf, by daylight recognisable
as a road by hoof marks, and the fret of feet over the turf.
By night it could be followed only by observing stones set
up at intervals and capped with whitewash. Stones had
been picked off the roadway and thrown on one side, so
that the turf was smooth almost as a racecourse. The head
of the horse was turned now somewhat easterly. The
sky above the rugged moor range was silvery, and from
behind a rocky crest rose the moon, doubled in size by the
haze that hung over the moor, and seemed like a mighty
flame of the purest white light.

"There, there!" said Urith. "Do you see, Anthony;
the moon is up above that old Lyke Way, along which we
made our first journey together."

She disengaged her hand from his belt, and put it round
his waist.

He raised his head and looked away to the east, at the ridge of moor and rock, black against the glittering orb. He remembered then how he had mounted her on his horse—how he had stood by her and looked into her eyes! He recalled the strange magic that had then come over him—a longing for her, mingled with a presentiment of evil—a fear lest she were drawing him on to destruction. That fear was verified—she had lured him on to his ruin. He was a ruined man; he had lost all that he valued—the esteem of his fellows, the comforts and luxuries of life. Then began again the odious and monotonous enumeration of the sacrifices he had made.

Why did Urith remind him of that ride? Did she want to find occasion to reproach him? Was it not enough that he was scourging himself with the whips of his own thoughts for his precipitate folly in marrying her?

But Urith was not at that moment thinking of reproach. She breathed moor air, was beyond hedges and enclosures, in the open, vast, uncultivated heather-land, and there her brain had cooled, and her heart had recovered composure. The atmosphere was other than that of a ball-room, which had filled her with intoxication, and had bred phantoms that had affrighted her.

As he rode on, with the light of the rising moon on his face, Anthony felt the pressure of Urith's hand below his heart. The pressure was slight, and yet it weighed heavy on him, and interfered with his breathing; that light hand, as it rose and fell with the motion of the horse, and at each inhalation, seemed to strike reproachfully against his side, to knock, and bid him open to better thoughts.

How was it that he was so changed—that he, who had forced himself on the reluctant Urith, had not let her alone till she had yielded to his persistency to precipitate the marriage—that he should be trying to shift the blame on her? If he had made sacrifices to win her, she had not invited him to do so; he had done it with his eyes open—he had done it moved by no other influence, urged by his own caprice solely.

It had never occurred to him that Urith had made sacrifices on her part; that he had demanded them of her, and given her no rest till they were made. He had made her marry him against her conscience and wishes, too quickly after her mother's death, and against her mother's dying orders. But he considered that what was done could not be undone, that as he had made his bed, so must he lie, as he had laden himself, so he must trudge. What then was the use of repining, and fretting over the past?

"Yet—it was the Lyke Way," he said, in a low tone, "the way of death, on which we set our feet together."

"No," she said, "not altogether." She released her hand from his heart, and placed it on the arm that held the bridle. "Stay the mare a moment, Tonie."

"Why?"

"I have something to tell you."

"Can you not say it as we ride on—it is late?"

"No—stay the mare."

He drew rein.

"Well—what is it?" he asked, a little impatiently.

She looked round.

"We are quite alone?"

"Yes—of course—who else could be here?"

Then she put her hand on his shoulder. "Turn your ear to me, Tonie. I will not say it aloud."

He did as required. But she did not speak for a few moments.

He showed signs of impatience.

Then she gathered resolution, and whispered something into his ear; only a word or two, but he started, and turned in his saddle.

"What! Urith—is it true?"

"I must not ride with you more after to-night," she said, and her eyes fell.

Then he put his arm round her, and drew her to him, and kissed her on one cheek, then on the other, then on her mouth, and laughed aloud.

"Hold tight!" he said. "Put both arms round me, both hands on my heart! O Urith! Urith! What will my father say when he knows this? He will relent. He must."

CHAPTER XXXI.

FAMILY JARS.

"What is the meaning of the strange talk that is about concerning thee and Elizabeth Cleverdon?" asked Julian of her brother, at breakfast next morning.

"Nay, that is putting on me more than I can do. I should be sorry to account for all the idle talk that blows and drifts about on the stream of conversation, like leaves of autumn on a trout pool."

"I heard it yesterday, and you certainly showed her great attention so long as you were at the dance."

"Did I show her more attention than you showed to one I do not name? Faith! if I had listened to and picked up the scraps of scandal cast about, I might have filled an apron with what wanton words I heard concerning thee."

He looked hard at Julian, and their eyes met. She coloured, but shook off her embarrassment, and turned to her father and said: "The saying is that my brother is setting his cap to catch Bessie Cleverdon."

Mr. Crymes became grave, and looked at his son. He was a stern and Puritanical man, who had kept himself aloof from his children, never entering into their amusements, and concerning himself with what they did. Julian's fortune was assured to her, and his son would inherit something, the relics of the paternal estate, and what he had saved when managing for Julian.

"Is there anything in this, Anthony?" he asked. "On my honour, I am surprised."

"There is truth and there is falsehood in it," answered Fox, carelessly. "It has come to this, that as Julian cannot be Anthony Cleverdon's wife, it lies open to her to become his mother. Old Master Cleverdon is nothing loth, and, if she will accept him, she will have the opportunity of bringing the father to good terms with the son, for, from what I have seen, the happiness of Tonie lies very near to my sister's heart. If she declines the old man, I shall try my fortune with his daughter."

"This is absurd, Fox," said Julian, highly incensed.

"Absurd it may be—but the old gentleman has his head full of it, and has commissioned me to sound his way with you."

"Be silent," said Julian, very red, very angry, "I do not believe one word of this; but that you are aiming at Bessie, that I do believe, though when I asked her about it, she had no knowledge of anything of the kind."

"Before we proceed to consider my affairs, let us settle yours," said Fox. "Am I to tell Squire Cleverdon of Hall that you will not favour his suit, being already too deep gone in attachment to the son?"

"Silence to that slanderous tongue!" said Mr. Crymes, wrathfully. "Julian at one time was thought of in reference to young Tony Cleverdon, but he did not fancy her, but took Urith Malvine. From that moment the name of Tony Cleverdon, in connection with my daughter and your sister, is not to be employed in jest or earnest, by you or any other. Understand that."

"Then," said Fox, with his eye on his father, out of the corner, "let her keep herself out of folks' mouths, and not be like a rat I saw 'tother day, that ran into the jaws of my terrier, mistaking his open mouth for a run."

"What is he aiming at?" inquired Mr. Crymes, turning to his daughter. "I know he has a wicked tongue, but I cannot think he can speak without some occasion."

"There is nothing—that is to say——" Julian became confused. "Why may I not speak to—why not dance with an old, old friend?"

"I have no command to lay on you not to speak to, not to dance with an old friend," said her father, "but everything in moderation; take notice from your brother that evil eyes look out for occasion, therefore give none. If Ahab had no weak places in his armour, the bow drawn at a venture would not have sent an arrow to him with death at the point. No bluebottles are bred where carrion is not found."

Julian looked down abashed, then, with woman's craft, shifted the subject.

"It is nonsense that Tony speaks. I do not believe for an instant that Master Cleverdon has any suit for me in his head—if he has, no marvel if folk talk, but God be wi' me, it will not be I who occasion it."

"What do you mean by this?" asked the father, now turning to his son. "Has my friend Cleverdon said aught to justify you?"

"My dear father, if you wish it, and Julian does not object, he will step from the position of good friend into son. He has cast an eye on Kilworthy, and as Kilworthy cannot be had without Julian, i' faith, he will take both."

"Let him dare to offer this to me!" exclaimed Julian, "and until he does, pass it over. I refuse to accept any message through such a go-between."

"It is no fault of mine," said Fox, "if the father thinks that some of the overspill of love and languishment for his son may rebound to him. I do not see how Jule, if she desire to chastise her faithless lover for having despised her charms, can do so more effectually and more cuttingly than by taking his father. Then Tony Cleverdon is in her hands absolutely. She can reconcile her father to him or tear them apart for ever. She can bring him, if she will, to bite the dust at her feet, to fawn at her knee, and to a woman such power is precious."

"That suffices," said Mr. Crymes; "you heard what was her answer. She will speak no more on this matter with you. If Cleverdon comes to me with the suit, I will know what reply to make; if he goes to Julian, she can answer him herself. Meanwhile do you keep silence thereon. I but half trust what thou sayst. Such fancies breed in thy perverse mind. Come now to the other matter. Is it true that you see Elizabeth Cleverdon? For her sake I trust not, for I esteem her exceeding well, as much as I reckon thee below the general level of good men. If I thought there was aught mendable in thee that could be shaped by the hands of a good wife, I would say God prosper thee. But I fear me thou art over-rotten at the heart to be ripened to any good, over-hard to be moulded to a vessel of honour."

"I do not see why you should think so ill of me, father," said Fox, sullenly; "unless it be that your ear has drunk in all the complaints Julian has poured out against me. What she says you accept, what I say you cast away. Then, I fancy, the time is come when you will be glad to have me married and got rid of."

"You do seek marriage?"

"I seek to be away from those who flout and despise me, who cross me and mistrust me. At least Squire Cleverdon and I understand each other, and regard each other."

"Yes," broke in Julian; "for in each is the same yeast of sourness."

"Be silent, Julian," commanded her father. "Let me hear the boy out."

"What concern me the quirks and hints I hear concerning Jule?" pursued Fox, unable, in spite of his father, to contain himself from a stroke at his sister; "let them fly about thick as midges, they are naught to me—they do not sting me. Why, father, you should grudge me Bessie Cleverdon, I cannot see. If you respect her so highly—think so excellent well of her—I doubt but no other maid would so content you as a daughter-in-law as she."

"A better girl does not exist," answered Mr. Crymes. "I would desire her a better fate than to be united to thee."

"She is not comely, that is a fact," continued Fox, "but she will be the richest heiress in all the Tavistock district—between here and Plymouth and Exeter. Now that Master Cleverdon has fallen out with his son, and that there is no riddance by Anthony of the wife with whom he has saddled himself, not to please his father, or himself—or Jule yonder——"

Mr. Crymes brought his fist down on the table.

"I will drive thee out of the room at another word against thy sister."

"Do you notice, father," exclaimed Julian, with flaming cheeks, "it is poor Bessie's money and the lands of Hall that he covets, and he seeks this by levering out of his place his best friend and old comrade."

"Did I lever him out of his place?" retorted Fox. "He did it himself, and never a little finger did I put to help in his upsettal."

"No, but you are ready to profit by his loss; ready, if you could, to get me as your confederate in fencing every inlet by which he might return to his father," said Julian, vehemently.

"Because one man is a fool, is that reason why his friend—as you choose to term me—should not be wise? Because one man throws away a diamond, why his comrade should not pick it up and wear it on his finger?"

"The case is not the same. It is taking the jewel, and smiting the rightful owner in the face when he puts forth his hand to reclaim it, and that rightful owner—your friend."

"My friend!" exclaimed Fox, angrily. "Why should you call Anthony Cleverdon 'my friend?' Was it an act of a friend—a dear, considerate friend—to strike me in the eye and half blind me? Look!" Fox turned his left side towards his sister. "Do I not carry about with me a mark of friendship—a pledge to be redeemed? Trust me, I shall return that blow with usury some day, when the occasion comes."

· "And you will employ poor Bessie as your lash wherewith you filip him in the face. You are a coward—a mean——"

"Silence!" commanded Mr. Crymes. "There is no grain of brotherly love between you two——"

"Not a grain," threw in Julian, hotly.

Fox bowed sarcastically.

"You observe, father," he said, "that here I am at a disadvantage, between a sister who spars at me and a father who treads me down."

"I do not tread on you save when you grovel in the dirt," answered Mr. Crymes, "in base and dishonest matters, and I do esteem this suit of Elizabeth Cleverdon as one such."

"Opinions vary. You make me willing to leave my home, though it be not mine, nor thine neither, father, but that of sister Julian, who stuffs my pillow with thorns and the seats of her chairs with nettles. I would be away at any price, and if I can go to Hall and live there with Squire Cleverdon, I doubt not I shall be more content than I be here."

"You will live there?" said his father.

"No doubt. Master Cleverdon has ever had his daughter Elizabeth with him. He might have sent her packing, as he sent his own sister packing, when he needed her no more, and that would have been when Anthony brought home a wife to his taste. As he has not—if Julian still persists in declining to be my mother-in-law—why, I reckon that Bess will remain at Hall. A man must leave father and mother and cleave to his wife—so it will be scriptural, and that should content thee, father."

The old man drew forth his 'kerchief and wiped his face.

"I suppose, father," continued Fox, "that you will hardly let me go penniless out of the house? That would be a pretty comment on your professions. You must have saved something, and there is that little scrap of land still ours in Buckland——"

Mr. Crymes again wiped his face. He did not know what answer to make.

"Or, is the fashion set by Squire Cleverdon of cutting his son off without a shilling infectious, that my father has taken it, and will follow suit, and sicken into the same green infirmity?"

"No," said Mr. Crymes, "I will do what is right; but you spring this on me, I am taken aback——"

"I did not spring it on you. That is one of the many kindnesses I have received from Jule."

"I do not know what to say. You must give me time to consider. This journey to London has cost me a considerable sum of money."

"There comes the usual excuse for shirking out of a money obligation which cannot be enforced by law. Say on, father—the times have been bad, the hay was black with rain, the corn did not kern well, the mottled cow dropped her calf, the tenants have not paid, and so my poor boy gets nothing but advice in bushels and exhortations in yards."

"Having insulted your sister, now you throw your jibes at me. That is not encouraging to me to deal handsomely towards you."

"I did not think, father, that you needed to be coaxed and caressed to do an act of justice."

"I do not ask that of thee, but I must consider. It ill pleases me that you should have thought of Bessie Cleverdon."

"If I had chosen some worthless wench without a penny to bless herself withal, you would have shaken the head and broken the staff over me. Now that I have chosen one who is in all ways unexceptional, who is a wealthy heiress of irreproachable manners of life, the favourite of everybody, a dutiful daughter, it is all the same—you disapprove. Is there aught I could do—any change that I could make—that would give thee pleasure?"

"None—till I saw there was an amendment in thyself."

"If I can give satisfaction in no way to thee, father, I may assuredly make choice for myself. Bess may not be beautiful, but she pleases me—she has what is better than beauty, all Hall estate on her back. It will be to your advantage and to that of Jule that I should take her—you will thus be rid of me, who content neither of you, simply because my tongue has a point to it, and I do not suffer it to lie by and be blunted."

Then Julian laughed out.

"What avails all this reckoning and debating over a matter that cannot be settled till the main person concerned has been consulted? Bessie, I am very sure, has not the faintest waft of a notion that such schemes are being spun about her, or had not till I spoke with her yestreen. She will never take thee, Fox. Bessie has a good heart and a shrewd understanding, and neither will suffer her to take thee."

"You think not?" asked Fox, superciliously.

"I am sure she will not," answered Julian.

"We shall see," said Fox. "She is not as was her brother, one to fly in the face of a father. He has set his mind to it, and if Julian will not have him, then he will yet have an Anthony Cleverdon to sit on his seat, and reign in his stead, when he has been gathered to his old yeoman fathers."

"How mean you?"

"Why, thus—I am Anthony. I was thus christened. And if I take Bess, I will throw aside my surname of Crymes, which brings me little—and take that of my father-in-law. So he will have an Anthony Cleverdon to carry on the name, and I—" his face assumed a malevolent expression— "I shall have spoiled for ever his own son's chances. It shall be down in black-and-white, and bound as fast as I can bind him. See if I cannot manage for myself."

He stood up, took his hat, and set it jauntily on his head, then at the door turned, and with a mocking laugh, said:

"There, sister Jule! Is not that a slap in the face for Anthony that will make his cheek tingle?"

He left the room.

Mr. Crymes laid his brow in his hand, and his elbow on the table.

"'Fore heaven!" he sighed, "I curse the day that gave me such a son."

CHAPTER XXXII.

MORE JARS.

A drizzling rainy day. A day on which nothing could be seen but a wavering veil of minute dust of water. A drizzle that was wetting, and which penetrated everywhere. The air was warm, laden with moisture, oppressive, and depressing. From a window could be seen nothing beyond a hedge. Trees seemed to be bunches of cotton wool; the drizzle crawled or was drawn along by a damp wind over the grass along the hedge, beading every blade and twig with the minutest drops of moisture. The shrubs, the plants stooped, unable to support the burden deposited on them, and shot the impalpable water-dust down on the soil in articulate drops.

Although the drizzle was excluded by roof and walls from the house, the moisture-charged atmosphere could not be shut out, and it made the interior only less wretched than outside the house. The banisters, the jambs of the door, the iron locks were bedewed, and the hand that touched them left a smear and came off clogged with water. The slates of the floor turned black, and stood with drops, as though the rain had splashed over them. Wherever there was a stone in the wall of a slatey or impervious nature, it declared itself by condensing moisture, sweating through plaster and whitewash, and sending tears trickling down the walls. The fireirons became suddenly tarnished and rusty. The salt in the cellar and salt-box was sodden, and dripped brine upon the floor, as did the hams and sides of bacon hung up in the kitchen. The table-linen and that for the beds adhered to the fingers when touched.

Anthony stood at the window in the hall looking out, then he went to the fire; then took down a gun from over the mantel-shelf, and looked at the lock and barrel; stood it in the corner of the fire, and resolved by and by to clean it.

Then he went to the window again, and wrote his initials on the window-pane, or tried to do so, and failed, for the condensation of moisture was not inside but without, on the glass.

He had nothing to occupy him ; no work could be done on the farm, and employment or amusement lacked in the house.

Where was Urith? She might come and talk to and entertain him.

What is the good of a wife, unless she sets herself to make home agreeable to her husband, when he is unable to go out-of-doors ?

Where was Solomon Gibbs? He might have talked, fiddled, and sung, though, indeed, Anthony had no relish just then for music, and he knew pretty well all the topics on which Uncle Sol had aught to say. His anecdotes had often been retailed, and Anthony loathed them. He knew when Sol was preparing to tell one, he knew which he was about to produce, he was acquainted with every word he would use in telling his tale.

Anthony had grown irritable of late with Sol, and had brushed him rudely when he began to repeat some hacknied anecdote. On such a day as this, however, even Uncle Sol were better than no one.

At length, Anthony, impatient and out of humour, went upstairs and called Urith. She answered him faintly from a distance.

"Where are you hidden? What are you about?" he called.

"In the lumber-room," she replied.

He followed the direction of her voice, and came to a sort of garret full of every kind of discarded article of domestic use, old crocks that had lost a leg, broken-backed chairs, a dismantled clock, corroded rushlights, bottles that were cracked, a chest of drawers which had lost half the brass handles by which the drawers could be pulled out.

In the obscurity, dishevelled, covered with dust, and warm with her exertions, stood Urith. She put her hand to her face, and pushed her strayed hair from her eyes.

"I want thy help, Tony," she said. "I have been searching, and at length, I have found it. But I cannot carry it forth myself."

" Found what ? "

" O—how can you ask ? Do you not see what it is ? "

It was an old, dusty, cobweb-covered, wooden cradle.

" What do you want, Urith, with this wretched bit of rummage ? "

" What do I want it for ? O—Tony, of course you know. It is true I shall not need it immediately—not for some months, but I shall like to have it forth, and clean it well, and polish its sides, and fit it up with little mattress and pillows, and whatsoever it need, before the time comes when it is required to be put in use."

" I will not have this wretched old cradle," said Anthony. " It is not meet for my son—the heir to Hall and Willsworthy." ·

" You are reckoning too soon—" laughed Urith. " Perhaps you may have a daughter, not a son."

" A daughter ! I do not want a maid ; no—I shall never forgive you, if it be not a boy. Urith, My—everything depends on that. When there is a new Anthony Cleverdon, my father can hold out in his obstinacy no longer. He must give way. An Anthony Cleverdon of Willsworthy, and *not* of Hall ! It would go against all his pride, against his most cherished ambition. It cannot, it shall not be. Urith, a boy it must be, and what is more, he shall not lie in that dusty, cobweb-clad pig-trough. It would not become him."

" But, Tony," laughed Urith, " it was mine, I was rocked in that. It was not so bad that I could not sleep therein."

" Oh, you ! " he spoke disparagingly in tone. " You were only heiress of Willsworthy, but my young Anthony will be something much different from that."

" I want my child to lie in the same crib in which I was rocked. It will be a pleasure to me."

" I will not have it. This is too mean."

" What does it signify ? "

" If it does not signify, then let me go and buy a new cradle."

" No," said Urith. " No—there I lay when a poor little feeble creature ; and there, in the same, it shall lie when it comes."

" I will go into Peter Tavy to the carpenter, and order a new cradle."

"I will not use it if you do. We have not the money to waste on luxuries. A child will sleep as well in this as in a painted cradle."

All at once, Anthony flushed to the roots of his hair. A thought had struck him, that if he bought a new cradle he must do so with his wife's money. He had nothing of his own. He was her pensioner. There stood at his side an old rusty bar of iron ; in his anger and disgust he grasped this, raised it, and brought it down on the cradle, breaking down its side.

"Anthony !" exclaimed Urith. "Anthony ! you would not have done that had any love, any respect remained in your heart for me. You would have loved the little crib in which I was laid, if you loved me."

He did not answer her. Ashamed at his own conduct, embittered at her opposition to his wishes, discontented with his lot, he left the garret and descended the stairs.

On reaching the hall, he found Solomon Gibbs there ; he had been out in the rain, and had come in very wet. His face was red and moist, proclaiming that he had been drinking, but he was not intoxicated, only hilarious. He had cast his hat on the table, a broad-brimmed felt hat that had absorbed the rain like a sponge, and was now giving it forth in a stream that made a puddle on the table and ran over the side, dripped on to a bench, and having formed a slop there fell again to the floor, there producing another pool. The water ran off Uncle Sol's dress and oozed from his boots that were rent, and had admitted water within, which now spirited forth from the gaps at every step. Solomon had taken down a single-stick, with basket handle, from the wall, and was making passes, wards, and blows in the air at an imaginary opponent, and, as he delivered his strokes, he trilled forth snatches of song :—

I'm a hearty good fellow, as most men opine.

Then he whacked from right to left—

So fill up your bumpers, and pass round the wine,
Singing, Tol-de-rol-lol-de-rol.

He fell to the ward.

"Come on, Tony lad! 'Tis cursed moist weather, and no fun out of doors. I've been to the Hare and Hounds, but no one there, and not even I can drink when there be no comrades with whom to change a word. Come, Tony, take a stick and let us play together, perhaps it will dry me, for I am damp, uncommon damp."

"Take your hat off the table," said Anthony, in ill-humour. He was accustomed to order and cleanliness in his father's house, and the ramshackle ways of Willsworthy displeased him; Uncle Sol was a prince of offenders in disordering and befouling everything. "Take your hat off. We shall have the board spread shortly, and how can we eat off it when it is slopped over by the drainage of your dirty beaver?"

"Nay, Tony, boy; let it lie. See—here I be. I will stand on the defence, and you take t'other stick; and, if you beat me off, you shall remove my hat; but, if I remain master, you shall pull off my boots. Can't do it myself, by heaven, they be so sodden with water."

"I will make you both remove your hat and kick off your own boots," said Anthony, angrily. "Dost think because I have married the niece that I am abased to be the uncle's serving-man? 'Fore heaven, I'll teach thee the contrary."

He went to the wall, took down a stick, and attacked Solomon Gibbs with violence.

Uncle Sol, for all the liquor he had drunk, was sober enough to be able to parry his blows, though handicapped by his drenched garments, which weighed on his shoulders and impeded rapid movement.

Anthony was not an accomplished single-stick player; he had not a quick eye, and he had never possessed that application to sports which would render him a master in any. Satisfied if he did fairly well, and was matched with inferiors who either could not or would not defeat him, he had now small chance against the old man, who had been a skilful player in his youth—who, indeed, had stuck to his sports when he ought to have held to his studies.

The old man held the stick between his hands over his head jauntily—carelessly, it seemed—but with perfect assurance; whereas Anthony struck about at ramdom and rarely touched his antagonist. Anthony was in a bad temper—he faced the window; whereas Uncle Sol stood with his back to the light, and to the table, defending his soaked hat. Anthony was the assailant; whereas Sol remained on the defensive, with an amused expression in his glossy face, and giving vent at intervals to snatches of melody—showing his unconcern, and heightening his opponent's irritability, and causing him every moment to lose more control over his hand and stick.

Once Anthony struck Uncle Sol on the side, and the thud would have showed how dead with wet the old man's coat was, even had not water squirted over the stick at the blow.

"Well done, Tony! One for thee!" Then Mr. Gibbs brought his stick down with a sweep, and cut Anthony on the left shoulder.

The sting and numbness roused Anthony's ire, and he made a furious attack on his antagonist, which was received with perfect equanimity and the hardly-broken strain of—

> I sing of champions bold,
> That wrestled—not for gold.

With ease, and without discontinuing his song, Sol caught a blow levelled at his skull, dealt with such force that Tony's hand was jarred by it.

> And all the cry
> Was Will Trefry,
> That he would win the day.
> So Will Trefry, huzzah!
> The ladies clap their hands and cry—
> Trefry! Trefry, huzzah!

Down came Sol's stick on his antagonist's right shoulder.

"There, there! You are no match for me," laughed the old man. "Will you give over—and pull off my boots?"

"Never!" shouted Anthony, and struck at him again, again ineffectually.

"Look out, Tony! save your head!"

The old man, by a dexterous back-handed blow, struck up Anthony's staff, and with a light stroke he touched his ear. He had no intention to hurt him, he might have cut open his head had he willed; but he never lost his good-humor, never took full advantage of the opportunities given him by the maladroitness of his antagonist.

It was exasperating to the young man to be thus played with, trifled with by a man whom he despised, but who he felt was, at all events at single-stick, his master.

"Hah!" shouted Anthony, triumphantly. His stick had caught in Sol's wig, and had whisked it off his skull, but instantly the old man with a sweep of his staff smote his stick from the hand of Anthony, leaving him totally disarmed.

"There, boy, there! Acknowledge thyself vanquished."

Then the old fellow threw himself down on the bench, with his back to the table.

"Come, lad, pull off my boots."

"I will not," said Anthony, savagely, "you had unfair odds. You stood with your back to the window."

"I was guarding my hat. Leave it where it lies, dribble, dribble—drip, and take my place on the floor, and try another bout, if thou wilt. Come on, I am ready for thee."

Mr. Solomon Gibbs stood up, resumed his single-stick, and stepped into the midst of the hall. Anthony, with face on fire with annoyance and anger, stooped for his own weapon, and then took the place with the table behind him, where previously Mr. Gibbs had stood.

"Ready!" called Sol. "Come along! so be I."

Another bout, staves whirling in the air, feet dancing forward, backward, to this side, then to that.

Reports as of pistols, when the sticks met.

Anthony was no match for the old gentleman even now that he had the advantage of the light. Sol was without his wig, he had not resumed it, and his shaven pate exhibited many a scar, the mark of former encounters in which he had got the worst, but in which also he had acquired his skill.

"My foot slipped!" said Anthony, as, having dealt an ineffectual blow from which Uncle Sol drew back, Anthony went forward to his knee, exposing himself completely to the mercy of his antagonist. "It is that cursed wet you have brought in—not fair."

"Choose a dry spot," said Sol.

"You have puddled the whole floor," answered the young man.

"Then it is equal for both of us. I have given thee many advantages, boy."

"I want none. I will have none."

His eye was on the old man's bald head; the sting of the blows he had received had exasperated him past consideration of what was due to an aged man, the uncle of his wife. The blows had numbed in him every sense save anger. He longed to be able to cut open that smooth round skull, and so revenge his humiliations and relieve his ill-humour. But he could not reach that glossy pate, not smite which way he would, so dexterous was the ward of Uncle Sol, so ready was his eye, and quick his arm in responding to his eye.

Not an advantage of any kind could he get over his adversary; he rained his blows fast, in the fury of his disappointment, hoping to beat down his guard by mere weight of blows; and Uncle Sol saw that he was blinded with wrath and had lost all sense of play, having passed into angry earnest. Then he twirled the stick from Anthony's hand once more, so that it flew to the ceiling, struck that, and fell by the hearth.

Mr. Gibbs laughed. "Mine again, Tony, boy!" He cast himself into the settle by the fire, stretched forth his legs, and said, "Come, pull off my boots."

Anthony stood lowering at him, panting and hot.

> " He strip't him to the waist,
> He boldly Trefry faced,
>   I'll let him know
>   That I can throw
>   As well as he to-day !
>   So little Jan, huzzah !
> And some said so—but others, No,
>   Trefry, Trefry, huzzah ! "

Sol sang lustily, with his hands in his pockets and his legs extended.

"Come, lad, down on your knees, and off with my boots."

Anthony did stoop, he went on one knee, not on both, and not to pull off the old man's boots, but to pick up his single-stick, whirl it round his head, and level a blow at the head of the undefended Uncle Sol; the blow would have fallen, had not Urith, who had entered the room at the moment, sprung forward, and caught it in her hand.

"Coward!" she exclaimed, "coward!—my uncle! an old man! I hate you. Would God I had never seen you!"

He had hurt her hand, he saw it, for she caught it to her bosom, then put it to her mouth, but her eyes glared at him over her hand like white lightning.

"A scurvy trick, lad—did not think thee capable of it," said Uncle Sol. "Has he hurt thee, child?"

He stood up.

Anthony flung the single-stick from him with an oath, put his hand to his brow, stood for a minute confronting Urith, looking into her fiery eyes, without exculpation, without a word. Then he turned, took up Uncle Sol's hat, without observing that it was not his own, flung it on his head, and went forth.

CHAPTER XXXIII.

INTO TEMPTATION.

Never is man so inflamed with anger, so overflowing with gall against others, as when he is conscious that he has laid himself open to animadversions. Anthony was bitter at heart against his wife and against her uncle, because he was aware, without being ready to acknowledge it, that he had acted ill towards both.

Why should not Urith have yielded at once to his wishes about the cradle? How obtuse to all delicate and elevated feeling she was to think that such a dusty, dingy, worm-eaten crib would suffice for his son, the representative of the house of Cleverdon—the child who was to be the means of reconciliation between himself and his father—the heir of Hall, who would open to him again the paternal mansion, and enable him to return there and escape from Willsworthy, a place becoming daily more distasteful, and likely to become wholly insupportable! That he had seen the cradle under disadvantage, in its abandoned, forgotten condition, and that it could be made to look well when a little feminine skill and taste had been expended on it, did not occur to him.

Moreover, his wife had no right to resist his wishes. He knew the world better than she—he knew what befitted one of the station his child would assume better than she. What might do for an heir to Willsworthy would be indecent for the heir to Hall—what might have suited a girl was not adapted to a boy. A wife should not question, but submit; the wish of her husband ought to be paramount to her, and she should understand that her husband in requiring a thing acted on his right as master, and that her place was to bow to his requisition. The old sore against his father that had partially skinned over broke out again, festered and hot. He was angry against his father, as he was against Urith. He was angry also with Mr. Gibbs for having proved a better man than himself at single-stick. Of old, Anthony had shown himself a tolerable wrestler, runner, single-stick player, thrower of quoits, player at bowls, among the young men of his acquaintance, and he had supposed himself a match for any one. Now he was easily disarmed and defeated by a half-tipsy old loafer, who had done no good to himself or any one in his life.

He had gone down in public estimation since his marriage—he who had been cock of the walk. And now he was not even esteemed in his own house; resisted by his wife, who set at naught his wishes, played with and beaten by that sot—her uncle.

There was no one who really admired and looked up to him any longer, except Julian Crymes.

He had wandered forth in the wet, without a purpose, solely with the desire to be away from the house where he had met with annoyance, where he had played—but this he would not admit, though he felt it—so poor a figure. He took his way to Peter Tavy, and went into the little inn of the Hare and Hounds at Cudliptown, the first hamlet he reached.

No one was there. Uncle Sol had sat there, and tippled and smoked; but had finally wearied of the solitariness, and had gone away. Now Anthony sat down where he had been, and was glad to find no one there, for in his present humour he was disinclined for company. The landlord came to him and took his order for *aqua vitæ*, brought it, and seated himself on a stool near him. But Anthony would not speak, or only answered his questions shortly, so as to let the man understand that his society was not desired. He took the hint, rose, and left the young man to his own thoughts.

Anthony put his head in his hand, and looked sullenly at the table. Many thoughts troubled him. Here he had sat on that eventful night after his first meeting and association with Urith on the moor. Here he had sat, with his heart on fire from her eyes, smouldering with love—just as an optic-glass kindles tinder. Here he had drunk, and, to show his courage, had gone forth to the churchyard and had broken down her father's head-post. He had brought it to this house, thrown it on this table—there! he doubted not, was the dint made by it when it struck the board.

How long was it since that night? Only a little over a twelve-month. Did Urith's eyes burn his heart now? There was a fire in them occasionally, but it did not make his heart flame with love, but with anger. Formerly he was the well-to-do Anthony Cleverdon, of Hall, with money in his pockets, able to take his pleasure, whatever it cost him. Now he had to reckon whether he could afford a glass before he treated himself to one, was warned against purchasing a new cradle as a needless expense, a bit of unpardonable extravagance.

He tossed off his glass, and signed for it to be refilled.

Then he thought of his father, of his rebellion against him, and he asked whether any good had come to him by that revolt. He, himself, was like to be a father shortly. Would his son ever set him at defiance, as he had defied his father? He wondered what his father was thinking of him; whether he knew how straitened his circumstances were, how clouded his happiness was, how he regretted the unretraceable step he had taken, how he was weary of Willsworthy, and how he hungered to hear of and to see Hall once more. There was little real conscious love of his father in his heart. He did not regret the breach for his father's sake, think of the desolation of the old man, with his broken hopes, his disappointed ambitions; he saw things only as they affected himself; he was himself the

pivot about which all his meditations turned, and he con-
doled with, lamented over, himself as the worst-used of
men, the man most buffeted by misfortune.

Anthony kicked the legs of the table impatiently. The
host looked at him and smirked. He had his own opinion
as to how matters stood with Anthony. He knew well
enough that the young man was unlike Mr. Gibbs, was no
toper; he had rarely stepped within his doors since his
marriage. As the host observed him, he chuckled to himself and said, "That fellow will come often here now. He
has a worm at the heart, and that worm only ceases to
gnaw when given *aqua vitæ* or punch."

What if the old Squire were to remain obdurate to the
end? What if he did not yield to the glad news that he
was grandfather to a new Anthony Cleverdon? Anthony's
heart turned sick at the thought. His son to be condemned to a toilful life at Willsworthy! But what if Urith
should at some future time be given a daughter, then her
estate would pass away from the young Anthony, and the
representative of the Cleverdons would be adrift in the
land without an acre, with hardly a coin—and Hall would
be held by an alien.

He stamped with rage.

His father was possessed with madness; the whole blame
fell on his father. Why was the old grudge against Richard Malvine to envenom the life of the son and grand-
children of the Squire? By the course he took the Squire
was not hurting the man whom he hated, who was in his
grave and insensible to injury, but his own living direct
descendants! Anthony was stabbing at his own family, in
his insensate malice. He thought over his quarrel with
the old man, and he regretted that he had not spoken
plainer, given his father sharper thrusts than he had—that
he had not dipped his words in pitch, and thrown them
blazing into his father's face.

His cheeks were burning; he clenched his fists and
ground his teeth, and then bowed his hot brow upon his
clenched hands. No doubt his father would hear how ab-
surdly Urith had danced at the Cakes, and would laugh
over it. He held up his head and looked round him,
thinking he heard the cackle of his father, so vividly did
he portray the scene to his imagination. No one was in

16

the room save the taverner ; but Anthony caught his eye
fixed on him, and he turned impatiently away.

Urith was not—there was no blinking the matter—a wife
suitable to him.   He compared her with his sister.   Bessie
was sweet, gentle, and with all her amiability dignified ;
Urith was rough, headstrong, and sullen.   She was uncouth,
unyielding—did not understand what were the tastes and
requirements of a man brought up on a higher plane of refinement.   He was weary of her lowering brow, of her silence, her dark eyes with a sombre, smouldering fire in
them.   He wondered how he could ever have admired her !
He never would feel content with her.   He had sacrificed
for her the most splendid prospects that any man had, and
she did not appreciate the sacrifice, and bow down before
him and worship him for it.

He knocked over his glass and broke it.   By heaven !
He wished he had never married Urith.

Anthony stood up, and threw down some coin to pay
for his brandy and for the broken glass.   He had knocked
over the glass in the gesture and start of disgust, when
he had wished himself unmarried, and now—he must pay
for the glass with money that came to him from Urith.
He knew this, it made him writhe, but he quickly
deadened the spasm by the consideration that for every
groat he had of his wife, he had given up a guinea.   She
was in debt to him, and the ridiculous little sums placed at
his disposal were but an inadequate acknowledgment of
the vast indebtedness under which she lay.

He stood for a few minutes irresolute in the rain, uncertain in which direction to turn.   Home ?—To Willsworthy ?   To the reproaches of Urith, to the tedious jests
and drawled-out songs of Mr. Gibbs ?   To the sight of
Urith ostentatiously holding her hand in a sling to let him
know that he had hurt her, when she intercepted the blow
aimed at her uncle ?

"Pshaw ! " said Anthony.   "She is not hurt, she cannot
be hurt.   She caught the stick in her palm.   It stung her,
no doubt, but will pass.   But what an outcry and fuss will
be made over it."

Yet his heart reproached him for these complaints.   He
knew that it was not the way with Urith to make an outcry and a fuss.   If he had hurt her, she would disguise

the fact. Anyhow, he resolved not to go back to Willsworthy.

Should he go on to Peter Tavy, and visit his cousin Luke?

No—he had no desire for the society of a parson. Luke
had married him to Urith; Luke was in part to blame for
his present condition of dissatisfaction. Luke might surely; if he had poked about in his books, have discovered
some canonical reason why the marriage could not have
taken place, at least as early as it did. Then—with delay
—his love might have abated, his head would have become
cooler, he would have been better able to balance loss and
gain.

"Loss and gain!" scoffed Anthony; "all loss and no
gain!"

Luke would surmise that all was not right, he was keen-
sighted—he had already had the impertinence to give an
oblique admonition to Anthony to be tender and forbear-
ing to his wife. If he went to him now, Luke would nail
him, and hammer remonstrances into him.

By heaven! no—he wanted no sermons preached to him
on week-days.

He walked to the door of Farmer Cudlip. The Cudlips
had been on that estate much as the Cleverdons had been
at Hall, for centuries, but the Cudlips had owned their own
land, as yeomen, whereas the Cleverdons had been tenant-
farmers. Now the Cleverdons had taken a vast stride up
the ladder, whereas the Cudlips, who had given their name
to the hamlet, had remained stationary. The Cudlips,
though only yeomen, were greatly respected. Some of
the gentle families were of mushroom growth compared
with them. It was surmised that the Cudlips had originally been Cutcliffs, and that this yeoman family had issued
from the ancient stock of Cutcliffe of Damage, in North
Devon, which had gone forth like a scriptural patriarch
and made itself a settlement on the verge of the moor, and
called the land after its own name; but there was no evidence to prove this. It was at one time a conjecture of a
Rector of Peter Tavy, who mentioned it to the Cudlip then
at Cudliptown, who shrugged his shoulders and said, "It
might be for ought he knew." In the next generation the
descent was talked about as all but certain, in the third it
was a well-established family tradition.

Anthony stood in the doorway of the old ancestral farm.
He had knocked, but received no answer ; no one had
come to the door in response. He knew or guessed the
reason, for overhead he heard Mistress Cudlip putting the
youngest child to bed ; he had heard the little voice of the
child raised in song, chanting its evening hymn :—

> Matthew, Mark, Luke and John,
> Bless the bed that I lay on.
> Four angels to my bed,
> Two to bottom, two to head ;
> Two to hear me when I pray,
> Two to bear my soul away.

Probably Farmer Cudlip was not within. Had he been,
the knock of Anthony would have been responded to by a
loud and hearty call to come in.

Anthony did not repeat the knock. It was of no use his
entering that house if the master were out ; he did not
want to pass words with women folk. But he halted
where he was in order to make up his mind whither he
should go. He craved for—not exactly flattery, but something of that adulation which had been lavished on him by
all alike—old and young, men and maids—when he was
Anthony Cleverdon of Hall, and which had been denied
him since he had become Anthony Cleverdon of Willsworthy.

Under the humiliation he had received in his own house,
under the sense of disgrace which he had brought on himself, first by his anger over the cradle, and the breaking it
down with a blow of an iron bar ; then, by his hand raised
over an old man, defenceless ; he felt a real need for adulation. He could not hold up his head, recover his moral
elasticity till he had encountered some one who did not
flaunt and beat him down. Fox—should he go and see Fox
at Kilworthy ? Fox was his friend ; Fox had a sharp tongue
and could say cutting things that would make him laugh,
would shake the moths out of his fretted brain. Yes, he
would go to Kilworthy and see Fox.

As he formed this resolution he was conscious that he
was false to himself. He did not want to see Fox. Fox
would not look up to him with eyes full of loving devotion.
Fox's colour would not flush to the cheek when he entered.

Fox's pulses would not bound when his step was heard on the gravel. Fox would not in words encourage him to think well of himself, to esteem himself again as the old cock of the walk in plumage, instead of a wretched draggled fowl. No—he did not want to see Fox, but Fox's sister. He would go to Kilworthy to see, to hear Julian Crymes, but he repeated to himself—"I must have a talk with Fox."

Then he heard the little child's voice upstairs repeating the Prayer of Prayers after its mother.

"Forgive us our trespasses," said Mistress Cudlip.

"Tespusses," said the child.

"As we forgive them that trespass against us."

"As we 'give them——" a pause. The mother assisted the little one, and it completed the sentence.

"And lead us not into temptation."

"And lead us not——"

Anthony drew his cloak closer about him, shook the water from Solomon's hat, that he wore, and set it again on his head.

"Into temptation," said the mother.

"Lead us not into temptation," repeated the child. Anthony bent his head, and went out into the rain, went heedless of the warning that hammered at his heart, went wilfully—into temptation.

CHAPTER XXXIV.

A COLD WOOING.

"Get yourself ready," ordered Squire Cleverdon, looking at Bessie across the table. "Your aunt is unwell, and I have sent word that we would come and see her. A wet day, and nothing better to be done, so we can find out what is the matter with her."

"Certainly, father," answered Elizabeth, with alacrity. "I hope nothing serious is the matter with her?"

"Oh, serious, no."

The manner of the Squire was never gracious to his daughter; always imperious, but this day there was a peculiarity in it that struck her. There was, she felt instinct-ively, something in the background.

"What is it, father? I pray you tell me. She is not in any danger?"

"Oh, danger? No." A twitching of his cheeks marked inner uneasiness.

Bessie looked anxiously at him. "I am sure, father, you are hiding something from me."

"Go at once and get ready! Do not stop chattering here like a parrot," he roared forth, and Bessie fled.

Elizabeth had no anxiety over the weather. That was not the day of umbrellas, but then, neither was it the day of fine bonnets. The skirts were worn short, and did not trail in and collect the mud. A woman pinned up her gown, or looped it at the girdle, exposing a bright coloured petti-coat, and below that her ankles, and there were many inches between the mud and the petticoat. A thick serge mantle covered gown and petticoat; it was provided with a hood that was drawn over the head, and bright eyes looked out of the hood and laughed at the rain and cold.

We sometimes wonder now how the world got on before the introduction of the umbrella. Very well. It was dryer, warmer, better protected in former days. It is only since the invention and the expansion of the parapluie, that those marvels of millinery, the nineteenth-century bonnet, piled up of feathers and flowers, and bead and lace, became pos-sible. The umbrella has been a bell-shade under which it has grown.

Mr. Cleverdon was not communicative on the ride to Tavistock. Now and then he growled forth a curse on the weather, but said nothing against Magdalen. This sur-prised his daughter, who was accustomed to hear him grum-ble at his sister if she occasioned him any inconvenience; but she charitably set it down to real concern for Magdalen, and this increased her fear that more was the matter with her aunt than her father chose to admit.

Aunt Magdalen really was indisposed; but the indispo-sition was partly, if not chiefly, due to her distress of mind about her niece. She knew that her brother had resolved to act upon her own to marry Bess to young Crymes, and that he expected his sister to help him to overcome any op-position that might be encountered from Bessie. Poor

Elizabeth had as little suspicion, as she accompanied her father to Tavistock, that he was about to sacrifice her, as had Isaac when he ascended Moriah at the side of Abraham.

When Mr. Cleverdon and Bessie arrived at the house of Miss Magdalen, near the Abbey Bridge, they observed a man's hat and cloak hung up in the hall.

"Oh!" exclaimed Elizabeth, "the doctor is here! I am sure my aunt is really very ill."

At the same moment the side door opened, and the old lady appeared, and caught her niece in her arms.

"He is here," said Magdalen—"arrived only a minute before you."

"Who is here?" asked Bessie. "What do you mean?"

"Come aside with me into my snuggery," said her aunt. "I have a word with you before I speak with your father, and in the parlour he will find Anthony."

"Anthony! My brother!" with a joyful flash from Bessie; and she flung her arms round her aunt. "Oh, you dear—you good Aunt Magdalen! You have——"

"Have done with this folly," said the Squire, angrily. "Are you still such a fool as to think that when I say a thing I shall change about? No—your brother is not in there, but your bridegroom."

Miss Cleverdon put up her hand entreatingly to stop her brother, and hastily brought her niece into the adjoining room and shut the door.

"What is the meaning of this?" asked Bessie, with some composure. She had now a suspicion that the visit concerned herself, and not her aunt.

"My dear," said Magdalen, "do seat yourself—no, not in that chair; it is hard, and there is something wrong with the back—the bar comes exactly where it ought not, and hurts the spine—at least, I find it so. I never sit in it myself, never. Take that seat by the fireplace. I am so sorry there is nothing burning on the hearth, but, on my word, I did not expect to have you in here. I thought I might have spoken a word with you in the parlour before he came, or—but, bless my heart, Bess! I am so distracted I hardly know what I thought."

Bessie shook down her skirt over her dark-blue petticoat, and seated herself where her aunt desired, then laid her hands in her lap, and looked steadily at Miss Cleverdon.

"You are not ill, then?" she said.

"Oh, my dear, ill! I have not slept a wink, nor had a stomach for aught. I should think I was indeed ill, but all about you. You must remember that the commandment with promise is that which refers to the submission of a child to the parent; but, Lord! Bess, I would not have you forced against your wishes. Your father's mind is made up, and he has met with a sore disappointment in the case of Anthony. I do think it will be a comfort to him, and heal over that trouble somewhat, if he finds you more pliant than was Anthony. But, Lord! Bess, nothing, I trust, hinders you—no previous attachment. Lord! I did at one time think that your heart was gone a-hankering after Luke."

Bessie, who had become very pale, flushed, and said, "I entreat thee, aunt, not to have any fancies concerning me. I never gave thee grounds for any such opinion."

"I know that, I know that, child. But, Lord! an old woman like me must have her thoughts about those she loves and wishes well for."

"Aunt," said Bessie, "I think I can understand that my father desires to have me married, and has asked you to see me thereon. I have had some notions thereupon myself, but I would gladly hear from you whom he has fixed on, though, indeed, I think I can guess."

"It is Fox," answered Miss Cleverdon, and looked down on the floor, and arranged her stool, which was slipping from under her feet. "There, there, I have told thee; thy father put it on me. And I can only say to thee that which thou knowest well thyself. He belongs to an ancient family, once well estated, but now sadly come down; nevertheless, there is something of the old patrimony remaining. He is thy father's friend's son; and as it has come about that the families that were to be united by my nephew have not been thus joined, it is not wonderful that your father would see them clipped together by thee."

"I cannot indeed take Fox," said Bessie, gravely.

"Well—well—the final choosing must be with thee, wench. All that thy father can do is to say he desires it, and all I can do is to support him. God forbid that we should constrain thee unwilling, and yet a blessing does rain down from above the clouds on the heads of such children as be obedient. Now look to Anthony, and see if he be happy, having gone against his father's wishes."

"Is he unhappy?" asked Bessie.

"I do not think him the same at all. He is restless, and his mood has lost all brightness. I have not seen much of him, but what I have seen has made me uneasy concerning him, and what Fox tells me still further disconcerts me."

"I may not go to Willsworthy. I may not see my brother nor Urith—except by very chance I meet them," said Bessie, heaving a sigh, and her eyes filling. "My father seems no nearer forgiving than he was at first."

"I do not think that aught will move him to forgiveness save, perchance, the finding of ready obedience in thee."

"I cannot—indeed I cannot, in this," said Bess.

"Lord! I would not counsel thee against thy happiness," pursued Magdalen. "But see how ill it has worked with Anthony. He followed his own will, and went against the commandment of his father, and it eats as a canker into his heart, I can see that; now if then——"

Then the door was thrown open, and the Squire appeared in it, with Fox behind his back in the passage.

"Sister," said old Cleverdon, "time enough has been spent over preparing Bess for what must be. As you have not brought her unto us, to the parlour, we've come in here to you. Come in, Tony! Come in! Look at her —there she sits; kiss her, lad! She is thine!"

But Fox did not offer to do what he was required; Bessie started and drew back, fearing lest he should, but was at once reassured by his deprecatory look and uplifted hand.

"May I enter?" asked Fox.

"Come in, boy, come in!" said the old man, answering for his sister, as though the house were his own; and his own it might be considered, for it was paid for and furnished out of Hall; the maintenance of Miss Cleverdon fell on him and his estate.

"Come!" said the Squire, roughly, "shut the door behind you, boy. Go over beside her. Take her hand. Hold out yours, Bess. Do y' hear? It is all settled between us."

Fox entered the room, fastened the door, and remained
fumbling at the lock, with his face to it, affecting great
diffidence.   Mr. Cleverdon took him by the arm and thrust
him away, and pointed imperiously to where Bess sat, near
the fireplace, on which burnt no spark ; her hands lay in
her lap folded, and her eyes on the hearth.   The window
was behind her.   The little room was panelled with dark oak
that was polished.   There were no pictures, no ornaments
on the wall—only one oval pastel over the mantelshelf of
Magdalen when she was a girl.   The colour had faded from
this, the pink gone wholly—it was a poor bleached picture
of a plain maiden ; and now beneath it sat one as blanched,
for all the colour had gone out of Bessie's face, and she had
assumed the same stiff attitude that her aunt had maintained when drawn by the artist.

Fox, with apparent reluctance, went over to the fireplace ;
Elizabeth looked at her father with great drops formed on
her brow, as though the damp of the atmosphere had condensed on that surface of white alabaster.

"Give him your hand.   Are you deaf?"

Elizabeth remained with her hands folded as before, her
eyes wide open, fixed reproachfully on her father.   She
had given her young life to him, borne his roughness, experienced from him no love, no consideration—in every
way sacrificed herself to make his home happy, and now he
cast her happiness from him, gave her up to a man for
whom she had no regard, without considering her feelings
in the smallest degree.   Then Magdalen looked at the
crayon drawing of herself and down at Bessie, and some
reminiscence at once painful and yet sweet in its bitterness
came back to her—a remembrance, may be, of some sacrifice she had been called to make when about Bessie's age,
and the tears came into her eyes.

"Brother," she said, "you are too hasty.   The poor
child is overcome with surprise.   You handle her too
roughly.   Tell her that her well-being is dear to you, tell
her that this plan of yours has been considered by you as
the best for her, but do not attempt to drive her, as you
might a sheep into the fold to be shorn, with a crack of
whip and bark."

"You keep silence, Magdalen," said the Squire.   "You
have had time to say what you had, and have, it seems,

wofully mismanaged the task set thee. I ought to know how to deal with my children."

"Nay, brother, I cannot be sure of that, after what has fallen out with Anthony."

Magdalen regretted having made this sharp reply when it was too late to recall it.

"You understand me, Bess," said the old man; "I have let you see by the way in which I have treated that rebellious son of mine, that my wishes are not to be slighted, my commands not to be disobeyed. You do as I tell you. Give your hand to Tony Crymes, or else——"

Bessie's calm, steadfast eyes were on him. He did not finish his sentence.

"Or else, what, father?" she asked.

He did not answer her; he put out one hand to the table, leaned on it, and thrust the other behind him under the coat-tails. His brows were knit, and his eyes glittered into stony hardness and cruel resolve.

"I cannot obey you, father," said Bessie.

"You will not!" shouted the old man.

"Father, I neither will, nor can obey, you. I have known Fox, I mean Anthony Crymes, ever since I have been a child, but I have never cared for him." She turned to Fox apologetically; even then, in that moment of trial and pain to herself, she could not endure to say a word that might seem to slight and give a pang to another. "I beg your pardon, Fox, I mean that I have never cared for you more than, in any other way than, as a friend, and as Julian's brother."

"Pshaw! What of that?" asked the old man, somewhat lowering his voice, and attempting to keep his temper under control. "Love comes after marriage where it did not precede it. See what love comes to when it is out of place before it, in your brother's case."

"I cannot promise Anthony Crymes my love, for I know it never will come. I am glad he is the friend of my brother, and as such I regard him, but I esteem him only for what merits he has in him. I never can love him— never—never!"

"Disobedient hussy!" exclaimed the old man, losing the slight control he had exerted momentarily over himself. "Am I to be set at defiance by you as well as by Anthony?

By heaven, I did not think there was such folly in the family. It did not come from me—not from my side. I will be obeyed. I will not have it said in the town that I cannot have my own way with my children."

He looked so angry, so threatening, that Fox interfered. He slipped between Bessie and her father, and said:

"Master Cleverdon, I will have no constraint used. If you attempt to coerce Bessie, then I withdraw at once. I have known and loved her for many years, and would now have hardly dared to offer myself, but that you cast out the suggestion to me. I saw that Bessie did not love me, and I held back, hoping the time might come when she would, perhaps, be guided less by the feelings of the heart and more by the cool reason of the brain. If she refuses me, it shall be a refusal to me, to an offer made in my own way, with delicacy and consideration for her feelings, not with threat and bluster. Excuse plain speaking, Squire, but such are my views on this matter, and this is a matter that concerns Bessie and me first, and you, Master Cleverdon, afterwards."

"Yes," said Magdalen, "your violence, brother, will effect nothing. You will only drive your remaining child from under your roof, as you drove Anthony."

"Be silent, you magpie!" shouted old Cleverdon, but he looked alarmed.

"Now," said Fox, "you have frightened and offended Bessie, and effected no good. Let her walk home, although it is raining, and I will accompany her part of the way, if not the whole, and speak to her in my own manner, and hear her decision from her own lips."

Bessie stood up.

"I am content," she said; "but do not for a moment think that my determination is to be changed. Have with you, Fox. Father, you will follow when your business in the town is over, and will catch me up. You said, I think, that you were going up to Kilworthy to see Mr. Crymes."

CHAPTER XXXV.

A WET WOOING.

Bessie and Fox walked side by side, but without speaking, as long as they were in the street of Tavistock, with houses on both sides. Here there were, perhaps, more mud, more numerous puddles, than outside the town. Moreover, the water that fell on the roofs dripped or shot in streams down on the heads of such as ventured to walk near the walls, and the only escape from these cataracts and douches was in the well-worn midst of the street where the dirt was deepest because the roadway was there most trampled. The douching from the descending shoots of water, the circumventing of the pools, caused the walk of the two to be no more than approximately side by side. No walk could be direct, but must consist of a series of festoons and loops; but on passing the last house, Fox came boldly up to the side of Elizabeth Cleverdon, and said :

"Bessie, I am at a disadvantage; who can be the lover in such weather, and how can I lay myself at thy feet when the road is ankle-deep in mire? I should sink into the slough of despond and the mud close over my head and back or ever I had an answer from thee."

"There can and will be no romance in the matter," answered Elizabeth. "It is to me a sad and serious business, for if there be truth in what you say—that you have cared for me, then I am sorry to disappoint you; but, on my honour as a maid, Fox, I never suspected it."

"That may well be, for thou art so modest," replied Fox Crymes. "Yet I do assure thee the attachment has been of a long time, and has thrown its roots through my heart. Even now—or now least of all, would I have held my tongue had not thy father encouraged me to speak."

"Why least of all now?"

"Because now, Bessie, that thy brother Anthony is out of favour thou art an heiress with great prospects; and neither would I seem to make my suit to thee because of these prospects, nor to step into the place and profits that should have belonged to Anthony."

Bessie looked round at him gratefully.

"I am glad you think of Anthony," she said.

"Of course I think of him. He is my friend. None have mourned more than I at his estrangement from his father. It has affected him in many ways. Not only is he cut off from Hall and his father, but disappointment has soured him, and I do not believe he is happy with his wife."

"What!—Anthony not happy with his wife!" Bessie sighed and hung her head. She remembered the dance at the Cakes, Anthony's neglect of Urith, and the attention he paid to Julian. No doubt this had occasioned a quarrel when he reached his home. Poor Anthony! Poor Anthony!

"And now," said Bessie, gently—"now that we are quite alone together, let me assure you that, though I am thankful to you for the honour you have done me by asking for me, that yet I must beg you to desist from pressing a suit that must be unsuccessful. I can—after what you have said, and after the good feeling you have shown —I will, respect you. I can do no more."

"You have given your heart to another?" half-asked Fox, with a leer that she did not notice.

"No—no one has my heart, for no one has thought it worth his while to ask for it, except you; and, alas! to you I cannot give it."

"But, if it is still free, may I not put in a claim for it?"

"No—it can never be yours."

"I will not take such a refusal. At bob-apple any boy may jump for the fruit, till it is carried away. Your heart is hung up to be jumped for, and I will not be thrust aside, and refused permission to try my luck along with the rest."

"No one else will think of coming forward."

"There you are mistaken, Bess. Consider what you are now—at all events what you are esteemed to be. You will inherit Hall and all your father's savings. Your father has made no secret of his determination to disinherit Anthony. He has told several persons that he has made his will anew, and constituted you his heiress, your husband to take the name of Cleverdon. This is known and talked about everywhere. Do you suppose that with such a prospect there will not be a score of aspirants ready to cast off their names and become at once the husband of the most charming girl anywhere in South Devon, and a rich Squire Cleverdon of Hall ? "

Bessie was infinitely hurt and shocked. She to rob her brother of his birthright ! God forbid !

"Fox," she said, "this can never be. If I should at any time become owner of Hall, I would give it up immediately to dear Anthony."

"But," said Fox, with a mocking laugh on his face, "is it not likely that your father knows what you would do, and will take precautions against it, by settling the estate through your husband on your eldest son ? You could not, were the estate so settled, do as you propose."

Bessie was silent, looking down into the mud, and forgetting to pick her way among the puddles. The rain had formed drops along the eave of her hood, and there were drops within on the fringes of her eyes.

"You will be persecuted by suitors," Fox continued, "and I ask you is there any you know about here whom you would prefer to me ?"

She did not answer him, she was thinking, with her hood drawn by one hand very close about her face, that no one approaching, nor Fox, should see her distress.

"Do not speak of others," said Bessie, at length ; "suffi-cient to let things be till they come. I am, and you need not pretend it is not so—I am but a plain homely girl, and that will dampen the ardour of most young men who sigh for pretty faces."

"You do yourself injustice, Bessie. For my part I look to the qualities of the heart and understanding, and you have a generous and noble heart, and a clear and sound understanding. Beauty withers, such qualities ripen. I never was one to be taken with the glitter of tinsel. I look to and love sterling metal. It was your good qualities which attracted my admiration, and, 'fore Heaven, Bess, I think you uncommon comely."

" I pray you," urged Bessie, "desist from your suit. I have told thee it is fruitless."

" But I will not desist without a reason. Give me a reason, and I am silent. Without one, I will press on. I have a better right than any of the unknown who will come about thee like horseflies after awhile."

" I do not love thee. Is not that a reason ? "

"None at all. I do not see why thou mayest not come
to like me."

Bessie walked on some way in silence.

Presently she said, in a plaintive, low voice : "I will give
thee, then, a reason ; and, after that, turn on thy heel and
leave me in peace. I have——" Her voice failed her, and
she stepped on some paces before she could recover it.
"I tell thee this, Fox, only because thou hast been frank
with me, and hast shown me a generous heart. My reason
is this—and, Fox, there must, I reckon, be some confidence between two situated as we are—it is this, that long,
long ago I did dearly love another, and I love him still."

"Now, Bessie!" exclaimed Fox, standing still in the
road, and she halted also, "you assured me that you had
given your heart to none."

"I have given it to none, for none asked it of me."

"I do not understand. You speak riddles."

"Not at all. Cannot a poor, ugly girl love a man—
noble, wise and good—and never let him know it, and
never expect that it will be returned? I have heard a
tale of a Catholic saint, that he wore a chain of barbed
iron about his body, under his clothing, where it ate into
his flesh and cankered his blood ; but none suspected it.
He went about his daily tasks, and laughed with the merry-
makers ; yet all the while the barbs were working deeper
into him, and he suffered. There may be many poor, ill-
favoured—ay, and well-favoured—wenches like that saint.
They have their thorny braids about their hearts, and hide
them under gay bodices, that none suspect aught. But—
God forgive me," said Bessie, humbly, with soft, faltering
voice—"God pardon me that I spoke of this as a chain of
iron barbs, festering the blood. It is not so. There is no
iron there at all, and no fester whatsoever—only very long-
drawn pains, and now and then, a little pure, honest blood
runs from the wound. There, Fox, I have shown this only
to thee. No one else knows thereof, and I have shown it
thee only as a reason why I cannot love thee."

Fox Crymes made a grimace.

Bessie stepped along her way. Fox followed.

Presently she turned, hearing his steps, with a gesture
of surprise, and said, "What, not gone yet?"

"No, Bessie, I admire thee the more, and I do not even

now give over the pursuit. I would yet learn, hast thou
any thought that he whom thou lovest will be thine."

"No! no! never; I do not desire it."

"Not desire it?"

"Nay, for he has loved another; he has never given me
a thought. I must not say that. Kind and good he has
ever been—a friend; but he can and will be nothing more."

"There you mistake, Bessie. When he learns that you
are the heiress to Hall his eyes will be wonderfully opened
to your charms, and he will come and profess he ever loved
thee." He spoke bitterly, laying bare his own base motives in so doing. But Bessie was too guileless to suspect
him. She reared herself up; his words conveyed such a
slight on the honor of Luke that she could not endure it.

"Never! never!" she said, and her eyes flashed through
her tears. "Oh, Fox! if you knew who he was you would
never have said that."

"But if he should come and solicit thy hand?"

"He cannot. He has told me that he loved another."

She resumed her walk.

Fox continued to attend her, in silence. He was puzzled
what line to adopt. What she had told him had surprised
and discomfited him. That Bessie—the ordinary, plain-
faced, methodical Bessie—should have had her romance
was to him a surprise.

How little do we know of what passes under our very
feet. Who dreamed of magnetic currents till the mag-
netometer registered their movements? Waves roll
through the solid crust of earth without making it tremble
at all; magnetic storms rage around us without causing a
disturbance in the heavens, and but for the unclosing of
our eyes through the scientific instrument we should know
nothing about them—have laughed at the thought of their
existence.

"I must needs walk on with thee," said Fox; "for I cannot leave thee till thy father come and overtake thee. And
if I walk at thy side, well—we must talk, at all events I
must, for my tongue has not the knack of lying still behind
my teeth."

Fox was at heart angry at his ill-success; he had hoped
to have made a great impression on Bessie by the declaration of his love. She was but an ordinarily-favoured girl, as

17

he knew well enough had never been sought by young men, always thrust aside, accustomed to see others preferred to herself—at a dance to be left against the wall without a partner, after church to be allowed to accompany her father home, without any lad seeking to attach himself to her and disengage her from the old man. To a girl so generally disregarded his addresses ought to have come as a surprise, and have been accepted with eagerness. He was in a rage with her for the emphatic and resolute manner in which she refused him.

"Let us talk of Anthony," said he.

"With all my heart," she replied, with a sigh of relief.

"Do you see any way in which your brother can be received again into favour?" he inquired.

She shook her head. "Nothing that I can say has any effect on my father. He will not permit me to go near Willsworthy."

"Then I can say what is the only way in which peace and good will may be brought back into the family. It lies in your hands to build a bridge between your father and Tony. I am certain that in his heart the old Squire is discontented that things should remain as they are, but he has spoken the word, and he is too proud to withdraw it. If it could have come to pass that you took my hand, then I do not believe that your father would resist our united persuasion. See how much weight we could have brought to bear on him, how we could have watched our opportunities, how—if it should happen at any time that Tony should have a child, we might have brought it to the old man, set it on his knees, and then together have taken the right moment to plead for Anthony."

Bessie drew a long breath.

"I would do a great deal, almost anything, to bring about what you speak of, but this means is beyond my power. It cannot be. I know now how good and faithful a friend you are to my dear, dear brother Anthony. I must again speak very plainly. I do desire, Fox, in all ways to spare you a wound, but you will take no refusal. You said, 'Let us talk of Anthony,' and you work it round to the same point. I shall never marry; I cannot marry you; I shall take no one else. I pray you desist from your pursuit. You heard what Aunt Magdalen said, that my father, if he

persisted, would drive me to run away, as did Anthony.
It will be so. If my father will not accept my refusal, then
I must go. I shall go to Anthony and his wife, or to my
aunt. I could not swear what is false to you or to any one
else. Before the minister of God I would not promise
love, and love to my husband only, knowing that I could
not love, for my love was elsewhere. No," added Bessie,
shaking her head, " I must be true, always true, to myself,
and before God."

As she spoke, both heard the clatter of horse's hoofs.
They halted, parted, one on each side of the road, and
looked back. A man was galloping along with his head
down against the rain, he did not look up, but remained
bowed as he approached.

"Father!" called Bessie, for she recognised both the
horse and the rider. He did not draw rein, apparently he
did not hear her. Certainly he saw neither her nor Fox.
Wrapped in his own thoughts, forgetful of his daughter,
of his promise to take her up, he galloped past, and sent
the mud flying from his horse's hoofs, bespattering her as
he passed.

CHAPTER XXXVI.

IN TEMPTATION.

Anthony entered the little parlour, or bower, of Kilworthy. It looked comfortable and bright. A fire of logs
burnt on the hearth, with turf thrust into the interstices
between the logs, and the pleasant fragrance of the peat
filled the room, without being strong enough to be offensive. Outside, everything was grey and moist and dull,
within a red and yellow sparkle, and a sense of dryness.
The walls were hung with good paintings, in silvered
frames, richly carved. A crimson mat was on the polished
floor and embroidered crimson curtains hung by the
window.

Julian was doing no work. She was sitting by the fire
in a day-dream, in much the attitude that was assumed by
Bessie at that very time in the little parlour of Aunt Magdalen's house, beside her cold, cheerless hearth.

Anthony had thrown off his wet cloak and sopped hat; and was fairly dry beneath them, he wore high and strong boots, and these he had made as clean as was possible on the mats before entering.

"How are you, Julian? Where is Fox?"

Julian started as he spoke. Her mind had been engaged on him, and the sound of his voice came on her unwelcome at that moment.

Sitting over her fire she had been considering her conduct, asking herself whither she was going, what was to be the end of her encouragement of Anthony.

She repeated to herself as excuse, that she had thrown the glove at Urith, and that the challenge had been accepted. The contest was a fair and open one; each used what weapons she had. If men might call each other out and fight, why not women also contend on their own special ground, in their own manner?

Urith had won in the first round, had carried off the prize, but in this second round, she—Julian—was beating her adversary. She could not take the prize over to herself, and wear it as her own; that she knew well enough; but she could render it worthless in the eyes of Urith— spoil irretrievably her pleasure in it.

Was she justified in pursuing her advantage? Was the result she would arrive at one to fill her with content? She would destroy the happiness of Urith, perhaps that also of Anthony, break in pieces all domestic concord for ever in Willsworthy, to satisfy her own pride and revenge. She loved Anthony, always had loved him, but had sufficient cool resolution not to go a step with him beyond what she would allow herself, to establish the completeness of her triumph over Urith. She loved him out of pure selfishness, without the smallest regard for his well-being, hardly more compunction for the torture she was administering than has the child that plays with a cockchafer by thrusting a pin through it, attaching a thread to the pin, and whirling the insect round his head. But Julian was not suffered to proceed without some qualms of conscience, some warnings given by her better nature, and when Anthony entered it was at a moment when she had almost resolved to give up the contest, satisfied with what she had gained.

Fox was out, answered Julian to Anthony's inquiry, he had gone into the town. Then she was silent.

Anthony went into the window, where was a box seat, and planted himself there, not looking at her, but looking away, at the door; and he took his knee between his hands. Both remained silent. He was weary, not with the length of his walk, but with walking wrapped in a cloak that had become heavy with moisture, and with the closeness of the day. He was, moreover, in no good mood, dissatisfied with himself, discontented with the world, and at a loss what to say, now that he found himself in the company of the girl he had come to see.

Julian pouted, and looked at the fire. The day, with its continuous drizzle, had been one of tedium to her. She was not accustomed to work, like Bessie, whose hands were never idle. She took up some embroidery, tried to paint, attempted knitting, and threw all aside, after ten minutes, with restless impatience. She had taken a book in the afternoon, read a chapter, remembered that she had read the same book before, and cast it into the window seat. She did not even replace it on its proper shelf. Then she had fallen to her desultory musings, to listening languidly to her conscience, and answering its remonstrances evasively. She had, as already said, almost resolved to leave Anthony alone, and to be content with what mischief she had already done. But the resolution was no more than *almost* arrived at; for she had not the moral courage to make a final resolution to which she would force herself to adhere.

Anthony, on his side, had been spoiled, so, on her side, had Julian. He had been flattered and made much of as the heir to Hall; she had been treated in a similar manner as heiress to Kilworthy. Her mother had died early, her father was an unpractical political and religious dreamer, who had exercised no control over her; and she had been brought up chiefly by servants, who had fawned on her, and given her whatever she wanted. She was therefore wayward, wilful, and selfish, with no fixed principles, and no power of self-control—a feminine reflex of Anthony, but with more passion and latent force of character than he.

The two sat silent for full ten minutes, each looking in

an opposite direction, and each with a shoulder turned to
the other. Anthony had come hoping to be received with
pleasure; but Julian showed no alacrity in receiving his
visit, and this helped to depress him.

Presently Julian turned her face over her shoulder, and
said, "I suppose you do not know where Fox is, or you
would not have come to his lair."

"Certainly I do not know."

Anthony looked at the window-glass. Either the fire
had considerably heated the atmosphere of the room, or
the wind without had veered northward and made the air
colder, for breath had condensed on the glass. He put up
his finger, and wrote on a pane "A. C."

"I know, for he was too full of his plans to keep them
from bursting forth at his mouth," said Julian.

"I dare be bound it was so," answered Anthony, list-
lessly; then on another pane he wrote "J. C."

"And you are not interested to know whither he has
gone and what he seeks?"

"No," said Anthony, "I came here to see him. I
found no one at Cudliptown, and Sol Gibbs is dull company at Willsworthy."

"You have other company there than Sol Gibbs."

"Whom do you mean?"

"There is Urith—your wife," with a sharp flash of her
eye out of the corner; and insensibly she put one knee up
and hugged it as did Anthony.

"Oh! Urith," he repeated, in a tone in which she discerned something like a sneer.

"Your wife."

"One cannot be talking to a wife all day," he said, peevishly, and let fall his leg and loosened his plaited fingers.
She instinctively did the same.

"Can you not? Oh, indeed, that is news to me. I
should have thought that you would never have lacked
material for talk. Flames, darts—hymeneal altars smoking."

He looked sullenly out of the window, turning his back
to her, and made no reply. She waited for a response,
then said,

"If not these subjects, then chickens and goslings."

He turned his head impatiently, and said,

"You are mocking me. You!—and I came here for comfort from you—you, Julian!"

There was pain in his manner and expression, and she was somewhat touched.

"Oh, Anthony, you said you had come here after Fox, and now you say you came to see me."

He passed his hand over his forehead to wipe away the drops formed there. He did not answer her, to correct the effect of his words, but put up his hand to the glass, and with a shaking finger drew on the diamond pane, between the initials, a lover's knot.

"Anthony," she said, after a pause, "I suppose I must tell you why Fox has gone into Tavistock, for it concerns you mightily, and you should not be kept in the dark concerning him. Do you recall what I said when we were dancing together at Wringworthy?"

"No, Julian, nothing. That was a bright and delightful dream. I have awaked out of it, and remember nothing."

"I told you that Fox had set his mind on Bessie—your Bessie. You scouted the notion, but I spoke the truth. And he has been as open to his father and me thereon as is possible for him. You, Anthony, have a good and kind nature—you are too ready to trust any one. Always upright and straightforward yourself, never thinking evil in your heart, never putting forth a foot to trip up an enemy—certainly never a friend."

Anthony's head was raised. This was what he wanted—a few words of commendation came down as warm rays of sunshine on his depressed and drooping heart.

"You, Tony, have never mistrusted Fox, for it was not in you to mistrust any one. But I know his real nature. He is seeking his own ends. He has been over at Hall two and three times a week, and——" she laughed, "will you believe it? has been cajoling the old man, your father, into the belief that it is possible he may win and wear me, as—as—" she hesitated. "As he was disappointed——"

Anthony turned and looked at her, and their eyes met. Hers fell, and he looked again hastily at the window-pane—at the initials, and the lover's knot between them. The moisture had collected in the figures he had described, and had formed drops at the bottom of each downstroke.

"That is not all. Whether your father builds greatly on

this or not I cannot say ; but Fox has dangled the prospect before him, whilst he snatched at something for himself—even at Bessie, the heiress of Hall, now that you are thrown out into the wet and cold."

Anthony sighed involuntarily. Yes, he was out, indeed, in the wet and cold at Willsworthy—not metaphorically only, but actually as well.

"Now," continued Julian, "you shall hear the whole plan as worked out. Fox has gone in to-day to meet Bessie and your father at your Aunt Magdalen's house, and your aunt has been inveigled into uniting her persuasion to the commands of your father to induce Bessie to jump down the Fox's throat."

"It cannot be," said Anthony. "Bess will never—and she does not care for Fox."

"She may not have the power to resist. Girls have not the daring and independence of you men. When Fox has got his way, then he intends to change his name, and live at Hall with your father, who will re-settle the property on him and his heirs, that so there may still be an Anthony Cleverdon of Hall."

"Never! No—never!" exclaimed Anthony, springing to his feet. "He cannot—he shall not do that. Fox will never play me such a base trick as that! Bessie never will lend herself to be made a tool of like that!"

"Bessie is true to you—that never doubt; but do not lean on my brother : he is false to every one."

"He never shall become a Cleverdon. What! Good heavens! He take my name, my place, my rights, my inheritance, my everything?"

"Not everything," said Julian, maliciously. "He does not stretch a hand for your Urith and for Willsworthy— only for what you tossed away as valueless."

Anthony uttered an oath, and cast himself back where he had been before, in the seat in the window, and put his hands to his brow and clasped them there, leaning his head against the window sill.

Then, for some while, both remained silent, but Julian turned herself about in her seat to look at him.

Was that the same Anthony she had loved and admired? This dejected, sad man, with his head bowed, his face pale, and lined with trouble? it was certain that he was vastly altered. Her woman's eye detects a difference in his clothing. Formerly he had been ever dapper; without foppishness, his dress always of the best and well cared for; now it was old and worn, in places threadbare. Nor was it, though poor, yet with the merit of being attended to. Timely stitches had not been given where they had been needed, nor tags and buttons added that had fallen off. His boots were shabby and trodden down at the heel. The wet and dirt undoubtedly gave to them a special shabbiness on that day, but Julian could see that they were out of shape and past their best days. The trimness and gloss had gone out of Anthony's outer case and his spirit within had lost as much, if not more. There was none of the ancient merriment, none of the self-conscious swagger, none of the old assurance of manner in him. He had become morose, peevish; he showed a diffidence which was the reverse of his former self. It was a diffidence mingled with resentment, the product of his consciousness that the world was turned against him, and of his bitterness at knowing this. Anthony's nature was one that required sunshine, as a peacock demands it that its beauty and splendour may appear. Come rain, and how the feathers clog and droop and draggle—how squalid a fowl it appears! So was Anthony now—a faded disconsolate shadow of his old self, without the nerve to bear up against what depressed him, the adaptability to shape himself to his new surroundings.

As Julian looked at him she pitied him. Her love for him warmed her, and made her forget the cruelty of the part she was playing. The child of impulse, feeling this qualm of compassion, she rose and gently came across the room to him.

He heard her not, coming in her light slippers on the carpet, so engrossed was he in his wretched thoughts. Every one had turned against him—every one in whom he had trusted. His friend Fox, the only man who had seemed not to be affected by the general adverse tone of opinion, he had given him the most stinging blow of all. He was now at variance with his father, with his friend— if Bessie consented to take Fox, he could never regard her with esteem again; at home he had quarrelled with Uncle Solomon, and raised his hand against him; he had alienated from him his wife; his aunt was in league against him; the servants at Willsworthy would take sides with their mistress. What wretchedness! what hopelessness was his! There was no one—no one but Julian who had a word of kindness, a spark of feeling for him. He heard the rustle of her gown and looked up.

She was standing by him, looking down on his ruffled hair, that hung over his hands, clasped upon his forehead. He hastily brushed away the scattered locks.

"Oh, Anthony!" she said, "what have you been doing here? What drawn on the glass?"

He slightly coloured, put his hand to the panes and covered them.

"Nay," she said, taking hold of his hand, and drawing it away, "nay, let me read it."

"I have writ," said he, bitterly, "what might have been, and then——" he gulped down his rising emotion, "then I had been——"

She stooped and kissed him on the brow, "Poor boy!"

Instantly he threw his arms round her neck and drew her face to his, and kissed her cheeks and lips, passionately. She—she alone remained to him—and yet—how far apart they were.

She sprang away with a cry.

The door was open, and in it stood old Anthony Cleverdon.

CHAPTER XXXVII.

ANOTHER TEMPTATION.

Anthony rose, when he saw his father, with instinctive filial respect, but he did not look him in the face. He could not do this.

"Hah!" said the old man, entering the room, and closing the door behind him. "I had come here with an intent that is now set aside. I had come, Julian, to tell thee that it was yet in thy power to weld together the estates of Hall and Kilworthy, notwithstanding what has occurred —that is, if thou wouldst overlook a certain disparity in years, and keep thine eye fixed on the main advantage.

But that is over. I am glad I came when I chanced, and in time to save me from running a great risk. Thou art too free with thy kisses, too lavish in thy love to please me."

He spoke as though what he said must wither Julian, crush her under the sense of her great loss. His assurance that she must be attracted by the same ambition as himself was so grotesque that Julian at once rallied from the confusion that had covered her, laughed, and said :

"You do me a mighty honour."

"Not at all—I decline to show you the honour."

"So much the better. When I walk through a wood I do not not like to have the bramble claw at me. If it does, then I must turn and put my foot on it. Let the bramble hug the nettle, and not aim at the lady."

Her impudence staggered him.

"It is mighty sport," she continued, "to hear that little Hall desired to hitch itself on to the skirts of Kilworthy. But Master Cleverdon, if thou art in a marrying mood, prithee go to the next giglet fair, and choose thee there a wench."

Her insolence had its effect ; the effect designed. Instead of being attacked by the old Squire, she was the assailant, and she hit him where she knew she could keenly wound him, so as to draw off his thoughts from what he had just seen. He was offended and angry.

"There," said she—"sit down in my seat by the fire. I meant no harm ; but as you were absurd on your side, I made grimaces on mine. I am glad you are here, and face to face with Anthony, for, mayhap, I can persuade you to that which, unpersuaded, you were loth to do."

The old man was so angry that he did not answer her. He remained near the door, doubtful whether to retire or to come forward. He had not expected to meet his son there, and was unprepared for an interview ; though hardly regretting it, for, in his bitter and resentful spirit he was willing that Anthony should hear from his own lips what he designed—learn to the full the completeness of the severance between them.

"Whatever persuasion you may attempt," said he, looking at Julian, "comes at a wrong time, after you have shown me that you are a person who, not respecting herself, deserves no respect from another, and after you have grossly insulted me. But I will listen to you, though, I tell you, what you say will not weigh with me as a feather."

"If that be so," laughed Julian, "I will spare myself the trouble. But look at your son; look at him calmly, and tell me whether I was wrong in pitying him, ay, and if, in consideration of old, tried friendship, that has been almost cousinship—so well have we known each other since child-hood—was I so very wrong in lightly touching his brow with my lips, for from my heart I was sorry for him. Think what it would have been for you, when you married, had your father lived and treated you as you have treated Anthony! Is a man to be cast out of every home because he has committed one folly? I dare stake my word that Anthony has rued his act almost daily; and is all his regret to count for nothing?"

"A man must take the consequences of what he has done."

"Julian, I do not wish you to plead my cause," said Anthony, coming before his father; "I will speak to him myself. I want to ask of him a question or two."

"I will answer them," said the old man. "Say on."

"I desire to know for certain whether you intend to give Bessie to Fox Crymes?"

"Yes, I do."

"And she consents?"

"All are not so disobedient as yourself."

"And if she refuses?"

"She will not refuse. I can but let her go, as I let you go. But she will not refuse; I have that to say to her which will make her give way."

"Then if she takes Fox, do you intend to take him into Hall?"

"Yes, I do."

"And under my name?"

"Certainly. He changes his name of Crymes to that of Cleverdon when he becomes my son."

"Then I tell you it shall not be. There shall not be an-other Anthony Cleverdon in Hall. I give you and Fox fair warning. There cannot—there shall not—be a sup-planter in Hall bearing my name."

"We shall see."

"Yes you shall see. Tell Fox what I have said."

"Tell him yourself. I will be no bearer of messages between you."

"Mr. Cleverdon," said Julian, "I cannot let you meet and part in my presence, spoiling all my pleasure in this little room forever with the remembrance of this scene, without one more effort to bring you to agreement. Come, now—what if Anthony returns to you?"

"Returns to me?"

"Yes, what if he throws up all connection with Willsworthy? He is wretched there—poverty-stricken. He is unhappy in a hundred ways. Look at his face. Where is the old brightness—where the old pride? He has lost all the ancient merry Anthony, and now is a sad one. Let him come back to Hall, and leave Urith to manage with her uncle—to manage, or mismanage—as before, till all goes there to pieces. He has committed a boyish folly, and he knows it. He has thrown away gold for dross, and he has found it out. He will now be twice the Tony to you that he was. Then he was thoughtless, careless, devilmay-care; now he has learned a lesson, and learned it so sharply that he will never forget it again. He has learned what disobedience costs—what it is to go against a father—what boy's fancies are compared with matured plans in the head of a man. Give him that chance. Come, you do not know Fox as I know him. Take him into your house, and he will not be more dutiful to you than has been your own Tony. He will make you unhappy, and your Bessie wretched. I saw by Tony's face, when he came here, that he had quarrelled with his wife. He came here because his home was hateful to him—because it was unendurable to him to be there any more. We cannot retain him here. Let him go to thee, and there will be an end to Fox and his story with Bessie. Anthony will be dutiful and loving henceforth, and cling to thee, and esteem thee, as he never clung to thee and esteemed thee heretofore."

Anthony was speechless. The blood rushed into his face. Everything might be as it was—or almost everything.

Old Anthony Cleverdon stood irresolute.

He had misgivings relative to Fox. One crafty malevolent nature mistrusts another of the same quality. His daughter's peace of mind troubled him little, but he was by no means certain that Fox, once in the house, might not presume, and that there would not be sharp contests between them.   Moreover, when Fox was there, married to his daughter, his place would be assured, and the old man could not well drive him from it.   There were other reasons which made the old Squire feel that, to some extent, Fox would be unassailable, and might be eminently disagreeable.

The suggestion made by Julian was inviting.   In the depths of his heart lurked love for his only son ; his old pride in him was there, and was wounded and sore with the spectacle of the lad humbled, sinking out of men's favour, and out of his old dignity.   He looked at him, and saw what an alteration had taken place in him—how oldened and worn in face he was, how shabby in his clothing.

"Do you know, Mr. Cleverdon," pursued Julian, "why it was that poor Tony caught me by the neck and kissed me?   It was because he was so utterly forlorn and disconsolate ; he had lost all his friends, his heart was void through bereavement from his father ; he was estranged from that Jacob, that supplanter, Fox ; he saw his own sister turning against him, and—I doubt not he has not found that solace and sufficiency in his own home that would make up for these mighty losses.   He held me, because he had none other.   I do not want him, I have no right to him—let me cast him off—but only on to his father's bosom, into his father's arms."

The old man went to the window and looked forth.   His face was agitated.   He must have time to consider.

Anthony, moreover, remained mute, and his face was troubled.   A terrible temptation was presented to him.   He believed that now, were he to throw himself at his father's feet, take his hand, and ask his forgiveness, the old man would receive him back at once into favour on the terms proposed by Julian.   That he would forgive him on any other, he might not expect.   That he knew full well.

And the old man saw that an opportunity was offered to deal the most insulting and cruel stroke to the daughter of the man who had incurred his undying hatred.   He could by a word rob her of her husband, of the prize she had laboured to win, but which he could prevent her from retaining.

To Julian was offered the most complete and open triumph over her enemy. A triumph more complete than she could have hoped to gain. Anthony could be nothing to her, he would remain as a friend, that was all; but she would see, and show to Urith, her threat made good to wrench Anthony away from her.

Anthony stood with downcast eyes. The temptation was a strong one—strong, to a young man who had been humoured and allowed to have his own way uncontrolled, allowed to follow his pleasure or whim without hindrance. He could not return home without having to face his wife, angered and resentful, without having to acknowledge himself to have been in the wrong. Anthony Crymes was playing him a treacherous and cruel trick, and here was a chance offered him of at once recovering his old position, wiping out his past mistake, and discomfiting Fox when on the eve of success. Was he sure that he could ever be on the same terms as before with Urith? Had she not been gradually estranged from him, till she had declared to him that she hated him, that she wished she had never seen him? Would it not be a relief to be rid of him, to be spared any more domestic broils?

Old Anthony Cleverdon was at the window, and as he stood there he marked the initials drawn on the fogged glass, and turned and looked at his son. Young Anthony noticed the look, and observed what had attracted his father's attention. He moved hastily to the window, and his father drew away, went to the fireplace, and rested his elbow against the mantel-shelf and fixed his eyes intently on his son. So also did Julian. Both saw that the moment was a crucial one. The young man was forced to make up his mind on a point which would determine his whole after-life. It was more than that, it was a crucial moment in his moral life. He must now take a step upward or downward, in the path of right or that of wrong. This neither Julian nor his father considered, intent only on their selfish ends. But this appeared clearly to Anthony. His inner consciousness spoke out and told him plainly where went the path of duty and where lay the deflexion from it. But the path of duty was a painful one full of humiliations, promising no happiness, only a repetition of contests with a sulky wife, and jars with the foolish Solomon Gibbs, of struggle against poverty, of labour like a common hired workman, of loss for ever of his old position, and deprivation of all the amusements that had filled his former life.

He and Urith did not suit each other. His temperament was sanguine, his spirit mirthful; he was sociable, and full of the sparkle of youth; whereas she was moody, almost morose, had no humour and laughter in her soul, brooded over imagined wrongs as well as those that were real, and could as little accommodate herself to his mood as could he to hers. Surely it were best, under these circumstances, that they should part.

Now Anthony was standing at the window where he had stood before when he drew those initials on the panes, in the place occupied recently by his father. So full was he of his thoughts, of the rolling of conflicting waves of feeling, that he forgot where he was, forgot the presence of his father and of Julian—the very sense of the lapse of time was gone from him. Though he looked through the window, he saw nothing.

Then, all at once, uncalled for, there broke and oozed forth in his heart the old vein of love which had been filled with so hot and full a flood when he was Urith's suitor; he saw her with the old eyes once more, and looked in mental vision once more into the sombre eyes, as he had on the moor, when he lifted her into his saddle, and there came over him that sensation of mingled love and fear. It seemed to him that now only did he understand the cause of that fear; it was fear lest he himself should prove a wreck through lack of love and devotion to her. He thought now of how, after their wedding, on his coming to Willsworthy, he had taken her in his arms, how her dark head had lain on his bosom, and he had stooped and kissed her brow, and she had looked up into his face with eyes expressive of perfect confidence, of intensest love. He thought now how he had forced her against her will, against her conscience, to marry him prematurely, after her mother's death, and against the dying command of that mother. He thought how that he had lived on her estate, had been, as it were, her pensioner. He thought also of the efforts she had made, efforts he had perceived, to accommodate herself to him, to meet his humour, to overcome her own gloom, to struggle against the bad habits of slovenliness into which the household had fallen, and to correct her own want of order, because she saw it pained her husband. She had done a great deal for him, and what had he done for her? Grumbled, been peevish, disappointed her. He recalled that evening at the Cakes, where he had slighted her. He thought of how he had trifled with his old regard for Julian, allowed her to lure him away from his wife, and had let her see that he was no more at one with Urith, and that he wished he could have undone the marriage and re-tied the old threads that had bound him to Julian. She—this Julian, had been playing with him—she, for her own ends, had been making mischief between him and his wife—and what had he done?

His eyes were opened, and he saw the initials on the glass, and the love-knot between them.

With the blood surging to his brow and cheeks, and a fire in his eye, he raised his hand, and angrily brushed his palm over the three panes, effacing utterly the characters there inscribed, then he remained with uplifted hand and forefinger extended, still, as in dream, unconscious that he was being watched.

A new thought had occurred to him—that he was about to become a father.

A father! and he away at Hall, while the deserted Urith sat at Willsworthy—wan, with tears on her cheek, drip, drip, over the cradle he had treated so insultingly— her cradle, which he had deemed unworthy of his child, and which, for all that, with his child in it, he was inclined to abandon!

Then the blood went out of Anthony's face, went back to his heart, as he grew pale and still with the thought of the infamy of the conduct that had been his, had he yielded to the temptation.

And tears, tears of shame at himself, of love for Urith, of infinite longing for that little child that was to be his, and to nestle in his arms, filled his throat and choked him. With a trembling finger on another clouded pane he drew an U and interlaced with it an A, twisting and turning the initials about, weaving them inextricably together, till the U was lost in the A, and the A confounded with the U.

He could not speak. He did not look round. With his

18

eyes fixed before him, and his mind full of the thoughts that opened to him, he went out of the room, out of the house, and spoke to no one.

But old Anthony and Julian knew his decision—knew it from his finger-writing on the little diamond pane.

Yet the old man would not accept it—he called after his son.

"I give thee three days. I will do no more for three days in the matter."

But Anthony did not turn his head or answer.

CHAPTER XXXVIII.

ON THE ROAD.

Fox Crymes walked on toward Hall with Bessie. He could not well leave her to take the rest of her course alone, after the old man, her father, had ridden past, forgetting her, and leaving her to make her way home without him. They therefore walked on together, speaking at intervals and disconnectedly to each other. Bessie feeling the irksomeness of her position, and he unwilling further to jeopardize his suit by pressing it on her any more. He had said what was sufficient and he left the father to use pressure to force her to comply with his wishes.

The two had not, however, proceeded more than a mile before they saw Squire Cleverdon riding back to meet them. He had recalled his promise before he reached home, and then remembered having passed two persons whom he did not particularly observe, but whom he concluded were his daughter and Fox.

The first impression he had received from Anthony's conduct was that he put the offer from him altogether; and yet, on further consideration, he persuaded himself that he had been mistaken. Had Anthony finally decided to reject his offer, why had he not said so in words? The old man's nature was coarse—he could not understand the struggles of a generous mind and resistance to mean motives. Anthony had not spoken, because he did not choose to speak before Julian, because he thought it seemly to affect difficulty of persuasion, because he wanted time in which to consider it, because—because—the father could find many reasons why Anthony should not immediately close with the proposal.

The more the old Squire turned the matter over, the more obvious it became to him that Anthony would do as he wished. It was inconceivable to him that he should persist in a course of opposition to his best interests. The boy was proud; but he had learned, by sore experience, that pride brought to misery. He had tried his strength against his father's—had shown what he could do; and now, if he gave way, he was not humiliated. Why, in the Civil Wars, when Salcombe Castle was held by Sir Edmund Fortescue for five months against the Roundheads, and held after every other fort in the country had been taken or had surrendered; and then, when starved into yielding, it was on the most honourable terms, and Sir Edmund marched forth with all the honours of war, bearing away with him the key of the castle he had so gallantly defended. This was no disgrace to him, it was a proud act of which all Devon men would speak with elation. Why then should not Anthony surrender? He should march forth with flying colours, and it would be no blow to his self-respect, no jar to his pride. The old man, having worked himself into the conviction that his case was won, was full of elation, and, with the petty spite of a mean mind, he resolved at once to show Fox he had no longer need of him. Then it was that he remembered that Fox and Bessie were to walk towards Hall till he caught them up, and he turned his horse's head and rode back till he met them.

"Heigh, there!" shouted the old man; "how goes the suit, Tony Crymes? Hast thou won her consent?" He paused for an answer.

"Her mother brought her naught," he continued, when Fox remained silent, not well knowing what answer to make.

"That I know," said Fox; "but he who wins Bessie Cleverdon wins a treasure."

"I am glad thou thinkest so. I hope that will satisfy thee. Come, Tony, lend a hand to the maid's foot, and help her up on the pillion behind me."

Fox obeyed; the dirty road had soiled Bessie's boot so that he could not preserve a clean hand.

"Find her heavy, eh?" asked the Squire, in a mocking tone.

"Much gold and many acres stick to thy hand when thou puttest it forth to her, eh?"

Fox looked questioningly at the old man. His tone was changed.

"Bessie will bring luck that will adhere to whatever hand holds her," said the young man.

"No doubt—no doubt," said the Squire. "You may walk at our side, and I will have a word with thee. Come on to Hall if it give thee pleasure. The road is well known to thee, thou hast trod it many a time of late. I doubt but soon thou thinkest to set up thy home there, and not to have to run to and fro as heretofore."

Fox looked again inquiringly and uneasily at the old man. He did not understand this new style of banter.

"Thou hast helped Bessie now into pillion, and I suppose thou art reckoning on the stuffing of the pad on to which thou thinkest her hand will help thee up, eh?"

Fox, usually ready with a word, was uncertain how to meet these sallies, and still remained silent.

The old man rode on, casting an occasional glance, full of cynicism, at young Crymes, who walked at the side of the horse.

Fox would not return till he was enlightened on this change in his manner; nor would he say much, resolving on silence as the best method of forcing old Cleverdon to show what was in his mind.

"What dost say to Anthony coming home?" asked the Squire of his daughter, turning his head over his shoulder.

"Anthony—is he really coming to Hall?" gasped Bessie, her heart leaping with gladness.

"It will be a pleasure to thee to be able to retain the name of Crymes," sneered the Squire, turning to the walker. "A fine, ancient, gentle name; thou did'st doubt about exchanging it for one less venerable—that of Cleverdon, though of better sound, and the name that goes up, whilst Crymes goes down?"

Anthony Crymes's colour changed; "I do not understand what you aim at," he said, in uncertain tone.

"Nay, there is naught hard to be understood in what I say. If Anthony should come back to me, then there will be no need for Tony Crymes to spend some forty guineas to obtain license to call himself Cleverdon."

"Then Anthony is coming back! Oh, father!" exclaimed Bessie, "this is glad tidings." She disregarded all his hints and allusions to her marriage with Fox.

"This it is—you, Bess, say you are pleased to hear it, and I am very sure it will delight Tony Crymes. This it is—my Anthony has had the offer made him by me that he shall return to Hall, and all be forgiven and forgot that was between us."

"Oh, father, and you will receive Urith!"

"Not so fast, Bess. Anthony comes back, but never, never, will I suffer that hussy to cross my threshold. I swore that when he married her, and I will not go from my oath. No—Anthony returns, but not with that creature—that beggar wench. He comes himself. He comes alone."

"He cannot, father; he cannot—she is his wife."

"She is, as his madness made it to be—she is his wife. But he is tired of the folly; he repents it. He will be glad to be quit of her. He comes back to me, and she remains in her beggary at Willsworthy."

"Never, father! never. Anthony could not have agreed to that."

"I tell thee he did; that is, he has almost agreed to it. He did not close with the offer I made at once, but, for appearance sake, made some difficulty—yet only for appearance sake. I have given him three days, and in that time he will have let the matter be noised abroad, have broken his intention to the girl, and have made himself ready to return to me."

"Father!" said Bessie, in a voice choked with agitation, "I can never regard—never think of Anthony again, in the old way, if he do this. He must not leave his wife. He swore before God to hold to her in poverty or in wealth till death, and thou wilt make him forswear himself?"

"His first duty he owes to me—nay, he owes it to himself, to return from the evil ways in which he has gone. Heaven set him in Hall, and he went against Heaven when he left it; now he is the prodigal that has been among swine, but comes back to his father. That is Scripture—that is the Word of God, and stands before all foolish words said in oath, without weighing what they meant."

Fox Crymes caught the bridle, and stayed the horse.

"Is this jest, or is it earnest?" he asked, huskily.

"It is most serious and solemn earnest," answered the Squire.

"Then I insist on a word with thee, and I will hold the bridle till thou dismount. I will not let thee go on till I have spoken alone with thee. Let Bessie go forward, we must say somewhat together."

Squire Cleverdon had no whip, but he struck spurs into the flanks of his horse; but Fox held the rein, and, though the beast plunged and kicked out, he would not let it break away. Bessie was almost thrown off, and in her danger threatened to drag her father with her.

"Nay, thou shalt not escape me," said Fox. "Dismount, Master Cleverdon, and tell me plainly what this new matter is between thee and thy graceless fool of a son, or I will make the horse fling thee into the mud, and perhaps break thy neck."

The old man thought best to comply, and, growling, he dismounted. Then Fox let go his hold of the rein, and bade Bessie ride forward beyond earshot.

"What is the meaning of this?" asked Fox, who was livid with rage and mortification, so livid, that the freckles on his face stood out as black spots on the hide of a coach-dog. "It is ill to trifle with me. You arranged all with me. I was to have your daughter, and succeed to Hall, I was to take your name, and step into all the rights forfeited by Anthony. You brought me face to face with Bessie at her aunt's, and then sent me walking back toward Hall with her, to press my case. When all is nearly over, then you turn round, cast me over, and reinstate that son who has maltreated and half-blinded me, and make a mock of me for my pains?"

"It is you who have trifled with me," retorted the Squire, with less heat, but more bitterness. "You told me that you would urge my suit with your sister; you brought me weekly accounts of how she was becoming more disposed to think of me, you flattered and encouraged me, and all the while you knew——"

"I knew what? I knew nothing, save that you are old, and she young."

"That is not it," said the Squire, peevishly, "that is

not what I refer to. You knew that she was encouraging my son, and that the old attachment that subsisted before this hateful affair with Urith Malvine had reasserted itself."

"It is false," answered Fox, furiously, "not content with making your sport with me, you insult my sister."

"I suppose you will not dispute the testimony of my own eyes," sneered old Cleverdon.

"And to what do they bear testimony?"

"To what I said. I entered the parlour where they were, she standing over him, at the window; he seated, with his arms thrown about her neck, kissing her, and above them on the glass, scrawled by his finger, their initials woven together, with a true lover's knot."

Fox glared at him, in speechless wrath.

"Now—what say you to that?" asked the old man. "With such proceedings, allowed, connived at in your house, I am to be lured on to offer myself to your precious sister, and then to be laughed at, and scouted for my folly —a folly into which you were drawing me."

"It is false"—that was all Fox could say, so disconcerted, so choked was he with rage.

"It is not false. I have but just come from your house, and saw that, and because I saw it, I made overtures to Anthony to return. It was clear to me that all the fever of fancy for that hussy at Willsworthy was dead as ashes. That the reputation of Julian will need looking to, should he return to me, and be separate from Urith, is naught to me."

"He has enough to answer to me without this," gasped Fox. Then, by an effort, he steadied his voice and resumed his usual manner. "Now," said he, "let us have all brought into measure and rhyme between us. You tell me that Anthony comes back to Hall and abandons his wife."

"Aye! That is my offer to him. Let him leave Willsworthy and return to me, and all shall be forgiven. 'Tis a misfortune that he cannot be rid of his wife, but the tie by law alone will remain. She shall never be mentioned between us."

"And he agrees to this?"

"I have granted him three days to consider. In three days he gives me his answer, but who can doubt what that

answer will be? Is he not wearied with his toy? Has
he had good cheer at Willsworthy? Has he aught there
now to retain him?"

"And what about Bessie?"

"Oh! you are welcome to her, as I said before; but after
my death Hall will go to Anthony, only the reversion to
thee and any child thou hast by Bess. Should my Anthony
survive Urith and marry again, then to his son by his second wife, never—that I have ever maintained—never to any
child of his by Urith Malvine."

Fox laughed contemptuously.

"A poor prospect for Bess and her husband."

"A poor prospect, mayhap, but the only one on which
they can look through their windows when they set up
house together."

"And what allowance will you make Bessie when she
marries?"

"But a trifle—I cannot more."

"So her husband and she are to live on the expectation
of succession should they survive Anthony, and should
Anthony not be remarried."

"That is all."

"But what if Anthony refuses your offer?"

"Then all remains as before. He will not refuse."

"I will hear that from his own mouth. Where is he?"

"I did not overtake him on the road. He had not yet
left the town. I doubt not he has gone to his Aunt Magdalen."

"One word more. Hold up your hand to Heaven and
swear that he dared—dared to put his arms round and kiss
my sister! He—he—Anthony Cleverdon!"

"I will do it! It is true!"

Fox remained in the midst of the road, and his hand con-
vulsively caught and played with his hunting-knife that
hung to his belt. His red, thick brows were knitted.

As old Cleverdon looked at his mottled face, he allowed
to himself that Bess would have bad taste to choose such
an one wittingly; and that, unwilling, it would take some
compulsion to drive her to accept him.

"And, if Anthony does not come within three days, all
remains as heretofore?" again asked Fox, looking furtively
up at the father, and then letting his eyes fall again.

"Yes, all as heretofore. Should he dare to disappoint me in this, not a thread from my coat, nor a grass-blade from my land, shall fall to him."

Fox waved his hand. "That will do," he said, and turned away.

He was at the junction of the road or track that led from Willsworthy with the main highway along which Squire Cleverdon had been riding. He remained at this point, waiting till the old man had remounted, and had trotted away, with Bessie behind him. There he stood, still playing with the handle of his hunting-knife, his red, lowering brows contracted over his small eyes, watching till the riders disappeared over the hill. Then he turned along the track-way that led to Willsworthy, with his head down against the drizzling rain, which had come on again, after having ceased for an hour; which came on again thick, blotting out the scenery—all prospect within a hundred feet—as effectually as though veils of white gauze had been let down out of the heavens, one behind another.

CHAPTER XXXIX.

TWO PARTS OF A TOKEN.

Anthony had, as his father surmised, gone to see his Aunt Magdalen. His heart was soft within him—softened at the sense of his own unworthiness, and with the return flow of his old love to Urith. And as he did not desire at once to go back to Willsworthy, and at the same time remembered that some time had elapsed since he had seen his aunt, he went to her house. There he found his grandmother, Mistress Penwarne. Some of the bitterness of the old woman seemed to be rubbed away. Perhaps daily association with the gentleness of Luke Cleverdon had done this.

She was in tears when Anthony entered. Magdalen had been talking with her over the plan mapped out for Bessie, to the complete, final exclusion of Anthony from return to his father's house.

"Now—now does the righteous God pay back to old

Anthony Cleverdon all the wrong he did my daughter," she said. "See—drop for drop of gall. Where there fell one on my child's heart, his own son spirts a drop on to his father's heart. There is retribution in this world."

"Oh, Mistress Penwarne," remonstrates Magdalen. "How can you take delight in this?"

"I delight only in seeing justice done," answered the old woman. "You hold with your brother—naturally—to some extent; but you never loved my daughter. You never showed her kindness——"

"Indeed, now," interrupted Magdalen, "there you do me a wrong. It was Margaret who would not suffer me to enter the house and be of any consequence more in Hall, who withstood me when I would draw near to my brother."

"She had no power to withstand any one. That you know full well. She weighed naught with her husband. But let that be. If you sinned against her, God is bringing the whip down on your shoulders as well, for I know that what is now falling out is to you great pain and affliction."

"That it is indeed," sighed Magdalen.

"Anthony is used by the hand of Providence as its rod with the father; Heaven rewards on the proud Squire of Hall every heartache, every humiliation to which he subjected my child. You know not how I have prayed that I might be suffered to see the day when the rod should fall and beat and bruise the back of the offender."

"You do not reckon," said Magdalen, "that the chief suffering falls, not on my brother, but on your daughter's son. Is not Anthony the very image of his mother? Has he not her eyes and hair—all the upper part of his countenance? Does not her blood run in his veins? You have desired revenge on my brother, and you have got it through the breaking to pieces of your own grandson."

Mistress Penwarne was silent. It was as Magdalen said.

"Yes, and whom does Bessie resemble most? She has none of the handsomeness of your Margaret. It is true that she is her child, but she has inherited the plain homeliness of the Cleverdons. Look at yonder picture over the mantel-shelf. That was drawn of me when about her age. Does she not so resemble me at that time that you would say she had taken nothing of the Penwarnes, that she was altogether and only Cleverdon? Yet to her will come Hall. She will be mistress there, and to her child it will descend, to the utter exclusion of Anthony. Nay, I cannot think that the judgment of God, to which thou appealest ever, is falling all to thy side in its weighted scale."

The old woman was about to answer when Anthony entered. He was pale, and his pallor reminded her of her daughter as the wan picture recalled Bessie. Mrs. Penwarne rose from her chair and stepped up to him, took him by both his hands, and looked him steadily in the face. As she did so great tears formed in her eyes and rolled down her wrinkled cheeks.

"Ah!" said she, seeing in him her dead daughter, and her voice quivered, "how hardly did the Master of Hall treat her, but Magdalen—aye, and Bessie—know that better than thou. He was rough and cruel, and now thou hast felt what his roughness and cruelty be—now thou canst understand how he behaved to thy poor mother; but thou art a man and able to go where thou wilt, fight thine own way through the world, carve for thyself thine own future. It was not so with my poor Margaret. She was linked to him—she could not escape, and he used his strength and authority and wealth to beat and to torment and break her. And Margaret had a spirit. Have you seen how a little dog is mended of lamb-worrying? It is attached to an old ram—linked to it past escape, and at every moment the ram lets drive at the little creature with his horns, gets him under his feet and tramples him, kneels on him and kneads him with his knees, ripping at him all the while with his horns. Then, finally, the little dog is detached and taken away, covered with wounds and bruises, before the ram kills it. It was so with my Margaret, but she was no lamb-killer—only had a high spirit —and she was tied to that man, your father. He rent her away from Richard Malvine, whom she loved, just because it was his pleasure, and he broke her heart. Look here."

The old grandmother drew from her bosom a token, a silver crown-piece of Charles I., on which the King was figured mounted on horseback; but the coin was broken, and to her neck hung but one half.

"Look at this," said Mrs. Penwarne. "Here is the half-token that Richard Malvine gave to my daughter, and the other half he kept himself. That was the pledge that they belonged to each other. Yet Anthony Cleverdon **of Hall** would not have it so. He took her away, and on her marriage day she gave me the broken half-token. She had no right to retain that; but with her broken heart she could not part so readily. As if it were not enough that he had torn her away from the man she loved, your father left not a day to pass without ill-treating her in some way. He was jealous, because he thought her heart still hung to Richard Malvine; though, as God in heaven knows, she never failed in her duty to him, and strove faithfully to cast out from her heart every thought of the man she had loved, and to whom the Squire of Hall had made her unfaithful. As he could not win her love, he sought to crush her by ill-treatment. Now, O my Lord! how it must rejoice my poor Margaret, and Richard also, in Paradise, to think that their children should come together and be one —be one as they themselves never could be."

She ceased and sobbed. Then with shaking hands, she put the ribbon to which the broken token depended round Anthony's neck.

"Take this," she said. "I never thought to part with it; but it of right belongs now to thee. Take it as a pledge of thy mother's love, that her broken heart goes with thee to Willsworthy, and finds its rest there; and with it take my blessing."

Anthony bowed his head, and looked at the silver coin, rubbed very much, and placed it on his breast, inside his coat.

"Thank thee, grandmother," he said. "I will cherish it as a remembrance of my mother."

"And tell me," said she, "is it so, that thou art forever driven away from Hall, that thy father will take thy name, even, and give it to another, and that thou and thy children are forever to be shut off and cast away from all lot and inheritance in the place where thy forefathers have been?"

"It is even so," answered Anthony. "But hark!"

A horn was being blown in the street, and there was a tramp of running feet, and voices many in excitement.

"What can be the matter?" exclaimed Magdalen, going to the window. "Mercy on us! What must have taken place?"

Anthony ran out of the house. The street had filled; there were people of all sorts coming out of their houses, asking news, pressing inward toward the man with the horn. Anthony elbowed his way through the throng.

"What is this about?" he inquired of a man he knew.

"The Duke of Monmouth has landed at Lyme in Dorsetshire. Hey! wave your hat for Protestantism! Who'll draw the sword against Popery and Jesuitism?"

More news was not to be got. The substance of the tidings that had just come in was contained in the few words—the Duke has landed at Lyme; with how many men was not known. What reception he had met with was as yet unknown. No one could say whether the country gentry had rallied to him—whether the militia which had been called out in expectation of his arrival had deserted to his standard.

Anthony remained some time in the street and market-place discussing the news. His spirits rose, his heart beat high; he longed to fly to Lyme, and offer himself to the Duke. His excitement over, the tidings dispelled his concern about his own future and gloomy thoughts about his troubled home. In that home there was at the time much unrest. After he had departed from Willsworthy, Uncle Sol Gibbs had burst into laughter.

"Ah, Urith!" said he, "I hope, maid, thy hand is not hurt. It was not a fair hit. The lad was nettled; he thought himself first in everything, and all at once discovered that an old fool like me, with one hand behind my back, could beat him at every point. Your young cockerells think that because they crow loud they are masters in the cockpit. It disconcerts them to find themselves worsted by such as they have despised. There, I shall bear him no grudge. I forgive him, and he will be ashamed of himself ere ten minutes are past in which his blood has cooled. None of us are masters of ourselves when the juices are in ferment."

He took his niece's hand and looked at the palm; it was darkened across it, by the stroke of the stick.

"So! he has bruised thee, Urith! That would have cracked my old skull had it fallen athwart it, by heaven! Never mind, I kiss thee, wench, for having saved me, and I forgive him for thy sake. Look here, Urith, don't thou go taking it into thy noddle that all married folks agree like turtle-doves. Did'st ever hear me sing the song about Trinity Sunday?

> When bites the frost and winds are a blowing,
>   I do not heed and I do not care.
> When 'Tony's by me—why let it be snowing,
>   'Tis summer time with me all the year.
> The icicles they may hang on the fountain,
>   And frozen over the farmyard pool,
> The east wind whistle upon the mountain,
>   No wintry gusts our love will cool.

That is courtship, Urith—summer in the midst of winter. Now listen to matrimony—what that is :—

> I shall be wed a' Trinity Sunday,
>   And then—adieu to my holiday !
> Come frost, come snow on Trinity Monday,
>   Why then beginneth my winter day.
> If drudge and smudge on Trinity Monday,
>   If wind and weather—I do not care !
> If winter follows Trinity Sunday,
>   It can't be summer-time all the year.

That's the proper way to regard it. After marriage storms always come ; after matrimony nipping frosts and wintry gales. It can't be summer-time all the year. Now just see," continued Uncle Sol, climbing upon the table and seating himself thereon, and then fumbling in his pocket. " Dos't fancy it was ever summer-time with thy father and mother after they were wed ? Not a bit, wench—not a bit. They had their quarrels. I don't say that they were exactly of the same sort as be yours, but they were every whit as bad—aye ! and worse, and all about this." He opened his hand and showed a broken silver crown piece of Charles I., perforated, and with a ribbon holding it. "I'll tell thee all about it. Afore thy father was like to be married to my sister, he was mighty taken in love with someone else. Well, Urith, I won't conceal it from thee— it was with Margaret Penwarne, that afterward married old Squire Cleverdon, and became the mother of thy Anthony. Everyone said they would make a pair, but he was poor and she had naught, and none can build their nest out of love ; so it was put off. But I suppose they had passed their word to each other, and in token of good faith had broken a silver crown and parted it between them. This half," said Uncle Sol, " belonged to thy father. Well, I reckon he ought, when he married thy mother, to have put away from his thoughts the very memory of Margaret Cleverdon. I could not see into his heart—I cannot say what was there. Maybe he had ceased to think of her after she was wed to Anthony Cleverdon, and he had taken thy mother ; maybe he had not. All men have their little failings—some one way, some another. Mine is—well, you know it, niece, so let it pass. I hurt none but myself. But thy father never parted with the broken half-token, but would keep it. Many words passed between them over it, and the more angry thy mother was, the more obstinate became thy father. One day they were terrible bad—a regular storm it was, Urith. Then I took down my single-stick, and I went up to Richard, and said I to him, ' Dick, thou art in the wrong. Give me up the half-token, or, by the Lord, I'll lay thy head open for thee!' He knew me, and that I was a man of my word. He considered a moment, and then he put it into my hand—on one condition, that I should never give it to my sister. I swore to that, and we shook hands, and so peace was made for the time. There "——said the old man, descending from the table. "I will give thee the half-token, maid, for my oath does not hold me now. Thine it shall be ; and when thou wearest it, or holdest it, think on this—that there is no married life without storms and vexations, and that the only way in which peace is to be gotten is for the one in the wrong to give up to the other."

He put the half-token into Urith's hand.

She received it without a word, and held it in her bruised palm. Her face was lowering, and she mused, looking at the coin.

Yes, he who is in the wrong must abandon his wrongful way—give up what offended the other. What had she to yield? Nothing. She had done her utmost to retain Anthony's love. She had not been false to him by a moment's thought. She had striven against her own nature to fit herself to be his companion. She loved him—she loved him with her whole soul ; and yet she hated him—hated him because he had slighted and neglected her at

the Cakes, because he was suffering himself to be lured
from her by Julian, because he was dissatisfied with his
house, resented against her his quarrel with his father.
She could hardly discriminate between her love and her
hate. One merged into the other, or grew out of the other.

"Come!" said the old man, looking about for his hat.
"By the Lord! the boy has gone off with my wet cap.
Well, I shall wear his, I cannot tarry here. I will go seek
out my friend Cudlip at the Hare and Hounds. I shall
not be late, but I want to hear news. There is a wind that
the Duke of Monmouth has set sail from the Lowlands. The
militia have been called out and the trainbands gathered.
Come, Urith, do not look so grave. Brighten up with
some of the humours of the maid who sang of winter on
Trinity Monday. It cannot be summer-time all the year—
why, neither can it be winter."

Then he swung out of the house trolling :—

> So let not this pair be despised,
>   That man is but part of himself ;
> A man without woman's a beggar,
>   If he have the whole world full of wealth,
> A man without woman's a beggar,
>   Tho' he of the world were possessed,
> But a beggar that has a good woman,
>   With more than the world is he blessed.

CHAPTER XL.

"THIS FOR JULIAN."

Urith was left alone looking at the broken token. It did
not bring to her the cynical consolation that her uncle intended it to convey. It was not even poor comfort, it was
no sort of comfort whatever to learn that others had been
unhappy in the same way as herself—that there had been
discord between her father and mother. The broken token
was to her a token of universal breakage—of broken trust,
broken ambitions, broken words, broken hearts—but that
all the world was in wreck was no relief to Urith, whose
only world for which she cared was contained within the
bounds of Willsworthy.

She had dreamed with reverence of her father; but Uncle Sol had shown her that this father had been false in heart to her mother. Her own story was that of her mother. Each had married one whose heart had been pre-engaged. After a little while, no doubt of sincere struggle, the heart swung back to its eldest allegiance. As Urith sat in the hall window, looking out into the court, her eyes rested on the vane over the stables. Now that arrow pointed to the west! Sometimes it veered to other quarters, but the prevailing winds came from the Atlantic, and that vane, though for a few days it may have swerved to north or south, though for a whole month, nay—a whole spring it may have pointed east, as though nailed in that aspect, yet round it swung eventually, and for the rest of the year hardly deviated from west. So was it with the heart of Anthony; so had it been with the heart of her father. Each had had a first love; then there had come a sway towards another point, and eventually a swing round into the direction that had become habitual.

Fox's words at the dance in the house of the Cakes returned to her:—"You cannot root out old love with a word." With Anthony it had been old love. Since childhood he and Julian had known each other, and had looked on each other in the light of lovers. It was a love that had ramified in its roots throughout his heart and mind. It was with this love as with the coltsfoot in the fields. When once the weed was there, it was impossible to eradicate it; the spade that cut it, the pick that tore it up, the sickle that reaped it down, only multiplied it; every severed fibre became a fresh plant—every lopped head seeded on the ground and dispersed its grain. For a while a crop of barley or oats appeared, and the coltsfoot was lost in the upright growth; but the crop was cut and carried, and the coltsfoot remained.

Was this a justification for Anthony? Urith did not stay to inquire. She considered herself, her anguish of disappointment, her despair of the future—not him. With all the freshness and vehemence of youth, she had given herself wholly to Anthony. She had loved—cared for—no one before; and when she loved and cared for him it was with a completeness to which nothing lacked. Hers was a love infinite as the ocean, and now she found that his had

19

been but a love, in comparison with hers, like a puddle that is dried up by the July sun.

She did not consider the matter with regard to Anthony's justification, only as affecting herself—as darkening her entire future. The coltsfoot must go on growing, and spread throughout the field. It could not be extirpated, only concealed for a while. She could never look into Anthony's face—never kiss him again, never endure a word of love from him any more, because of that hateful, hideous, ever-spreading, all-absorbing, only temporarily-coverable weed of first love for Julian. An indescribable horror of the future filled her—an inexpressible agony contracted her heart as with a cramp. She threw up her hands and clutched in the air at nothing; she gasped for breath as one drowning, but could inhale nothing contenting. Everything was gone from her with Anthony, not only everything that made life happy, but endurable. Down the stream belonging to the manor was a little mill, furnished with small grinding-stones, and a wheel that ever turned in the stream that shot over it. No miller lived at the mill. When rye, barley, or wheat had to be ground, some person from the house went down, set the mill, and poured in the grain. Night and day the wheel went round, and now in her brain was set up some such a mill—there was a whirl within, and a noise in her ears. The little manor-mill could be unset, so that, though the wheel turned, the stones did not grind unless needed; but to this inner mill in her head there was no relaxation. It would, grind, grind as long as the stream of life ran—grind her heart, grind up her trust, her hopes, her love, her faith in God, her belief in men—grind up all that was gentle in her nature, till it ground all her nobler nature up into an arid dust.

The day declined, and she was still looking at the broken token.

The mill was grinding, and was turning out horrible thoughts of jealousy, it ground her love and poured forth hate, it ground up confidence and sent out suspicion. She sprang to her feet. Where was Anthony now? What was he doing all this while? He had been away a long time; with whom had he been tarrying?

The mill was grinding, and now, as she threw in the jealous thoughts, the hate, the suspicions, it had just turned out, it ground them over again, and sent forth a wondrous series of fancies in a magic dust that filled her eyes and ears; in her eyes it made her see Anthony in Julian's society, in her ears it made her hear what they said to each other. The dust fell into her blood, and made it boil and rage; it fell on her brain, and there it caught fire and spluttered. She was as one mad in her agony—so mad that she caught at the stanchions of the window and strove to tear them out of the solid granite in which they were set, not that she desired to burst through the window, but that she must tear at and break something.

Why had Anthony marred her life, blistered her soul? She had started from girlhood in simplicity, prepared to be happy in a quiet way, rambling over the moors in a desultory fashion, attending to the farm and garden and the poultry yard. She would have been content, if left alone, never to have seen a man. Her years would have slipped away free from any great sorrow, without any great cares. Willsworthy contented her where wants were few. She loved and was proud of the place; but Anthony, since he had been there had found fault with it, had undervalued it, laughed at it; had shown her how bleak it was, how ungenerous was the soil, how out of repair its buildings, how lacking in all advantages.

Anthony had taught her to depreciate what she had highly esteemed. Why need he have done that?

The wheel and the grindstones were turning, and out ran the bitter answer—because Willsworthy was *hers*, that was why he scorned it, why he saw in it only faults.

She paced the little hall, every now and then clasping her hands over her burning temples, pressing them in with all her force, as though by main strength to arrest the churn of those grindstones. Then she put them to her ears to shut out the sound of the revolving wheel.

On the mantel-shelf was a brass pestle for crushing spices. She took it down. Into it were stuffed the old gloves of Julian Crymes. It was a characteristic trait of the conduct of the house; nothing was put where it ought to be, or might be expected to be. After these gloves had lain about, at one time in the window, at another on the settle, then upon the table, Urith had finally thrust them out of the way into the pestle, and there they had re-

maimed forgotten till now. In the train of her thoughts
Urith was led to the challenge of Julian, when she recalled
where the gloves were, and these she now took from the
place to which she had consigned them.

She unfolded them and shook the dust from them.
Then she stood with one foot on the hearthstone, her
burning head resting against the granite upper stone of
the fireplace, looking at the gloves. Had Julian made good
her threat? Was she really, deliberately, with determinate
malice, winding Anthony off Urith's hand on to her own?
And if so—to what would this lead? How would she—
Urith—be tortured between them? Every hair of her head
was a nerve, and each suffering pain.

She lifted her brow from the granite, then dashed it
back again, and felt no jar, so acute was the inner suffering she endured. It were better that Anthony, or she—
were dead. Such a condition of affairs as that of which
the mill in her head ground out a picture, was worse than
death. She could not endure it, she knew—she must go
mad with the torment. Oh, would! oh—would that Fox's
fuse had been left to take its effect in the ear of Anthony's
horse, and dash him to pieces against the rocks of the
Walla!

She could no longer bear the confinement of the house.
She gasped and her bosom laboured. She put the gloves
between her teeth, and her hands again to her head, but
her dark hair fell down about her shoulders. She did not
heed it. Her mind was otherwise occupied. In a dim
way she was aware of it, and her hands felt for her hair,
how to bind it together and fasten it again, but her mind
was elsewhere, and her fingers only dishevelled her hair
the more.

The air of the room oppressed her; the walls contracted
on her; the ceiling came down like lead upon her brain.
She plucked the gloves out of her mouth and threw them
on the table, then went forth.

The rain had ceased. Evening had set in, dark for
June, because the twilight could not struggle through the
dense vapours overhead.

"Where is Anthony? I must see Anthony!" Her
words were so hoarse, so strange that they startled her.
It is said that when one is possessed, the evil spirit in the

man speaks out of him in a strange voice, utterly unlike
that which is natural. It might be so now. The old de-
mon in Urith that had gone to sleep was awaking, re-
freshed with slumber, to reassert his power.

Where was Anthony? What delayed his return? Had he
on leaving Willsworthy gone direct to Julian to pour out
into her sympathetic ear the story of his domestic troubles? Was he telling her of his wife's shortcomings?—of
her temper?—her untidiness?—her waywardness? Were
they jeering together in confidence at poor little moorland
Willsworthy? Were they talking over the great mistake
Anthony had made in taking Urith in the place of Julian?
Were they laughing over that scene when Anthony led out
Urith for the dance at the Cakes? She saw their hands
meet, and their eyes—their eyes—as at the Cakes.

Then there issued from her breast a scream—a scream
of unendurable pain; it came from her involuntarily; it
was forced from her by the stress of agony within, but the
voice was hoarse and inhuman. She was aware of it, and
grasped her hair and thrust it into her mouth to gnaw at,
and to stifle the cries of pain which might burst from her
again.

She had descended the hill a little way when she thought
she discerned a figure approaching, mounting the rough
lane. It might be Anthony—it might be Solomon Gibbs.
She was unprepared to meet either, so she slipped aside
into the little chapel. The portion of wall by the door was
fallen, making a gap, but further back grew a large sycamore, out of the floor of the sacred building, near the an-
gle formed by the south and west walls. Behind this she
retreated, and thence could see the person who ascended
the path, unobserved.

She was startled when Fox Crymes stepped through the
gap where had been the door. There was sufficient light
for her to distinguish him, but he could not observe her,
as the shadows thrown by the dense foliage of the sycamore from above, and the side shadows from the walls,
made the corner where Urith stood thoroughly obscure.

She supposed at first that Fox had stopped there for a
moment to shake out his wet cloak and readjust it; he
did, in fact, rearrange the position of the mantle, but it
was not so as more effectually to protect himself from rain

as to leave his right arm free. Moreover, after that he had fitted his cloak to suit his pleasure, he did not resume his ascent of the lane to Willsworthy.

For a while Urith's thoughts were turned into a new channel. She wondered, in the first place, why Fox should come to Willsworthy at that hour; and next, why Fox, if Willsworthy should be his destination, halted where he was, without attempting to proceed.

His conduct also perplexed her. He seated himself on a stone and whistled low to himself through a broken tooth in front that he had—a whistle that was more of a hiss of defiance than a merry pipe. Then he took out his hunting-knife, and tried the point on his fingers. This did not perfectly satisfy him, and he whetted it on a piece of freestone moulding still in position, that formed a jamb of the old door, of which the arch and the other jamb were fallen.

This occupied Fox for some time, but not continuously, for every now and then he stood up, stole to the lane, and cautiously peered down it, never exposing himself so as to be observed by any person ascending the rough way.

The air was still, hardly any wind stirred, but what little there was came in sudden puffs that shook the foliage of the sycamore burdened with wet, and sent down a shower upon the floor. Urith could not feel the wind, and when it came it was as though a shudder went through the tree, and it tossed off the burden of water oppressing it, much as would a long-haired spaniel on emerging from a bath.

Bats were abroad. One swept up and down the old chapel, noiseless, till it came close to the ear, when the whirr of the wings was as that of the sails of a mill.

An uneasy peewhit was awake and awing, flitting and uttering its plaintive, desolate cry. It was not visible in the grey night-sky, and was still for a minute; then screamed over the ruins; then wheeled away, and called, as an echo from a distance, an answer to its own cry.

Fox stood forward again in the road, and strained his eyes down the lane; then stole a little way along it to where he could, or thought he could, see a longer stretch of it; then came back at a run, and stood snorting in the ruins once more. Again, soft and still, came on a comminuted rain—the very dust of rain—so fine and so light that it took no direction, but floated on the air, and hardly fell.

Fox turned to the sycamore-tree. No shelter could be had beneath its water-burdened leaves, that gathered the moisture and shot it down on the ground. But he did not look at it as wanting its shelter. He stepped toward it, then drew back; exclaimed, "Ah! Anthony. Here's one for Urith," and struck his knife into the bole. The blade glanced through the bark, sheering off a long strip, that rolled over and fell to the ground attached to the tree at the bottom. "You took her and Willsworthy from me," said Fox, drawing back. Then he aimed another blow at the tree, cursing, "And here is for my eye!"

Urith started back; each blow seemed to be aimed at and to hit her, who was behind the tree. She felt each stroke as a sharp spasm in her heart.

Fox dragged at his knife, worked it up, down, till he had loosened it; then withdrew it. Then he laid his left hand, muffled in his cloak, against the sycamore trunk, and raised his knife again. "That is not enough," he whispered, and it was to Urith as though he breathed it into her ear. He struck savagely into the side of the tree, as though into a man, under the ribs, and said, "And this for Julian."

Before he could release his blade, Urith had stepped forth and had laid her hand on him.

"Answer me," she said: "What do you mean by those words, 'And this for Julian?'"

CHAPTER XLI.

"THAT FOR URITH."

Fox cowered, and retreated step by step before Urith, who stepped forward at every step he retreated. He seemed to contract to a third of his size before her eyes, over which a lambent, phosphorescent fire played. They were fixed on his face; he looked up but once, and then, scorched and withered, let his eyes fall, and did not again venture to meet hers.

Her hands were on his shoulders. It might have been thought that she was driving him backward, but it was not so. He recoiled instinctively; but for her hands he might have staggered and fallen among the scattered stones of the old chapel that strewed the floor.

"Answer me!" said Urith, again. "What did you mean, when you said—'This for Julian?'"

"What did I mean?" he repeated, irresolutely.

"Answer me—what did you mean? I can understand that in thought Anthony stood before you when you struck —once because I had cast you over, and had taken him— once because he touched and hurt your eye—but why the third time for Julian?"

He lifted one shoulder after the other, squirming un- easily under her hands, and did not reply, save with a scoffing snort through his nostrils.

"I know that you are waiting here for Anthony—and like yourself, waiting to deal a treacherous blow. It is not such as you who meet a foe face to face, after an open challenge, in a fair field."

"An open challenge, in a fair field!" echoed Fox, re- covering some of his audacity, after the first shock of alarm at discovery had passed away. "Would that be a fair field in which all the skill, all the strength is on one side? An open challenge! Did he challenge me when he struck me with the gloves in the face and hurt my eye? No—he never warned me, and why should I forewarn him?"

"Come!" said Urith, "go on before—up to Wills- worthy; I will not run the chance of being seen here talk- ing with you, as if in secret. Go on—I follow."

She waved him imperiously forth, and he obeyed as a whipped cur, sneaked through the broken doorway forth into the lane. He looked down the road to see if Anthony were ascending, but saw no one. Then he turned his head to observe Urith, hastily sheathed his knife, and trudged forward in the direction required.

Urith said nothing till the hall was entered, when she pointed to a seat, and went with a candlestick into the kitchen to obtain a light. She returned directly, having shut the doors between, so that no servant could overhear what was said. The candlestick she placed on the table, and then planted herself opposite Fox Crymes. He was sitting with his back to the table, so that the light was off his face, and such as there was from a single candle fell on Urith ; but he did not look up. His eyes were on the skirt of her dress and on her feet, and by them he could see that she was quivering with emotion. He seemed to see her through the flicker of hot air that rises from a kiln. He wiped his eyes, thinking that his sight was disturbed, but by a second look ascertained that the tremulous motion was in Urith. It was like the quiver of a butterfly's wings when fluttering at the window trying to escape.

"I am ready," said Urith. "What did you mean when you said 'This for Julian?'"

He half-lifted his cunning eyes, but let them fall again. He had recovered his assurance and decided on his course.

"I suppose," sneered he, "that you will allow that I have a right to chastise the man who insults our good name, to bring my sister into the mouths of folk?"

"Has he done so?"

"You ask that?" he laughed, mockingly. "How remote this spot must be to be where the breath of scandal does not blow. You ask that? Why, 'fore heaven, I supposed that jealousy quickened and sharpened ears, but yours must be singularly blunt, or, mayhap, deadened by indifference."

"Tell me plainly what you have to say."

"Do you not know that your Anthony was engaged, or all but engaged—had been for some fifteen years—to my sister? Then he saw you under remarkable circumstances, saw and attended you along the Lyke Way that night of the fire on the moor. Then a spark of the wild fire fell into his blood, and he forgot his old, established first love, and in a mad humour took you. Take a scale," pursued Fox. "Put in one shell my sister with her wealth, her civilized beauty, her heritage, the grand old house of Kilworthy, and her representation of a grand old line. Put in also"—he suited the action to his word, in imaginary scales in the air before him, and saw the shrink of Urith's feet at each item he named—"put in also his father's favor, Hall—where he was born and bred, the inheritance of his family for many generations, with its associations, his sister's company, the respect of his neighbours; all that and more that I have not named into the one shell, and into the other.—Come, come!"—he crooked his finger, and made a sign with his knuckle, and a distorted face full of mockery and malice—"come, skip in and sit yourself down with a couple of paniers of peat earth, that grows only rushes. What say you? Do you outweigh Julian and all the rest? And your peat earth, sour and barren, does that sink your scale heavier than all the bags of gold and rich warm soil of Kilworthy and Hall combined?"

He glanced upward hurriedly, to see what effect his words had. All this that he said Urith had said it to herself; but though the same thoughts uttered to herself cut her like razors, they were as razors dipped in poison, when coming articulate from the lips of Fox.

"Do you not suppose," continued he, "that after the first fancy was over, Anthony wearied of you, and went back in heart out from this wilderness, back to Goshen and to the Land of Promise rolled into one, with the flesh-pots, and without hard labour? Of course he did. He were a fool if he did not, or your hold over him must be magical indeed, and the value of Willsworthy altogether extraordinary."

Again he furtively looked at her. Her eyes were off him, he felt it, before he saw it. She was looking down at the floor, and her teeth were fastened into her clenched hands. She was biting them to keep under the hysteric paroxysm that was coming over her. He took a malevolent delight in lashing her to a frenzy with his cruel words, and so avenging himself on her for his rejection, avenging himself on her in the most terrible way possible, by making her relations with her husband henceforth intolerable.

She could no longer speak. He saw it, and he waited for no words. He went on: "You married him; you married him, notwithstanding that he had offered the grossest insult to the memory of your father. You married him indecently early after your mother's death, and that was an outrage on her memory. Whether you have the blessing of father and mother on your union is more than doubtful. I should rather say that out of heaven they fling their united curses on you for what you have done."

A hoarse sound issued from her throat. It was not a cry, nor a groan, but like the gasp of a dying person.

"And now the curse is working. Of course Anthony is hungering after what he has thrown away. But he cannot get Kilworthy. You stand in the way. He can get Hall only by casting you over. That he will do."

Suddenly Urith became rigid as stone. She could not speak, she dropped her hands, and looked with large fixed eyes at Fox. He saw, by the cessation of the quiver of her skirt, that she had become stiff as if dead.

"That," repeated Fox, "he is prepared to do. His father made him the offer. If he would leave you, then, said the old Squire, all should be as before. Anthony should go back to Hall, live with his father, be treated as heir, and command his pocket—only you were to be discarded wholly, and he was not to see you again."

Fox paused, and began his hissing whistle through his broken tooth. He waited to let the full force of his words fall on her to crush her, before he went on still further to maltreat her with words more terrible than blows of bludgeons or stabs of poisoned knife.

Now he twisted his belt round, and laid the scabbarded hunting knife before him on his lap, played with it, and then slowly drew forth the blade.

"But now—" he said leisurely, "now I reckon you can see why I took out my knife, and why I would strike him down before he leaves you and returns to Hall. Already has there been talk concerning him and my sister. He gave rise to it at the dance at the Cakes. But you know better than I what happened there, as I went away with my father, who arrived from London. When young blood boils, it is forgotten that the sound of the bubbling is audible. When hearts flame, it is not remembered that they give out light and smoke. I suppose that Anthony and my sister forgot that they were in the midst of observant eyes when they met again, as of old so often ; just as they forgot that you existed and were a bar between them. I tell you I do not know what took place then, as I was not there, but you had eyes and could see, and may remember."

He put the knife upright with the haft on his knee, and set his finger at the end of the blade, balancing it in that position. She saw it, her eyes were attracted by the blade; the light of the candle flashed on the polished steel; then Fox turned the blade and the light went out, then again it flashed, as the surface again came round over against the candle.

"When Anthony is back at Hall, I know well what will take place. Even now he comes over often to Kilworthy, too often, forgetful of you, forgetful of all save his old regard, his love for Julian, that draws him there; he cannot keep away even now. When he is at Hall nothing will retain him, and he will bring my sister's fair name into the dirt. Have I not a cause to take out this knife? Must I not stand as her guardian? My father is old, he has no thoughts for aught save the Protestant cause and Liberty and Parliamentary rights. He lets all go its own way, and, unless I were present to defend my sister, he would wake, rub his eyes, and find—find that all the world was talking about the affairs of his house, and his grey hairs would be brought in shame to the grave. Julian has no mother, and has only me. She and I have bickered and fought, but I value the honour of my family, and for that I can, when need be, strike a blow. You know now what it is I fear; you know what it is I meant when I took out my knife and waited in the chapel for the man who would bring my sister to dishonour. I could tell you more—I could tell you that which would make you kiss the blade that tapped his blood, that entered his false heart and let out the black falsity that is there, but——" He looked hesitatingly at her, then slowly rose, and, watching her, went backwards to the door.

She stood motionless, white, as though frozen, and as still; her hands were uplifted. She had been about to raise them to her mouth again, but the frost had seized them as they were being lifted, and were held rigid, in suspense. Her eyes were wide and fixed, her mouth half-open, and her lower jaw quivered as with intense cold, the only part of her in which any motion remained. So stiff, so congealed did she seem, that it occurred to Fox, as he looked at her, that were he to touch and stir her wild flowing hair, it would break and fall like icicles on the floor. He stepped back to the door, then held up his finger, with a smile about his lips—

"I am coming back again. I am not going to run away."

A convulsive movement in her arms. Her hands went up with a jerk to her mouth.

"No," said Fox; "do not bite your pretty hands. There"—he turned to the table and picked up the old pair of gloves that lay there—"if you must tear something, tear these. They will do you good."

He put the gloves to her hands, and they mechanically closed on them. Her eyes were as stones. All light had deserted them, as fire had deserted her blood, had died out of her heart.

Fox went out, and remained absent about five minutes. Suddenly the door was dashed open, and he came in excitedly. "He is coming—he is hard at hand. I have more to say. Do you mistrust me? Do you think I am telling lies? I will say it to his face; and then——" He drew his knife and made a stroke with it in the air, then sheathed it again. "Go," said he, "go in yonder." He pointed to the well-chamber that opened out of the hall. "Remain there. The rest I will tell Anthony to his face."

He caught her by the wrist and led her to the door, and almost forced her into the little chamber.

Then he went across the hall to the door that led to the kitchen, opened it, and looked into a small passage; crossed that to another door communicating with the kitchen, and turned the key in it. He returned to the hall, and was shutting the door behind him when Anthony entered from outside.

Anthony raised his brows with surprise at the sight of Fox there, and flushed with anger. This was the man who was going to displace him at Hall, occupy his inheritance, and take his very name. And Fox—this treacherous friend —had the daring to come to his house and meet him.

"What brings you here?" asked Anthony, roughly.

"An excellent reason, which you might divine."

Fox had completely recovered his assurance. He came across the room toward the seat he had occupied before, and, with a "By your leave," resumed it. He thus sat with his face in shadow, and his back to the door of the well-chamber.

"And, pray, what are you doing in my house? Hast come to see me or Master Gibbs?"

"You—you alone."

Anthony threw himself into the settle; his brow was knit; he was angry at the intrusion, and yet not altogether unwilling to see Fox—for he desired to have a word with him relative to his proposed marriage with Bessie, and assumption of his name.

"And I," said he; "I desire an explanation with you, Fox."

"Come, now!" exclaimed young Crymes. "I have a desire to speak with you, and you with me. Which is to come first? Shall we toss? But, nay! I will begin; and then, when I have done, we shall see what desire remains in you to talk to me and pluck thy crow."

"I want then to know what has brought you here? Where is my wife? Where is Urith? Have you seen her?" Anthony turned his head, and looked about the room.

"What!" said Fox, with a jeer in his tone, "dost think because thou runnest to Kilworthy to make love to my sister Julian, that I came here to sweetheart thy wife?"

"Silence!" said Anthony, with a burst of rage, and sprang from his seat.

"I will not keep silence," retorted Fox, turning grey with alarm at the hasty motion, and with concentrated rage. "Nay, Anthony, I will not be silent! Answer me; hast thou not been this very day with Julian?"

"And what if I did see her? I went to Kilworthy to find you."

"You go there oftentimes to find me, but, somehow, always when I am out, and Julian is at home. When I am not there, do you return here, or go elsewhere? Nay, you console yourself for my absence by her society—bringing her into ill-repute in the county."

"You lie!" shouted Anthony.

"I do not lie," retorted Fox. "Did you not remain with her to-day. Where else have you been? Who drew your initials on the glass beside hers, and bound them together with a true lover's knot?"

Anthony's head fell. He had planted himself on the hearthstone, with his back to the fireplace—now without burning logs or peat in it. The flush that had been driven by anger to his face deepened with shame to a dark crimson.

Fox observed him out of his small keen eyes.

"Tell me this," he pursued. "Was it not indiscreet that thy father should come in and find thee and Julian locked in each other's arms, exchanging lovers' kisses?"

Anthony looked suddenly up, and in a moment all the blood left his face and rushed to his heart. He saw behind the chair in which sat Fox, the form of his wife. Urith—grey as a corpse, but with fire spirting from her eyes, and her nostrils and lips quivering. Her hand was lifted, clenched, on something, he could not see what.

"Tell me," repeated Fox, slowly rising, and putting his hand to his belt. "Tell me—can you deny that?—can you say that it is a lie? Your own father told me what he had seen. Did he lie?"

Anthony did not hear him, did not see him; his eyes were fixed in sorrow, shame, despair, on Urith. Oh, that she should hear this, and that he should be unable to answer!

"Strike—kill him!" her voice was hoarse—like that of a man; and she dashed the gloves, torn to shreds by her teeth, against his breast.

Instantly, Fox's arm was raised, the knife flashed in the candle-light, and fell on him, struck him where he had been touched by the gloves.

"That," the words attended the blows, "that for Urith."

Anthony dropped on the hearthstone.

Then, as Fox raised his arm once more—without a cry, without a word, Urith sprang before him, thrust him back with all her force, that he reeled to the table, and only saved himself from a fall by catching at it, and she sank consciousless on the hearthstone beside Anthony.

CHAPTER XLII.

ON THE BRIDGE.

Fox soon recovered himself, and seeing Anthony moving and rising on one hand, he came up to him again and thrust him back, and once more stooping over him, raised the knife.

"One for Urith," he said, "one for myself, and then one for Julian."

Before he could strike he was caught by the neck and dragged away.

Luke Cleverdon was in the hall; he had entered unobserved. Fox stood leaning against the table, hiding his weapon behind him, looking at Luke with angry yet alarmed eyes.

"Go," said Luke, waving his left hand. "I have not the strength to detain you, nor are there sufficient here to assist me were I to summon aid. Go!"

Fox, still watching him, sidled to the door, holding his knife behind him, but with a sharp, quick look at Anthony, who was disengaging himself from the burden of Urith, lying unconscious across him, and raising himself from where he had fallen. Blood flowed from his bosom and stained his vest.

"It was she. She bade me!" said Fox, pointing towards Urith. Then he passed through the door into the porch, and forth into the night.

Luke bent over Urith, who remained unconscious, and raised her to enable Anthony to mount to his feet, then he gently laid her down again, and said:

"Before any one comes in, Anthony, let me attend to you, and let us hide, if it may be, what has happened from other eyes."

He tore open Anthony's vest and shirt, and disclosed his breast. The knife had struck and dinted the broken token, then had glanced off and dealt a flesh wound. So forcible had been the blow that the impress of the broken crown, its part of a circle, and the ragged edge were stamped on Anthony's skin. The wound he had received was not dangerous. The token had saved his life. Had it not turned the point of Fox's knife, he would have been a dead man; the blade would have entered his heart.

Luke went to the well-chamber, brought thence a towel, tore it down the middle, passed it about the body of Anthony, and bound the linen so fast round him as to draw together the lips of the wound, and stay the flow of blood.

He said not one word whilst thus engaged. Nor did Anthony, whose eyes reverted to Urith, lying with face as marble and motionless upon the floor.

When Luke had finished his work, he said, gravely, "Now I will call in aid. Urith must be conveyed upstairs; you ride for a surgeon, and do not be seen. Go to my house, and tarry till I arrive. Take one of your best horses, and go."

Anthony obeyed in silence.

When Mistress Penwarne had returned from the visit to Magdalen Cleverdon, she had communicated the intelligence of Fox's suit, and of the old Squire's resolution, to Luke, and he at once started for Willsworthy, that he might see Anthony. Of the offer made by the father to Anthony he, of course, knew nothing; but the proposal to marry Bessie to Fox, and for the latter to assume the name of Cleverdon, filled him with concern. Bessie would need a firmer supporter than her Aunt Magdalen to enable her to resist the pressure brought upon her. Moreover, Luke was alarmed at the thought of the result to Anthony. He would be driven to desperation, become violent, and might provoke a broil with Fox, in which weapons would be drawn.

He arrived at Willsworthy in time to save the life of Anthony, and he had no doubt that the quarrel had arisen over the suit for Bessie, and the meditated assumption of the Cleverdon name. Anthony was hot-headed, and would never endure that Fox should step into his rights. But Luke could not understand what had induced Fox to run his head into danger. That he was audacious he knew, but this was a piece of audacity of which he did not suppose him to be capable.

Anthony saddled and bridled the best horse in the stable, and rode to Tavistock, where he placed himself in the hands of a surgeon. He did not explain how he had come by the wound, but he requested the man to keep silence concerning it. Quarrels over their cups were not infrequent among the young men, and these led to blows and sword thrusts, as a matter of course.

The surgeon confirmed the opinion expressed by Luke. The wound was not serious, it would soon heal; and he sewed it up. As he did so, he talked. There was a stir in the place. Squire Crymes of Kilworthy had been sending round messages to the villages, calling on the young men to join him. He made no secret of his intentions to march to the standard of the Duke of Monmouth.

20

"It is a curious fact," said Surgeon Pierce, "but his Lordship the Earl of Bedford had been sending down a large quantity of arms to his house that had been built out of the abbey ruins. His agent had told folks that the Earl was going to fit up a hall there with pikes, and guns, and casques, and breastplates, for all the world like the ancient halls in the days before Queen Elizabeth. Things do happen strangely," continued the surgeon. "All at once, not an hour ago it was whispered among the young men who were about in the market-place talking of the news, and asking each other whether they'd fight for the Pope or for the Duke, that there were all these weapons in his Lordship's hall ; and that no one was on the spot to guard them. Well, they went to the place, got in, and no resistance offered, and armed themselves with whatever they could find, and are off the Lord knows where."

When Anthony left the surgeon's house, he considered what he should do, after having seen his cousin. To Luke's lodgings in the rectory at Peter Tavy he at once rode. His cousin he must speak to. To Willsworthy he could not return. The breach between him and Urith was irreparable. She knew that he had tampered with temptation, and believed him to be more faithless to her than he really had been. He would not, indeed he could not, explain the circumstances to her, for no explanation could make the facts assume a better colour. It was true that he had turned for a while in heart from Urith. Even now, he felt he did not love her. But no more did he love Julian. With the latter he was angry. When he thought of her, his blood began to simmer with rage. If he could have caught her now in his arms, he would have strangled her. She had played with him, lured him on, till she had utterly destroyed his happiness.

What had he done ? He had kissed Julian. That was nothing ; it was no mortal crime. Why should he not kiss an old friend and comrade whom he had known from childhood ? What right had Urith to take offence at that ? Had he written their initials on the glass, and united them by a true lovers' knot ? He had ; but he had also effaced it, and linked his own initial with that of Urith. He loved Urith no longer. His married life had been wretched. He had committed an act of folly in marrying her. Well,

was he to be cut off from all his old acquaintances because
he was the husband of Urith? Was he to treat them with
distance and coldness? And then, how Julian had looked
at him! how she had bent over him, and she—yes, she—
had kissed him! Was he to sit still as a stone to receive
the salutation of a pretty girl? Who would? Not a Puritan,
not a saint. It was impossible—impossible to young flesh
and blood. A girl's kiss must be returned with usury—tenfold. He was in toils—entangled hand and foot—and he
sought in vain to break through them. But he could not remain thus bound—bound by obligation to Urith, whom he
did not love—bound by old association to Julian, whom he
once had loved, and who loved him still—loved him stormily,
fervently. What could he do? He must not go near Julian
—he dare not. He could not go back to Urith—to Urith
who had given to Fox the mandate to kill him! He had
heard her words. It was a planned matter. She had
brought Fox to Willsworthy, and had concerted with him
how he, Anthony, was to be killed. And yet Anthony knew
that she loved him. Her love had been irksome to him—
so jealous, so exacting, so greedy had it been. If she had
desired and schemed his death, it was not that she hated
him, but because she loved him too much—she could not
endure that he should be estranged from her and drawn
towards another.

But one course was open to him. He must tear—cut
his way through the entangled threads. He must free
himself at one stroke from Urith and from Julian. He
would join Monmouth.

He rode, thus musing, towards Peter Tavy, and halted
on the old bridge that spanned in two arches the foaming
river. The rain that had fallen earlier had now wholly
ceased, but the sky remained covered with a dense grey
blanket of felt-like cloud. A fresher air blew; it came
from the north, down the river with the water, and fanned
Anthony's heated brow.

His wound began now to give him pain; he felt it as a line
of red-hot iron near his heart. It was due to pure accident
that he was not dead. If matters had fallen out as Urith
desired, he would now be lying lifeless on the hearthstone
where he had dropped, staggered and upset by the force
of Fox's blow, when unprepared to receive it

Now he recalled that half-challenge offered on the moor when first he met Urith, and had wondered over her bitten hands. He had half-threatened to exasperate her to one of her moods of madness, to see what she would do to him when in such a mood. He had forgotten all about that bit of banter till this moment. Unintentionally he had exasperated her, till she had lost all control over herself, and, unable to hurt him herself, had armed Fox to deal him the blow which was to avenge her wrongs.

He could not go back to the house with the girl who had sought his life. No—there was nothing else for him to do than throw in his lot with Monmouth, and, at the moment, he cared little whether it should be a winning or a losing cause.

"Anthony?"

"Yes. Is that you, Luke?"

A dark figure stepped on to the bridge, and came to the side of the horse.

"I have been home," said the curate. "Urith is ill; she scarce wakes out of one faint to fall into another. I have sent your grandmother to Willsworthy to be with her."

"It is well," answered Anthony. "And, now that we have met here, I wish a word with you, Luke. I am not going back to Willsworthy."

"Not—to Urith?"

"No, I cannot. I am going to ride at once to join the Duke of Monmouth. You have the Protestant cause at heart, Luke, and wish it well; so have I. But that is not all—I must away now. I do not desire to meet Fox for a while."

"No," said Luke, after a moment of consideration; "no, I can understand that. But Bessie must not be left without some one to help her."

"There is yourself. What can I do? Besides, Bess is strong in herself. She will never go against what she believes to be right. She will never step into my shoes, nor will she help Fox to draw them on."

"You cannot ride now, with your wound."

"Bah! That is naught. You said as much yourself."

"Tony, there is something yet I do not understand," said Luke, falteringly. "Did you first strike Fox?"

"No—no. I had my hands behind me. I stood at the hearth."

"But the quarrel was yours with him, rather than his with you. If you did not strike him, why did he aim at you?"

"Luke, there were matters passed of which you need know naught—at least no more than this. My father had offered to receive me back into his good-will once more, to let the past be blotted out, no longer to insist on Bess being wed to Fox, and to return to live at Hall."

"Indeed!" exclaimed Luke, joyously. "Now can I see why Fox came to you, and why he struck you."

"It was on one condition."

"And that was——"

"That I should leave Urith, and never speak to her again."

"Anthony!" Luke's tone was full of terror and pain. "Oh, Anthony! Surely you never—never for one moment —not by half a word—gave consent, or semblance of consent, to this! It would—it would kill her! Oh, Anthony!"

Luke put up both his hands on the pommel of the saddle, and clasped them. What light there was fell on his up-turned, ash-grey face.

"Anthony, answer me. Has she been informed of that? She never thought you could be so cruel—so false; and she has loved you. My God! her whole heart has been given to you—to you, and to no one else; and you have not valued it as you should have done. Because you have had to lose this and that, you have resented it on her. She has had to bear your ill-humour—she has suffered, and has been saddened. And now—no! I cannot think it. You have not let her know that this offer was made."

The sweat drops poured and rolled off Luke's brow. He looked up, and waited on Anthony for a reply.

"She did know it," answered the latter, "but that was Fox's doing. He told her; and told her what was false, that I intended to accept the offer, and leave her. No, Luke, I have done many things that are wrong, I have been inconsiderate, but I could not do this. And now I bid you go to-morrow to my father, see him, and tell him my answer. That is expressed in one word—Never."

Luke seized his hand, and wrung it. "That is my own

dear cousin Anthony!" he said, and then added, "But why away at once, and Urith so ill?"

"I must away at once. I cannot return to her." Anthony hesitated for some while; at last he said, in a low tone, "I will tell you why—she thinks me false to her, and in a measure I have been so. She thinks I no longer love her—and it is true. My love is dead. Luke—I cannot return."

"Oh, Urith—poor Urith!" groaned the curate, and let his hands fall.

"Now I go. Whatever haps, naught can be worse than the state of matters at present. If you can plead in any way for me, when I am away, do so. I would have her think better of me than she does—but I love her no more."

Then he rode away.

Luke remained on the bridge, looking over into the rushing water—the river was full.

"Poor Urith! My God—and it was I—it was I who united them." Then he turned into the direction of Hall. "I will go there, and bear Anthony's message to his father at once."

CHAPTER XLIII.

AN EXPIRING CANDLE.

When Squire Cleverdon arrived at Hall, he found there awaiting him a man booted, spurred, whip in hand, bespattered with mire. The old man asked him his business without much courtesy, and the man replied that he had ridden all day from Exeter with a special letter for Master Cleverdon, which he was ordered to deliver into his hands, and into his alone.

Old Cleverdon impatiently tore away the string and broke the seal that guarded the letter, opened it, and began to read. Then, before he had read many lines, he turned ghastly white, reeled, and sank against the wall, and his hands trembled in which he held the page.

He recovered himself almost immediately, sufficiently to give orders for the housing and entertainment of the messenger; and then he retired to his private room, or office, into which he locked himself. He unclosed a cabinet that contained his papers, and, having kindled a light, brought forth several bundles of deeds and books of accounts, and spread them on the table before him. Some of the documents were old and yellow, and were written in that set courthand that had been devised to make what was written in it unintelligible save to the professionals. Squire Cleverdon took pen and a clean sheet of paper and began calculations upon it. These did not afford him much satisfaction. He rose, took his candle, opened and relocked the door, and ascended the stairs to his bedroom, where he searched in a secret receptacle in the fireplace for his iron box, in which were all his savings. Thence he brought the gold he had, and, having placed the candle on the floor, began to arrange the sovereigns in tens, in rows, where the light of the candle fell. After the gold came the silver, and after the silver some bundles of papers of moneys due that had never been paid, but which were recoverable.

Having ascertained exactly what he had in cash, and what he might be able at short notice to collect, the old man replaced all in the iron case, and reclosed the receptacle.

In the mean while, during the evening, after darkness had set in, to Bessie's great annoyance, Fox appeared. Directly he left Willsworthy, he thought it advisable to visit Hall before going home, and forestall with old Cleverdon the tidings of what had occurred. He did not doubt that the story of his attack on Anthony would be bruited about—that Anthony, or Luke, or both, would tell of it, to his disadvantage, and he determined to relate it his own way at once, before it came round to the ears of the Squire, wearing another complexion from that which he wished it to assume.

"You desire to see my father," said Bessie. "He is engaged, he is in his room; he would not be disturbed."

"I must see him, if but for a minute."

Bessie went to the door and knocked, but received no answer. She came back to the parlour. "My father is busy; he has locked himself into his room. You had better depart."

"I can wait," said Fox.

"Then you must pardon my absence. There has come a messenger this evening for my father, with a letter that has to be considered. I must attend to what is fitting for the comfort of the traveller."

When left to himself, Fox became restless. He stood up, and himself tried the door of old Anthony's apartment. It was locked. He struck at the door with his knuckles, but received no answer. Then he looked through the key-hole; it was dark within. The old man was not there, but at that moment he heard him cough upstairs. He was therefore in his bedroom, and Fox would catch him as he descended. He returned to the parlour.

Presently Bessie entered with Luke; she had gone to the door, had stood in the porch communing with herself, unwilling to be in the room with her tormentor, when Luke appeared, and asked to see her father. "Verily," said she, with a faint smile, "he is in mighty request this night; you are the third who have come for him—first a stranger, then Fox——"

"Fox here?"

"Yes, he is within."

"I am glad. A word with him before I see your father, and do you keep away, Bessie, for a while till called."

Fox started to his feet when Luke came in, but said nothing till Bessie left the room, then hurriedly,

"You, raven—what news? But mark you. I did it in self-defence. Every man must defend his own life. When he knew that I was to take his place in Hall, he rushed on me, and I did but protect myself."

"Anthony's wound is trifling," said Luke, coldly.

"So! and you have come to prejudice me in the ear of his father."

"I am come with a message from Anthony to his father."

"Indeed—to come and see his scratch, and a drop of blood from it; and then to clasp each other and weep, and make friends?"

"The message is not to you, but to his father."

"And—he is not hurt?"

"Not seriously hurt."

"I never designed to hurt him. I did but defend my own self. I treated him as an angry boy with a knife."

"No more of this," said Luke. "Let the matter not be mentioned. I will say naught concerning it, neither do you. So is best. As for Anthony, he is away."

"Away? Whither gone?"

"Gone to-night to join Monmouth. Your father is gathering men for the Protestant cause, Anthony will be with him and them."

Fox laughed. His insolence had come back, as his fears abated.

"Faith! he has run away, because I scratched him with a pin. At the first prick he fainted."

Luke went to the door, and called in Bessie. He could not endure the association with Fox.

"Bess!" he said, "can I see your father?—I have a message for him from Tony."

"He is upstairs—in his bedroom," said Bessie. "I will tell him you are here when he descends."

"Come here," exclaimed Fox, who had recovered all his audacity, and with it boisterous spirits. "Come here, Bess, my dear, and let Cousin Curate Luke know how we stand to each other."

"And, pray," said Bessie, colouring, "how do we stand to each other?"

"My word! you are hot. We shall be asking him ere long to join our hands—so he must be prepared in time— he will have a pleasure in calculating the amount of his fee."

"Cousin Luke," said Bessie, "I am not sorry that he has mentioned this, for so I can answer him in your presence, and give him such an answer before you as he has had from me in private, but would not take. Never, neither by persuasion, nor by force, shall I be got to give my consent."

In spite of his self-control, Fox turned livid with rage.

"Is that final?" he asked.

"It is final."

"We shall see," sneered he. "Say what you will, I do not withdraw."

"For shame of you!" exclaimed Luke, stepping between Bessie and Fox. "If you have any good feeling in you, do not pester her with a suit that is odious to her, and after what has happened to-night, should, to yourself, be impossible."

"Oh!" jeered Fox, "you yourself proposed silence, and are bursting to let the matter escape."

"Desist," said Luke. "Desist from a pursuit that is cruel to her, and which you cannot prosecute with honour to yourself."

"I will not desist!" retorted Fox. "Tell me this. Who first sought to bring it about? Was it I? No. Magdalen Cleverdon was she who prepared it, then came the Squire himself. It's the Cleverdons who have hunted me—who try to catch me; not I who have been the hunter. You call me Fox, and you have been hue and tally ho! after me."

"There is my father!" gasped Bessie, and ran from the room. She found the old man in the passage with his candle, unlocking his sitting-room door.

"Oh, father!" she said, breathlessly, for the scene that had occurred had taken away her breath, "here is Luke come—he must see you."

"What! at night? I cannot. I am busy."

"But, father, he has a message."

"A message? What, another? I will not see him."

"For a moment, uncle. It is a word from Anthony," said Luke, entering the passage. "One word, shall I say it here, or within?"

"I care not—if it is one word, say it here; but only one word."

He was fumbling with the key in the lock. His hand that held the candle shook, and the wax fell on his fingers and on the cuff of his coat. He had the key inserted in the door, and could not turn it in the wards.

"Very well," said Luke. "You shall have it in one word—Never."

The old man let the key fall—he straightened himself. His voice shook with anger. "It is well. It is as I could have wished it. I take him at his word. Never. Never—let me say it again. Never, and once again, never; and each never shuts a door on him for all time. Never shall he have my forgiveness. Never shall he inherit an acre or a pound of mine. Never will I speak to him another word. Nay, were he dying, I would not go to see him; could I by a word save his life, I would not do it. Go tell him that. Now go—and Elizabeth, hold the candle. I will open the door; go in before me to my room; I'll lock the door on us both. Now all is plain. The wind has cleared away

the mists, and we must settle all between us this night,
with the way open before us."

He managed to unfasten the door, and he made his
daughter pass in, carrying the light. Then he turned the
key in the lock.

The little table was strewn with deeds and papers and
books. Bessie cast a glance at it, and saw no spot on which
she could set the candle. She therefore held it in her
hand, standing before her father, who threw himself into
his chair. She was pale, composed, and resolved. He
could have nothing further to urge than what had been
urged already, and she had her answer to that. The candle
was short, it had swaled down into the tray, and could not
burn for more than ten minutes.

"Elizabeth," said her father, "I shall not repeat what
has been said already. I have told you what my wishes,
what my commands are. You can see in Anthony what
follows on the rebellion of a child against the father. Let
me see in you that obedience which leads to happiness as
surely as his disobedience has brought him to misery.
But I have said all this before, and I will not now repeat it.
There are further considerations which make me desire that
you should take Anthony Crymes without delay." He drew
a long breath, and vainly endeavoured to conceal his agitation. "I bought this place—Hall—where my forefathers
have been as tenants for many generations; I bought it,
but I had not sufficient money at command, so I mort-
gaged the estate, and borrowed the money to pay for it.
Then I thought soon and easily to have paid off the debt.
The mortgagee did not press; but having Hall as mine
own was, I found, another thing to having Hall as a tenant.
My position was changed, and with this change came increased expenditure. Anthony cost much money, he was
of no use in the farm, and he threw about money as he
liked. But not so only. I rebuilt nearly the whole of the
house; I might have spent this money in paying off the
mortgage, or in reducing it, but instead of that I rebuilt
and enlarged the house. I thought that my new position
required it, and the old farmhouse was small and inconve-
nient, and ill-suited to my new position. But I had no
fear. The mortgagee did not require the money. Then
of late we have had bad times, and I have had the drag of

the mortgage on me. A little while ago I had notice that I must repay the whole amount. I did not consider this as serious, and I sought to stay it off. The messenger who has now come from Exeter, comes with a final demand for the entire sum. The times are precarious. The Duke of Monmouth has landed. No one knows what will happen, and the mortgagee calls in his money. I have not got it."

"Then what is to be done?"

Bessie became white as the wax of the candle, and the flame flickered because the candle shook in her hand.

"Only one thing can be done. Only you can save Hall —save me."

"I! Oh, my father!" Bessie's heart stood still, she feared what she should hear.

"Only you can save us," pursued the old man. "You and I will be driven out of this place, will lose Hall, lose the acres that for three centuries have been dressed with our sweat, lose the roof that has covered the Cleverdons for many generations, unless you save us."

"But—how, father?" she asked, yet knew what the answer would be.

"You must marry Anthony Crymes at once. Then only shall we be safe, for the Crymes family will find the money required to secure Hall."

"Father," pleaded Bessie, "ask for help from some one else! Borrow the money elsewhere."

"In times such as this, when we are trembling in revolution, and none knows what the issue will be, no one will lend money. I have no friend save Squire Crymes. There is no help to be had anywhere else. Here"— said the old man, irritably—"here are a bundle of accounts of moneys owed to me, that I cannot get back now. I have sent round to those in my debt, and it is the same cry from all. The times are against us—wait till all is smooth, and then we will pay. In the mean time my state is desperate. I offered to Anthony but this day to forgive the past and receive him back to Hall—but the offer came too late. Hall is lost to him, lost to you, lost to me, lost forever, unless you say yea."

"Oh, Luke! Luke!" cried Bessie; "let me speak first with him;" then suddenly changed her mind and tone,

"Oh, no! I must not speak to him—to him above all, about this."

"Bessie!" said the old man; his tone was altered from that which was usual to him. He had hectored and domineered over her, had shown her little kindness and small regard, but now he spoke in a subdued manner, with entreaty. "Bessie! look at my grey hairs. I had hoped that all future generations of Cleverdons would have thought of me with pride, as he who made the family; but, instead, they will curse me as he who cast it forth from its home and brought it to destruction."

Bessie did not speak, her eyes were on the candle, the flame was nigh on sinking, a gap had formed under the wick, and the wax was running down into the socket as water in a well.

"I have hitherto commanded, and have usually been obeyed," continued the old man, "but now I must entreat. I am to be dishonoured through my children, one—my son—has left me and taken to himself another home, and defies me in all things. My daughter, by holding out her hand, could save me and all my hopes and ambitious, and she will not. Will she have me—me, an old grey-headed father, kneel at her feet?" He put his hands to the arms of his seat to help him to rise from the chair that he might fall before her.

"Father!" She uttered a cry, and, at the shock that shuddered through her, the flaming wick sank into the socket, and there burnt blue as a lambent ghost of a flame. "O father!—wait!—wait!"

"How long am I to wait? The answer must be given to-night; the doom of our house is sealed within a few hours, or the word of salvation must be spoken. Which shall it be? The messenger who is here carries my answer to Exeter, and, at the same time, if you agree, the demand for a licence, that you may be married at once. No delay is possible."

"Let me have an hour—in my room!"

"No; it must be decided at once."

"Oh, father—at once? She watched the blue quiver of light in the candle socket. "Very well—well—when the light goes out you shall have my answer."

He said no other word, but watched her pale face, looking weird in the upward flicker of the dying blue flame, and her eyes rested on that flame, and the flicker was reflected in them—now bright, then faint, swaying from side to side as a tide.

Then a mass of wax fell in, fed the flame, and it shot up in a golden spiral, revealing Bessie's face completely.

"Father! I but just now said to Fox Crymes 'Never! never! never!'"

She paused, the flamed curled over.

"Father! within a few minutes must I go forth to him and withdraw the 'Never?'"

He did not answer, but he nodded. She had raised her eyes from the dying flame to look at him.

Again her eyes fell on the light.

"Father! If I withdraw my 'Never,' will you withdraw yours about Anthony?—never to forgive him—never to see him in Hall—never to count him as your son?"

The flame disappeared—the old man thought it was extinguished, but Bessie saw it still as a blue bead rolling on the molten wax; it caught a thread of wick and shot up again.

"Father! I do not say promise, but say perhaps."

"So be it—Perhaps."

The flame was out.

Bessie walked calmly to the door, felt for the key, turned it, went forth, still holding the extinguished candle in her hand. It was to her as if all that made life blessed and bright to her had gone out with that flame.

She went into the parlour and composedly put out her hand to Fox.

"Take me," she said. "I have withdrawn the 'Never.' I am yours!"

CHAPTER XLIV.

LADING THE COACH.

Fox hastened back to Kilworthy. He also knew that time was precious. His father was in a fever of excitement about the landing of Monmouth, and was certain to give him all the assistance in his power both with men and with money. Not only so, but he would so compromise himself that, in the event of the miscarriage of Monmouth's venture, he would run the extremest risk of life and fortune.

He had for some time past been acting for the Duke in enlisting men in his cause. The whole of the West of England was disaffected to the King—was profoundly irritated at his overbearing conduct, and alarmed lest he should attempt to bring the realm back to Popery. The gentry were not, however, disposed to risk anything till they saw on which side Fortune smiled. They had suffered so severely during the Civil War, and at the Restoration had encountered only neglect, so that the advisability of caution was well burnt into their minds. The Earl of Bedford, who owned a vast tract of property about Tavistock, secretly favoured Monmouth, but was indisposed to declare himself. He had not forgotten—he bitterly resented the execution of his son, Lord William Russell, for complicity in the Rye House Plot—a plot as mythical as the Popish Plot revealed by Titus Oates, and which he attributed to the resentment of the Catholic party. He was willing that Squire Crymes should act for him, and run the risk of so doing.

Fox had the shrewdness to see this, but his father was too sincere an enthusiast, and too indifferent to his own fortunes to decline the functions of agent for Monmouth pressed on him by the Earl of Bedford.

"What dost want? I cannot attend to thee," said Mr. Crymes, when his son entered the room. On the table lay piled up several bags tied with twine, and sealed.

"What do I want?" retorted Fox. "Why, upon my honour, you have forestalled my thought. I came for money; and, lo! there it is."

"I am busy," said the old man. "Dost see, though it be night, I am ready for a journey? I have the coach ordered to be prepared. I must travel some way ere daydawn."

"If you are going away, father, so much the more reason why you should give ear to me now."

"Nay, I cannot. I have much to do—many things to consider of. I would to God thou wast coming with me! But, as in the case of those that followed Gideon, only such as be whole-hearted and stout may go to the Lord's army."

"I have the best plea—a scriptural one—for biding at home," laughed Fox; "for I am going to be married. Ere ten days be passed, Bess Cleverdon will be my wife."

"I am sorry for her. I esteem her too well," said the old man, impatiently. "But away with thy concerns; this is no time for marrying and giving in marriage, when we approach the Valley of Decision in which Armageddon will be fought. Go out into the yard and see if any be about the coach."

"I passed through the court in coming here. The coach was there—no horses, no servants."

"I must take the coach," said the old man. "I was a poor rider when young; I cannot mount a horse now in my age."

"Then, verily, father, thy coach and four will be out of place in the Valley of Decision," scoffed Fox. "Of what good canst thou be in an army—in a battle—if unable to mount a horse? Stay at home, and let the storm of war blow across the sky. If thou wantest Scripture to justify thee, here it is: 'Rebellion is as the sin of witchcraft.'"

"The cause of true religion is in jeopardy," retorted the father. "I know what is right to be done, and I will do it. Go I must, for, though I cannot fight myself, my counsel may avail; and I bear to the Duke the very nerves of war." He pointed to the money-bags.

"I did not know thou hadst so much gold by thee, in the house," said Fox, going to the table, taking up, and weighing one of the bags.

"A hundred pounds in each," said his father; "and good faith! I had not the coin. There, thou art right. But it has fallen out that the Earl of Bedford has called to mind certain debts to me, or alleged debts for timber, wool, and corn, and has sent orders to the steward to pay me for the same in gold. The Earl—" he stopped himself. "But there, I will say no more. The money is not mine."

"What, no real debt?"

"I say nothing. I take it with me, whether mine or not signifies naught to thee; it goes to the Duke of Monmouth."

"It concerns me, father, for I want, and must have

money. I am shortly to be married, and I cannot be as a beggar. I have sent to the College of Arms for licence to change my name, and that will cost me a hundred pounds. I want the money."

"I cannot let you have it."

"But it is here. Let me toll it."

"Never—get thee away, I cannot attend to thee now."

"But, father; I cannot be left thus, your clearing away all the money in the house, and I about to marry; who can say but Armageddon may turn all contrary to your expectations."

"Put off the marriage till I return."

"It cannot be put off. What if all goes wrong, and the land be given up to the Jesuits? What then with thy neck? What with thy money? Will either be spared? Give me, at least, the gold, and take care of thy neck thyself; then one will be safe at all events."

"If it be the Lord's will," said the old man, with a look of dignity, "I am well content. If I follow Lord William Russell's steps, I follow a good man, and die in a righteous cause. I shall seal my faith with my blood."

"And the Jesuits will lay their hands on all thou hast——"

"I have nothing. Kilworthy belongs to thy sister. As for what I have saved, it is not much. I have some bills, I have contributed to the suffering saints, I have helped the cause of the Gospel with my alms——"

"More the reason, if so much has been fooled away that this should be secured. The cause of the Gospel is the providing for thine own household, and there never yet was a more suffering saint than myself. I will lay hands on this coin, and take it as my wedding portion!"

"Hands off!" shouted the old man, half drawing his sword. "Though thou art mine own son, I would run thee through the body or ever thou shouldst touch this, which is for the justest, truest, holiest cause, and I am a steward that must give account for the same. I will give thee twenty pounds."

"That will not pay the clerks of the Herald's College."

"I will not pay for that—to change the ancient name of Crymes for another."

"What! Not when one name brings to me a vile twenty

pounds, and the other name will give me a thousand pounds a year!"

"Heaven gave thee to me, for my sorrow," said the old man, "and in giving thee to me, covered thee with my name. It is tempting heaven to cast it off and take another. But there! I have no time for talk. Would God I could persuade thee to draw a sword for the good cause."

"Not a bodkin!" mocked Fox, who was very angry. The sight of the bags of money fevered him. "But you have one after your own heart ridden forward, and that is 'Tony Cleverdon. I heard as much from Luke."

"'Tony Cleverdon!" repeated Mr. Crymes. "I am rejoiced at that. Ah! would that Providence had given him to me as a son! 'Tony Cleverdon! That is well. He will take my place at the head of a brigade from this region. My infirmities and age will not suffer me to ride, but I will speak to the Duke, and he shall be the captain over our men from Tavistock. But come now, and be of good mind for once, and help me, lad." The old man took up one of the money bags. "I have sent the men to the kitchen for their supper, and I would remove all these to the carriage whilst they are away, as they know naught about the treasure, and it is well that they should remain ignorant. Not that I misdoubt them, they be honest men and true, and would not rob me of a shilling, but their tongues might clack at the taverns, and so it get noised that there was money in the coach, and come to the ears of scoundrels, and we be waylaid. Not but that we shall be well provided against them ; for I shall be armed, so also the footman on the box beside the driver, and there will be two riders armed, with each a horse led to hitch on when we go up the hills, so as to have six to pull the coach up. And I shall have two of our recruits to go on, with carbines, ahead, and spy about, that there be no highwaymen awaiting us on the road. So! Anthony Cleverdon is gone on without tarrying for me to ask him. That is like the lad. 'Fore Heaven! even were a party of footpads to waylay us, if I said, 'Gentlemen of the Road, I am travelling for the Protestant cause, bearing specie to the camp, and we are rising against the Jesuits and the Inquisition, and the Pope of Rome, join us and march along!' I believe not one of them would touch a coin, but all would give a cheer and come along. Why, who will stay us? There is but the High Sheriff, John Rowe, is a Catholic, and perhaps three or four more among the gentry, and among the common, simple folk ne'er an one that would stay us, and not wish us God speed! Come, lend a hand with the bags; I will hold the candle. Let all be stowed away whilst the men are supping."

In the courtyard of Kilworthy stood the glass coach of Mr. Crymes—a huge and cumbrous vehicle, so cumbrous that it required four horses to draw it along the roads, and six to convey it to the top of a hill. Travelling on the highways was not smooth and swift in those days; the roads were made by filling the ruts with unbroken stones of all sizes, unbroken as taken off the fields. Where there was a slough, faggots were laid down, and the horses stumbled over the faggots and soused into the mire between them as best they could. Travelling in saddle was in those days slow, especially in wet weather, but travelling in a coach was a snail-like progress, and the outrunners had not to exert themselves extraordinarily to distance the horses, for they could trip along on the turf at the side of the ways, which were part slough, part rubble-beds of torrents, without the inconvenience and perils that assailed the travellers on wheels.

Mr. Crymes always journeyed in his coach, for, owing to an internal malady, he was unable to sit a horse; but a coach-journey tried him greatly, owing to his age, and the jolting he went through in his conveyance.

The courtyard was deserted, the monstrous vehicle looked in the darkness like a hearse, so black and massive was it, only the flicker from the reflection of the light relieved its sombreness as Mr. Crymes crept round to the back with his lantern, and a bag of gold under one arm.

Fox sulkily obeyed his father. At the back of the carriage was the boot that had a flap which, when unlocked, fell down. The old man fumbled for and produced the key, unfastened the receptacle, and thrust his bag inside.

"Now give me thine, and go for two more," said he, "and I will tick them off in my note-book as they are placed in the boot."

"It is a pity, father," said Fox, "that you have not a stouter lock."

"Nay, it sufficeth," answered Mr. Crymes. "None will know what is fastened within. If we were—and the chance is not like to come—overpowered by highwaymen, I trow they would demand the key and open the boot though the lock were twice as strong. My own luggage shall travel in the front boot. Go, lad, fetch me more of the gold. Even in the best cause men will fight faintly unless they be paid."

Fox obeyed, and brought all the bags in pairs to the carriage, and saw the old man stow them away. He was in an ill-humour, and cursed his father's folly in his heart.

"How if the venture fails?" he asked, "and then you be led to Tyburn. It will be a sorry end to have lost all this gold as well as thy life. Thy life is thine own to throw away, but the gold I may claim a right to. I am thy son, I want it; I am about to be married, and have a use for the money; now it will all go into the pockets of wretched country clowns, who will shoulder a musket and trail a pike for a shilling—if it were given to me, I could put it to good usage."

"Come with me to my study," said the old man. "Here come Jock and Jonas from the kitchen. Come along with me, and thou shall have twenty pound in silver and gold, and a hundred more in bills that may be discounted when the present troubles are over."

"I will ride with thee, father, some part of the road as thy guard—till the daybreak."

CHAPTER XLV.

UNLADING.

The hour was past midnight and before dawn when the great coach of Squire Crymes approached the long hill of Black Down. The road from Plymouth to Exeter was one of singular loneliness for a considerable part of its course, but in no part did it traverse country so desolate and apart from population as in the stretch, a posting stage between Tavistock and Okehampton, a distance of sixteen miles. It ran high up on the flanks of Dartmoor, mounting it nearly nine hundred feet above the level of the sea, with the trackless waste of the forest on one hand, and on the other a descent by ragged and rugged lanes to distant villages. Lydford, almost the sole one at all near the road, was severed from it by ravines sawn through the rock, through which the moor rivers thundered and boiled, ever engaged in tearing for themselves a deeper course.

Precisely because this track of road was the most inhospitable and removed from human haunts, was it one of the safest to travel even in the most troublous times, for no one dreamed of traversing it after nightfall, when aware that for sixteen miles he would be cut off from help in the event of a breakage of his carriage or the laming of a horse ; and as no one ever thought of taking this road except in broad day, when it was fairly occupied by trains of travellers, no footpads and highwaymen thought it worth their while to try their fortunes upon it.

Roads in former days to a large extent made themselves, or were made by the travellers. In the first place the bottoms of valleys were deserted by them as much as might be, because of the bogs that were there, and the lines of communication were laid on the ridges of hills above the springs that undermined and made spongy the soil. Then the roads were traced before the enclosures were made, and originally were carried as directly as possible from point to point. But obstacles, sometimes temporary, intervened : perhaps a slough, perhaps a rut of extraordinary depth had torn into the road, and became the nucleus of a pool ; perhaps an unduly hard and obstinate prong of rock appeared after the upper surface had been worn through. Then the stream of travellers swayed to one side, and gave the course of the road a curve, which curve was followed when hedges were run up. These hedges following the curves stereotyped the line of road, which thenceforth became permanently irregular in course.

A roadway in those days was about as easy to go over, and to go over with expedition, as the beach of Brighton. Consequently it was slow work journeying on such highways on horseback ; and it was journeying like a snail, when travelling in a coach. The outrunner had no very arduous task to outstrip the horses. He put his foot on the turf by the road-side, and tripped along at his ease, leaping the puddles and stones which were occasional by the road-side; whereas they were continuous in the road-way.

Fox rode sulkily beside the coach, as it rolled and rocked along the highway from Tavistock to the North. The night was overcast, after midnight, as it had been before the turn of the night; no wind was blowing, nor did rain fall, but the aspect was utterly sombre and uncheering. Every light was out in such houses as were passed, and not a passenger was met, or overtook the carriage that lumbered along, sending squirts of muddy water to this and that side as the wheels plunged into ruts. Fox came occasionally to the coach window, and said something to his father, and was bespattered from head to foot, boots, clothes, and face.

Presently the point was attained where the road left the valley of the brawling Tavy and climbed Black Down. There was a directness in the way in which old roads went at hills that was in keeping with the characters of our forefathers. A height had to be surmounted, and the road was carried up it with a rush, and with none of our modern zig-zags and easy sweeps. The hill must be ascended, and the sooner it was surmounted the better. Now, the great road to the North from Plymouth by Tavistock had the huge hogsback of Black Down to surmount, and it made no hesitating and leisurely attempts at it; it went up four hundred feet as direct as a bow-line.

On reaching the foot of the Down, the driver paused and the footman on the box dismounted. The men with the spare horses went ahead and hitched on their beasts. Then ensued loud cries and shouts, and the cracking of whips, each man attending to a horse, and encouraging it to do its uttermost to haul the great coach up the hill. The only men who kept their places were the driver on the box, and Mr. Crymes within.

Now, a good many other coaches had halted at the same spot, and halting there had ground away the soil, so as to make a very loose piece of road; moreover, the water falling on the road had run down it to the lowest level, and finding this rotten portion there had accumulated and done its utmost to assist the disintegration. The result was that the wheels sank in liquid mire to the axles, and six horses did little more than churn the filth and jerk the coach about.

Mr. Crymes having been subjected to several violent relapses as the coach was half pulled out of the pit and then sank back again, thrust his head out of the window and called :—"Wilkey! will it not be best to have all the horses harnessed? There is rope in the box."

"Well, perhaps it were best, your worship."

Thereupon much discussion ensued, and much time was spent in attaching ropes; and finally, with great hooting, and with imprecations as well, and some words of encouragement, the whole team was set in motion, and the coach was hauled out of the slough, and began slowly to snail the way up the two-mile ascent.

Again Mr. Crymes thrust forth his head.

"Wilkey! Perhaps if Mr. Anthony were to ride forward, it might be an encouragement to the horses to go along with more spirit."

"Your worship, I do not see Mr. Fox! I beg pardon, Mr. Anthony. I think he has returned."

"What! without a farewell? The boy is unmannerly, and inconsiderate of what is due to a father. But such is the decay of the world, alas! Go on, Wilkey! there was no necessity for all the men and horses to halt to hear what I had to say to thee."

Again there ensued a cracking of whips, objurgations, and cheers, a great straining at ropes, and a forward movement of the coach.

The vehicle proceeded some way with more ease, for the stream of water that had here flowed over the road had smoothed it, and cleared it of obstructions.

Presently the men and horses came to a dead halt, and there ensued ahead much conversation, some expostulation, and commotion.

Again Mr. Crymes' head was thrust out of the window, and he called, "Wilkey! I say; come here, Wilkey! What is the matter? Why dost thou not go on? Has any rope broken?"

But several minutes elapsed before Wilkey responded to his master's call, and when finally, in answer to further and more urgent shouts, he did come, it was not alone, but attended by several of the other men, dragging with them by the arms a man whom they had found in the road.

"What is it? Who is he? What does he here?"

"Oh, I will be good! I promise—I swear, I will be good! I'll say my prayers! I'll not get drunk any more! I do not want to go inside—I'd rather walk a hundred miles and run by night and day, than have this carriage stop for me, and hear——"

"Who are you? What are you doing here?" asked Mr. Crymes. "Some of you bring the lantern. Let me look at him. Is he a footpad?"

"No—never—never robbed any one in my life. I pray you do not ask me to step in. I thank thee, I had rather walk than gather to thy side. I really will be good. 'Pon my soul I will. Drive on, coachee!"

"Why—'fore Heaven!" exclaimed Mr. Crymes, "this is Mr. Solomon Gibbs—and, the worse for liquor. Mr. Gibbs, Mr. Gibbs!"

"Eh!" said the gentleman, coming to the coach door, "why, by cock! it isn't my Ladye at all! By my soul, you must excuse me, Master Crymes. I was in that state of fright! At this time of night, and on Black Down! I thought it could be no other than the Death Coach, and that my Ladye wi' the ashen face was inside, and would make me ride by her."

Then half-humorously, but half-scared still, and not wholly sober, Mr. Solomon Gibbs trolled forth in broken tones,

> I'd rather walk a hundred miles
> And run by night and day,
> Than have that carriage halt for me
> And hear my Ladye say—
> "Now pray step in and make no din,
> Step in with me to ride;
> There's room I trow, by me for you,
> And all the world beside."

"Why, how came you here?" asked Mr. Crymes. "My men took you for a highwayman, and might have fired their holsters or carbines at you."

"And I might ask, how came you here at night, in your coach! By cock! You do not know the scare you gave

me, at the very midnight—too—and I on the very road
that my Ladye goes over in her Death Coach! But—I
thought it stopped for me, and that upset my mind altogether. When I saw something—black horses, and a coach
coming along, I tried to skip out of the way and hide
somewhere, but, not a hiding-place could I find on the
moor. I did suppose at first that it was on its way for my
poor niece—for Urith, but when it stopped—when it
stopped—" he shivered. "I felt my heart go into my
boots. And I have been looking for him everywhere, in
every ale-house, and not so much as a thread of his coat,
nor the breath of a word as to his whereabouts, and she—
so ill—dying. I should not be surprised, dead. By cock!
when I saw the coach come along, and at or about midnight, I made sure my Ladye was on her way to Willsworthy, to fetch Urith; but when the coach stopped—when
it stopped—" again he shuddered.

"Whom are you seeking?" asked Mr. Crymes.

"Anthony, to be sure, my nephew-in-law. But I say,
Justice, thou art a religious man and a bit of a Puritan;
now solve me this. When I thought this was my Lady's
coach, and that she was about to put out her bony hand,
and to wave me to come in, then I swore and protested
I'd not touch another drop of drink and be good as any
red-letter day saint. Now, as the carriage is not hers, but
yours, and instead of the Lady wi' the Ashen Face it is the
Right Worshipful Justice Crymes, what say you? Does it
hold? Mind you, the oath was taken under misapprehen-
sion. Does it hold?"

"What is that you say, Master Gibbs, about your niece?
Is she really so ill?"

"Ill! So ill that I made sure the coach was on its way
for her. I've been running about the world all night like
the Wandering Jew, to first one ale-house and then another, after Anthony. Confound the fellow! what does he
mean, running away, hiding where none can find him, when
Urith is so ill?"

"What ails her?" asked Mr. Crymes. "Step in by
me——"

"No. 'Fore Heaven, I don't like the risk. You may be
my Lady in disguise, and I may rub my eyes and find that
a trick has been put on me. I will into no coach what-

ever to-night. I will keep to my own feet, though, indeed, they are so shaken with much running about that I can't rely on them. I'll to the surgeon and have him examine them, and let me know why they do not hold up under me as they was wont."

"How long has Urith been ill?"

"Now, look here!" said Mr. Solomon Gibbs, approaching the window closer, and lowering his voice. "Poor thing, poor thing! Prematurely, and the babe dead—she out of her mind, crazed like—the house upside down, and me running about the country, looking into every ale-house I can call to mind, to make inquiries after Anthony, and not a footprint of him anywhere, and he has gone off with a horse—the apple-grey—you know him."

"I can tell thee where Anthony Cleverdon is—he has followed the highest call—the voice of religion and of his country's need. He has ridden away to join the Duke of Monmouth."

"Whew!" whistled Solomon. "And his wife like every minute to die! I'll go back and tell her. This is ugly tidings—he tried to give me a blow 'gainst all laws of the game, this past day, but that I forgive him. But to run off and never leave a word at home, and Urith dying! That I'll never forgive."

"If I encounter him in the camp I will tell him the tidings; and now I must along. This delay has been great. Wilkey! what are you standing there agape for? Urge the horses on; by this time we should have been at the top of Black Down. Fare thee well, Master Gibbs."

He waived his hand out of the window.

The whips were cracked, shouts, oaths, and entreaties recommenced, and the vehicle was again in motion. Mr. Solomon Gibbs remained standing.

But the carriage had not gone forward many yards before Mr. Gibbs came striding up to the window; he put his head through and said, "Your worship! Are you aware that the boot-flap behind is down?"

"Boot—behind!" almost screamed Mr. Crymes. "Let me out! Heigh! Stay the horses! Wilkey! the door!"

He scrambled out of the coach, called for the lantern, and ran behind.

The flap was down, the boot open—and empty.

The coach had been unladen either at the slough at the foot of the hill, or during the commotion occasioned by the discovery of Mr. Solomon Gibbs.

CHAPTER XLVI.

AN EVENING SO CLEAR.

Luke paced his room at the parsonage, Peter Tavy, the greater part of the night. He had much, very much to trouble him. Urith was seriously ill. Mistress Penwarne was with her, otherwise she would have been left to servants who, with the best intentions, might not have known what to do. Her fainting fits had continued one after another, and then had been succeeded by an event which left her in fever and delirium.

Luke's hands clenched with wrath as he thought of Anthony—Anthony, to whom had been entrusted the care of this precious jewel, who had undervalued her, wearied of her, neglected her, and broken her heart, perhaps destroyed her young life. He was gone before, indeed, that he suspected how ill Urith was, and unaware of the danger she was in. Luke could not communicate with him, and if he did send a message after him, this might reach him when too late, or when unable to return. Urith's life hung on a thread; and, as Luke paced his room, he could not resolve whether it were better to pray that it should be spared or taken.

If her life were spared, it would be to what? To a renewal of misunderstandings, to the greatest of unhappiness, probably to deep-seated, embittered estrangement. Anthony and Urith were unsuited to each other—she sullen, moody, and breaking forth into bursts of passion; he impulsive, reckless, and without consideration for others. Was it conceivable that they could become so tempered and altered as to agree? He did not think this possible, and he folded his hands to pray for her release; but again he shrank from framing such a prayer lest, by making it, he should bring upon himself a sense of guilt, should his petition be answered.

What was to become of Urith if she lived? Best of all that Anthony should fall on the battle-field fighting for liberty and his religion. That would ennoble a life that lacked dignity, that had been involved in one disaster after another, that had alienated the hearts most attached—his father's, his own, Luke's, and, lastly, his wife's. But what if it were so? What if Urith were left a widow?

Luke's heart gave a leap, and then stood still and grew faint. She would then be free. Dare he—he, Luke—think of her, love her, once more? He had the strength of moral power to think out the situation, and he saw now that it must ever remain impossible that they should unite. He had his sacred calling, that brought on him obligations he dare not cast aside; and Urith's husband must be one to live at Willsworthy, and recover her property from the ruin into which it had fallen by devoting thereto all the energies of his mind and body. Moreover, the radical difference in their characters, in the entire direction of their minds, must separate them, and make them strangers in all that is best and stoutest in the inner nature. No, not even were she left a widow, could Luke draw nearer to her.

With his delicate conscientiousness, he took himself to task for having for a moment anticipated such a contingency springing out of the possible death of Anthony. Then Luke turned his thoughts to Bessie, and saw almost as dark a cloud over Hall as that which hung upon Willsworthy. If Anthony and Urith were unsuited for each other, far greater was the difference which existed between Fox and Bessie. Luke knew Fox—knew his unscrupulousness, his greed, his meanness, his moral worthlessness; and he valued no woman he knew higher than he did Bessie, for her integrity, her guilelessness, and self-devotion. By no right could Fox claim the hand of Bessie, for by no possibility could he make her happy. To unite her to him was to ensure the desolation of her whole life, the blighting of all that was beautiful in her. It was to consign her to inevitable heartbreak. She would take an oath to do what was impracticable; she could neither honour nor love such a man as Fox; she would strive to do both, but must fail. Luke vowed that nothing would induce him to pronounce the marriage benediction over their heads.

Luke was still up and awake, but kneeling at his table, and with his head in his hands, when a rattle of gravel at his window-panes brought him to his feet with a start, and he went to see who was in want of him. He opened the casement and looked out, to see Mr. Solomon Gibbs below. Luke descended and unfastened the door.

"Is Urith worse?" was his breathless question.

"Whew! I can say nothing," answered Mr. Gibbs. "I am cold. Always chillest before dawn, it is said, and daybreak cannot be a bowshot off. What dost think? Highway robbery on Black Down—this night Justice Crymes plundered whilst on his way to Exeter in his glass coach. The rascals prised open the boot behind, and though there were six men with the carriage, no one either saw the robber or heard him at work. It must have been done whilst they were urging the horses up the ascent; but it is passing strange. The highwayman must have been mounted, for he could not have escaped with the plundered goods had he not bestrid a horse. How it was done, when it was done, by whom, no one can tell anything, and by cock they're all talking, and every one has an opinion."

"Where is Mr. Crymes now?"

"Gone on. He was as one distraught—what with losing his money, and the call of the business he was on."

"His money taken!"

"Ay, and more than his own—in all about four hundred pounds, that was to be conveyed to the Duke of Monmouth at Taunton. He told me about it, as I have to go to Mr. Cleverdon about it, and see that the neighbourhood be searched for footpads. It must have been done quickly, for Fox rode behind the carriage, and now and then alongside it, to the rise of Black Down, when he turned and went back to Kilworthy. 'Twas dexterously done, and must have been the deed of a skilled hand. Now, what I am come here for is that I do not care myself to go to Squire Cleverdon. There has not been pleasantness between him and my family, so seeing your light, I came here to ask you to do the matter. Tell him that steps must be taken to have the neighbourhood searched for strangers—strangers they must be. We've none here could do the trick; all honest folk. And I can be of better service going round to the ale-houses. I am well known there, and there I can pick up information that may be of use. Every cobbler to his bench, and that is mine. Will you go to Hall as soon as you can in the morning?"

"I will do so, certainly. Now tell me about Urith."

"Urith! I cannot. I have not seen her; nor been near Willsworthy since you came away. I have been going about the country, to the taverns looking for Anthony, and not hearing any tidings of him."

"I can tell you where he is."

"I know myself now. Squire Crymes informed me that he had ridden across the moor towards Exeter, also bound for Taunton. Let me sit down. Nothing can be done yet; every one sleeps. The Hare and Hounds at Cudliptown will be closed. Do you hap to have any cider that can be got at? I am dry as old hay."

Mr. Gibbs took a seat.

"Lord, I have had a day," said he, "enough to parch up all the juices of the body. There was the affair with Tony to begin with, and I should not be surprised if the cut of the single-stick he gave her——"

"What!" exclaimed Luke, with a cry. "He strike her!"

"Well—not that, exactly. He and I were playing at single-sticks, when he gave me a cut out of all rules, and might have laid my skull bare had not Urith caught it on her hand. I doubt not it stung. It must have stung, and that may have begun the trouble. No—he never ill-treated her to that extent, intentionally, but they have not been happy together, and she has been very miserable of late."

Luke sighed, and said nothing. He had covered his face with his hand.

"Poor wench!" continued Uncle Sol, "she has no pleasure in anything now—that is to say, she has not for some while, not even in my stories and songs. Everything has gone contrary. Anthony has found fault with all I do—has complained of the state of the farm and the buildings, as if I could better matters without money. He has been discontented with everything, and Urith has seen it and fretted over it, and now things are at their worst; he is away; she dying, if not dead; and, Heavens help us—here, have you any cider? I am dried up with troubles."

"Come!" said Luke, "I can bear to be here no longer;

I will go with you to Willsworthy ; I must know how Urith is. I cannot endure this uncertainty longer."

Luke walked to Willsworthy with Mr. Gibbs, who was somewhat reluctant to pass Cudliptown without knocking up the taverner of the Hare and Hounds to tell him what had happened that night on Black Down, and to obtain from him a little refreshment before he traversed the last stage of his walk.

The grey of dawn appeared over the eastern ridge of moors by the time Willsworthy was reached, and the birds were beginning to pipe and cry.

No one had gone to bed that night in the house, a rush-light was burning in the hall, unregarded, a long column of red-hot snuff. The front door was open. Mr. Gibbs strode into the kitchen, and found a servant-maid there dozing on the settle. He sent her upstairs to call Mrs. Penwarne down, and the old lady descended. When she saw Luke, she was glad, and begged him to come upstairs with her and see Urith. It was possible that his presence might calm her. She was excited, wandering in mind, and troubled with fancies.

Luke mounted to the room where Urith was.

By the single candle contending with the grey advancing light of dawn he saw her, and was alarmed at her condition. Her face was pale as death, save for two flames in her cheeks, and her eyes, unusually large, had a feverish fire in them. She was sitting up. Mrs. Penwarne had striven all night to induce her to lie down, but Urith incessantly struggled to rise, and she had taken advantage of her nurse's absence to do so.

Luke went to her side and spoke. She looked up at him with hot eyes, and without token of recognition.

"I have killed him," she said. "I did it so !"—she raised her hand, clenched it, and struck downwards, imitating the action of Fox. "He fell on the hearthstone, as mother said he would, and then I tried to strike him again, and again, but was torn away." She began to grapple in the air with uplifted hands—"Where is the knife ? Where are the gloves ? That for Urith !"

Luke took her burning right hand, and said, " Lie down, lie down and sleep. You must be very quiet, you must not distress yourself. Anthony is well."

"Anthony is dead. I killed him. And my baby is dead. They killed it, because I had killed Anthony."

"Anthony is alive, he is but little hurt."

"Where is he? You have carried him away and buried him. I know he is dead. Why does he not come if he is not dead. I am sure he is dead. Look!"—she again struggled with her hand to be free, and show how the blow was struck—Look! You shall see how I did it!"

"No—Urith, lie down! Hush! I will pray with you."

Luke knelt at her side, but she turned her head impatiently away. "I will not be prayed for. I cannot pray. I killed him. I am glad I killed him, he was untrue to me. He had always loved Julian, and he grew tired of me. I killed him. I would not give him up. Julian should not have him back."

"Listen—I will pray."

"It is of no use. I do not regret that I struck him—I struck him to the heart. Answer me. Is there forgiveness if there be no repentance?"

She looked eagerly, almost fiercely, at Luke, who did not know what to answer. She was, it seemed to him, partly conscious, but partly only, of what had taken place —to be in a state of half dream. She knew him, she could reason, but she believed herself to have done that which was done actually by Fox Crymes.

"There!" she exclaimed, and threw back her head on the pillow. "It cannot be. I am glad I killed him. I could not do other. He brought it on himself. He was untrue to me. He loved Julian all his life, all but for a little while, when he fancied me. But you—you gave him to me at the altar. He could not remain mine. He was drawn away. But I could not let Julian have him. She defied me—it was a fair strife. She won up to a certain point, then I won the last point. Look! I will show you how I did it."

Once more she strove to sit up in the bed, and raised her hand, and clenched it.

"Do not be afraid. I have no knife now. They have taken it away to wash off the blood. I have heard them cleaning it. But my hand has the stain. That they cannot clean away. I had his blood on me once before—at the Drift. But then I did not know what that meant.

See—this is how I did it. Here is a feather, a feather from my pillow. That will do. I will let you see how I killed him. I will strike him with the feather. Then take that and clean it too."

Luke held her wrist, and gently forced her back on her pillow.

"Urith!" he said, "leave him to God. Commit the matter to God. Do not take the revenging of your wrongs, real or fancied, into your own hands."

She allowed him to compose her for a moment, and closed her eyes. But presently opened them again, and they were as full of fire as before.

"All is to pieces," she said, "all is broken, and Anthony broke it. Look here!" she plucked at her neck, and drew forth the halved token that was suspended there. "Look, he gave me this—but it was false. He has only given me one half, he has given the other to Julian. If she comes here, I will put my hand in between the ribbon and her throat and throttle her. Then there will be three dead—Anthony and my baby and she; and I will die next. I hope I shall. I long to die."

"You must not desire death, it is sinful."

"But I do; I have nothing to live for. I have killed Anthony, and my baby is dead; they say it was born dead. Then I will kill Julian. Look! you shall see how I killed Anthony."

Again she struggled to sit up. Luke rose from his knees, and said, peremptorily, "Lie down."

She obeyed, and he laid his cool hand on her burning temples. Below could be heard Solomon Gibbs tuning his fiddle, and then playing a few snatches.

Urith began to struggle under Luke's hands. "Do you hear? He is playing Anthony's song. Let him play it out and sing it also."

Mrs. Penwarne went to the head of the stairs and told Mr. Gibbs the request of Urith; then he put the violin to his chin and played:

An evening so clear
I would that I were
To kiss thy soft cheek
With the faintest of air.

22

The star that is twinkling
So brightly above,
I would that I were
To en-lighten my love.

He played very softly, and as he played the words of
the song formed and passed faintly over Urith's lips. She
may have recalled that evening when Anthony sang it,
coming up the hill, and so was carried away from the torturing present back into a pleasant past.

If I were the seas,
That about the world run,
I'd give thee my pearls,
Not retaining of one.
If I were the summer,
With flowers and green,
I'd garnish thy temples,
And would crown thee my queen.

She was quieter, lying with eyes closed, murmuring the
words as Uncle Sol played in the room below.

If I were a kiln,
All in fervour and flame,
I'd catch thee, and then be
Consumed in—the—same.

Luke lightly raised his hand, and put his finger to his
lip.
Urith was asleep.

CHAPTER XLVII.

IN THE HALL GARDEN.

Bessie was in the garden, the following afternoon, with
scissors and an apron pinned up, trimming her flowers, yet
with her mind away from the plants ; she was unhappy on
her own account, yet strove after resignation, and she felt
the consciousness of having done right in sacrificing herself for her father. He must now behave more kindly
towards her ; be more ready to listen to her intercession

for poor Anthony. Poor Anthony! she had heard that morning that he was gone, gone to extreme risk, and that Urith was in danger. She had resolved that now she must go to Willsworthy and see her sister-in-law, and be of what use to her she could. Her father could no longer forbid that. Even if he did, in that she would not obey him.

She was stooping over her plants, with tears in her eyes, snipping, picking off dead flowers and leaves, and tying up the carnations, when she heard behind her the voice of Fox.

"What!—busy?"

She winced, but rose, and with a little hesitation, held out her hand to him.

"Yes," she said, "I must do something with my hands to keep my thoughts from resting on troubles."

"Troubles! what troubles?"

Bessie gave him a look of reproach. "I must feel anxious about my brother, and also for Urith. How is it that you did not go as well as your father and my Anthony, to draw a sword for the good cause?"

"You ask that? Why, you are my attraction. I cannot leave you to venture my precious life in crack-brain undertakings. Before either of them returns, I suppose we shall be married."

"I am ready to fulfil my promise at any time," said Bessie.

"The sooner the better. Your father has already sent a messenger for a licence. I shall not rest till you are mine."

Bessie knew that what Fox desired was to have his foot in Hall, and be established there in the position of heir, and that his pretence of caring for her was hollow. A colour came into her cheeks like the carnations she was tying up. "Enough of that," she said; "you know the conditions on which I take you?"

"Conditions! On my soul I know of none."

"I told you that I did not love you, that I never had felt any love for you."

"You had the frankness to inform me of that, and to say that you had thrown your heart away on some one else, who declined the gift altogether."

Bessie bowed her head over her flowers.

" Yes, you told me that as we walked in the mud on the road ; and then you refused me, but changed your mind before many hours had passed. I have no doubt that, when I am your husband, you will learn to love and admire me. However, this is no condition."

"No condition ? " asked Bessie, rising, and looking him in the face. " Surely it is. I will take you, as you insist on it, and as my father desires it ; but it must be on the understanding that you do not ask of me at once what is not in my power to give. I will try to love you, I promise you. I will strive with my whole heart to give you all I undertake ; but I cannot do that at once."

"Oh! you call that a condition. It is well. I accept it." There was a veiled sneer in his tone.

"Then, again," continued Bessie, "I made my father promise, if I gave my consent, that he would try to forgive Anthony."

"What!—forgive and reinstate him ? " asked Fox, sharply.

"There was nothing said about reinstating him. I suppose that my father and you have talked about Hall, and everything that concerns the property, and that you understand the circumstances fully."

" To be sure I do," said Fox.

"Then, of course, I said nothing to him about reinstating Anthony, except in his old place in my father's heart. I believe that he will, himself, be glad to forgive the past. He cannot have cast out all the old love for, and pride in Anthony."

" And he has promised that ? "

"He has promised to try and forgive him. And now, Fox—I mean Tony Crymes—you are ready to take me, knowing that I do not love you, and can only try to render you that love which will be due from a wife to a husband ? "

"Oh, yes ! I take you as you are."

Of course he would. It was indifferent to him whether Elizabeth loved him or not, so long as his ambition and greed were satisfied.

" You see, Bess, I have a sharp tongue, and have made many enemies with it, who say in return sharp things of me, but with this difference—I say these things to their **faces**, they malign me behind my back. **When we are** married you will know me better, and not believe all you hear said of me."

Bessie slightly shook her head, and stooped again over her carnations.

"There is one thing further," she said ; "you must help me to persuade my father to be completely reconciled to Anthony."

"To be sure I will," answered Fox. "You want to see how good a fellow I am, in spite of all that is said of me. Here, take my hand, in token that I will do all you ask of me."

He gave her a cold, moist hand.

"And you promise me," she said, taking it, " on your honour that you will stand by me and back me up when I try to bring Anthony and my father together once more on the old terms ? "

His mistrust was roused, and he did not answer at once. Her frank grey eyes rested full on his face, and his eyes fell before her steady glance.

"I will do what you will," he said ; "but I do not suppose that your father will prove as wax in our hands, to mould as we like. Anthony has too deeply offended him, and Urith he will never see."

They dropped hands, for at that moment Julian entered the garden.

"I will go, see your father at once, and make trial in this matter," said he.

"You will find him in his room ; he is looking at some papers."

Fox walked away, giving Julian a nod and a sneer as he passed, and entered the house.

Julian came hastily up to Bess.

"My dear Bessie ! Is it true ? Are you really going to take my brother? It cannot—it must not be. It is intolerable to be in the house with him when one is master, and he there only on sufferance ; but to have him lord superior, and to be his slave !" Julian shivered.

"It is settled. I have passed my word, and I will not withdraw it."

"Bess ! And after the lesson you have had from Anthony ! "

"How a lesson, Julian ?"

"Why, dear child, a lesson that it does not answer to marry without love."

"Surely, Julian, there was love there, on both sides."

"Oh! love! A passing caprice. Do you not know that Anthony always loved me? Why has he gone off to join the Duke of Monmouth? Do you suppose it is because he cares so greatly for the Protestant cause? Nay, wench, it is that he may escape from me—and from the sight of Urith. I am dangerous, Urith is odious to him. Better be where balls are flying than where my eyes flash with temptation and Urith's dart with jealousy."

"Julian! how canst thou speak thus?" Bessie stepped back from her visitor, without offering to take her extended hands.

"Nay! do not be so offended. What I speak is the truth, and it all comes of marrying where there is no true affection. I am holding up thy brother as a warning to thee. Dost think that Fox cares a rush for thee? Not half a rush—all he looks to is Hall; he takes thee because he cannot have Hall without thee; and to have Hall is double pleasure to him, for he will have the place as his own, spiced with the satisfaction of having robbed his friend of it."

"I cannot help myself. I have passed my word, and stand to it."

"Look how things are now at Willsworthy. There is Urith dying, maybe; and Anthony far away. I hope she may die. It is best so, for she will have no happiness any more with Anthony. He is weary of her, he has found out that he cannot find his rest in her, his heart is with me. It has come back to me. It flew away a little while, and now it has returned. Anthony is mine. He does not belong any more to Urith."

"Shame on you!" said Bessie. "But I am glad you have spoken on this matter. You have acted sinfully, you have striven to turn Anthony from his duty."

"I have done so. Urith and I have wrestled a hitch together, and I have given her the turn, a fair back—three points. That is what she knows, and she is eating her heart out at the thought."

"Do you know what has happened? Urith has become a mother of a dead child."

"Is it so?" Julian was startled and changed colour. She had not heard this, she only knew that Urith was ill.

"She is in high fever and derangement of mind. If you have driven Anthony away, driven him to his death in the battle-field, and Urith also dies, then there will be the lives of all three you will be answerable for. It may be that Anthony was too hasty in marrying Urith, but once married, you should have left him alone. I do not believe, Julian, that he ever loved you. No, you may look at me in anger and doubt, but I am sure of it; I am his sister, I have seen and heard him, and if you fancy that he ever loved you, you are utterly in error. He never did. He never loved any girl till he saw Urith. She was his first love, not you. No, you never stirred his heart. He liked you. It flattered his vanity to see that you admired, almost worshipped him, but love you he did not. No, Julian, never—never! Urith was his first love, and, please God! will remain his only love."

Julian Crymes turned deadly white, and clenched her hands against her bosom.

"I saw what you were doing at that dance at the Cakes. Then you strove to draw him from his wife—then you threw the seeds of mistrust into her heart! You played a cruel and wicked game. But do not think, even although you may for a while have lured Anthony away from his wife, that you will separate them for ever. No! She was his first love, and to her he will return with redoubled love when this misunderstanding, this estrangement, is at an end—that is to say, if they live."

Bessie did not speak reproachfully, but sadly.

"Julian, you have been thoughtless, not malicious. I can tell you what the end will be, if Anthony do come back and find Urith dead. He will not go to you, and throw himself at your feet. No; he will hate you with a hatred that will be lasting as his life. He will look on you as—if not his wife's murderer—at all events, as one who engalled the last hours of her life—who drew briars and thorns between them, tearing their hearts when they last met. What passed between them I cannot say; but something must have—something terrible—to account for her present condition, and for his absence. You are answerable for that. Your thoughtlessness, and Anthony's love of flattery, have contrived to ruin a home. Anthony and Urith might have been happy parents of a sweet, innocent little one, who would have bowed the heart of his grandfather, and wiped off it all the rust that has gathered there. That little life, with all it might have been to itself, or to others, is destroyed—by you! You and Anthony broke the heart of Urith, and brought about what has taken place. You cannot give back the little life—you cannot mend the wreckage of happiness you have brought about. Pray to God to have pity on you, and forgive you your sins!"

"I have no cause to repent," answered Julian; but she did not speak with her old confidence, and she spoke with veiled eyes, resting on the gravel of the walk. "I am sorry Urith is ill. I am sorry that she and Anthony are disappointed in their hopes. I have always loved Anthony. There is no sin in that. If Urith succeeded in drawing him away from me to whom he was all but assured, must I not feel it? May I not resent it? She stole him from me, and the blessing at the altar does not hallow her theft."

"What are you saying!" exclaimed Bessie, fixing her eyes on Julian. "Is it not a sin to love a man who has sworn before heaven that he will be true to one, and one only, and that not yourself? Is it not a sin to endeavour to make him false to his oaths?"

"I cannot force him to be true to Urith, and to love her. You are going to marry Fox. You will swear to love and honour him, and you know you can do neither. You will swear and be false to your oath, for it is an impossibility to keep it. Anthony swore, but he could not keep his oath, he found out that he had make a mistake——"

"You tried to persuade him that he had. Be sure he will return to Urith with tenfold deeper, sincerer love, and will bitterly rue that he let himself be deluded by you."

Julian stood brooding, with her eyes on the ground. She recalled how Anthony had brushed out her initials linked with his, and interwoven in their place his own with those of Urith.

"There," said she, hastily, "I came here for something else than to be judged and condemned by you."

"I neither judge nor condemn you," answered Bessie,

"but I tell you the truth. Anthony can never be yours, not even if Urith dies. He never did love you."

Julian stamped. "You do not know—he did, and I loved him."

"What token did he give that he cared for you?—answer me now."

"I loved him, I love him still. In love all is fair. If I thought he did not love me——"

"Well," said Bessie, "what?" She looked steadily into Julian's eyes.

"I would dash my head against the stones, and kill thought for ever."

CHAPTER XLVIII.

A WEDDING DAY.

The marriage took place so speedily after the report of the engagement as to take every one by surprise; for everywhere a wedding is expected to be much discussed and prepared for beforehand. In the case of Fox and Bessie, all was over almost as soon as it was known to be in the air.

No great ceremony was made of it. Indeed, there was not time to make great preparations; nor did Squire Cleverdon care for display, or, on this occasion, for expense. His one desire was to have it over, and Fox settled in his house, for his affairs were causing him the utmost alarm—they were gathering to a crisis. It was with them but a matter of days; and, unless Fox were married to Bessie before the crisis arrived and became known, it was possible that the engagement, on which now all his hopes for the salvation of the property hung, might be broken off.

The licence was obtained, and almost simultaneously came the grant from the Garter King of Arms, and Clarenceaux King of Arms, "of the South, East, and West parts of England, from the River Trent southwards," to the effect that "whereas His Majesty, by warrant under his Royal Signet and Sign Manual, had signified to the Most Noble the Earl Marshal that he had been graciously pleased to give and to grant unto Anthony Crymes, Gent., son and heir apparent to Fernando Crymes, Esquire," the licence to bear henceforth the arms and name of Cleverdon, in lieu of that of Crymes; that therefore a patent to this effect was issued, etc. Consequently, Anthony Crymes was married, not in his paternal name, but in that which he had acquired.

The day was grey and sunless, with a raw northeast wind blowing.

Bessie returned, after the marriage, to the house where she had been born, and Fox came with her. She went to her old room, and there laid aside her wedding-dress, and then came quietly down the stairs into her father's chamber, where she patiently awaited him.

The old man had been giving orders without, and she heard his voice in the passage. She had not long to wait before he came in.

He looked at her with lifted eyebrows, and took off his hat, and asked what she wanted there.

"One word with you, dear father," said she, gently.

"Very well; make haste—I am busy. There is much to see to to-day. Where is Fox?"

He threw himself into his armchair, and crossed his feet.

"Father," said Bessie, "I have done what you desired, and with this day a new life begins with me. I have come to ask your pardon for any grief, annoyance, or trouble I may have at any time caused you. I also ask you to forgive me for having opposed your wishes at first when you wanted me to marry Fox. I did not then understand your reasons. But it has been a hard thing for me to submit. I dare say, dear father, you can have no idea how hard it has been for me. Now I have sworn to love Fox, and I will try my best to do so."

"Oh, love! love!" said the old man; "that is a mere word. You will get accustomed to each other, as I am to this chair."

"That may be. And yet—there is love—love that is more than a word. I suppose you loved my mother."

The old man made a deprecatory motion with his hand.

"Oh! father, without love in the house, how sad life is! I ought to know that, for I have had but little love shown me by you. Do not think I reproach you," she said, hastily, a little colour mounting into her pale face; "but I have felt the want of what, perhaps, I was not worthy to receive."

"Come—come!" said the old man; "I have no time for such talk that leads to nothing."

"But it must lead to something," urged Bessie; "for that very reason have I come here. You know, my dear father, that you made me a promise when I gave my consent, and I come now to remind you of it."

"I made no promise," said the old man, impatiently.

"Indeed, father, you did; and on the strength of that promise I found the force to conquer my own heart, and make the sacrifice you required of me."

"Oh, sacrifice! sacrifice!" sneered Squire Cleverdon. "I have been a cruel father, to be sure; I have required you to offer yourself up as a victim! Pshaw! You keep your home—it becomes doubly yours—you get a husband, and retain your own name of Cleverdon. What more do you require? It is a sacrifice to become heiress of Hall! Good faith! Your brother would give his ears for such a sacrifice as this. Go and get ready for the guests."

"I cannot go from you, father," answered Elizabeth, with gentleness, and yet, withal, with firmness. "I should be doing an injustice to myself, to my brother, and to you, were I not now to speak out. There was a compact made between us. I promised to take him whom you had determined on for me because it was your wish, and because it was necessary for the saving of the estate. I suppose Fox made it a condition. He would not help you out of your difficulties unless I gave him my hand."

"Fox knows nothing about them."

"What!" Bessie turned the colour of chalk. "Father! you do not mean what you say? He has been told all. He is aware that the mortgage is called in, and must be paid."

The old man fidgetted in his chair; he could not look his daughter in the face. He growled forth:

"You wenches! what do you understand of business—of money concerns—mortgages, and the like? Say what you have to say and be gone, but leave these money-matters on one side."

"I cannot, father," exclaimed Bessie, with fluttering

heart; "I cannot, indeed, father. Is it so that Fox has been drawn on to take me without any knowledge of how matters stand with regard to the property?"

"All properties are burdened more or less with debts. He knows that. He does not keep his wits in his pocket. I have told him nothing, but he must know that there are mortgages. Show me the estate without them. But there, I will not speak of this matter with you; if you will not leave the room, I shall." He half rose in his seat.

"Very well, father, no more of that now. Time will show whether he was aware of, or suspected the condition Hall is in; and I trust that he may not then have to reproach you or me. That is not what I desired to speak of when I came here. I came about Anthony."

"I know but one Anthony Cleverdon, and he is your husband."

"I came in behalf of my brother and your very flesh and blood, which Fox is not. Father, you must—you must indeed suffer me to pour out my heart before you."

He growled and turned uneasily in his chair, and began to scrape the floor with his heel. His brows were knit, and his lips close set.

"Father," said Bessie, with her clear, steady eyes on him, "you speak of love as empty air, but it is not so. What but love induced me to submit myself to your will? I love you. To me Hall is nothing; a cottage with love in it, where I might sit at your feet and kiss your hand, were a thousand times dearer to me than this now, cold house, where all is hard, and love does not settle to live." She drew a long breath. "I love you, therefore I have bowed myself before you; and I love Anthony, and for his sake I have made the greatest sacrifice any mortal can make. I have given my life up to another, whom as yet I can neither love nor respect, that I might by so doing obtain from you pardon for my brother."

"A fine pattern of love Anthony has shown!"

"Father, there is great sorrow and sickness in his house, and he is far away, venturing his life for a cause that he thinks right. He may never return. His babe is dead, his wife ill. See what misery there is hanging over him! Nothing but my love for my brother, my desire to see him again in your arms, has kept me here. When I was plagued about Fox—that is to say, when I first heard about him as seeking me—I had resolved never to marry him, and rather than marry him, I would have run away to Anthony; he would have taken me in. But I thought of you alone in this house, deserted by both your children, and I thought that by staying here I might do something for Anthony, find a proper time for speaking in his favour, and so I stayed; and then, father, when you told me in what peril the property stood, when I saw what agony of mind was yours, when I thought that with the break down of the whole ambition of your life, your grey hairs would certainly be bowed to the dust—then I conquered myself and gave up my will to yours. There is love that is more than a mere word, it is a mighty force, and oh! father, I would that you knew more of it! Father, you—your own self—have suffered most of all through your lack of love. I have seen how the consequences of your harshness towards Anthony have fallen on you, and you have suffered. I dare say you may have loved him, but I think, as you say love is nought but a word, that you can have had only pride in him, and not love—for love suffereth long and is kind. He rebelled against you because you showed him pride—not love. He offended your ambition because you had set your heart on his taking Julian and winning with her Kilworthy; he embittered your heart because he married the daughter of a man that was your enemy. What has been wounded in you has been ambition, not love. Well, Anthony has done wrong. He ought to have considered you. He has ill repaid you all that was lavished upon him from infancy. But, father, if you had given him love, instead of setting your ambition on him, it would not have been so light a matter for him to resist your will. I feel his conduct more than do you. It is because of him that I have married Fox. I have loved and cared for him since he was an infant, as though I were his mother as well as his sister. I promised my mother and his to be his guardian angel, and I have been what I could to him, and now, dutiful to my promise to her and my love of him, and my desire for your own happiness, I have given up myself. So now, father, accept the sacrifice I have made, and forgive Anthony his inconsiderate offence against you."

The old man felt rather than saw that she was nearing

him with extended hands, with tearful eyes fixed entreatingly on him. He thought how he had almost gone on his knees to her to obtain her consent to marry Fox, and he was ashamed of his temporary weakness, the outcome of his distress; now he thought he must compensate for this weakness by obstinate perseverance in his old course.

"Now, Bess," said he, roughly, "no more of this. What I did promise that I will keep. I did not undertake to forgive Anthony. I never—no, not for one instant—gave way to your intercession for that girl—that Urith. Her I will never forgive!"

"What, father! Not if she dies?"

"No, never! not if she dies!"

"Then how can you expect forgiveness for your transgressions? Father, consider that it was not her will to marry Anthony. It was his. You taught him to be headstrong, self-willed, imperious. You taught him to deny himself nothing that he wished. He acted on the teaching you gave, and yourself is answerable for the result."

The old man drew back in his armchair and clenched his hands on the arm of the seat, so that the tendons stood out as taut strings, and the dark veins were puffed with blood.

"Father! You have now a son-in-law, taking the place in the house that should have been—that was—Anthony's. He takes his place, occupies his seat, wears his very name. Compare the two. Which is the most worthy representative of the Cleverdons, of whom you are so proud? Which is the finest man—the tall, strong, splendidly-built Tony, your own son, with his handsome face and honest eyes, or this other Anthony—this Fox who has stolen into his lair? Which is the better in heart? Tony, with all his faults, has a thousand good qualities. He has been vain, self-willed, and self-indulgent, but all this came on him from outside; you and I, and all who had to do with him, nurtured these evil qualities. But in his inner heart he is sound, and true, and good. What is Fox? What good do we know of Fox? Will anything make of him a generous and openhearted man?"

It seemed to Bessie as though the hands of her father that clenched the chair-arms were trembling. He moved his fingers restlessly; and for a moment she caught his eye, and thought she saw in it a tender look. She threw her arms about him, and, stooping, kissed the backs of his hands. It was the first time she had dared to kiss him. He thrust her from him.

"Pshaw!" said he. "Do you suppose I am to be cajoled against my judgment?"

"Is that all you have to say?" asked Bessie, drawing back. "No, father, you shall not put me off. I will not be put off. I have won a right to insist on what I ask being heard and granted."

"Indeed!" He looked up at her with recovered hardness in his eye, and with his hands nerved to the same icy grip. "Indeed! You have acquired a right over me?"

"I have, father. I will be heard!"

"Very well; I hold to what I promised. Perhaps," he laughed bitterly, "perhaps I may think of the possibility of Anthony obtaining my forgiveness. Yes," said he, as a sudden access of better feeling rushed over him, as in his mind's eye the form of his handsome son rose up before him; "yes, let him come to me as the prodigal son, and speak like the prodigal, and desert his swine-husks, and then I will kill the fatted calf and bring forth the ring."

Still the same. He could see no fault in himself—no error in his treatment of his son.

Bessie would have answered, but that the door was thrust open, and in came Fox, agitated, angry, alarmed.

"What is the meaning of this?" he shouted, addressing the Squire, regardless of the presence of Bessie. "What is this about? Here is that fellow—that man from Exeter —here again at the door, with two others—and——"

"And what?"

"He says they are bailiffs, come to take possession."

"What! to-day! Then, son-in-law, you must pay them off. I cannot. Save Hall for yourself."

CHAPTER XLIX.

THE PIGEON-COTE.

"What is the meaning of this?" asked Fox. "Are these wedding-guests invited to help to make merry?"

Old Cleverdon looked at Fox, then at the door, in which, behind his son-in-law, entered the stranger from Exeter.

"This is Master French," said the Squire.

"I do not care what be his name, but what his business?" said Fox, rudely. "Come in, Master French, and let us have this load winnowed. You had better go." The last words were addressed to Bessie.

"This is what I have come about," said the stranger, entering: "The bill for foreclosure has been filed; and, unless the mortgage-money be paid within fourteen days, then, Master Cleverdon, you stand absolutely debarred and precluded from all rights, title, suit, and equity of redemption in or to the premises, which thenceforth become the absolute property of the mortgagee."

"And this," exclaimed Fox—"this is the meaning of my being constituted heir to Hall! Come, Squire, you must take me into council; for, please to know that now you have hooked me into your family and house, I must eat off the same trencher as you. You don't suppose I married Bess for her beauty, do you? What have you there?"

The old man had gone to his desk, and unlocked it.

Fox pressed after him, put his hand on his shoulder, and thrust him aside. "Let me see your accounts, your mortgages, and whatever you have beside stuffed into that cabinet of mysteries."

"Is there no means of raising the requisite money?" asked French. "Times are bad; but—still money is to be had somewhere. You must have friends and relatives who can help."

"Relatives—none," said the old man. "Friends—I have but Justice Crymes."

"And he is away," said Fox, looking over his shoulder.

"Away, putting his head into a noose."

"You have a fortnight," said French. "I was sorry for
you, but—I must perform my duty. If in a fortnight the
sum be not forthcoming——"

"A pretty sum it is!" shouted Fox, who had got hold
of the mortgage. "And this is what my father is to be cajoled into finding? That is the meaning of all the hurry
and scramble of the marriage?"

"I have debts due to me, but I cannot get the money in
—in time," said old Cleverdon.

"If not in time, then as well never," said Fox. "Come,
you French, tell me all about it."

The stranger—an attorney from Exeter—looked at Mr.
Cleverdon, who nodded his head. He knew that eventually the whole matter must be made known to his son-in-
law, but he had not reckoned on it coming to a crisis so
soon.

Mr. French plainly stated all the circumstances. A
large sum had been borrowed on the property some years
ago when purchased by Anthony Cleverdon, the elder, and
this sum had been called in. His client, the mortgagee,
was dead, and the executors were resolved, obliged, in fact,
to realise the estate, and could not be put off. Mr. Cleverdon had been given due notice, and had neglected to
attend to it; the mortgage money had not been paid, consequently a bill had been filed in Chancery, and unless the
entire sum were forthcoming within fourteen days, the
Cleverdons would have to leave the place, which would
pass over to the executors, who would sell it.

Fox followed what was said with close attention, and
without interruption. The only token of his feelings was
the contraction and twitching of his hard sandy eyelashes.
When Mr. French ceased speaking, he laughed aloud,
hoarsely and hysterically, and became deadly white. His
eyes turned to old Cleverdon, and with lips curled and
livid over his teeth, he looked at him in speechless rage for
some minutes. He was like a mean and angry beast,
driven to bay, and watching his opportunity to fly out and
bite.

Then all at once, with a voice half in a scream, half-
choked, he poured forth reproaches on the Squire.

"By heaven! I did suppose that no one could get the
better of me; but I had not reckoned on the craft of an

23

old country farmer, in whom sharp dealing has gone down from father to son, and roguery has been an heritage never parted with, never diminished, always bettered with each generation. And I have had to take this scurvy name of Cleverdon so as to involve me in the disgrace of the family, and mated with it to a maid with an ugly face and no wit —all to get me entangled so that I must with my own hands pull the Cleverdons—the Cleverdons," he sneered and spat on the floor, "pull with my hands, these Cleverdons out of the ditch into which they have tumbled, or lie down and be swallowed up in the mire with them. I will not do it. I will neither help you nor go into the dirt with you. I will leave you to yourselves, and laugh till my sides crack when you are turned out of the house. Where will you go—you and your beggarly daughter? Shall I see if there be room in the poorhouse at Peter Tavy? Listen!" he screamed and turned to the attorney, "listen to what this man, this old grey-haired rascal has done. He comes of a breed of sheep-dealers, accustomed to get a wether between the knees and sheer her; got horny hands from the plough-tail, boots that smell of the stables, arms accustomed to heave the dung-fork—this is what they have been, and he goes and buys Hall with other folks' money, and buys himself a coat of arms with other folks' money, and builds a mansion in place of his old tumble-about-the-ears farmhouse with other folks' money, and puts what money he will into the hands of that brag and bombast talker, his son, to humble and insult the young gentles of good blood and name—and, mark you, it is other folks' money—and then—then he offers to make me his heir if I will take his daughter, whom no one else will look at and give a thank-you for, and assume his name—his name that reeks of the stable-yard. When I do so, then I find I am heir to nothing but beggary!" He shrieked with rage, and held out his hands threateningly at the old man.

The Squire became at first purple with rage; he rose from his seat slowly. His eyes glittered like steel. He was not the man to be spoken to in this manner, to be insulted in himself and his family! His hand clenched. Old though he was, his sinews were tough and his hands were heavy.

Fox came at him with head down between his shoulders,

his sharp chin extended, his hand like the claws of a hawk catching the air.

The attorney stepped between them, or father and son-in-law would have done each other an injury. He laid hold of Fox by the shoulder and thrust him back, and bade him cease from profitless abuse of an unfortunate man, who was, moreover, his father, and to collect his thoughts, consider the situation, and decide whether he and his father would find the money and save Hall.

"Find the money!" said Fox. "Do you not hear that my father is away on a fool's errand, gone to join the rebels; was taking them money, several hundreds of pounds, when he was robbed by the way." He burst into harsh, hysterical laughter once more. "My father will not be home for a fortnight if he does come home at all. How am I to find the money? Kilworthy is not mine. It belongs to my sister."

"Cannot your sister assist you?"

"She would not if she could, but she can touch nothing, it is held in trust, and my father is trustee. Let Hall go, and the Cleverdons along with it. What care I?"

"You are now yourself a Cleverdon," retorted the Squire.

"By heavens," gasped Fox, "that I—that I should be outwitted, and by you!" Then he swung through the door and disappeared.

The old man remained standing with clenched hands for some minutes. The sweat had broken out on his brow, his grey hair, smoothed for the wedding ceremony, had bristled with rage and shame, and become entangled and knotted on his head. If it had not been for the convulsive twitching of the corners of the mouth, he might have been supposed a statue.

Presently he put his hands down on the arms of his chair, and slowly let himself sink into the seat. The colour died out of his cheeks and from his brow, and he became ashen in hue. His hands rested on the chair-arms, motionless. His lips moved as though he were speaking to himself; and he was so—he was repeating the insolent words—the words wounding to his pride, to his honour, that had been shot at him from the envenomed heart of Fox; and these hurt him more than the thoughts of the disaster that menaced.

"Do not be overcome by his spite," said French. "He is disappointed, and his disappointment has made him speak words he will regret. He must and will help you. My clients would not deal harshly with you—they respect you, but are forced to act. They do not want your estate but their money—that they are compelled to call together. If this young gentleman be your son-in-law and heir, it is his interest to save the property, and he will do it if he can. His father can be found in a couple of days, and when found can be induced to lend the money, if he has the means at his disposal. Perhaps in a week all will be right."

Squire Cleverdon did not speak.

"And now," said French, "with your consent I will refresh myself, and leave you to your own thoughts. It is a pity that you did not take steps earlier to save yourself."

"I could not—I could not. I was ashamed to ask of any one. I thought, that is, I never thought the demand was serious."

Fox had gone forth to the stable to saddle a horse; finding no one about in the yard, he seated himself on the corn-box, and remained lost in thought, biting his nails. All the men connected with the farm were in the kitchen having cake and ale, and drinking the health of the bride heartily, and secretly confusion to the bridegroom, whom they detested, both for his own character, which was pretty generally judged, and also, especially, because he had stepped into the place and name of their beloved young Anthony, who, though he had tyrannised over them, was looked up to, and liked by all.

All was silent in the stable save for the stamp occasionally of a horsehoof and the rattle of the halters at the mangers. Bessie's grey was nearest to Fox, and the beast occasionally turned her head and looked at him out of her clear, gentle eyes.

Fox put his sharp elbows on his knees, and drove his fingers through his thin red hair. He was in a dilemma. He was married to Bessie, and adopted into the family. As the old man had said to him, he was now a Cleverdon. It had cost him a large sum to obtain this privilege, and he could not resume his patronymic without the cost of a fresh grant from the College of Arms. Moreover, that would not free him from his alliance.

Nothing, perhaps, so galled the thoughts of Fox as the consciousness that he had been over-reached—he who had deemed himself incomparably the shrewdest and keenest man in the district ; who had despised and laughed at old Cleverdon—never more than when luring him on with the hopes of winning Julian. He had done this out of pure malice, with the desire of making the old man ridiculous, and of enjoying the disappointment that was inevitable. He had played his trick upon his father-in-law ; but the tables had been turned on him in compound degree.

His father-in-law was right—he was a Cleverdon, and his fortunes were bound up with Hall. If Hall were lost, he had lost all but the trifle he was likely to receive from his father. If Hall was to be saved, it must be saved by him ; and, had he known that it was likely to be sold, he would never have encumbered himself with a wife—with Bessie—and degraded himself to take the name of Cleverdon instead of his own ancient and honourable patronymic. He would have waited a fortnight ; and, if he could get the money together, would have bought Hall, and enjoyed the satisfaction of turning the Cleverdons out of it.

It was now too late. He must decide on his course of conduct. He did not think of doing what Mr. French supposed he would—ride in quest of his father. He would not venture himself near the quarters of Monmouth, and run the risk of being supposed to have any sympathy or connection with the rebellion. Moreover, he very much doubted whether his father could, if he would, assist in this matter.

Presently he stood up, went to the grey, saddled her, and rode to Kilworthy.

On reaching that place he put up the horse himself, and stole up the steps to the first terrace, on which grew a range of century-old yews, passed behind the yews to the end of the terrace, where was an abandoned pigeon-house, a circular stone building, with conical roof. The door was open, and Fox went in. The wooden door had long disappeared, for the pigeon-house had been given up. Within were holes in tiers all round the building, in which pigeons had formerly built and laid. But the owls and rats had so repeatedly and determinedly invaded this house, and had wrought such havoc among the pigeons, that at last it had been abandoned wholly, and the pigeons were accommodated in the adjoining farm-yard, on casks erected on the top of poles, where, if not out of reach of owls, they were secure from rats. The neglected pigeonry was too strongly built to fall to ruin, but the woodwork was rotted away, and had not been replaced. It was a dark chamber, receiving its light from the door, and was not used for any purpose.

Into this, after looking about him cautiously, Fox entered. A short ladder was laid against the wall, and this he took, and after carefully counting the pigeon-holes, set the ladder, and after ascending it, thrust his hand into one of the old resting-places, and drew out a canvas bag. It had been sealed, but the seal was broken. It had been opened and then tied up again. Then Fox went to the next pigeon-hole, and felt in that, and again drew forth a bag similar to the first.

"Here is the money," muttered he. "Enough to save Hall, but whether I shall risk doing it is another matter."

Suddenly the place was darkened—the light entering by the door was intercepted.

Fox's heart stood still. For a moment only he was in darkness. He fell rather than climbed down the ladder, hastily put it back where he found it, and ran outside.

At the further end of the terrace was Julian. As he caught sight of her he attempted to withdraw, but she had seen him, and she beckoned, and came to him with quick steps.

"Why, Fox! you here!—and you were married but an hour or two agone! Why here? Why not at the side of Bessie at table answering the toasts?"

"Where have you come from?" retorted Fox, uneasily.

"Nay? that is for me to ask. I have but just come to walk up and down for air, and you—you spring out of the earth. What has brought you back? Quarrelled already with your bride?"

"I have returned for you, Julian. Bess is pained and aggrieved that you have not come to Hall to be with her. She has none as a friend but you."

"What! you have come after me?"

"For what else should I come?"

"Nay," laughed Julian; "who can sound thy dark and deep thoughts, and thread thy crooked mind? I cannot believe it."

"I have ridden Bess's own mare."

"That may be. And you came here to fetch me? And for that only?"

"I did."

"I won't go." Julian looked at Fox with twinkling eyes. "Oh, Fox! I do love and pity Bess too greatly to bear to see her at thy side. So you came for me? You came out here on the terrace after me?"

"I have told you so. How long have you been here?"

"But this minute. I took one walk as far as the old pigeon-house and back, and then—saw you. Did you come up the other way? From the yard?"

"I did."

"Oh! I will not go with you. Return to Bess. Tell her I love her and wish her well, but I cannot see her; I cannot now, I love her too well. Get thee gone, Fox."

CHAPTER L.

ANOTHER FLIGHT.

The day was drawing to its decline before Fox returned to Hall. He had been alarmed at having been seen by his sister in the dove-cote, and he tried by craft to extract from her whether she had observed what he had been doing in it. He hung about Kilworthy for several hours, uncertain what course to pursue. He could draw nothing from Julian to feed his alarm, and he persuaded, or tried to persuade, himself that she had no suspicions that he had been in the dove-cote; then he considered what he had best do with the money-bags concealed there. He could remove them only at night, and if he removed them, where should he hide them? No more effectual place of concealment could well be imagined than the pigeon-house with its many lockers, the depths of which could not be probed by the eye from below, and only searched by the hand from a ladder. He puzzled his brain to find some other place, but his ingenuity failed him. He was angry with Julian for having come on the terrace at the inopportune moment when he was in the pigeon-house, and he was angry with himself for having gone there in daylight.

He asked, was it probable that Julian, had she suspected anything, would not at once have assailed him with inquiries wherefore he had gone to that deserted structure, and what he was doing within it, on the ladder. It would be unlike her not immediately to take advantage of an occasion either against him, or of perplexity to him, and he almost satisfied himself that she had believed his account, and was void of suspicion that there was concealment behind it. Even if she did suspect and search the lockers of the pigeon-cote, he must know it. He would find she had been there, and he deemed it advisable not to disturb his arrangement, but leave the money hidden there till he was given fresh cause for uneasiness relative to its safety, at all events for a few days, till he could discover another and more secret place for stowing it away.

He remained for some hours, lurking about and watching; for he argued that, if Julian entertained any thought that he had been in the dove-cote on private ends, like a woman she would take the earliest occasion of trying to discover his ends, and would go, as soon as she thought she was unobserved, to the place and explore its lockers.

But though he kept himself hidden, and narrowly watched her proceedings, he could find no cause for mistrust. She left the terrace and went off to the stables to see her horse; she ordered it out for a ride; then, as rain began to fall, she countermanded it; then she went to the parlour, where she wrote a letter to her father to give him an account of the marriage of his son, and to express her views thereon.

Finding her thus engaged, and with his mistrust laid at rest, Fox left Kilworthy and went to Tavistock, where he entered a tavern and called for wine. He had not resolved what to do about the mortgage money on Hall.

He believed that, with the five hundred pounds stowed away in the pigeon-holes at Kilworthy, and with what money old Cleverdon was able to raise, sufficient, or almost sufficient, could be paid to secure Hall. If more had to be found, it could perhaps be borrowed on the security of the small Crymes estate in Buckland; but Fox was most averse to having his own inheritance charged for this purpose. If Hall were let slip, then he was left with nothing save his five hundred pounds and the small Buckland property.

He sat in the tavern for long, drinking, and trying to reach a solution of his difficulty, consumed with burning wrath at the manner in which he had been imposed upon, and entangled in the embarrassments of a family into which he had pushed his way, believing that by so doing he was entering into a rich heritage.

When he reached Hall, at nightfall, he had drunk so much, and was in such an inflamed and exasperated frame of mind, as to promise trouble.

Bess saw the condition he was in the moment he entered the door, and she endeavoured to turn him aside from her father's room, towards which he was making his way, unsteadily.

The serving-men and maids were about, and a few guests. Comments, unfavourable to Fox, had passed with some freedom, and not inaudibly, relative to his absence on that afternoon. No one desired his presence, and yet the fact of his being away provoked displeasure. It was taken as an insult to those present. That some trouble had fallen on Squire Cleverdon, that his position in Hall was menaced, was generally known and commented on in the house, by guests and servants alike. That Fox had left in connection with this difficulty was admitted but nevertheless not excused.

French was there disposed to make himself merry, with a fund of good stories to scatter among the guests. When Fox appeared, all present, guests and servants, were in jovial mood, having eaten and drunken to their hearts' satisfaction; some were in the passage, some in the dining-room that opened out of it, with the door open. Mr. Cleverdon was with the guests, and when he beheld his son-in-law in the entrance, he started up and came towards him. Fox saw him at once, and hissed, caught at the side-posts of the door with his left, and pointed jeeringly at the Squire.

"I want to have a talk with you, my plump money-bag,

my well-acred Squire father-in-law, and if there are others
by, so much the better. It is well that all the world should
see the bubble burst. Ha! ha! ha! This is the man who
was a little farmer, and pushed himself to become a justice! The little shrivelled toad who would blow himself
out to be like an ox. His sides are cracking, mark you!"

"Take him away," said the old man, "he is drunk."

"Go—I pray you go!" pleaded Bessie. "Prithee, respect him, at least in public, look at his grey hairs, consider the trouble he is in."

"His grey hairs!" retorted Fox. "Why should I respect them? They have grown grey in rascality. So many
years of sandy locks, so much roguery, so many more with
grey hair, double the amount of roguery. Why should I
respect an old rogue? I would kick and thrash a young
one out of the house. His trouble—forsooth! His trouble is naught to mine, hooked on to a disreputable, drowning family, and unable to strike out in their faces, and
wrench their hands away, and let them swallow the brine
and go down alone."

The Squire and the guests stood or sat spell-bound.
What was to be done with the fellow? How could he be
brought to silence? The stream of words of a drunken
man is no easier stopped than is a spring by the hand laid
against it.

"Ha! ha!" jeered Fox, still pointing at his father-in-law;
"there is the man who has ruled so tyrannically in his house,
who drove his son out-of-doors because he followed his own
example and married empty pockets. But his son did better than the father, he did take a girl with a few lumps of
granite and a few shovelfuls of peat, but the father's own
wife had nothing. What he suffered in himself he would
not suffer in his son."

The old man, shaking with rage as with the palsy, and
deadly white, turned to the servants, and called to them to
take away the fellow.

"Take me away!" screamed Fox. "Take and shake
me, and see if there be any gold in my pockets that will
fall out, and which he may pick up. I tell you I am rich;
I have the money all ready, I could produce that in an hour,
which would save Hall, and send that fellow there, the lawyer, and his men back to Exeter to-night, if they cared to

go over Black Down in the dark, where robbery is committed and coaches stopped and plundered. I have the gold all ready, but do not fancy I will give one guinea to help a Cleverdon. I hate them all—father, daughter, and son; I curse the whole tribe, I dance on their heads, I trample on their hearts, I scorn them. They hold out their hands to me, but I will not pick them up."

Bessie put her arms about him, and, with eyes that were full of tears, and face blanched with shame, entreated him to go, to control himself, to remember that this old man that he insulted was his father-in-law, and that, for better, for worse, in riches or poverty, he was her husband.

"I am not like to forget that," hissed Fox. "O, troth, no! Linked to thee—to thee, with thy ugly face and empty purse; thee, whom no one else would have, who has been hawked about and refused by all, and I am to be coupled to thee all my life. 'Fore heaven, I am not like to forget that."

This, addressed to Bessie, whom every servant in the house loved, and every guest who knew her respected, passed all bounds of endurance.

An angry roar rose from the men and maids who had crowded into the entrance-hall from the kitchen, from the courtyard, from the stables. The guests shouted out their indignation, and a blow was aimed at Fox from a groom behind, that knocked him over, and sent him down on his knees into the dining-room. He was not seriously hurt—not deprived of his senses—but other blows would have followed from the incensed servants had not Bessie thrown herself in the way to protect him.

"Take him up—throw him into the horse-pond!"

"Get a bramble, and thrash him with it till he is painted red."

"Cast him in with the pigs."

Such were the shouts of the servants, and, but for the interposition of Bessie, serious results would have followed. She gave Fox her hand, and, leaning on her shoulder, he was able to stagger to his feet. The blow he had received had driven the final remains of caution he had about him from his brain; he glared around in savage rage, with his teeth showing, and his short red hair standing up on his head like the comb of an angry cock.

"Who touched me? Bring him forth, that I may strike him." He drew his hunting-knife, and turned from side to side. "Ah! let him come near, and I will score him as I did Anthony Cleverdon."

Bessie uttered a cry and drew back.

Fox looked at her, and, encouraged by her terror and pain, proceeded. "It is true, I did. We had a quarrel and drew swords, and I pinked him."

"A lie!" shouted one present. "Thou wearest no sword."

Fox turned sharply round, and snarled at the speaker. "I have not a bodkin—a skewer—but I have what is better—a carving-knife; and with that I struck him just above the heart. He fell, and ran, ran, ran"—his voice rose to a shriek—"he ran from me as a hare, full of fright, lest I should go after him and strike him again, between the shoulder-blades. Farmer Cleverdon! Gaffer Cleverdon! Thou hast a fool for a son—that all the world knows—and a knave as well, and add to that—a coward."

He stopped to laugh. Then, pointing with his knife at his father-in-law, he said:

"They say that he has gone to join the rebels. It is false. He is too great a coward to adventure himself there, and add to that I have cut too deep and let out too much white blood. He is skulking somewhere to be healed or to die."

Bessie had staggered back against the wall. She held her hands before her mouth to arrest the cries of distress that could barely be controlled. The old man had become white and rigid as a corpse.

"I would he were with the rebels. I hope he will be so healed, and that speedily, that he may join them, and then he will be taken and hung as a traitor. I' faith, I would like to be there! I would give a bag of gold to be there—to see Anthony Cleverdon hung. I'd sit down on the next stone and eat my bread and cheese, and throw the crusts and the rinds in his face as he hung.—The traitor!"

An hour later there came a tap at the door of Willsworthy. Uncle Sol opened, and Bessie Cleverdon entered, pale.

She asked to see her grandmother, Mistress Penwarne, who was still there.

"I am come," she said, "to relieve you. Go back to Luke, and I will tarry with Urith. Luke must need you, and I can take your place here. I will not lay my head under the roof of Hall whilst Fox is there. It is true that I promised this day to love and obey him, but I promised what I cannot perform. He has forfeited every right over me! Till he leaves Hall I remain here—with Urith—both unhappy—maybe we shall understand each other. My poor father! My poor father! I cannot remain with him whilst Fox is there!"

CHAPTER LI.

ON THE CLEAVE AGAIN.

Ever full of pity and love for others, and forgetfulness of self, Bessie sat holding Urith's hand in her own, with her eyes fixed compassionately on her sister-in-law.

Urith's condition was perplexing. It was hard to say whether the events of that night when she saw Anthony struck down on the hearthstone, and her subsequent and consequent illness, with the premature confinement and the death of the child, had deranged her faculties, or whether she was merely stunned by this succession of events.

Always with a tendency in her to moodiness, she had now lapsed into a condition of silent brooding. She would sit the whole day in one position, crouched with her elbows on her knees and her chin in her hands, looking fixedly before her, and saying nothing: taking no notice of anything said or done near her.

It almost seemed as though she had fallen into a condition of melancholy madness, and yet, when spoken to, she would answer, and answer intelligently. Her faculties were present, unimpaired, but crushed under the overwhelming weight of the past. Only on one point did she manifest any signs of hallucination. She believed that Anthony was dead, and nothing that was said to her could induce her to change her conviction. She believed that everyone was in league to deceive her on this point.

And yet, though sane, she had to be watched, for in her absence of mind and internal fever of distress, she would put her hands into her mouth, and bite the knuckles, apparently unconscious of pain.

Mrs. Penwarne, who was usually with her, would quietly remove her hands from her mouth, and hold them down. Then Urith would look at her with a strange, questioning expression, release her hands, and resting the elbows on her knees, thrust the fingers into her hair.

The state in which Urith was alarmed Bessie. She tried in vain to cheer her; every effort, and they were various in kind, failed. The condition of Urith resembled that of one oppressed with sleep before consciousness passes away. When her attention was called by a question addressed to her pointedly by name, or by a touch, she answered, but she relapsed immediately into her former state. She could be roused to no interest in anything. Bessie spoke to her about domestic matters, about the rebellion of the Duke of Monmouth, about the departure of Mr. Crymes, finally, after some hesitation, about her own marriage, but she said nothing concerning the conduct of Fox on the preceding evening, or of her desertion of the home of her childhood. Urith listened dreamily, and forgot at once what had been told her. Her mind was susceptible to no impressions, so deeply indented was it with her own sorrows.

Luke, so said Mistress Penwarne, had been to see her, and had spoken of sacred matters; but Urith had replied to him that she had killed Anthony, that she did not regret having done so, and that therefore she could neither hope in nor pray to God.

This Mrs. Penwarne told Bessie, standing over Urith, well aware that what she said passed unheeded by the latter, probably unheard by her. Nothing but a direct appeal could force Urith to turn the current of her thoughts, and that only momentarily, from the direction they had taken.

"She has been biting her hands again," said Mrs. Penwarne. "Bessie, when she does that, pull out the token that hangs on her bosom and put it into her palm. She will sit and look at that by the hour. She must be broken of that trick."

Urith slowly stood up, with a ruffle of uneasiness on her dull face. She was conscious that she was being discussed, without exactly knowing what was said about her. With-

out a word of explanation, she went out, drawing Bessie
with her, who would not let go her hand; and together,
in silence, they passed through the court and into the lane.

Their heads were uncovered, and the wind was fresh
and the sun shone brightly.

Urith walked leisurely along the lane, accompanied by
Bessie Cleverdon, between the moorstone walls, thick-
bedded with pink and white flowering saxifrage, and
plumed with crimson foxgloves. She looked neither to
right nor to left till she reached the moor-gate closing the
lane, a gate set there to prevent the escape of the cattle from
their upland pasturage. The gate was swung between
two blocks of granite, in which sockets had been cut for
the pivot of the gate to swing. Urith put forth her hand,
thrust open the gate, and went on. It was characteristic
of her condition that she threw it open only wide enough
to allow herself to pass through, and Bess had to put forth
her disengaged hand to check the gate from swinging back
upon her. This was not due to rudeness on the part of
Urith, but to the fact that Urith had forgotten that any
one was with her.

On issuing forth on the open waste-land among the
flowering heather and deep carmine, large-belled heath, the
freedom, the fresh air seemed to revive Urith. A flicker
of light passed over her darkened face, as though clouds
had been lifted from a tor, and a little watery sunlight had
played over its bleak surface. She turned her head to the
west, whence blew the wind, and the air raised and tossed
her dark hair. She stood still, with half-closed eyes, and
nostrils distended, inhaling the exhilarating breeze, and enjoying its coolness as it trifled with her disordered locks.

Bessie had tried her with every subject that could
distract her thoughts, in vain. She now struck on that
which nearly affected her.

"Urith," she said, "I have heard that a battle is expected
every day, and Anthony is in it. You will pray God to
guard him in danger, will you not?"

"Anthony is dead. I killed him."

"No, dear Urith, he is not dead; he has joined the Duke
of Monmouth."

"They told you so? They deceived you. I killed him."

"It is not so." Bessie paused. Her hand clenched

that of Urith tightly. "My dearest sister, it is not so. Fox himself told me, and told my father—*he* struck Anthony."

"I bade him do so—I had not strength in my arm, I had no knife. But I killed him."

"I assure you that this is not true."

"I saw him fall across the hearthstone. My mother wished it. She prayed that it might be so, with her last breath; but she never prayed that I should kill him."

"Urith! Poor Anthony, who is dear to you and to me, is in extreme danger. There is like to be bloody fighting and we must ask God to shield him."

"I cannot pray for him. He is dead, and I cannot pray at all. I am glad he is dead. I would do it all over again, rather than that Julian should have him."

"Julian!" sighed Elizabeth Cleverdon. "What has been told you about Julian?"

"She threatened to pluck him out of my bosom, and she has done it; but she shall not wear him in hers. I killed him because he was false to me, and would leave me."

"No—no—Urith, he never would leave you."

"He was going to leave me. His father asked him to go back to Hall."

"But he would not go. Anthony was too noble."

"He was going to desert me and go to Julian, so I killed him. They may kill me also; I do not care. God took my baby; I am glad He did that. I never wish for a moment it had lived—lived to know that its mother was a murderess. It could not touch my hand with his blood on it; so God took my baby. I am waiting; they will take me soon, because I killed Anthony. I am willing. I cannot pray. I have no hope. I wish it were over, and I were dead."

On her own topic, on that which engrossed all her mind, on that round which her thoughts turned incessantly, on that she could speak, and speak fairly rationally; and when she spoke her face became expressive.

They walked on together. Bessie knew not what to say. It was not possible to disturb Urith's conviction that her husband was dead, and that she was his destroyer.

They continued to walk, but now again in silence. Urith again relapsed into her brooding mood, went forward, threaded her own way among the bunches of prickly gorse, now out of flower, and the scattered stones, regardless of Bessie, who was put to great inconvenience to keep at her side. She was forced to disengage her hand, as it was not possible for her to keep pace with her sister-in-law in such broken ground. Urith did not observe that Bessie had released her, nor that she was still accompanying her.

She took a direct course to Tavy Cleave, that rugged, natural fortress of granite which towers above the river that plunges in a gorge, rather than a valley, below.

On reaching this she cast herself down on the overhanging slab, whereon she had stood with Anthony, when he clasped her in his arms and swung her, laughing and shouting, over the abyss.

Bessie drew to her side. She was uneasy what Urith might do, in her disturbed frame of mind ; but no thought of self-destruction seemed to have crossed Urith's brain. She swung her feet over the gulf, and put her hands through her hair, combing it out into the wind, and letting that waft and whirl it about, as it blew up the Cleave and rose against the granite crags, as a wave that bowls against a rocky coast leaps up and curls over it.

Bessie allowed her to do as she liked. It was clearly a refreshment and relaxation to her heated and overstrained mind thus to sit and play with the wind.

Rooks were about, at one moment flashing white in the sun, then showing the blackness of their glossy feathers. Their nesting and rearing labours were over : they had deserted their usual haunts among trees, to disport themselves on the waste lands.

The roar of the river came up on the wind from below— now loud as the surf on reefs at sea, then soft and soothing as a murmur of marketers returning from fairing, heard from far away.

Something—Bessie knew not what—induced her to turn her head aside, when, with a start of alarm, she saw, standing on a platform of rock, not a stone's throw distance, the tall full form of Julian. Her face was turned towards her and Urith. She had been watching them. The sun was on her handsome, richly-coloured face, with its lustrous eyes and ripe pouting lips.

Bessie's first impulse was to hold up her hand in caution.

24

She did not know what the effect produced on Urith might be of seeing suddenly before her the rival who had blighted her happiness ; and the position occupied by Urith was dangerous, on the overhanging ledge.

Bessie rose from her place and walked towards Julian, stepping cautiously among the crags. Urith took no notice of her departure.

On reaching Julian Crymes, Bessie caught her by the arm and drew her back among the rocks, out of sight and hearing of Urith.

"For heaven's sake," she entreated, "do not let her see you! Do you see what has fallen on her? She is not herself."

"Well," retorted Julian, "what of that? She and I staked for the same prize, and she has lost."

"And you not won."

"I have won somewhat. He is no longer hers, if he be not mine."

"He is not, he never was, he never will be yours," said Bessie, vehemently. "Oh, Julian! how can you be so cruel, so wicked! Have you no pity? She is deranged. She thinks she has killed Anthony—dead; but you have seen —she cannot speak and think of anything now but of her sorrow and loss."

"We played together—it was a fair game. She wrested from me him who was mine by right, and she must take the consequences of her acts—we must all do that. I— yes—Bess, I am ready. I will take the consequences of what I have done. Let me pass, Bess, I will speak to her."

"I pray you!" Bess extended her arms.

"No—let me pass. She and I are accustomed to look each other in the face. I will see how she is. I will! Stand aside."

She had a long staff in her hand, and with it she brushed Bess away, and strode past her, between her and the precipice, with steady eye and firm step, and clambered to where was Urith.

She stood beside her for a minute, studying her, watching her, as she played with her hair, passing her fingers through it, and drawing it forth into the wind to turn and curl, and waft about.

Then, her patience exhausted, Julian put forth the end of her staff, touched Urith, and called her by name.

Urith looked round at her, but neither spake nor stirred. No flush of anger or surprise appeared in her cheek, no lightning glare in her eye.

"Urith," said Julian, "how stands the game?"

"He is dead," answered Urith, "I killed him."

Julian was startled, and slightly turned colour.

"It is not true," she said hastily, recovering herself, "he has gone off to serve with the Duke of Monmouth."

"I killed him," answered Urith composedly. "I would never, never let you have him, draw him from me. I am not sorry. I am glad. I killed him."

"What!" with a sudden exultation, "you know he would have been drawn by me away! I conquered."

"You did not get him away," said Urith, "you could not—for I killed him."

Julian put out her staff again, and touched Urith.

"Listen to me!" she said, and there was triumph in her tone. "He never loved you. No never. Me he loved; me he always had loved. But his father tried to force him, he quarrelled with him, and out of waywardness, to defy his father to show his independence, he married you; but he never, never loved you."

"That is false," answered Urith, and she slowly rose on the platform to her feet. "That is false. He did love me. Here on this stone he held me to his heart, here he held me aloft and made me promise to be his very own."

"It was naught!" exclaimed Julian. "A passing fancy. Come—I know not whether he be alive or dead. Some say one thing and some another, but this I do know, that if he be alive, the world will be too narrow for you and me together in it, and if he be dead—it is indifferent to both whether we live, for to you and me alike is Anthony the sun that rules us, in whose light we have our joy. Come! Let us have another hitch, as the wrestlers say, and see which gives the other the turn."

Urith, in her half-dreamy condition, in rising to her feet, had taken hold of the end of Julian's staff, and now stood looking down the abyss to the tossing, thundering water, still holding the end.

"Urith!" called Julian, imperiously and impatiently,

"dost hear what I say? Let us have one more, and a final hitch. Thou holding the staff at one end, I at the other. See, we stand equal, on the same shelf, and each with a heel at the edge of the rock. One step back, and thou or I must go over and be broken on the stones, far below. Dost mark me?"

"I hear what you say," answered Urith.

"I will thrust, and do thou! and see which can drive the other to death. In faith! we have thrust and girded at each other long, and driven each other to desperation. Now let us finish the weary game with a final turn* and a fair back."*

Urith remained, holding the end of the staff, looking at Julian steadily, without passion. Her face was pale; the wild hair was tossing about it.

"Art ready!" called Julian. "When I say three, then the thrust begins, and one or other of us is driven out of one world into the other."

Urith let fall the end of the staff; "I have no more quarrel with you," she said, "Anthony is dead. I killed him."

Julian stamped angrily. "This is the second time thou hast refused my challenge; though thou didst refuse my glove, thou didst take it up. So now thou refusest, yet may be will still play. As thou wilt: at thine own time—but one or other."

She pointed down the chasm with her staff, and turned away.

CHAPTER LII.

THE SAW-PIT.

At Hall, that same morning had broken on Squire Cleverdon in his office or sitting-room—it might bear either name—leaning back in his leather armchair, with his hands clasped on his breast, his face an ashen grey, and his hair several degrees whiter than on the preceding day.

* Terms in wrestling. A "turn" is a fall; a "fair back" is one where the three points are touched—head, shoulders, and back.

When the maid came in at an early hour to clean and tidy the apartment, she started, and uttered a cry of alarm, when she saw the old man in his seat. She thought he was dead. But at her appearance he stood up, and with tottering steps left the room and went upstairs. He had not been to bed all night.

Breakfast was made ready, and he was called; but he did not come.

That night had been one of vain thinking and torturing of his mind to find a mode of escape from his troubles. He had reckoned on assistance from Fox or his father, and this had failed him. Fox, may be, for all his brag, could not help him. The Justice might, were he at home; but he had gone off to join the Duke of Monmouth, and, if he did return, it might be too late, and it was probable enough that he never would reappear. If anything happened to Mr. Crymes, then Fox would step into his place as trustee for Julian till Julian married; but could he raise money on her property to assist him and save his property? Anyhow it was not possible for matters to be so settled that he could do this within a fortnight.

The only chance that old Cleverdon saw was to borrow money for a short term till something was settled at Kilworthy—till the Rebellion was either successful or was extinguished—and he could appeal to Fox or his father to secure Hall.

But to have, ultimately, to come to Fox for deliverance, to have his own fate and that of his beloved Hall in the hands of this son-in-law, who had insulted, humiliated him, publicly and brutally, the preceding night, was to drink the cup of degradation to its bitter and final dregs.

It was about ten o'clock when the old Squire, now bent and broken, with every line in his face deepened to a furrow, reappeared, ready to go abroad. He had resolved to visit his attorney-at-law in Tavistock, and see if, through him, the requisite sum could be raised as a short loan.

The house was in confusion. None of the workmen were gone to their duties; the serving-maids and men talked or whispered in corners, and went about on tip-toe as though there were a corpse in the house.

His man told the Squire that Fox was gone, and had left a message, which the fellow would not deliver, so grossly insolent was it; the substance was that he would not return to the house. The Squire nodded and asked for his horse.

After some delay it was brought to the door; the groom was not to be found, and one of the maids had gone to the stable for the beast, and had saddled and bridled it.

The old man mounted and rode away. Then he heard a call behind him, but did not turn his head; another call, but he disregarded it, and rode further, urging on his horse to a quicker rate.

Next moment the brute stumbled, and nearly went down on its nose; the Squire whipped angrily, and the horse went on faster, then began to lag, and suddenly tripped once more and fell. Old Cleverdon was thrown on the turf and was uninjured. He got up and went to the beast, and then saw why it had twice stumbled. The serving girl, in bridling it, had forgotten to remove the halter, the rope of which hung down to the ground, so that, as the animal trotted, the end got under the hoofs. That was what the call had signified. Some one of the serving-men had noticed the bridle over the halter as the old Squire rode away, and had shouted after him to that effect.

Mr. Cleverdon removed the bridle, then took off the halter, and replaced the bridle. What was to be done with the halter? He tried to thrust it into one of his pockets, but they were too small. He looked round; he was near a saw-pit a bow-shot from the road. He remembered that he had ordered a couple of sawyers to be there that day to cut up into planks an oak-tree; he hitched up his horse and went towards the saw-pit, calling, but no one replied. The men had not come; they had heard of what had taken place at Hall, and had absented themselves, not expecting under the circumstances to be paid for their labour.

The old man wrapped the halter round his waist, and knotted it, then drew his cloak about him to conceal it, remounted, and rode on. Had the sawyers been at the pit he would have sent back the halter by one of them to the stable. As none was there, he was forced to take it about with him.

Five hours later he returned the same way. His eyes were glassy, and cold sweat beaded his brow. His breath came as a rattle from his lungs. All was over. He could obtain assistance nowhere. The times were dangerous, because unsettled, and no one would risk money till the public confidence was restored. His attorney had passed him on to the agent for the Earl of Bedford, and the agent had shaken his head, and suggested that the miller at the Abbey Mill was considered a well-to-do man, and might be inclined to lend money.

The miller refused, and spoke of a Jew in Bannawell, who was said to lend money at high rates of interest. The Jew, however, would not think of the loan, till the Rebellion was at an end.

All was over. The Squire—the Squire!—he would be that no more—must leave the land and home of his fathers, his pride broken, his ambition frustrated, the object for which he had lived and schemed lost to him. There are in the world folk who are, in themselves, nothing, and who have nothing, and who nevertheless give themselves airs, and cannot be shaken out of their self-satisfaction. Mr. Cleverdon was not one of these, he had not their faculty of imagination. The basis of all his greatness was Hall; that was being plucked from under his feet; and he staggered to his fall. Once on the ground, he would be proper, lie there, an object of mockery to those who had hitherto envied him. Once there, he would never raise his head again. He who had stood so high, who had been so imperious in his pride of place, would be under the feet of all those over whom hitherto he had ridden roughshod.

This thought gnawed and bored in him, with ever fresh anguish, producing ever fresh aspects of humiliation. This was the black spot on which his eyes were fixed, which overspread and darkened the whole prospect. The brutality with which he had been treated by Fox was but a sample and foretaste of the brutality with which he would be treated by all such as hitherto he had held under, shown harshness and inconsideration towards. He had been selfish in his prosperity, he was selfish in his adversity. He did not think of Anthony. He gave not a thought to Bessie. His own disappointment, his own humiliation, was all that concerned him. He had valued the love of his children not a rush, and now that his material possessions slipped from his grasp, nothing was left him to which to cling.

He had ridden as far as the point where his horse had fallen, on his way back to Hall, when the rope twined about his waist loosened and fell down. The old man stooped towards his stirrup, picked it up, and cast it over his shoulder. The act startled his horse, and it bounded; with the leap the rope was again dislodged, and fell once more. He sought, still riding, to arrange the cord as it had been before about his waist, but found this impracticable.

He was forced to dismount, and then he hitched his horse to a tree, and proceeded to take the halter from his body, that he might fold and knot it together.

Whilst thus engaged, a thought entered his head that made him stand, with glazed eye, looking at the coil, motionless.

To what was he returning? To a home that was no more a home—to a few miserable days of saying farewell to scenes familiar to him from infancy; then to being cast forth on the world in his old age, he knew not whither to go, where to settle. To a new life of which he cared nothing, without interests, without ambitions—wholly purportless. He would go forth alone; Bessie would not accompany him, for he had thrown her away on the most despicable of men, and to him she was bound—him she must follow. Anthony—he knew not whether he were alive or dead. If alive, he could not go to him whom he had driven from Hall, and to Willsworthy, of all places under the sun, he would not go. Luke he could not ask to receive him, who was but a curate, and whom he had refused to speak to since he had been the means of uniting his son to the daughter of his deadly rival and enemy. What sort of life could he live with no one to care for him—with nothing to occupy his mind and energies?

How could he appear in church, at market, now that it was known that he was a ruined man? Would not every one point at him, and sneer and laugh at his misfortunes? He had not made a friend, except Mr. Crymes; and not having a friend, he had no one to sympathise with, to pity him.

Then he thought of his sister Magdalen. Her little annuity he would have to pay out of his reduced income; he might live with her—with her whom he had treated so unceremoniously, so rudely—over whom he had held his chin so high, and tossed it so contemptuously.

What would Fox do? Would he not take every occasion to insult him, to make his life intolerable to him, use him as his butt for gibes, anger him to madness—the madness of baffled hate that cannot revenge a wrong?

Anything were better than this.

The old man walked towards the saw-pit. The tree was there, lying on the frame ready to be sawn into planks, and already it was in part cut through. The men had been there, begun their task; then had gone off, probably to the house to drink his cider and discuss his ruin.

Below his feet the pit gaped, some ten or eleven feet, with oak sawdust at the bottom, dry and fragrant. Round the edges of the pit the hart's-tongue fern and the pennywort had lodged between the stones and luxuriated, the latter throwing up at this time its white spires of flower.

A magnificent plume of fern occupied one end of the trough. Bushes and oak-coppice were around, and almost concealed the saw-pit from the road.

That saw-pit seemed to the old man to be a grave, and a grave that invited an occupant.

He knelt on the cross-piece on which the upper sawyer stands when engaged on his work, and round it fastened firmly the end of the rope; then fixed the halter with running knot about his own neck.

He stood up and bent his grey head, threw his hat on one side, and looked down into the trough.

He had come to the end. Everything was gone, or going, from him—even a sepulchre with his fathers, for, if he died by his own hand, then he would not be buried with them, but near that saw-pit, where a cross-way led to Black Down. It was well that so it should be; so he would retain, at all events, six foot of the paternal inheritance. That six foot would be his inalienably, and that would be better than banishment to the churchyard of Peter Tavy. But he would make sure that he carried with him something of the ancestral land. He crept along the beam, with the rope about his neck, fastened near the middle of the saw-pit, like a dog running to the extent of his chain, and scrabbled up some of the soil, with which he stuffed his ears and his mouth, and filled his hands.

Thus furnished, he stepped back, and again looked down. He did not pray. He had no thought about his soul—about heaven. His mind was fixed on the earth—the earth of Hall, with which he must part, with all but what he held, and with which he had choked his mouth.

"Earth to earth!"

No words of the burial office would be said over him; but what cared he? It would be the earth of Hall that went back to the earth of Hall when he perished and was buried there. His flesh had been nourished by the soil of Hall, his mind had lived on nothing else. He could not speak as his mouth was full. How sweet, how cool tasted that clod upon his tongue under his palate!

Though he could not speak he formed words in his mind, and he said to himself—

"Thrice will I say 'Earth to earth!' and then leap down."

Once the words were said, and now he said them again, in his mind—

"Earth to earth."

There was a large black spider on the oak-tree, running up and down the chopped section, and now, all at once, it dropped, but did not fall—it swung at the end of its silken fibre. Mr. Cleverdon watched it. As the spider dropped, so, in another minute, would he. Then the spider ran up its thread. The old man shook his head. When he fell he would remain there motionless. What then would the spider do? Would it swing and catch at him, and proceed to construct a cobweb between him and the side of the pit? He saw himself thus utilised as a sidestay for a great cobweb, and saw a brown butterfly, with silver underwings, now playing about the pit-mouth, come to the cobweb and be caught in it. He shook his head—he must not yield to these illusions.

"Earth to——"

A hand was laid on his shoulder, an arm put about his waist; he was drawn to the side of the pit, and the rope hastily disengaged from his throat.

With blank, startled eyes old Squire Cleverdon looked on the face of his preserver. It was that of Luke, his nephew.

"Uncle!—dear uncle!"

Luke took the halter, unloosed it from where it had been fastened to the beam, knotted it up, and flung it far away among the bushes.

The old man said nothing, but stood before his nephew with downcast eyes, slightly trembling.

Luke was silent also for some while, allowing the old man to recover himself. Then he took his arm in his own and led him back to the horse.

"Let me alone! Let me go!" said old Cleverdon.

"Uncle, we will go together. I was on my way to you. I had heard in what trouble you were, and I thought it possible I might be of some assistance to you."

"You!" the Squire shook his head. "I want over a thousand pounds at once."

"That I have not got. Can I not help you in any other way?"

"There is no other way."

"What has happened," said Luke, "is by the will of God, and you must accept it, and look to Him to bless your loss to you."

"Ah, you are a parson!" said the old man.

Luke did not urge him to remount his horse. He kept his arm, and helped him along, as though he were conducting a sick man on his walk, till he had conveyed him some distance from the saw-pit. As the Squire's step became firmer, he said,

"A hard trial is laid on you, dear uncle, but you must bear up under it as a man. Do not let folk think that it has broken you down. They will respect you when they see your courage and steadfastness. Put your trust in God, and He will give you in place of Hall something better than that—better a thousand times, which hitherto you have not esteemed."

"What is that?" asked the old man, loosening his arm, standing still, and looking Luke shyly in the face.

"What is that?" repeated Luke. "Wait! Trust in God and see."

CHAPTER LIII.

On reaching Hall, the first person that came to meet them was Bessie. She had returned, anxious about her father, and to collect some of her clothes. On arriving, she had been told that he had not gone to bed all night, that he looked ill and aged; that he had ordered his horse and had ridden away without telling any one whither he was going, and that some hours had elapsed without his re-appearing. Bess was filled with uneasiness, and was about to send out the servants to inquire as to the direction he had taken, and by whom he had been last seen, when the old man returned on foot, leaning on Luke, who led the horse by the bridle.

"Has any accident happened?" she asked, with changing colour. The old man gave a shy glance at her, then let his eyes fall to the ground. He said nothing, and went into the house to his room. Bess's uneasiness was not diminished. Luke spared her the trouble of asking questions. He told her that he had met her father on the way, and that they had come to an understanding, so that the estrangement that had existed between them since Anthony's marriage was at an end.

Bessie's colour mounted to her temples, she was glad to hear this; and Luke saw her pleasure in her eyes. He took her hand.

Then she lowered her eyes and said :—"Oh, Luke! what am I to do? Can I withdraw the promise made yesterday? I cannot fulfil it. I did not know it then. Now it is impossible. I can never love Fox—never respect him. He has behaved to my father in a manner that even if forgiven is not to be forgotten. And, indeed, I must tell you. He said he had struck Anthony and half killed him. I do not know what to think. Urith——"

"I know what Urith says. I was present. I saw the blow dealt. Fox did that—Urith bade him do it."

Bessie's breath caught. Luke hastened to reassure her.

"Anthony was not seriously hurt. Something he wore

—a token on his breast—turned the point of the knife; but I am to blame, I am greatly to blame, I should have come and seen your father before your marriage and told him what I knew, then you would not have been drawn into this——"

"Oh, Luke!" interrupted Bessie, "I do not think anything you said would have altered his determination. He was resolved, and when resolved, nothing will turn him from his purpose. As we were married at Tavistock and not in your church, you were not spoken to about it."

"No—but I ought to have seen your father. I shall ever reproach myself with my neglect, or rather my cowardice, and now I have news, and that sad, to tell you. It is vague, and yet, I believe, trustworthy. Gloine, who went from my parish to join the Duke of Monmouth, has come back. He rode the whole way on a horse that belonged to some gentleman who had been shot. There has been a battle somewhere in Somersetshire. Gloine could not tell me the exact spot, but it does not matter. The battle has been disastrous—our side—I mean the side to which nearly all England wished well, has been routed. There was mismanagement, quarrelling between the leaders: bad generalship, I have no doubt; it was but a beginning of a fight; and then a general route. Our men—I mean the Duke's—were dispersed, surrendered in batches, were cut and shot down, and those who fled were pursued in all directions, and slain without mercy. What has happened to the Duke I do not know, Gloine could not tell me. But Mr. Crymes is dead. He passed the coach and saw the soldiers plundering it, and the poor old gentleman had been shot and dragged out of it, and thrown on the grass."

"But Anthony!"

"Of him, Gloine could not tell me much. He was greatly in favour with the Duke and with Lord Grey. There was a considerable contingent of men from Tavistock and the villages round, who had been collected by the activity of Mr. Crymes and one or two others, whose names we will now strive to keep in the background; and, as Mr. Crymes himself was incapacitated by age and infirmity from officering this band of recruits, Anthony was appointed captain, and I am proud to say that our little battalion showed more determination, made a better fight, and was less ready to throw away arms and run, than was any other. That is what Gloine says."

"And he can say nothing of Anthony?"

"Nothing, Gloine says that when the route was complete, he caught a horse that was running by masterless, and mounting, rode into Devon, and home as hard as he could, but of Anthony he saw nothing. Whether he fell, or whether he is alive, we shall not know till others come in; but, Bess, we must not disguise from ourselves the fact that, supposing he has escaped with his life, he will stand in extreme danger. He has been one of the few gentlemen who has openly joined the movement, he has commanded a little company drawn from his own neighbourhood, and has given the enemy more trouble than some others. A price will be set on his head, and if he be caught, he will be executed—almost certainly. He may return here if alive, he probably will do so; but he must be sent abroad or kept in hiding till pursuit is over."

"O, poor Anthony!" said Bessie. "Will you tell my father?"

"Not at present. He has his own troubles now. Besides, we know nothing for certain. I will not speak till further and fuller news reaches me. But, Bess, you must be with him—he is not in a state to be left alone. Now, may be, in his broken condition, he may feel your regard in a manner he has not heretofore."

"Heigh, there. Have you heard?"

The voice was that of Fox. He came up heated, excited.

"Heigh, there! Luke, and you, Bess, too? Have you heard the tidings? There's our man, Coaker, come back—came on one of the coach-horses. There has been a pretty upset at the end, as I thought. My father is dead—the soldiers shot him as he sat in the coach, and proceeded to turn everything out in search of spoil. What a merciful matter," he grinned, without an audible laugh, "that the five or six hundred pounds had been lifted on Black Down instead of falling into the hands of the Papist looters! Aye?"

Neither Luke nor Elizabeth answered him.

"You know that now I am owner of the little estate in Buckland," said he, "such as it is—a poor, mean scrap that remains of what we Crymes——"

"You are now a Cleverdon," said Luke, dryly.

"But not for long. I shall change my name back, if it cost me fifty pounds. There is something more that I am. I am trustee for Julian till she marries—I step into my father's place. How do you suppose she will like that? How will she find herself placed under my management?" He laughed.

"Your father dead," said Luke, "one might expect of you some decent lamentation."

"Oh! I am sorry, I assure thee! But Lord! what else could I expect? And I thank Heaven it is no worse. I expected him to be drawn to Tyburn, hung, and disembowelled as a traitor. I swear to thee, Luke, I was rejoiced to hear he died honourably of a shot, since die he must. And Anthony dead——"

"Anthony! Have you heard?"

"Nay—I cannot swear. But Coaker says it is undoubted. The troopers were in full pursuit of our Tavistock company of Jack-Fools, cutting them down and not sparing one. Anthony cannot escape. If he ran from the field, he will be caught elsewhere. If they spitted the common men, they will not spare the commanding officer."

"Poor Anthony!" sighed Bess.

"Ay! poor Anthony, indeed, with nothing left at all now—not even the chance of life! But never mind poor Anthony, Bess; please to consider me. I know not but what now I shall be able at my ease to pay that attorney from Exeter—if I choose; but that shall only be to make Hall my own, and no sooner has my money passed hands than out turns your father. He and I will never be able to pull together. He has his notions and I mine. No man can serve two masters, as Parson Luke will tell thee; and neither can a land be held by and serve two masters, one choosing this and t'other that. No sooner is Hall cleared with my money than out walks the old Squire. Then you and I Bess——"

"You and I will remain as separate as we are at present," answered Elizabeth. "I go with my father. Never will I be with you."

"As you will," said Fox, contemptuously. "Your beauty is not such as to make me wish to keep you."

"Then so let it be. We have been married, only to part us more than ever," said Bess. Then, turning to Luke, she said, "I cannot help myself. I swore with good intention of keeping my oath, but I cannot even attempt to observe it. He——" she pointed to Fox, "he has shown me how impossible it is."

Luke did not speak. The words of Fox had made him indignant; but he said nothing, as any words of his he felt would be thrown away, and could only lead to a breach between him and Fox, in which he must get the worst, as unable to retort with the insolence and offensiveness of the latter. He looked with wonder at Bessie, and admired her quiet dignity and strength. He could see that, with all his rudeness to her, Fox stood somewhat in awe of her.

"Yes," said Fox, "Anthony is dead; I do not affect to be sorry, after having received from him a blow that has half blinded me—a continuous reminder of him."

"His sister strove to make amends for that yesterday," said Luke, unable further to control his wrath. "You then demanded of her an atonement far more costly than any wrong done you."

Fox shrugged his shoulders. "A pretty atonement—when she flouts me, and refuses to follow me."

Bessie, shrinking from hearing her name used, entered the house, and went into her father's room.

She found the old man there, lying on a long leather couch against the wall, asleep.

She stood watching him for a moment in silence, and without stirring. His hair was certainly more grey than it had been, and his face was greatly changed, both in expression and in age. The old hardness had given way, and distress—pain, such as never before had marked his countenance, now impressed it, even in sleep. He had probably hardly closed his eyes for many nights, as he had been full of anxiety about the fate of Hall, and the success of his scheme for its preservation. The last night had been spent in complete and torturing wakefulness. Now Nature had asserted her rights; weary to death, he had cast himself on his couch, and had almost immediately lost consciousness.

After observing her father for some little while, Bessie stepped lightly back into the passage, closed the door, then sought Luke, who was standing before the house with his finger to his lips, a frown on his brows, looking at the ground steadily. Fox was gone.

Bessie touched him, and beckoned that he should follow, then led him to her father's parlour, opened the door gently, and with a sign to step lightly and keep silence, showed him the sleeping Squire. A smile lighted her homely but pleasant face ; and then she gave him a token to depart.

For herself, she had resolved to remain there, her proper post now was by her father. She knelt at his couch, without touching him, and never turned an eye from him. In her heart swelled up a hope, a belief, that at length the old man might come to recognise her love, and to value it.

An hour—then another passed, and neither the sleeper nor the watcher stirred ; when suddenly the old man opened his eyes, in full wakefulness, and his eyes rested on her. He looked at her steadily, but with growing estrangement ; then a little hectic colour kindled in his pale face, and he turned his head away.

Then Bessie put her arm under his neck, and drew his head to her bosom, pressed it there, and kissed him, saying,

"My father ! my dear, dear father ! "

He drew a long and laboured breath, disengaged himself from her arms, and putting down his feet, sat up on the couch. She was kneeling before him, looking into his face.

"Go— " said he, after a while, "I have been hard with thee, Bess ! I have done thee wrong."

She would have clasped and kissed him again, but he gently yet firmly put her from him, and yet—in so doing kept his eyes intently, questioningly, fixed on her. Was it to be—even as Luke said, that in losing Hall he was to find something he had not prized hitherto ?

25

CHAPTER LIV.

A DAISY.

As briefly as may be, we must give some account of the venture of Monmouth, which ended in such complete disaster.

Charles, natural son of Charles II. by Lucy Walters, born in 1649, created Duke of Monmouth in 1663 by his father, was, as Pepys writes, " a most pretty spark ; " "very handsome, extremely well made, and had an air of greatness answerable to his birth, "says the Countess D'Aulnay ; was his father's favourite son, and for some time it was supposed that King Charles II. would proclaim his legitimacy and constitute him heir to the Throne. He was vastly popular with the nation, which looked up to him as the protector of the Protestant religion against the Duke of York, whose accession to the Throne was generally dreaded on account of his known attachment to the Roman Church. James therefore always regarded him with jealousy and suspicion—a jealousy and suspicion greatly heightened and intensified by a memorable progress he had made in 1680, in the West, when incredible numbers flocked to see him. He first visited Wiltshire, and honoured Squire Thynne, of Longleate House, with his company for some days. Thence he journeyed into Somersetshire, where he found the roads lined with enthusiastic peasants, who saluted him with loud acclamations as the champion of the Protestant religion. In some towns and villages the streets and highways were strewn with herbs and flowers. When the Duke came within a few miles of White Ladington, the seat of George Speke, Esq., near Ilminster, he was met by two thousand riders, whose numbers rapidly increased to twenty thousand. His personal beauty, the charm of his manners, won the hearts of every one, and thus the way was paved for the enthusiastic reception he was to receive later when he landed at Lyme, in Dorsetshire, as a defender of religion and a claimant for the Throne.

On June 14th, 1680, that landing took place. It had

been arranged between him and the Duke of Argyle that each should head an expedition with the same end, and that a landing should be effected simultaneously, one in Scotland, under Argyle, the other in England, under Monmouth. Money and nearly everything else was wanting, and Monmouth was dilatory and diffident of success. But finally, two handfuls of men were got together, some arms were purchased, and some ships freighted. Argyle sailed first, and landed before the Duke of Monmouth, loth to tear himself from the arms of a beautiful mistress in Brussels, could summon resolution to sail. Argyle was speedily defeated and lodged in Edinburgh Castle on June 20th. Six days before his capture, Monmouth landed in Dorsetshire. He had with him about eighty officers and a hundred and fifty followers of various kinds, Scotch and English. Lord Stair, who had fled from the tyranny of James when Duke of York and Commissioner in Scotland, did not join the expedition; but Lord Grey did, an infamous man, who was one main cause of its miscarriage. The ablest head among the party was that of Fletcher of Saltoun, who in vain endeavoured to dissuade the Duke from an enterprise which he saw was premature and desperate, but from which he was too brave and generous to withdraw.

On landing at Lyme, Monmouth set up his standard, and issued a proclamation that he had come to secure the Protestant religion, and to extirpate Popery, and deliver the people of England from " the usurpation and tyranny of James, Duke of York." This was dispersed throughout the country, was passed from hand to hand, and with extraordinary rapidity was carried to the very Land's End, raising the excitement of the people, who chafed at the despotism of King James II., and were full of suspicion as to his purposes. In the Declaration, promises were made of free exercise of their religion to all kinds of Protestants of whatever sect; that the Parliament should be annually chosen; that sheriffs should also be annually elected; that the grievous Militia Act should be repealed; and that to the Corporations of the towns should be restored their ancient liberties and charters.

Allured by these promises, the yeomanry and peasantry flocked to Monmouth's standard, and had the Duke entrusted the volunteers to the direction of a man of talent and integrity, it is not impossible that he would have met with success.

But the infamous Lord Grey was made commander, and when, shortly after landing, the Earl of Feversham, a French favourite of King James, threw a detachment of regular troops into Bridport, some six miles from Lyme, and Monmouth detached three hundred men to storm the town, Lord Grey, who was entrusted with the command, deserted his men at the first brush, and galloping back into Lyme, carried the tidings of defeat, when actually the volunteers, with marvellous heroism, had accomplished their task, and had obtained a victory.

Monmouth inquired of Captain Matthews, what was to be done with Lord Grey.

Matthews answered as a soldier, "You are the only General in Europe who would ask such a question."

The Duke, however, dared not punish Lord Grey, and actually entrusted to him the command of the cavalry, the most important arm he had. Having thus given a position of trust to the worst man he could, he lost the ablest man in his party, Fletcher, who had quarrelled with a Somersetshire gentleman about his horse, which led to a duel, in which the Somersetshire man was shot, and Fletcher had to be dismissed.

On June 15th, four days after landing, the Duke marched from Lyme with a force that swelled to three thousand men. He passed through Axminster, and on the 16th was at Chard ; thence he marched to Taunton, his numbers increasing as he advanced. At Taunton his reception was most flattering ; he was welcomed as a deliverer sent from heaven ; the poor rent the air with their joyful acclamations, the rich threw open their houses to him and his followers, his way was strewn with flowers, and twenty-six young girls of the best families in the town appeared before Monmouth, and presented him with a Bible. Monmouth kissed the sacred book, and swore to defend the truth it contained with his life's blood.

Here it was that he was met by the detachment from Tavistock and its neighbourhood. The men came in singly or in pairs, and somewhat later Mr. Crymes appeared in his coach. Anthony was immediately presented to the

Duke, who, taken by his manly appearance, at once appointed him to be captain of the contingent from Tavistock.

On June 20th Monmouth claimed the title of King. It was a rash and fatal mistake, for it at once alarmed his followers, and deterred many from joining him. Many of those who followed him, or were secretly in his favour, still respected the hereditary rights of kingship; and others had a lingering affection for Republican institutions. These two opposite classes were dissatisfied by this assumption. Moreover, the partisans of the Prince of Orange, already pretty numerous, considered this claim as infringing the rights of James's eldest daughter, Mary, Princess of Orange, who, by birth and by religion, stood next in order of succession.

On June 22d Monmouth advanced to Bridgewater, where he was agained proclaimed King; and here he divided his forces into six regiments, and formed two troops out of about a thousand horse that followed him.

We need not follow his extraordinary course after this, marked by timidity and irresolution.

Few of the gentlemen of the counties of the West joined him, and the influx of volunteers began to fail. Discouragement took possession of the Duke's spirits; and, when St. Swithin's rains set in before their proper time, not only was his ardour, but also that of his followers, considerably damped.

At length, on July 5th, it was resolved to attack the Royal army, encamped on Sedgmoor, near Bridgewater, where the negligent disposition made by Lord Feversham invited attack. Here the decisive battle was fought. The men following Monmouth's standard showed in the action an amount of native courage and adherence to the principles of duty which deserved better leaders. They threw the veteran forces into disorder, drove them from their ground, continued the fight till their ammunition failed them, and would at last have obtained a victory, had not the misconduct of Monmouth and the cowardice or treachery of Grey prevented it.

In the height of the action, when the fortune of the day was wavering, Lord Grey told Monmouth that all was lost —that it was more than time to think of shifting for himself. Accordingly, he and Monmouth, and a few other officers, rode off the field, leaving the poor enthusiasts, without order or instructions, to be massacred by a pitiless army. The battle lasted about three hours, and ended in a rout. The rebels lost about fifteen hundred men in the battle and pursuit; but the Royal forces had suffered severely.

Urith sat in the parlour at Willsworthy. She had reverted to the stolid, dark mood that had become habitual with her. Her hands were in her lap. She was plucking at the ring affixed to the broken token, through which passed the suspending ribbon. But for this movement of the fingers of the right hand she might have been taken to be a figure cut out of stone, so still was her face, so motionless her figure; not a change of colour, not a movement of muscle, not a flicker of the eyelid betrayed that she was alive and sentient; no tears filling the eye, no sigh escaping her lips.

The heat of her brow showed that she was labouring under an oppressive sorrow.

She spoke and acted mechanically when roused into action and to speech, and then instantly fell back into her customary torpor. Only when so roused did the stunned spirit flutter to her eyes, and bring a slight suffusion of colour into her face. Next moment she was stone as before.

She had been given, by Mrs. Penwarne, some flowers to arrange for the table.

"For his grave?" asked Urith, "and for my baby."

She took them eagerly, began to weave them, then they fell from her fingers into her lap, and she remained unconscious, holding the stalks.

The old lady came to her again, and scolded her.

"There! there! this is too bad. Take your token, and give me the flowers. I must do everything."

She put the broken medal again into Urith's hand; and left her, carrying the flowers away.

Urith was at once back again under her overwhelming cloud—the ever-present conviction that Anthony was dead, and that she had killed him.

She saw him at every moment of the day, except when

roused from her dream, lying across the hearthstone with his heart pierced. She had seen a little start of blood from the wound, when it was dealt, and this she saw day and night welling up inexhaustibly in tiny wavelets, flowing over his side, and falling in a long trickle sometimes connected, sometimes a mere drip upon the hearthstone, and then running upon the pavement in a dark line.

This little rill never dried up, never became full; it pushed its way along slowly, always about the breadth of the little finger, and standing up like a surcharged vein, hemmed in by grains of dust and particles of flue. Urith was ever watching the progress of this rivulet of blood, as it stole forward, now turning a little to this side from some knot in the floor, then running into a crevice and staying its onward progress till it had filled the chink, and converted it into a puddle. She watched it rise to the edge of a slate slab, swell above it, tied back, as it were, by each jagged in the slate edge, then overleap it, and run further. The rill was ever advancing towards the main entrance to the hall, yet never reaching it, making its way steadily, yet making no actual progress.

On more than one occasion Urith stooped to remove a dead wasp that stood in the way of its advance, or to sop up with her kerchief some plash of water which would have diluted its richness.

Now, on the floor, lay a daisy head that had fallen from the flower bunch Mistress Penwarne had brought to her and then had taken away. Urith's eyes were on the daisy, and it seemed to her that the red rill was touching it. It was nothing to Urith that she was in the parlour, and that Anthony had fallen in the hall. Wherever she went, into whatsoever room, into the garden, out on the moor—it was ever the hall she was in, and the floor everywhere, whether of oak boards or of soft turf, or of granite spar, was in her eyes the pavement of the hall, and ever over that pavement travelled the little thread of blood, groping its way, like an earthworm, as endowed with a half consciousness that gave it direction without organs of sense.

And now on the floor lay the garden daisy-head, and towards it the purple-red streamlet was pushing on; was the daisy already touched, and the edges of the fringe of petals just tinctured? Or was its redness due to the reflection on the pure white of the advancing blood? The dye or glow was setting inward, whatever it was, and would soon stain the petals crimson, and then sop the golden heart and turn it black.

How long this process would require Urith did not ask, for time was nothing to her. But she looked and waited, she fancied that she saw the clotting together of the rays, and their gradual discoloration as the red liquid rose up through the yellow stamens.

And now the flower-head began to stir and slide over the floor, and the blood-streak to crawl after it.

Urith slowly rose to her feet, and, with bent head, observing the flower, step by step followed it. There was a draught blowing along the floor from a back-door that was open, and this stirred and carried forward the light blossom. Urith never inquired what moved the daisy; it was natural, it was reasonable, that it should recoil from the scent and touch of blood.

As the daisy-head slid forward—now with easy motion, now with a leap and a skip—so did, in Urith's diseased fancy, the rill of blood advance in pursuit, always just touching it, but never entirely enveloping it.

Urith stepped forward slowly towards the hall-door and opened it, to let the flower-head escape. Had she not done so, in a moment the daisy would have been caught, and have sopped up the blood like a sponge, lost all its whiteness, and become but a shapeless clot in the stream.

The draught, increased by the opening of the door, carried the little delicate blossom forward rapidly, into the hall and along its floor, and after it shot the head of the rivulet, pointed, like that of a snake darting on its prey. Then the daisy was arrested suddenly; it had struck against an obstruction—a man's foot.

Urith rose from her stooping position, and saw before her the man whose foot had stopped the daisy—it was Anthony, standing on the hearthstone. To her dazed sense it was nothing that the blood-stream should run in the course opposed to that it might have been supposed to run, from the parlour to the hall, from the door to the hearth. To her mind the ideal hall and the actual hall only coincided when they overlapped.

And now, standing on the actual hearthstone, with the

fancied blood-stream running up to, and dancing about his foot, was Anthony.

"Urith!"

The voice was that of Anthony.

He had seen Luke, he knew in what condition he might expect to find her; and he had come to the house to see her, to let her light unsuspecting on him, in the hopes that the surprise might rouse her, and change the tenor of her thoughts.

He looked at her with love and pity in his heart, in his eyes, and with a choking in the throat.

Urith remained standing where she had risen from her bowed position, and for a long time kept her eyes steadily fixed on him; but there was neither surprise nor pleasure in them.

Presently she said slowly, with a wave of her hand, "No! I am not deceived. Anthony is dead. I killed him."

Then she averted her face, and at once fell into her usual trance-like condition.

CHAPTER LV.

FATHER AND SON AGAIN.

Anthony sat in the house of his cousin Luke, his head in his hand. Bessie had come there to see him. She had been told of his return, and Luke had advised her to meet him at the parsonage.

"O Tony!—dear, dear Tony! I am so glad you are back. Now, please God, all things will go better."

"I do not see any turn yet—any possible," said Anthony.

His tone was depressed, his heart was weighed down with disappointment at his inability to rouse Urith.

"Do not say that, my brother," said Bessie, taking his hand between both of hers, "God has been very good in bringing you safe and sound back to Willsworthy."

"No exceeding comfort that!" Anthony responded, "when I find Urith in such a state. She does not know me again."

"You must not be discouraged," urged Bess. "She

has this darkness on her now, but it will pass away as the clouds rise from off the moor. We must wait and trust and pray."

"Remember, Anthony," added Luke, "that she received a great shock which has, as it were, stunned her. She requires time to recover from it. Perhaps her reason will return gradually, just as you say she herself came groping along step by step to you. You must not be out of heart because at the first meeting she was strange. Perhaps some second shock is needed as startling as the first to restore her to the condition in which she was. I have heard of a woman thrown into a trance by a flash of lightning, unable to speak or stir, and a second thunderstorm, months after, another flash, and she was cured, and the interval between was gone from her recollection."

Anthony shook his head.

"You both say this because you desire to comfort me, but I have little expectation, Bess," said he, pressing his sister's hand. "God forgive me that I have never hitherto considered and valued your love to me, but have imposed on you, and been rough and thoughtless. One must suffer one's self to value love in others."

His sister threw her arms about his neck, and the tears of happiness flowed down her cheeks. "Oh, Tony! this is too much! and father also! He loves me now."

"And you, Bess, you have been hardly used. But how stands it now betwixt you and Fox?"

Bessie looked down.

"My father forced you to take him; I know his way, and you had not the strength to resist. Good heavens! I ought to have been at your side to nerve you to opposition."

"No, Tony, my father employed no force; but he told me how matters stood with regard to Hall, and I was willing to take Fox, thinking thereby to save the estate."

"And Fox, what is he going to do?"

"I cannot tell. Nothing, I think. He says he has the money, but he will not pay the mortgage; and yet I cannot believe he will allow Hall to slip away. I think he is holding out to hurt my father, with whom he is very angry because the state of matters was not told him before the marriage."

"You suffered her to throw herself away?" asked Anthony, turning to Luke.

"I did wrong," he said. "I ought to have spoken to your father, but he had forbidden me the house, and—but no! I will make no excuse for myself. I did wrong. Indeed—indeed, Anthony, among us all there is only one who stands blameless and pure and beautiful in integrity—and that is our dear Bessie. I did wrong, you acted wrongly, your father, Fox, all—all are blameworthy, but she—nay! Bess, suffer me to speak; what I say I feel, and so must all who know the circumstances. The Squire must have eyes blinder than those of the mole not to see your unselfishness, and a heart harder than a stone not to esteem your worth."

"I pray you," pleaded Bessie, with crimson brow, "I pray you, not another word about me."

"Very well, we will speak no more thereof now," said Luke, "but I must say something to Anthony. You, cousin, should now make an attempt to obtain your father's forgiveness."

"What has he to forgive?" asked Anthony, impatiently. "Are not his own hard-heartedness and his hatred of Richard Malvine, the cause of all this misery?"

"His hard-heartedness and hatred have done much," said Luke, "but neither of these is the cause of Urith's condition. That is your own doing."

"Mine?" Though he asked the question, yet he answered it to himself, for his head sank, and he did not look his cousin in the face.

"Yes—yours," replied Luke. "It was your unfaithfulness to Urith that drove her——"

"I was not unfaithful," interrupted Anthony.

"You hovered on the edge of it—sufficiently near infidelity to make her believe you had turned your heart away from her for another. There was the appearance, if not the reality, of treason. On that Fox worked, and wrought her into a condition of frenzy in which she was not responsible for what she said and did. From that she has not recovered."

"Curse Fox!" swore Anthony, clenching his hands.

"No, rebuke and condemn yourself," said Luke. "Fox could have fired nothing had not you supplied the fuel."

Anthony remained with his head bowed on the table. He put up his hands to it, and did not speak for some time. At last he lowered his hands, laid the palms on the table, and said, frankly, "Cousin! sister! I am to blame. I confess my fault freely, and I would give the whole world to undo the past."

"Then begin a new life, Tony," said Luke, "by going to your father and being reconciled to him."

"I cannot. I cannot. How can I forget what he has done to Bess?"

"And how can your Heavenly Father forgive you your trespass if you remain at enmity with your earthly father?" said Luke, sternly. "No, Tony, begin aright. Do what is clearly your first duty, and then walk forward, trusting in God."

A struggle ensued in Anthony's breast. Then Bess took his hand again between her own, and said, "You have been brave, Tony, fighting on the battle-field; now show your true courage in fighting against your own pride. Come!" She held his hand still, and drew him after her. She had risen.

"Very well!" said Anthony, standing up. "In God's name."

"He has heard that you are returned," added Bessie. "It will be a pleasure to him to see you again."

On reaching Hall, Elizabeth found her father in his room. He was seated at his table, engaged on his accounts, turning over the list of sums due to him, reckoning his chances of recovering those debts, considering what money he could scrape together by cutting down timber, and by the sale of stock. He thought that he might raise five or six hundred pounds at once, and perhaps more, but the time was most unpropitious for a sale. It was the wrong season in which to throw oak, and to sell the crops in the ground would at that time be ruinous at the prices they would fetch.

When the door opened and Bessie entered with Anthony, the old man looked up, and said nothing. His sleep had restored his strength, and with it something of his natural hardness. His lips closed.

"Well, father!" said Anthony, "here am I, returned, without a shot through me."

"So I see," said his father, dryly.

Anthony, disappointed with his reception, was inclined to withdraw, but mastered his disappointment, and going up to the table, extended his hand, and said,

"Come, father, forgive me, if I have vexed you."

Old Cleverdon made no counter-movement. The request had been made somewhat coolly.

"Father! what did you promise me?" asked Bessie, her heart fluttering between hope and discouragement. "Here is Anthony, whose life has been in jeopardy, come back, asking your forgiveness, and that is what you required."

Then the old man coldly placed his hand in that of his son; but he said no word, nor did he respond to the pressure with which Anthony grasped him. His hand lay cold and impassive in that of his son. Then Anthony's cheeks flamed, and a sparkle of wrath burnt in his eye. Bessie looked up to him entreatingly, and then turned pleadingly to her father, and implored him to speak. Anthony did not await the word, but drew his hand away.

"So," said the old man, "you are back. Take care of yourself; you are not yet out of danger." And he took up again the papers he had been examining.

"I am interrupting you," said Anthony; "anything is of more interest to you than your own son."

He would have left the room, but Bessie held him back. Then she went up to her father and drew the papers away from him. In her fear lest this meeting should prove resultless she became bold. The old man frowned at her audacity, but he said nothing.

"Father," said Anthony, "I came here as a duty to you, to tell you that I ask nothing of you but your forgiveness for having been hot-headed in marrying without and against your will."

"I have nothing else to give," answered Mr. Cleverdon. "I no longer call this place mine. The place where I was born, and for which I have toiled, which I have dreamed about, loved—I have nothing more, nothing at all." He was filled with bitter pity for himself. I, in my destitution, must thank you that it has seemed worth while to you to come and see me."

"Father!" gasped Bessie.

The old man proceeded: "I cannot forget that all this

comes to pass because you disregarded my wishes. Had you married Julian, had you even proposed to marry her, this could not have happened. It is this," his voice rang hard and metallic, and the light in his eye was the glisten of a flint ; "it is this that is the cause of all. It brings my grey head into the dust. It deprives the Cleverdons of a place in the county, it blots them out with a foul smear." The pen he had been holding had fallen on a parchment, and, with his finger, the old man wiped the blotch and streaked it over the surface.

"I could not marry Julian," said Anthony, with difficulty controlling himself. "A man is not to be driven to the altar as is a poor girl." He turned to his sister. "I am sorry for your sake that Hall goes—not for mine ; I do not care for it. It has been the curse that has rested on and blasted your heart, father, turning it against your own children, marring the happiness of my mother's life, taken all kindness and pity out of yours. It is like a swamp that sends up pestilential vapours, poisoning all who have aught to do with it."

The old man raised himself in his seat, and stared at him with wide-open eyes. This was not what he had deemed possible, that a child of his, a Cleverdon, should scoff at the land on which he was born, and which had nourished him.

"What has been cast into thankless soil ? "asked Anthony. "All good feelings you ever had for my mother, all, everything, has been sacrificed for it. But for Hall, she would have never taken you, but have been happy with the man of her heart. But for Hall, I would have been better reared, in self-restraint, in modesty, and kept to steady work. But for Hall, Bess's most precious heart would not have been thrown before that—that Fox ! Very well, father. I am glad Hall goes. When it is gone clean away, I will see you again, and then maybe you will be more inclined for reconciliation."

The old man's blood was roused.

"It is easy to despise what can never be yours. The grapes are sour."

"The grapes were never other than sour," retorted Anthony, "and have set on edge all teeth that have bitten into them. Sister—come ! "

He went out of the door.

CHAPTER LVI.

In the hall again, seated in the window, is Urith. The window is planted high in the wall, so high, that to look out at it a sort of dais must be ascended, consisting of a step. On this dais is an ancient Tudor chair, high in the seat, as was usual with such chairs, made when floors were of slate and were rush-strewn, calculated to keep the feet above the stone, resting on a stool. Thus, elevated two steps above the floor, to whit, on the dais and the footstool, sat Urith as an enthroned queen, but a queen most forlorn, deadly pale, with sunken eyes that had become so large as to seem to fill her entire face, which remained entirely impassive, self-absorbed.

She made no allusion to Anthony; after he had withdrawn, she forgot that she had seen him. His presence when before her rendered her uneasy, so that, out of pity for her distress, he removed, when at once she sank back into the condition which had become fixed. But Anthony was again in the hall on this occasion, resolved again to try to draw her from her lethargy.

She sat uplifted in her chair, trifling with a broken token. She was swinging it like a pendulum before her, and to do this she leaned forward that the ribbon might hang free of her bosom. Though her eyes rested on the half-disc, its movement did not seem to interest her, and yet she never suffered the sway entirely to cease. So soon as the vibration became imperceptible, she put a finger to the coin and set it swinging once more.

Anthony had seated himself on the dais step, and looked up into her face, and, as he looked, recalled how he had gazed in that same face on Devil Tor, when he had carried her through the fire. An infinite yearning and tenderness came on him. His heart swelled, and he said low, but distinct, with a quiver in his voice——

" Urith ! "

She slowly turned her head, fixed her eyes on him, and said, " Aye."

" Urith !   Do you not know me ? "

She had averted her head again.   Slowly, mechanically, she again turned her face to him, seemed to be gathering her thoughts, and then said :

"You are like Anthony.   But you are not he.   I cannot tell who you are."

"I am your Anthony ! "

He caught her elbow to draw her hand to him, to kiss it, but she started at the touch, shivered to her very feet, so as to rattle the stool under them, plucked her arm from him, and said quickly :

"Do not touch me.   I will not be touched."

He heaved a long breath, and put his hand to his head.

" How can you forget me, Urith.   Do you not recall how I had you in my arms, and leaped with you through the fire, on Devil Tor ? "

"I was carried by him—he is dead—not by you. "   She looked steadily at him.   "No—not by you. "

"It was I ! " he exclaimed, with vehemence.   "I set you on my horse, dearest.   It was I—I—I.   Oh, Urith ! do not pretend not to know me ! I have been away, in danger of my life, and I thought in the battle of you, only of you. Urith ! my love ! Turn your eyes on me.   Look steadily at me.   Do you remember how, when I had set you on my horse, I stood with my hand on the neck, and my eyes on you.   You dazzled me then.   My head spun. Urith ! dear Urith, then I first knew that you only could be mine, that nowhere in the whole world could I find another I would care for.   And yet—whilst I discovered that, I foresaw something dreadful, it was undefined, a mere shadow— and now it has come.   Look me in the eyes, my darling ! look me in the eyes, and you must know me."

She obeyed him, in the same mechanical, dead manner and said, " I will not thus be addressed, I am no man's darling.   I was the darling of Anthony once—a long time ago ; but he ceased to love me ; and he is dead.   I killed him."

"Anthony never ceased to love you.   It is false.   He always loved you, but sometimes more than at other times, for his self-love rose up and smothered his love for you— but never for long."

"Did Anthony never cease to love me? How do you know that? How can you know that? You are deceiving me."

"It is true. None know it as I do."

She shook her head.

"Listen to me, Urith. Anthony never loved any but you."

"He had loved Julian," answered Urith. "He had from a child, and first love always lasts, it is tough and enduring."

"No, he never loved her. I swear to you."

She shook her head again, but drew a long breath, as though shaking off something of her load. "I cannot think you know," she said, after a pause.

"I knew Anthony as myself." He caught her hand. "I insist—look me steadily in the face."

She obeyed. Her eyes were without light, her hand was cold and shrinking from his touch, but he would not let it go. For a while there was symptom of struggle in her face, as though she desired to withdraw her eyes from him, but his superior will overcame the dim, half-formed desire, and then into her eyes came a faint glimmer of inquiry, then of vague alarm.

"Urith?"

"It is a long way down," she said.

"A long way down? What do you mean?"

"I am looking into hell."

"What! through my eyes?"

"I do not know; I am looking, and it goes down deep, then deeper, and again deeper. I am sinking, and at last I see him, he is far, far away down there in flames." She paused, and intensity of gaze came into her eyes. "In chains." She still looked, the iris of each orb contracting as though actually strained to see something afar off. "Parched." Then she moaned, and her face quivered. "All because he loved Julian when he was mine, and I shall go there too—for I killed him. I do not care. I could not be in heaven, and he there. I will be there—with him. I killed him."

Anthony was dismayed. It seemed impossible to bring her to recognition. But he resolved to make one more attempt.

He had let go her hand, and as he withdrew his eyes, her head returned to its former position; and once more she began to play with the pendant token.

Her profile was against the window. The consuming internal fire had burnt away all that was earthly, common in her, and had etherialised, refined the face.

"Urith!"

"Why do you vex me?"

"Turn fully round to me, Urith. What is that in your hand?"

"A token."

"Who gave it you?"

"It belonged to my father."

"It is broken."

"Everything is broken. Nothing is sound. Faith—trust—love." She paused between each word, as gathering her thoughts. "Everything is broken. Words—promises—oaths—." Then she looked at the token. "Everything is broken. Hearts are broken—lives—unions—nothing is sound."

"Look at this, Urith."

Anthony drew from his breast the half-token that had belonged to his mother, and placed it against that which Urith held.

"See, Urith! they fit together."

It was so, the ragged edge of one closed into the ragged edge of the other.

She looked at it, seemed surprised, parted the portions, and reclosed them again.

"Everything broken may be mended, Urith," said Anthony. "Faith—trust—love. Do you see? Faith shaken and rent may become firm and sound again, and trust may be restored as it was, and love be closed fast. Unions—a little parted by misunderstanding, by errors, may be healed. Do you see—Urith?"

She looked questioningly into his eyes, then back at the token, then into his eyes again.

"Is it so?" she asked, as in a dream.

"It is so, you see it is so. See—this broken half-token belonged to your father; that to my mother. Each had failed the other. All seemed lost and ruined forever and ever. But it could not be—the broken pledge must be made whole, the promises redeemed, the parts must be re-united—and Urith! they are so in us."

He caught her by both hands, and looking into her face, began to sing, in low, soft times :—

An evening so clear
    I would that I were
To kiss thy soft cheek
    With the lightest of air.
The star that is twinkling
    So brightly above
I would that I might be
    To enlighten my love!

A marvellous thing took place as he sang.

As he sang he saw—he saw the gradual return of the far-away soul. It was like Orpheus in Hades with his harp charming back the beloved, the lost Eurydice.

As he sang, step by step, nay, hardly so, hair'sbreadth by hair'sbreadth, as the dawn creeps up the sky over the moor, the spirit returned from the abysses where it had lost its way in darkness.

As he sang, Anthony doubted his own power, feared the slightest interruption, the least thing to intervene and scare the tremulous spirit-life back into the profound whence he was conjuring it.

The soul came, slow as the dawn, and yet, unlike the dawn in this, that it came under compulsion. It came as the treasure heaved from a mine, responsive to the effort employed to lift it ; let that strain be desisted from, and it would remain stationary or fall back to where it was before.

An explosion of firearms, the crash of broken glass, and the rattle of bullets against the walls.

Instantly Anthony has leaped to his feet, caught Urith in his arms, and carried her where she was protected by the walls, for the bullets had penetrated the window and whizzed past her head.

At the same moment he saw Solomon Gibbs, who plunged into the hall, red, his wig on one side, shouting, "Tony! for God's sake, fly! the troopers are here, sent after you. I've fastened the front door. Quick—be off. They'll string you up to the next tree."

He was deafened by blows against the main entrance, a solid oak door on stout iron hinges let into the granite. It was fastened by a cross-bar—almost a beam—that ran back into a socket in the jamb, when the door was unbarricaded.

"Tony! not an instant is to be lost. Make off. But by the Lord! I don't know how. They are clambering over the garden wall to get at the back door. There are a score of them—troopers under Captain Fogg."

Anthony had Urith in his arms. He looked at her, her eyes were fixed on him, full of terror, but also—intelligence.

"Anthony!" she said, "what is it? Are you in danger?"

"They seek my life, dearest. It is forfeit. Never mind. Give me a kiss. We part in love."

"Anthony!" she clung to him. "Oh, Anthony! What does it all mean?"

"I cannot tell you now. I suppose it is over. Thank God for this kiss, my love—my love."

The soldiers were battering at the door; two were up at the hall window, ripping and smashing at the panes. But there was no possibility of getting in that way, as each light was protected by stout iron stanchions.

"By the Lord! Tony. I'll fasten the back-door!" shouted Gibbs. "Get out somehow—Urith! if you have wits, show him the trapway. Quick! not a moment is to be lost—whilst I bar the back-door." Solomon flew out of the hall.

"Come," said Urith. "Anthony! I will show you." She held his hand. She drew it to her, and pressed it to her bosom. It touched the broken token—and she had his half-token in her hand. "Anthony! when joined—to be again separate?"

They passed behind the main door, whilst the troopers thundered against it, pouring forth threats, oaths, and curses. They had drawn a great post from the barn over against the porch, and were driving this against the door. That door itself would stand any number of such blows, not so the hinges, or rather the granite jambs into which the iron crooks on which the hinges turned were let; as Anthony and Urith went by, a piece of granite started by the jar flew from its place, and fell at their feet. Another blow, and the crook would be driven in, and with it the upper portion of the door.

On the further side of the entrance passage, facing the door into the hall, was one that gave access to a room employed formerly as a buttery. In it were now empty casks, old saddles, and a variety of farm lumber, and, amongst them that cradle that Anthony had despised, the cradle in which Urith had been lulled to her infantine slumbers.

Urith thrust the cradle aside, stooped, lifted a trapdoor in the wooden-planked floor, and disclosed steps.

"Down there," she said, "fly—be quick—grope your way along, it runs in the thickness of the garden wall, and opens towards the chapel."

"One kiss, Urith!"

They were locked in each other's arms. Then Anthony disengaged himself.

A shout! The door had fallen in. A shot—it had been fired through the window by a soldier without who had distinguished figures, though seen indistinctly, through the cobwebbed, dusky panes of the buttery window. Anthony disappeared down the secret passage. Urith put her hand to her head a moment, then a sudden idea flashed through her brain; she caught with both arms the cradle, and crashed it down the narrow passage, blocking it completely, and threw back the door that closed the entrance.

Next moment she and Solomon Gibbs were in the hands of the troopers who had burst in.

"Let go—that is a woman!" called the commanding officer. "Who are you?" This to Mr. Gibbs. "Are you Anthony Cleverdon? You a rebel?"

"I!—I a rebel! I never handled a sword in my life," answered Mr. Gibbs, without loss of composure; "but, my lads, at a single-stick, I'm your man."

"Come!—who are you?"

"I am a man of the pen, Mr. Solomon Gibbs, attorney," answered the old fellow; "and, master—whatever be your name, I'd like to see your warrant—breaking into a house as you have done. I can't finger a sword or a musket, but, by Saint Charles the Martyr, I can make you skip and squeak with a goose-quill; and I will for this offence."

"Search the house," ordered Captain Fogg, the officer in command of the party. "I know that the rebel is here;

he has been seen. He cannot have escaped ; he is secreted somewhere. Meanwhile keep this lawyer-rascal in custody. Here—you, madame ! "—to Urith—" what is your name, and who are you ? "

" I am Anthony Cleverdon's wife."

" And he—where is he ? "

" Gone."

" Where is he gone to."

" I do not know."

" Who is this fellow in the hands of my men ? "

" He is my uncle, my mother's brother, Mr. Solomon Gibbs."

" Search the house," ordered the captain. " Madame, if we catch your husband, we shall make short work of him. Here is a post with which we broke open the door ; we will run it out of an upstair window and hang him from it."

" You will not take him ; he is away."

In the mean time the soldiers had overrun the house. No room, no closet, not the attics were unexplored. Anthony could not be found.

" What have we here ? " A couple of troopers had lifted the trap and discovered the passage.

" It is choked," said the captain. " What is that ? An old cradle thrust away there ? 'Fore heaven ! he can't have got off that way, the cradle stops the way. The bird had flown before we came up the hill."

CHAPTER LVII.

ANOTHER PARTING.

Immediately after Sedgemoor, a small detachment had been sent under Captain Fogg to Tavistock from the Royal Army to seek out and arrest, and deal summarily with, such volunteers as had joined the rebels from thence. Not only so, but the officer was enjoined to do his utmost to obtain evidence as to what gentlemen were disaffected to the King in that district ; and to discover how far they were compromised in the attempt of Monmouth. Mr.

Crymes's papers had been secured in his coach. They contained correspondence, but, for the most part, letters of excuse and evasion of his attempt to draw other men of position into the rebellion. With the letters were lists of the volunteers, and names of those who, it was thought, might be induced later to join the movement.

There existed in the mind of James and his advisers a suspicion that the Earl of Bedford, angry at the judicial murder of his son, was a favourer of Monmouth, and Captain Fogg was particularly ordered to find out, if such existed, proofs of his complicity.

The part Anthony had taken was too well known for him to remain neglected ; and Fogg had been enjoined to seize and make short work of him.

Between two of the tors or granite crags that tower above the gorge of the Tavy where it bursts from the moor, at the place called The Cleave, are to be seen at the present day the massive remains of an oblong structure connecting the rocks, and forming a parallelogram. This was standing unruined at the time of our story. For whatever purpose it may have served originally, it had eventually been converted into a shelter-hut for cattle and for shepherds.

There was a doorway, and there were narrow loophole windows ; the roof was of turf. At one end, against the rock, a rude fireplace had been constructed ; but there was no proper chimney—the smoke had to find its way as best it might out of a hole in the roof above, which also admitted some light and a good deal of rain. A huge castle of rock in horizontal slabs walled off the hut from the north, and gave it some shelter from the storms that blew thence. There was a door to the opening that could be fastened, which was well, as it faced the southwest, whence blew the prevailing wind laden with rain ; but the windows were unglazed—they were mere slots, through which the wind entered freely. The floor was littered with bracken, and was dry. The crushed fern exhaled a pleasant odour.

Outside the hut, in early morning, sat Anthony with Urith among the rocks, looking down into the gorge. The valley was full of white mist, out of which occasionally a grey rock thrust its head. Above the mist the moor-peaks and rounded hills glittered in the morning sun.

Anthony sat with his arm about Urith ; he had drawn

her head upon his breast, and every moment he stooped to kiss it. Tears were in her eyes—tears sparkling as the dewdrops on bracken and heather—tears of happiness. The dusky shadows of the past had rolled away: a shock had thrown her mind off its balance, and a shock had restored it. What led to that brief period of darkness, what occurred during it, was to her like a troubled dream of which no connected story remained—only a reminiscence of pain and terror. She knew now that Anthony loved her, and there was peace in her soul. He loved her. She cared for nothing else. That was to her everything. That he was in danger she knew. How he had got into it she did not dare to inquire. But one thought filled her mind and soul, displacing every other—he loved her.

It was so. Anthony did love her, and loved her alone. When he was away—in the camp, on the march, in the battle-field—his mind had turned to Urith and his home. Filled with anxiety about her from what he had heard from Mr. Crymes, he had become a prey to despair; and, if he had fought in the engagement of Sedgemoor with desperate valour, it had been in the hopes of falling, for he believed that no more chance of happiness remained to him.

After his escape, an irresistible longing to see Urith once more, and learn for certain how she was, and how she regarded him, had drawn him to Willsworthy. And now, that she was restored to him in mind and heart, he stood, perhaps, in as great peril as at any time since he had joined the insurgents. He knew this, but was sanguine. The vast extent of the moor was before him, where he could hide for months, and it would be impossible for an enemy to surprise him. Where he then was, on the cliffs above the Tavy, he was safe, and safe within reach of home. No one could approach unobserved, and opportunities of escape lay ready on all sides—a thousand hiding-places among the piles of broken rock, and bogs that could be put between himself and a pursuer. Nevertheless, he could not remain for ever thus hiding. He must escape across the seas, as he was certain to be proscribed, and a price set on his head. That he must be with Urith but for a day or two he was well aware, and every moment that she was with him was to him precious. She did not know this:

she thought she had recovered him for ever, and he did not undeceive her.

Now he began to tell her of his adventures—of how he had joined the Duke, and been appointed Captain of the South Devon band ; of how they had been received in Taunton ; how they had marched to Bristol, and almost attacked it ; and then of the disastrous day at Sedgemoor.

"Come ! " said Anthony, "let us have a fire. With the mists of the morning rising, the smoke from the hut will escape notice."

The air of morning was cold.

Holding Urith still to his side, he went with her into the hut. It was without furniture of any sort. Blocks of stones served as seats ; but there was a crook over the hearth, and an iron pot hanging from it. A little collection of fuel stood in a corner—heather, furze-bushes, dry turf—that had been piled there by a shepherd in winter, and left unconsumed.

Urith set herself to work to make a fire and prepare. They were merry as children on a picnic, getting ready for a breakfast. Urith had brought up what she could in a basket from Willsworthy, and soon a bright and joy-inspiring fire was blazing on the hearth.

Anthony rolled a stone beside it and made Urith sit thereon, whilst he threw himself in the fern at her feet, and held her hand. They talked watching and feeding the fire, and expecting the pot to boil. They did not laugh much, they had no jokes with each other. Love had ceased to be a butterfly, and was rather the honey-bearing bee, and the honey it brought was drawn out of the blossoms of sorrow.

To Urith it gave satisfaction to see how changed Anthony was from the spoiled, wayward, dissatisfied fellow who had thought only of himself, to a man resolute, tender, and strong. As she looked at him, pride swelled in her heart, and her dark eyes told what she felt. But a little time had passed over both their heads, and yet in that little while much had been changed in both. How much in herself she did not know, but she marked and was glad to recognise the change in him.

As they talked, intent in each other, almost unable to

withdraw their eyes from each other, the door opened, and
Mr. Solomon Gibbs entered.

"There!—there!" said he, "a pretty sharp watch you
keep. You might have been surprised for aught of guard
you kept."

"Come here," said Anthony; "sit by the fire and tell
me what is being done below."

Mr. Solomon Gibbs shook his head. "You cannot remain here, Tony; you must be off—over the seas—and I
will take care of Urith, and have the windows patched at
Willsworthy."

"I know I must," said Anthony, gloomily, and he took
Urith's hand and drew it round his neck; never had she
been dearer to him than now, when he must part from
her.

"Oh! uncle!" exclaimed Urith, "he must not indeed
go hence now that he has returned to me."

"I am safe here for a while," said Anthony, and he
pressed his lips to Urith's hand.

"Can you say that, with the rare look-out you keep?"
asked Mr. Gibbs. Then he gazed into the fire, putting up
his hand and scratching his head under the wig. He said
no more for a minute, but presently, without looking at
Anthony, he went on. "Those fellows under their Captain
—Fogg is his name—are turning the place upside down;
they have visited pretty nigh every house and hovel in
quest of rebels, as they call them. The confounded nuis-
ance is that they have a list of the young fellows who went
from these parts. As fast as any of them come home, if
they have escaped the battle, they drop into the hands of
the troopers."

Anthony said nothing, he was troubled. Urith's large
dark eyes were fixed on her uncle.

"The Duke of Monmouth has been taken, I hear; he
hid in a field, in a ditch among the nettles. No chance
for him. His Majesty, King James, will have no bowels
of compassion for such a nephew. For the Protestants of
England there is now no hope save in the Prince of
Orange."

Then Uncle Solomon put his hand round behind Anthony and nudged him, so as not to attract the attention
of Urith.

"And whilst we are waiting we may be consumed," said Anthony.

Then Solomon nudged Anthony again, and winked at him, and made a sign that he desired to have a word with him outside the door.

"'Fore Heaven, Tony!" said he, "we are as careless as before. I who bade you keep a watch have forgotten myself in talking with you. Go forth, lad, and cast a look about thee."

Anthony rose from the fern, and went to the door. He stood in it a moment, looking from side to side, then closed the door, and went further.

Mr. Gibbs took off his wig and rubbed his head. "The mist in the valley has taken the curl out, Urith. I wish you would dry my wig by the blaze, and I will clap my hat on and go out and help Anthony to see from which quarter the wind blows, and whether against the wind mischief comes."

Then he also went forth.

Urith at once set herself to prepare the food for breakfast; her heart was heavy at the thought of losing Anthony again as soon as she had recovered him, when all the love of their first passion had rebloomed with, if not greater beauty, yet with more vigour.

When Anthony re-entered the hut, he was alone, very pale, and graver than before; Urith saw him as he passed the ray of light that entered from one of the loop-holes, and she judged at once that some graver tidings had been given him than Uncle Sol had cared to communicate in her presence.

She uttered a half-stifled cry of fear, and started to her feet. "O Anthony! What is it? Are the soldiers drawing near?"

"No, my darling, no one is in sight."

"But what is it, then? Must I lose you? Must you go from hence?"

She threw herself on his breast and clung to him.

"Yes, Urith, I must go. You must be prepared to lose me."

"But I shall see you again—soon?"

"We shall certainly meet again."

She understood that he was no longer safe there, that

he must fly further, and that she could not accompany him on his flight; but her heart could not reconcile itself to this conviction.

He spoke to her with great affection, he stroked her head, and kissed her, and bade her take courage and gather strength to endure what must be borne.

"But, Tony!—for how long?"

"I cannot say."

"And must you cross the seas?"

He hesitated before he answered. "I must go to a strange land," he replied in a low tone, and bowed his head over hers. She felt that his hand that held her head was trembling. She knew it was not from fear, but from the agony of parting with her. She strove to master her despair when she saw what it cost him to say "Farewell" to her. If she might not share his fate, she could save it from being made more heavy and bitter by her tears and lamentations.

"Tony," she said, "you gave me that other half-token, take it again; hang it about your neck as a remembrance of me, and I will wear the other half—wherever we may be, you or I, it is to each only a half, a broken life, an imperfect life, and life can never be full and complete to either again till we meet."

"No," he said, and took the token, "no, only a half life till we meet."

He hung the ribbon round his neck, and placed the half token in his breast. Then he said:

"I must go at once, Urith. Come with me a part of the way. Uncle Sol will take you from me."

They left the hut together. Urith pointed to the food, but Anthony's appetite was gone. He drew her to his side, and so, silently, folded together with interlaced arms, they walked over the dewy short grass without speaking. After a while they reached a point where Solomon Gibbs was awaiting them, a point at which their several ways parted.

There Anthony stayed his feet. Overcome by her grief Urith again cast herself into his arms. He put his hands to her head and thrust it back, that he might look into her eyes.

"Urith!" he said.

"Yes, Anthony!" She raised her eyes to his.

He was pale as death.

"Urith, your forgiveness for all the sorrow I have caused you."

"Oh, Anthony!" she clung to him, quivering with emotion. "It is I—it is I—who must——"

"We have been neither of us free from blame. One kiss—a last—in token of perfect reconciliation."

A kiss that was long—which neither liked to conclude—but Anthony at length drew his lips away.

"We shall meet again," he said, "and then to part no more."

CHAPTER LVIII.

ON THE WAY TO DEATH.

Anthony had seen Urith for the last time. They would meet again only in Eternity. Though the moor was wide before him and he was free to escape over it, yet he might not fly. Captain Fogg had taken his father prisoner, had conveyed him to Lydford Castle, which he made his headquarters, and had given out that, unless Anthony Cleverdon the younger, the rebel, who had commanded the insurgent company from the neighbourhood of Tavistock, surrendered himself within twenty-four hours, he would hang the old man from the topmost window of the castle keep.

This was the tidings that Mr. Solomon Gibbs had brought to Anthony. Mr. Gibbs made no comment on it, he left Anthony to act on what he heard unpersuaded by him, to sacrifice himself for his father, or else to let the old man suffer in his stead.

There could be little doubt that Squire Cleverdon had done his utmost to forfeit the love of his children.

All the unhappiness that had fallen on Anthony, Urith, and Bessie was due in chief measure to his pride and hardness of heart; nevertheless, the one great fact remained that he was the father of Anthony, and this fact constituted an ineradicable right over the son, obliging him to do his utmost to save the life of his father.

Moreover, the old man was guiltless of rebellion. Anthony's life was forfeit, because he had borne arms against his rightful sovereign, and his father had not compromised his loyalty in any way. Anthony had never, as a boy, endured that a comrade should be punished for his faults, and could he now suffer his father to be put to death for the rebellious conduct of the son?

Not for one moment did Anthony hesitate as to his duty. But a struggle he did undergo. He thought of Urith. He had sinned against her, led astray by his vanity and love of flattery; and, after having suffered, he had worked his way to a right mind. And at the very moment of reunion, when his love and exultation over his recovered wife shot up like a flame—at that very moment he must pronounce his own sentence of death; at the moment that he had felt that she forgave him, and that all was clear for beginning a new and joyous life together, he must be torn from her, and exchange the pure and beautiful happiness just dawning on him for a disgraceful death, and the grave.

He knew that Urith's grief over his death would be intense, and, maybe, bring her down almost into the dust; but he knew, also, that the day would come when she would acknowledge that he had acted rightly, and then she would be proud of his memory. On the other hand, were he to allow his father to die in his room, he would remain for ever dishonoured in his own sight, disgraced before the world, and would lose the respect of his wife, and with loss of respect her love for him would also go.

The worst was over: he had bidden her farewell without betraying to her that the farewell was for ever. He took his way to Lydford, there to hand himself over to the Royal officers.

He had not left the moor, but was on the highway that crosses an outlying spur of it, when he suddenly encountered Julian Crymes.

Julian had heard of the return of Anthony before Captain Fogg and his soldiers arrived. She heard he was at Willsworthy, but he had not been to see her; and yet he had an excellent excuse for so doing—he must be able to tell her about her father. She had waited impatiently, hourly expecting him, and he had not come. She did not like to leave the house for a minute, lest he should come whilst she was away. Every step on the gravel called her to the window, every strange voice in the house caused her heart to bound. Why did not he come?

She went to the window of her little parlour and looked forth; and as she looked, her hot, quick breath played over the glass, and in so doing brought out the interwoven initials "A" and "U." They had long ago faded, and yet under the breath they reappeared.

When she had heard a rumour of his return, the life blood had gushed scalding through her veins, her eye had flashed, and her cheek flamed with expectation. Her father was dead, but the sorrow she felt for his loss was swallowed up in the joy that Anthony was home and in safety. Now all was right again, and in glowing colours she imaged to herself their meeting. She could hardly contain the exultation within; yet her reason told her that he could be no nearer to her than he was; he was still bound to Urith. The reproaches of Bess had stung her, but the sting was no longer felt when she heard that he was back.

But as she breathed on the window-pane, and first the interwoven initials "A" and "U" reappeared, and then the smirch where Anthony had passed his hand over her own initials linked to his, it sent a curdle through her arteries. He came not near her. He loved her no more—he had forgotten her. Little by little the suspicion entered, and made itself felt, that he did not love her. It became a conviction, forming as an iron band about her heart, rivetted with every hour, firmer, contracting, becoming colder. She was too haughty to betray her feelings, and she had not suffered a question relative to Anthony to pass over her lips.

Then she heard that Captain Fogg had arrived, and was searching the neighbourhood for Anthony, and was arresting every returned insurgent. The Captain visited Kilworthy, and explored the house for treasonable correspondence, but found none.

The anxiety and alarm of Julian for the safety of Anthony became overmastering. She could no longer endure imprisonment in her own house. Moreover, there was now no need for her to remain there. Anthony was in hiding somewhere, or he was taken—she knew not which —and could not come to her.

She had not slept all night, and when morning dawned she rode forth, unattended, to obtain some tidings about him. She would not go to Willsworthy. She could not face Urith, but she would hover about between Willsworthy and Hall, and wait till she could hear some news concerning him.

In this restless, anxious condition of mind, Julian Crymes was traversing the down when she lit on Anthony himself.

She greeted him with an exclamation of joy, rode up to him, sprang from her horse, and said, "But surely, Tony! this is reckless work coming on to the highway when they seek thy life."

"They will not have long to seek," said he.

"What do you mean?"

He made no answer, and strode forward to pass her, and continue his course to Lydford.

"Anthony!" exclaimed Julian, "you shall not meet and leave me thus. I have not seen you since your return."

"I cannot stay now."

"But you shall!" She threw herself in his road, holding the reins of her horse with one hand, and extending her whip in the other. "Anthony! what is the meaning of this?"

"I must pass," said he, stepping aside to circumvent her.

"Anthony!" she cried—there was pain and despair in her tone—"where are you going? and why will you not speak to me?"

He stood still for a moment, and looked steadily at her; then she saw how pale he was.

"Julian," said he, quietly, "you have acted towards me in a heartless——"

"Heartless, Tony!"

"In an utterly cruel manner, and have brought me to this. It was you who sowed the seeds of strife between Urith and me; you who drove her off her mind; you who forced me to leave home and go to the standard of the Protestant Duke; and it is you now who bring me to the gallows."

"The gallows!"

"The captain at the head of the troopers has taken my father, and threatens to hang him within a day unless I surrender to the same fate."

"But, Anthony!" She could hardly speak, she was trembling, and her colour flying about her face like storm-driven cloudlets lit by a setting sun, red and threatening. "Anthony!—not to—to death?"

"To death, Julian!"

She uttered a cry, let go the bridle, dropped her whip, and ran to him with extended arms. "Anthony! — O Anthony!"

He put forth his hand and held her from him. No; not on his breast where his Urith had just lain, that should never be touched by another—not by such another as Julian Crymes.

"Stand back," he said, sternly.

"Anthony! say you love me! You know you have—have always loved me."

"I never loved you, Julian. No—never."

She shook herself free, drew back, pressed her clenched fists against her bosom. "You dare to tell me that—you!"

"I never loved you," he said.

Her face became white as that of a corpse. She drew on one side and said, "Go—and may you be hanged! I hate you. I would I were by to see you die."

CHAPTER LIX.

A LAST CHANCE.

Julian was left alone. She watched Anthony depart, till he had disappeared round a turn of the road and a fall of the hill; then she cast herself upon the heather in a paroxysm of agony. She drove her fingers into the bushes of dwarf gorse, and the needles entered her flesh and drew the blood; but she heeded it not. The rough heather was against her cheek, a storm of sobs and tears shook and wetted the harsh, dry flowers. He did not love her! He never had loved her! She had fought against this conviction that, like a cold, gliding snake, had stolen into her heart and dripped its poison there.

Now she could resist it no more. It was not told her by Bessie—it was not a new conjecture formed on certain scribblings on the glass; it had been proclaimed by his own lips, and at a solemn moment when he would not lie—when he was on his way to death.

He had trifled with her heart, and he dared to reproach her! She had loved him before ever he had known Urith, and then he had shown her attention. Had she mistaken that attention for love? Had not her own flaming passion seen in the reflection it called up in him a real reciprocal flame?

After he was married she could not hide from her conscience that she had made a struggle to win back his heart—had disregarded the counsels of prudence and the teachings of religion in the furious resistance she had offered to the established fact that he had been given to another, and belonged to that other.

He did not love her! He never had loved her! And his life had been to her precious only because she loved him, and believed that he loved her.

She drew herself up in the heather; her cheeks were flaming, scratched by the heather branches, and her hair dishevelled. Her great dark eyes were like a storm-cloud full of rain, and yet with fire twinkling and flashing out of it. He was on his way to death. He would be no more in this life to be fought for, to be won by her or by Urith.

"I am glad he is going to die!" she cried, and laughed. Then she threw herself again on the ground in another convulsive fit of sobs.

Urith had won. She—Julian, had dared her to the contest for the prize. Each had come off ill; but Urith had gained the object—gained it only to lose it—won Anthony's heart, only to have it broken as her own brain was broken.

"It is well," moaned Julian, catching at the tufts of heath and tearing at them, but unable either to break them or root them up. "It is well! I would never have suffered her to regain him. I would have killed her!"

Rage and disappointment tore her, as the evil spirit tore

the possessed under Tabor, and finally left her, exhausted
and sick at heart. A cool air came down off the moor and
fanned her hot cheek, and dried the tears that moistened
them.

A few hours—perhaps only an hour—and Anthony would
be dead. She saw the gallows set up below Lydford Castle,
and Anthony brought forth, in his shirt; his eyes bandaged; his hands bound behind his back. She heard the
voices of the soldiers, and the hum of compassion from the
bystanders. She saw the rope fastened about his neck, and
cast over the crosstree of the gallows. Then one of the
soldiers leaped, and caught the free end of the rope, and
began to haul at it. Julian uttered a cry of horror, struggled to her knees, clasped her palms over her eyes, as
though to shut out a real sight from them, and swayed
herself to and fro on her knees.

The black 'kerchief, with the jerk, fell from his eyes, and
he looked at her. Julian threw up her hands to heaven,
and screamed, with horror, "My God, save him!"

Then she saw, indistinctly, through her tears, and out of
her horror-distended eyes, some one standing before her.
She could not see who it was; but, overmastered by her
terror, she cried, "Save him! Save him!"

"Julian!" said a voice; and it had a composing effect at
once on her disordered feelings.

"Bess! O, Bess! is that you? O, Bessie! do you
know? He has given himself up. Anthony! Anthony!"
She cowered no more; her bosom labored, and she bowed
herself, with her head in her lap, and wept again.

Bessie put her hand under her arm, and raised her.

"Stand up, Julian. I did not know it; but I was
quite sure he would do this. I am glad he has. It was
right."

"Bess, you are glad?"

"It is like himself; he has done right. He is my own
dear, dear Anthony."

"O Bess!—such a death!"

"The death does not dishonour; to live would have dishonoured. He has done right."

"He has betrayed my love!" gasped Julian, "and I
should be glad he died, yet—I cannot bear it. Indeed—
indeed, I cannot. O Bess! I would that it were I who was

to die—not he. Bess! will they take me and let him go? He has been false to me, and I am true to him."

"He has not been false to you," said Bessie; "he has come to a sense of the wrong course he was engaged in, into which you drew him. But he never was false to you, for he never cared for you. Come! poor unhappy girl. I know how full of sorrow you must be—so must all who love Tony."

"But, Bess! is there no way of saving him?"

Elizabeth shook her head, and said:—

"I do not suppose so. It is true that Gloine has got off, and there is a whisper that his uncle saw the captain, and some money passed, but——"

"Oh! if money were all——"

"But, remember, Gloine was only a common soldier, and Anthony was the captain who led the men from these parts. I do not think any money could save him."

"Let us try." Julian sprang to her feet.

"Where is money to be had? Enough, I mean. You know the state we are in."

"But Fox has it."

"Fox!" Bessie considered; then, turning colour, said, "I do not think that even to save Anthony's life I would ask a favour of Fox."

"Then I will. He can and must save Anthony. Where is he?"

"At Hall. He has gone over there; that is why I left, and I was on my way to Willsworthy when I saw your horse; I caught him by the bridle, I knew whose it was, and came in search of you. I feared some accident. But, Julian, I am very certain nothing can be done for Anthony, save by our prayers. I have heard that special orders were issued that he was to be hung. The captain came here on purpose to take and execute him. He cannot, he dare not spare him."

"O Bess!—we will try!"

"Prayer alone can avail," said Bessie, sadly.

"Come with me. Come back to Hall. You must be with me. I will see Fox. He alone can help us."

"I will go with you," said Bessie. "But I know that it is hopeless."

"He must be saved. He must not die!" gasped Julian.

She remounted her horse, mechanically, and Bessie walked at her side.

Julian said no more. She was a prey to conflicting emotions. A little while ago she had wished Anthony's death, and now she was seeking to save it. If she did succeed in saving it, it was for whom? Not for herself. He did not love her—he never had loved her. For Urith—for her rival, her enemy! She knew that Urith was in a strange mental condition. She did not know that she was recovered from it. But she gave no heed to the state in which Urith was. She thought of her as she had seen her, handsome, sullen, defiant. That was the girl Anthony had preferred to herself, and she would save Anthony to give him to the arms of Urith, that Urith might take him by the neck, and cover his face with kisses, and weep tears of joy on his breast. Julian set her teeth. Better that he should die than this! But, next moment, her higher nature prevailed. She had loved Anthony—she did love Anthony—and true love is unselfish. She must forget herself, her own wrongs, real or imagined, and do her utmost for him. How could she love him, and let him die an ignominious death? How could she let him die, when, by an effort, she might save him, and bear to live an hour longer? She would feel as though his blood lay at her door.

"Bessie, I cannot stay. You walk. I must ride on as fast as I can. Time must not be wasted. Every moment is important."

Then she struck her horse, and galloped in the direction of Hall. Her hair, wild and tangled, flew about her ears. Her hands were full of gorse-spikes, and every pressure on the bridle made the pain great, but she did not regard this. Her mind was tossed with waves of contrary feeling, and yet, as in a storm, when the surges seem to roll in every direction, there is yet a prevailing set, so was it now. There had been a conflict in her heart, but her nobler, truer nature had won the day.

As she drew up in the courtyard of Hall, Fox came out, and uttered an exclamation of surprise at seeing her.

He was in a high condition of excitement. Without waiting to hear her speak, he burst forth into a torrent of complaint.

"I will have the law of them—soldiers though they be,

and with a search-warrant, they are not entitled to rob—
we have been treated as though we were foreigners, and
subjected to all the violence of a sack. They have torn
open every cupboard, broken into every drawer and cabinet,
thrown the books and letters about—I can find nothing,
and what is worst, I cannot lay my hands on the money.
To-morrow is the last day, to-morrow the mortgage must
be paid, and I know that my father-in-law had some coin
in the house. By the Lord! I wonder whether he had
the wit to secrete it somewhere, or left it where any plun-
derer would go straight in quest of it. And he is to be
hanged in an hour, and I cannot ask him."

"Fox, it is not true; Master Cleverdon escapes."

"I know he will be hanged, and I do not suppose that
set of ruffians will let me see him and find out where the
money is. I have searched everywhere, and found nothing
but broken cabinets and overturned drawers, account-
books, title-deeds, letters, bills, all in confusion along with
clothing. It drives me mad. And—unless the money be
forthcoming to-morrow, Hall is lost. I have heard that the
agent of the Earl of Bedford will offer a price for it—and
that there is like to be another offer from Sir John Morris.
They would out-bid me. The mortgage must be paid, or
Hall lost, and if the old man be hanged to-day, Hall is
mine by this evening. It will drive me crazed—where can
the money be? He was fool enough for anything—to put
it in his cabinet, or in a box under his bed, or in the chimney, tied in an old nightcap like as would have done any
beldame. If he has done that—then the soldiers have
taken it. Who was to interfere? Who to observe them?
They drove all the servants out. They took the Squire in
custody, and I was not here. I was at Kilworthy, as you
know."

"Fox," said Julian. "It is no matter to me whether
Hall be saved or lost. Anthony has surrendered, and the
Squire is free."

"Anthony surrendered!" Fox fell back and stared at
her, then laughed. "'Fore heaven! we live in crack-
brained times when folk take a delight in running their
heads into nooses. There was my father did his best to
get hung, drawn, and quartered. A merciful Providence
sent him into the other world with a bullet in his heart,

and saved the honour of the family, and made a more easy
exit for him. And now there is Tony—runs to the gibbet
as though to a May-dance! Verily! there are more fools
than hares. For them you must hide the snare, for the
fools expose it, cross-piece, loop, and rope, and all complete,
and ring a bell and call—come and be hanged! Come!"

"Fox, we must save Anthony."

"Save him? Why, he will not be saved! He had the
world before him, and he might have run where he would;
now he has gone where he ought not, and must take the
consequences. Save him! Let him be hanged. I want his
father. I want to know what money he has, and where it
is. I can't find the whole amount. I know he has, or had,
some hundreds of sovereigns somewhere."

"Fox, you must assist me to save Anthony; we cannot
let him die. I will not! I will not! He must not die!"
Her passion overcame her, and she burst into tears.

"Pshaw! He is past salvation. If he is in the hands of
Captain Fogg, he is in a trap that has shut on him and will
not let him go. Besides—nothing can be done."

"Yes, there can. Gloine escaped. His uncle, the rich
old yeoman at Smeardon, bought him off."

"No money will buy Anthony off. Besides, where is
the money to come from?"

"You have some. Fogg let off Gloine, and he will let
Anthony off if he be paid a sufficient sum. If he was a
rascal in small game, he will be rascal in great."

"I do not care to have Tony escape; I owe him a grudge.
Besides, and that is just as well, his father is not here; what
money the old fellow has is hidden in some corner or other,
where I cannot find it, unless it has been carried off by
those vultures, those rats."

"If this is not available you must help."

"I! pshaw! I cannot, and I will not."

"You can; you have a large sum at your disposal."

Fox turned mottled in face. He stared at his sister with
an uneasy look in his eye.

"What makes you suppose that?" he said. "It is a
folly; it is not true. I am poor as the yellow clay of North
Devon. No small sum would serve, and I have but a couple
of groats and a crown in my pouch."

"You have the money; you yourself admitted it, two

minutes ago. You said that if you could find the money Squire Cleverdon had laid by, you would be able to make up the rest."

"Oh! that was talk! I would mortgage my Buckland estate."

"You have the money. Fox, this is evasive."

"What will satisfy you? Here is a crown, and here two groats, and, by Heaven—there is a penny as well. Take this and go—try your luck with Captain Fogg."

"I will have nothing under five hundred pounds. Fox, you can help me, and you will."

"I have not the coin. If I had I would not spare it. I will not throw Hall away. What is Tony to me? If he puts his neck into the noose, who is to blame if the rope be pulled and he dangles? No; here is the extent of my help—a crown, two groats, and one penny."

"Fox! I will sell you all my rights in Kilworthy. I will make over to you everything I have there—land, house—all—all—if you will give me five hundred pounds in gold."

Fox looked down, considered, then shook his head.

"There is not time for it. By the time we had got the transfer engrossed and signed, all would be over. Fogg won't let the grass grow under his feet, nor the rope rot for lack of usage. No; if there were time, I might consider your offer; but, as there is not, I will not. Let Tony hang: it is his due. He ran his head into the loop."

"Your final answer is—you will not help?"

"To the extent of one crown, two groats, and a penny."

"Then, Fox, I shall help myself."

CHAPTER LX.

EXIT "ANTHONY CLEVERDON."

Old Squire Cleverdon had spent the night in Lydford Castle. The Castle was more than half ruinous; nevertheless, there were habitable rooms still in it, and one or two of these served as prison cells. The walls were damp, and the glass in the windows broken; but it mattered not, he had but that night longer for earth, and the season was summer.

The Squire did not lose his gravity of deportment. He had held up his head before the world when things went well with him; he would look the world defiantly in the face as all turned against him. He knew that he must die. He did not entertain a hope of life; it may also be said that he was indifferent whether he lived or died. His only grievance was that the manner of his death would be ignominious. It was hardly likely that the news of his capture and of Captain Fogg's threat should reach Anthony. Where his son was he did not know, but he supposed that he had taken refuge in the heart of the wilderness of moors, and how could he there receive tidings of what menaced his father? Or, if the news did reach him, almost certainly it would reach him when too late to save his father. But, supposing he did hear, and in time, what was menaced, was it likely that he would give himself up for his father? His life was the more valuable of the two; it was young and fresh, he had a wife dependent on him, he had an estate—his wife's—to live on; and the old man was near the end of his natural term of life, was friendless, he had cast from him his children, and was aereless, he had lost his patrimony. Anthony would be a fool to give himself up in exchange for his father. What did the Squire care for the scrap of life still his? So little that he had been ready to throw it away; and if the mode of passage into eternity was ignominious, why it was the very method he had chosen for himself at the sawpit. He was an aged ruined man, who had failed in everything, and had no place remaining for him on earth. He did not ask himself whether he had been blameworthy in his conduct to his children, in his behaviour to Anthony. He slept better that night in Lydford Castle than he had for many nights, but woke early, and saw the dawn break over the peaks of the moor to the east. He would not be brought before the captain and sent to execution for a few more hours. From his cell he had heard and been disturbed by the riot and revelry kept up by the captain and some boon comrades till late.

The morning was well advanced when Julian Crymes rode to the Castle gates, followed by a couple of serving men and laden horses. At her command the men removed the valises from the backs of the beasts and threw them over their own shoulders. The weight must have been considerable, judging by the way in which the men walked under their burdens.

Julian asked for admittance. She would see Captain Fogg. The sergeant at the gate hesitated.

"Captain Fogg was at Kilworthy yesterday in search of papers—my father's papers. I have found them, and bring them to him—correspondence that is of importance."

The sergeant ascended to the room where was the captain, and immediately came down again with orders for the admission of Julian.

Followed by the men, she mounted the stone flight that led to the upper story, where Captain Fogg had taken up his quarters, and bade the servants lay their valises on the table and withdraw.

Captain Fogg sat at the table with a lieutenant at his side ; he was engaged on certain papers, which he looked hastily over, as handed to him by the lieutenant, and scribbled his name under them.

Julian had time to observe the captain ; he was a man of middle height, with very thick light eyebrows, no teeth, a blotched, red face, and a nose that gave sure indication of his being addicted to the bottle. He wore a sandy scrubby moustache and beard, so light in colour as not to hide his coarse purple lips. When he did look up, his eyes were of the palest ash colour, so pale as hardly to show any colour beside the flaming red of his face, and they had a watery and languid look in them. His appearance was anything but inviting.

He took no notice of Julian, but continued his work with a sort of sulky impatience to have it over.

Not so the younger officer, who looked at Julian, and was struck with her beauty. He turned his eyes so often upon her that he forgot what he was about, and Fogg had to call him to order. Then Fogg condescended to observe Julian.

"Well," said he, roughly, "what do you want? Are these papers? What is your name?"

"I sent up my name," answered Julian.

"Ah! to be sure—the daughter of that rebel. I know—I know. What do you want?"

"I have come to ask the life of Anthony Cleverdon," she answered. "He does not deserve death ; it was all my fault that he joined the Duke. He was no rebel at heart ; but I drove him to it. See what a man he is—to come and surrender himself in order to save his old father from death."

"Bah! A rebel! He commanded—a chief rebel! He shall die," answered Fogg, roughly.

"I implore you to spare him ! Take my life, if you will. It was all my doing. But for me he never would have gone. I sent him from his home—I drove him into the insurgent ranks. I alone—I alone am guilty."

"And who are you that you plead for him so vehemently?" asked the Captain, his watery eye resting insolently on her beautiful, flushed face. "Are you his wife?"

"No—no ; I am not."

"Ah, you are his sweetheart."

Julian's colour changed. "He does not love me. He is innocent, therefore I would buy his life."

"Buy!" echoed the Captain.

"Yes—buy it."

"It cannot be done. It is forfeit. In a quarter of an hour he dies ! Look here, pretty miss : I have my orders. He is to die. I am a soldier : I obey orders. He dies."

He put his hand to his cravat and drew it upwards. The action showed how Anthony was to die.

"I have brought you here something worthy of your taking," said Julian, lowering her voice—"documents of the highest value. Documents, letters, and lists—what you have been looking for, and worth more than a poor lad's life. What is his body to you when you have driven out of it the soul? A cage without a bird. Here, in these valises, I have something of much more substantial value."

"Let me look," said Fogg.

"By heaven !" he swore, after he had leaned across the table and taken hold of one. "Weighty matters herein."

Julian gave him the key, and he opened ; but not fully. Some suspicion of the contents seemed to have crossed his mind. He peered in and observed bags, tied up.

"Ah !" said he. "State secrets—State secrets only for those in the confidence of the Government. Friswell !" he turned to the lieutenant, "leave me alone for a few minutes with this good maiden. She has matters of importance to communicate that concern many persons high up—high up—and young ears like yours must not hear. Wait till you have earned the confidence of your masters."

The lieutenant left the room.

Then Captain Fogg signed to the soldiers at the door to stand without as well.

"So—matters of importance concerning the Government," said Fogg. "In confidence, tell me all—I mean about these valises and their contents."

"I have come here," said Julian, "to implore you to save the life of Anthony Cleverdon. I am come with five hundred guineas, some in silver, some in gold—some in five-guinea pieces, the rest in guineas; they are yours freely and heartily, if you will but grant me the life of your prisoner."

"Five hundred guineas!" exclaimed the Captain; and his pale eyes watered, and his cheeks became redder. "Let me look."

He thrust his hand into the saddle-bag before him on the table, and drew forth a canvas bag that was tied and sealed. He cut the string and ran out some five-guinea pieces on the table. A five-guinea piece was an attractive —a beautiful coin. James I. had struck thirty-shilling pieces, and Charles I. three-pound gold pieces, but the five-guinea coin had been first issued by Charles II. Noble milled coins, on the reverse with the shields arranged across, and each crowned. Captain Fogg took three in his hand, tossed them, rubbed one with his glove, put his hand into the bag and drew forth more.

"Five hundred guineas!" he said. "Upon my soul, it is more than the cocksparrow is worth. I wish I could do it. By the Lord, I wish I could. Give me up that other bag."

Julian moved another over the table to him.

"Why," said he, "what do you reckon it all weighs?"

"I cannot say for certain; one of my men thought about eighty pounds."

"More, I'll be bound; and mostly gold. Why, how come you by so much down here? You country gentry must be well off to put by so much; and all coins of his late Majesty. You may have been nipped and scraped under Old Noll, but under the King you have thriven. Five hundred pounds! Where the foul fiend did you get it? You have not robbed the Exchequer?"

Julian made no answer.

The Captain continued to examine, rub, weigh, and try the coins; he ranged them in rows before him, he heaped them in piles under his nose.

"Upon my word, I never was more sorry in my life," he said. "But I can't do it. My orders are peremptory. If I do not hang him I shall get into trouble myself. But I'll tell you what I'll do—give him a silk sash, a soldier's sword-sash, and hang him in that. It's another thing altogether —quite respectable. Will that do?" After a pause.

"Now look at me," said the Captain; "it is cursed unpleasant and scurvy treatment we gentlemen of the sword meet with. I know very well that such prisoners as we deliver over to be dealt with by the law, supposing they be found guilty and sentenced to transportation or death, will be given the chance of buying off. Why, I've known it done for ten or fifteen pounds. Look at me and wonder! Ten or fifteen pounds in the pocket of this one or that— may be a Lady-in-Waiting. But here be I—an honest, blunt, downright soldier, and five hundred guineas, and many of them five-guinea pieces, too, that smile in one's face as innocent as a child, and as inviting as a wench, and, by my soul! I can't finger them. Orders are peremptory, I must hang him. 'Tis enough to make angels weep?" *

He wiped his watery eyes.

"By the Majesty of the King, I'll do my best for you, saving my honour. I'll hang the old man, the father, and let the young one go free."

"Sir," said Julian, "Anthony will never accept life on those terms."

"Then, by my sword and spurs, I can't help you! But I'll do what I can for you—I will, upon my soul! I'll make him dead drunk before I hang him. Will that do? Then he won't feel. Not a bit. He'll go off asleep, and wake in

---

* This was the case. Among those sentenced by Judge Jeffreys, the majority escaped with a payment. The Queen had 98 delivered to her order, Jerome Nimo had 101, Sir Wm. Booth 195, Sir Christopher Musgrave 100, Sir Wm. Howard 205, and so on. They paid sums varying in amount, and got off clear. See Inderwick's "Sidelights on the Stuarts," 1889.

kingdom come, as easy as if he were rocked in a cradle.
No unpleasantness at all, and I'll stand the liquor. He
shall have what he likes. By Heaven, they're making noise
enough outside! Here, help to put this money into the
valise. I will call to order."

He set to work and pocketed as many five-guinea pieces
as he could, then thrust the rest into the bags.

Having assumed a grave manner, he knocked with the
hilt of his sword on the table, and roared to the sentinel to
open the door.

He was at once answered. The commotion without had
not ceased.

"I will go in. I insist!—I must see Captain Fogg."

"Who is without?" asked the Captain. "Who is that
creating such an uproar?"

"It is some one who desires to be admitted into your
presence, Captain!" said the Lieutenant. "He says he has
been robbed; he claims redress."

"I can't see him—I am busy—— State secrets? Very
well, let him in."

He changed his order as Fox burst into the room in spite
of the efforts of the sergeant and sentinel to stay him.

"Who are you? What do you here?" asked Fogg.
"Stand back. Guard, hold his hands. Take him into custody. What is the meaning of this?"

"I have been robbed," said Fox, his face streaming with
sweat and red with heat. "I have had my money taken;
she has brought it here; she is trying to bribe you with
it; she would buy off that fellow; he deserves to be hung.
I will denounce you if you take the money; it is mine.
You have come here to hang him, and hanged he shall be.
You shall not take my money and let him escape." He
gasped for breath; he had been galloping, and galloping
in a state of feverish excitement and rage. Some time after
Julian had left him at Hall, her final remark had occurred
to him, "Then I shall help myself," and he asked himself
what she could mean by that, what she possibly could do.

Suddenly he remembered his doubts about whether she
had seen him in the pigeon-cote, and at once he was over-
whelmed with fear. He mounted his horse and rode to
Kilworthy, to hear that his sister had left an hour before
with servants and horses. He flew to the dove-cote and

explored the pigeon-holes. Every one had been rifled.
Sick, almost fainting with dismay, with baffled avarice and
ambition, he remounted his horse, and rode at its fastest
pace to Lydford.

"You are an impudent scoundrel," said Captain Fogg;
"an impudent scoundrel to dare insinuate—but, who are
you, what is your name?"

"I am Anthony Crymes of Kilworthy," said Fox.

"It is a lie!" exclaimed Julian, starting forward. "Captain Fogg, take him, if you must have a victim. Take him.
He is Anthony Cleverdon, son of the old Squire, and heir
to Hall."

"What is that?—what is that? Clear the room," shouted Fogg. "Stand back you rascal!—traitor!—rebel!
Sergeant, keep hold of him till you can get a pair of man-
acles—or stay, take your sash, bind his hands behind his
back, and leave the room. Friswell, you need not stay;
I will call you when wanted. Matters of State importance,
secrets against the Government and his sacred Majesty the
King, are not for ears such as yours—till tried, tried and
proved worthy. Go."

When the room was cleared of all save Julian and Fox, the
Captain said, "Now, then, what is the meaning of this?"

"I have been robbed," said Fox, trembling between ap-
prehension and rage. "My sister has taken advantage of
having seen where I keep my money, and has carried it off
—therewith to bribe you to let off"—he turned fiercely at
Julian, his white teeth shining, his lips drawn back, and
his eyes glittering with hate—"to let off—her lover."

"You are quite mistaken," said Fogg, stroking his moustache. "These saddle-bags and valises contain documents
of importance, correspondence of the rebels——"

"They contain my money," screamed Fox—"five hundred pounds."

"Five hundred guineas," said the Captain, and thrust
his hand into his pocket, "and some of them five-guinea
pieces?"

"Even so. They are mine."

"And you are——?"

"Anthony Crymes. Most people know me as Fox
Crymes."

"Captain Fogg," said Julian, "that is false. I do not

deny that he was once called Crymes, but he obtained a royal license to change his name ; he is Anthony Cleverdon."

"Anthony Cleverdon !" echoed Captain Fogg. "By the Lord, you seem to be a breed of Anthony Cleverdons down here ! How many more of you are there ?"

"There are three," said Julian—"the father, the old squire ; there is his son, an outcast, driven by his father from his home ; and there is the Anthony Cleverdon of Hall, who has assumed the name, stepped into the rights and place of the other, and walks in his shoes."

"And, by Heaven!—why not wear his cravat? You swear to this."

" I will swear."

" Come—I must have another to confirm your word."

"Call up the old father, if he be not already discharged."

Fox for a moment was stunned. He realized his danger. He had run his head into the noose prepared for Anthony, and that five hundred pounds had saved Anthony and sold him.

The paralyzing effect of this discovery lasted but for a moment. Then he burst forth into a torrent of explanation, confused, stuttering in his rage and fear, now in a scream, then in a hoarse croak.

Captain Fogg rapped on the table.

"Gag him," ordered he, "stop his mouth. We have made a mistake—locked up the wrong man. This is the veritable Anthony Cleverdon, the rebel. Stop his mouth instantly. He deafens me."

Fox—writhing, plunging, kicking, struggling to be free —was quickly overmastered, his mouth gagged, his feet bound as well as his hands. He stood snorting, his eyes glaring, the sweat pouring from his brow, and his red hair bristling.

In another moment old Squire Cleverdon was introduced, looking deadly pale. He had not been released—had not as yet heard that his son had delivered himself up. He looked with indifference about him. He believed he was brought up to receive sentence, and he was prepared to receive it with dignity.

"Old man," said the Captain, "a word with you. Friswell, you may stay. Sergeant, keep at the door. I

want a short and direct answer to a question I put to you.
Prisoner, do you know that fellow there, with his hair on
end and his mouth stopped?"

"I know him very well. I have good reason to know
him," answered the Squire.

"What is his name?"

"His name is the same as mine—Anthony Cleverdon."

"And his place of residence?"

"Hall."

"Is he your son?"

"He is my son-in-law; he——"

"Enough. He is your son?"

"Yes; that is to say——"

"Exactly," interrupted Captain Fogg. "I want to hear
no more; the lady says the same. Say it again. This is
your assert——"

"Anthony Cleverdon, the younger, of Hall," said Julian.

"Sergeant," said Fogg, "is the beam run out?"

"Yes, your honour?"

"And the rope ready?"

"It is, your honour."

"Then take this prisoner—Anthony Cleverdon the
younger—and hang him forthwith. The two other prisoners are discharged. They were apprehended, or gave
themselves up, by mistake. That is the true Anthony
Cleverdon. Hang him—at once. He who steps into
another man's shoes may wear as well his cravat."

CHAPTER LXI.

EXEUNT—OMNES.

Anthony was in his cell. He expected every moment to
be called forth, and to hear his doom. He was perfectly
calm, and thought only of Urith. He had the half-token
about his neck, and he kissed it. Urith had given it to
him: it was a pledge to him that she would ever be heart-
aching for him, living in the love and thought of him.
Time passed without his noticing it.

Steps approached his cell, and he rose from his seat,
ready to follow the soldier who would lead him forth to
death. But, to his astonishment, in the door appeared

28

Julian, with the lieutenant. Anthony's face darkened, and he stepped back. Why should this girl—this girl who had poisoned his life—come to torment and disturb him at the last hour?

Perhaps she read his thoughts in his face by the pale ray of light that entered from the window; and, with a voice trembling with emotion, she said, "Anthony, you are free!"

He did not stir, but looked questioningly at her. She also was pale, deadly pale, and her whole frame was quivering.

"It is true," said Friswell. "You are free to depart, you and the old man; both are discharged. There has been a mistake."

"I do not understand. There can have been no mistake," said Anthony.

"Come, quick; follow me," said Julian. Then, in a low tone, turning to the lieutenant, she said, "Suffer me one moment to speak to him alone."

"You may speak to him as much as you will," said the young man. "I only wish I were in his place."

"Anthony," said she, "say not another word to anyone here. I have delivered you."

"You, Julian! But how?"

"I have bought your life, with gold and——"

"And with what?"

"With——but I will tell you outside, not here. Come, your father awaits you."

"I thank you for what you have done for me, Julian. If I have wronged you in any way hitherto, I ask your forgiveness. Indeed, we have been in the wrong on all sides —none pure, none—save Bessie."

"None, save Bessie," repeated Julian.

"Come with me," she added, after a silence; and he obeyed.

Near the castle stands the weather-beaten church of St. Petrock, with its granite-pinnacled tower. Outside this church, on a tombstone, sat the old Squire. He first had been released, not at all comprehending how he had escaped death; not allowed to ask questions, huddled out of the castle, and sent forth into the street, bewildered and in doubt.

Now, with wide-opened eyes, he stared at Julian and his

son as they came to him, as though he saw spirits from the dead.

"He is free, he is restored to you!" said Julian. The old man tried to rise, but sank back on the stone, extended his arms, and in a moment was locked in those of his son.

He could not understand what had taken place. He knew only that both he and Anthony were free, and in no further danger, but how that had come about, and how it was that Fox was in bonds, he could not make out. The reaction after the strain on his nerves set in. Great tears rolled out of his eyes, and he sobbed like a child on the breast of Anthony.

Then Julian told him how that his son had come and had surrendered himself to save his father. The old man listened, and as he listened, his pride, his hardness gave way. He put his hand into that of his son and pressed it. He could not speak, his heart was overfull.

But how had Anthony escaped? That he could not understand.

Then Julian told how that she had discovered that Fox had a hidden store of gold in the pigeon-cote at Kilworthy. She was convinced that this was the money that her father had lost, the money he was conveying to Monmouth at Taunton. Fox must have robbed the coach, robbed his own father, secreted the bags near the place where he had stolen them, and conveyed them by night, one by one, to the pigeon house at Kilworthy, where he had supposed they were safe, as the cote was deserted and no one ever entered it, least of all ascended a ladder to explore the pigeon-holes. She, by accident, had observed him, but had not allowed him to suppose that he had been seen.

When Anthony gave himself up, then Julian had entreated Fox to use this money to obtain the freedom of his friend and brother-in-law. As he had refused to do so, Julian had gone home, and taken the gold, brought it to Lydford, and with it had purchased Anthony's freedom.

As they spoke, the sexton passed them, rattling the keys of the church. He took no notice of them, nor they of him. They, indeed, were immersed in their own concerns.

"But," said Anthony, "you said something more to me. You had sacrificed something for me besides the gold. What was it——?"

"A life," answered Julian, in a low tone.

Hark ! as she said the word, the bell of the church began to toll.

"There is some one dying," said the old man, rising from the gravestone. "Let us pray for him as he passes."

There was a noise of voices in the street, exclamations, heard between the deep deafening notes of the bell.

Presently the old man said. "What did you say, Julian ! A life—whose life ? "

She did not answer. He looked round. She was gone.

"And what did the Captain mean," he added, "when he said—he who has stepped into another man's shoes must wear his cravat ? "

As he looked about, searching for Julian—he saw his question answered ; understood why the bell tolled, why the whole of the population of the little place was in the street, talking, gesticulating, crying out, and looking at the topmost window of the Castle.

He who had stepped into Anthony's shoes, assumed his name, occupied his place, was wearing the cravat intended for his neck.

But where was Julian ?

That was a question asked often, repeatedly, urgently, and it was a question that was never answered.

A shepherd boy declared that he had seen her going over the moor in the direction of Tavy Cleave. Search was made for her in every direction, but in vain.

When the writer was a boy, he was with a party at a pic- nic at Tavy Cleave, and was bidden descend the precipitous flank to the river to bring up water in an iron kettle. He went down—jumping, sliding, scrambling, and suddenly slid through a branch of whortleberry plants between some masses of rock that had fallen together, wedging each other up, and found himself in a pit under these rocks. To his surprise he there found a number of bones. His first im- pression was that a sheep had fallen from the rocks into this place, and had there died, but a little further examina- tion convinced him that the remains were not those of a sheep at all. Among the remains, where were the little bones of the hand, was a ring. The ring was of gold and delicately wrought. It probably at one time contained hair, but this had disappeared, and the socket was empty, within the hoop was engraved "Ulalia Crymes, d. April 6, 1665." It was clearly a mourning ring. Now Ulalia Glanville was the last of that family, the heiress who married Ferdinando Crymes, and the day of her burial was April 10th, therefore, probably she died about April 6th, in that very year, 1665. And this was the mother of Julian. Can this have been the ring commemorative of her mother worn by Julian Crymes, and does this fact identify the bones as the remains of that unhappy girl? If so she must have either slipped or precipitated herself from the rocks over head, and fallen between these masses of stone, where her crushed body escaped the observation of all searchers, and of accidental passers-by.

As already said in an earlier chapter, the parish church of Peter Tavy has gone through that process which is facetiously termed "restoration," on the principle of the derivation of *Lucus à non lucendo*; restoration meaning, in ninety-nine out of a hundred cases the utter destruction of every element of interest and loveliness in an ancient church. Among the objects on which one of those West of England wreckers, the architects, exhibit their destructive energies are the tombstones.

Now, in Peter Tavy Church, previous to its restoration, there were—in the interest of my story—two tombstones, fortunately transcribed before the wrecker began his work. Here is one, cut on a slate slab let into the floor :—

"To the Memory of

ANTHONY CLEVERDON, Gent.,

[*Then a pair of clasped right hands*]

and URITH, his Wife,

Daughter and Heiress of

RICHARD MALVINE, of Willsworthy, Gent."

Under this stone the corps of them abide
What lived and tenderly and love, and dyed.
Wedlock and Death had with the Grave agreed
To make for them an everlasting marriage bed,
Where in repose their mixed dust might lye.
Their souls be gone up hand in hand on high.

Curiously enough, there was no date to this tomb.

It would appear that for a hundred years the descendants of Anthony and Urith remained at Willsworthy, and then the family became extinct.   It would also appear that Hall passed completely out of the family of Cleverdon, the old Anthony Cleverdon, on his death, being entered in the register as "Anthony Cleverdon the Elder, once of Hall, but now of Willsworthy, Gentleman ;" and the date of his burial was 1689, so that he just survived the accession of the Prince of Orange.

It cannot be doubted that the few remaining years of his life saw him an altered man, and that he had discovered that with the loss of Hall he had gained something, as Luke had said, far more precious—the love of his children, and the knowledge how precious it was.

In the floor of the chancel, below the Communion-rails, was another Cleverdon monument, but not one of a Cleverdon of Willsworthy, but of a rector of Peter Tavy.   His Christian name was Luke.   We may therefore conclude that Luke from being curate became incumbent of the church and parish he had served so faithfully.   Beneath his name stood a second.   The inscription ran thus :— "Also of Elizabeth, his true helpmeet, daughter of Anthony Cleverdon, formerly of Hall."   There was no mention on it of the marriage with Fox.   Below stood the text from Proverbs :—

"Who can find a virtuous woman? for her price is far above rubies.   The heart of her husband doth safely trust in her.   She will do him good, and not evil, all the days of her life."

THE END